GENESIS

UNKNOWN9

GENESIS

BOOK ONE OF THE GENESIS TRILOGY

BY LAYTON GREEN

REFLECTOR

Published by Reflector Entertainment
Montreal, Quebec
www.reflectorentertainment.com

Distributed by Greenleaf Book Group
For ordering information or special discounts for bulk purchases, please contact Greenleaf Book Group at PO Box 91869, Austin, TX 78709, 512.891.6100.

Cover design by Reflector Entertainment Ltd
Interior book design by The Book Designers

Publisher's Cataloging-in-Publication data is available.
Print ISBN: 978-1-9992297-0-2
eBook ISBN: 978-1-9992297-1-9

Part of the Tree Neutral® program, which offsets the number of trees consumed in the production and printing of this book by taking proactive steps, such as planting trees in direct proportion to the number of trees used: www.treeneutral.com

Printed in the United States of America on acid-free paper
19 20 21 22 23 24   10 9 8 7 6 5 4 3 2 1
First Edition

To the seekers

Humans have learned that what they can touch, smell, see,
and hear is less than one-millionth of reality.

—R. BUCKMINSTER FULLER

FACT

Ettore Majorana, an Italian physicist born in Sicily at the turn of the twentieth century, was considered by many of his peers to be a genius on the level of Einstein and Newton.

In 1932, at the age of twenty-six, Ettore proposed a radical theorem to help solve the greatest mystery of modern-day physics, the theory of everything: a universal law that would unite the principle of general relativity with the strange workings of quantum mechanics. To this day, Ettore's hypothesis has been ignored in favor of competing ideas.

On the night of March 25, 1938, for reasons unknown, Ettore boarded a ship in Palermo. When the boat arrived in Naples, he was nowhere to be found—and was never seen again.

A famously reclusive scientist, nearly all of his work remains lost or deliberately hidden, though speculations abound as to the nature of his research and the cause of his disappearance.

The theory of everything remains unsolved.

PROLOGUE

TYRRHENIAN SEA
PALERMO-NAPLES ROUTE
MARCH 1938

Unused to the roll of the open sea, Ettore Majorana kept losing his footing as he hefted the leather satchel across the upper deck of the mail boat. Ettore was a theoretical physicist, not a sailor. Nor did he travel well. Adding to his disorientation, the ship at night was very dark, as dark as the Sicilian hilltops upon which he had stargazed as a boy.

When at last he managed to right himself, he clutched the satchel to his chest as if it were a long-lost child. Brine from the day's journey coated his tongue and crusted his lips. He had spent the afternoon leaning into the rail, gazing fiercely at the horizon and cringing as each new vessel approached, wondering if they had come for him.

Using the whisper of red luminescence from the port sidelight, he edged along the deck, all too aware of the restless bulk of the sea at his side. How easy to slip forever into that secret embrace. Inside the pocket of his wool coat, his fingers rubbed against his palm, over and over, a subconscious response to the stress of his decision.

The scouting journey from Palermo to Naples had revealed the private areas of the ship at night, invisible to the pilothouse and cabin windows. No one else was about. It was just Ettore, the salt and the sea, the unblinking cosmic eye of whoever or whatever had put the universe into motion—and the device in his satchel, built to probe the nature of that celestial machine.

Though built by a select group of scientists and engineers from the Society—Nikola Tesla himself had lent a hand—the device was conceived and designed by Ettore. Maybe now the world, which had so long ignored his theorems, would listen.

Or maybe other worlds would hear.

Ettore knelt beside a stack of wooden crates, the high sidewall of the pilothouse at his back. He eased the leather bag to the deck. A chill swept across him, and not just from the icy wind. Not even he understood the full nature of what was about to happen. The math and physics, yes. But the reality?

That raised the question, of course, as to the nature of reality. Einstein had taken the world through the looking glass and proven how little mankind really knew. Was reality this vast new spectrum of subatomic particles and electromagnetic waves hidden from the human eye—or something even more than that?

Was the march of human knowledge nearing the end line or just setting out on the journey?

Or perhaps mankind had seen all this before, eons ago, the knowledge lost in time or buried in the Arctic ice, a doomed cycle of enlightenment and loss.

That last bit of speculation did not sound as crazy to Ettore as it once would have. Because he had seen things. Objects from the past, in the possession of the Society. Things that made him question the course of human history. Things that had driven him to the limits of his sanity and compelled him to finish the project.

An icy gust of wind lashed his exposed face. Ettore's hands trembled so much as he unzipped the bag that he paused to collect himself. He had told the others they could test it first, in a safe house, with their charts and monitors and instruments. Stefan would have been there, of course, in the shadows, slipping an arm across Ettore's shoulders in the familiar, authoritative way of a master protecting his chattel.

Yet Ettore had disobeyed them. The blueprint he had given Stefan was misleading, and the very thought of the betrayal caused Ettore's pulse to hammer against his chest.

No. I must not turn aside.

Everyone thought he was weak. Frail and unstable. And perhaps he was. Yet two things drove him to press through his fear and open the satchel, extracting a silver sphere surrounded by a gangly mess of filament wires: desperation, and the one thing in life that moved him above all else, his sole fountain of strength in the face of adversity.

Curiosity.

Ettore had an aching desire to know what lay behind it all, to discover what had imagined the beauty of the cosmos, caused the music of the spheres to ring, formed the galaxies into spirals, conceived of genes and chromosomes and neurons, made the numbers align as they do.

The numbers. It was always the numbers. Speaking to him for as long as he could remember, whispering at the dinner table when he was a child, revealing themselves during his music lessons, demanding his attention. It was as if those arithmetical symbols were not just mental constructs but actual living entities. He did not fully understand it, could not give voice to the feeling. It was simply an itch he had to scratch, a pressure in his skull that threatened to drive him mad if left untended.

There was a pattern to it all; he could feel it. To *everything*. And he might have discovered an important piece.

Soon he would know for sure.

With his mind on his invention, freed from his constant worry of the people who would surely pursue him to the ends of the earth, his hands ceased to tremble as he untangled the wires—fine quartz string coated with silver—and attached the ends of the electrodes to his body at the twelve meridians. Once finished, he sat cross-legged and held the silver bauble, about the size of a cantaloupe, in his hands. A moment of profound reflection overcame him.

What would he see, once it began?

Would the place Stefan called the Fold reveal itself at last?

Were Ettore's calculations correct or the product of a diseased and desperate mind?

He took a deep breath to exhale his fear. A final glance at the sky revealed a swarm of stars flickering in those inky depths. They appeared so close together, yet an unfathomable distance separated each and every one.

Achingly alone, yet part of something greater.

With a serene smile, feeling truly at peace for the first time in his life, Ettore absorbed the sway of the ship as he pressed his fingers into the trigger points of the device.

Pinpricks of electricity flowed through him, and the silver sphere began to glow.

 PART ONE

Bologna, Italy

1

A serpent with mouths gaping at both ends loomed atop the arch of the portico, carved into centuries-old stone, its belly distended by a globe depicting a flattened distortion of the continents. The portico, one of thousands in the city, heralded the entrance to a lecture hall at the University of Bologna, the oldest institution of higher education in Europe.

Beneath the carving, Dr. James Corwin, professor emeritus of theoretical physics and astronomy at Duke University, guest lecturer for the week in Bologna, emerged carrying a brown leather briefcase and leaning on a mahogany cane that matched the color of his skin. A group of students and colleagues gathered around him. His lecture on Lorentz transformations and the geometry of space-time had drawn quite the crowd. Bologna was a wonderful city for academics: full of bright and eager students, a distinguished roster of international scholars, and gastronomical delights by which to relish the long sultry evenings. Dr. Corwin loved to discuss the latest theories while lingering in a mouthwatering *salumeria*, or a wine bar built into a medieval cellar.

This city, he thought. *Its timeless colonnades and courtyards, flowers in the windowsills, families strolling arm in arm. A window to a bygone era.*

The crowd lingered beneath the portico for some time. Eventually his colleagues wandered off, and then the younger professors. A slender postdoc, at least forty years his junior, stepped forward from the remaining students. She wore bangles on her wrist and a sleeveless yellow dress.

"And what is your opinion?" she asked in that formal lilting accent of the Italian elite. They were debating the merits of string theory versus loop quantum gravity, the two theories with the most promise for marrying relativity with quantum mechanics. Most physicists were fierce proponents of one or the other.

"Have you not read my papers?" Dr. Corwin said, bemused.

"Of course."

"And?"

She tucked a strand of brown hair behind her ears. Her mousy face possessed a proud, uncompromising intelligence that reminded the professor of Andie. She was about the same age and build too. But the similarities ended there. This young woman had innocence and privilege stamped all over her, a softness to her gestures that spoke of European gentry and private schooling and summers at Lake Como. Not the borderline obsessive drive of the woman he thought of as almost a daughter. Not the fierce independence born of necessity. Not the soul-churning insecurity of a child abandoned by her mother.

"I know you disfavor M-theory," she said, "but I thought I would take the opportunity to ask you in person. If that is okay?"

"I prefer to let my research speak for itself. I also prefer not to think too hard on an evening as lovely as this, at least before my first beer. But let me pose a broader question: Why favor a single theory?"

She blinked. "The current unification theories have no experimental backing. I did not think you would approve."

"I don't."

"I . . . don't understand."

"Macro- and microphysics, string theory and quantum gravity—are they not different facets of the same gem? I doubt the true shape will come in a blinding flash of inspiration, but by forging a diamond out of generations of research. Choose a theory that interests you," he advised, "and hack away."

After a thoughtful nod, the postdoc thanked him and left on the back of a scooter with a long-haired young man with glasses and tattooed forearms. After watching them disappear, Dr. Corwin realized the crowd had dispersed and he was alone on the street. How had he let this happen? The passion of the Bologna academics had swept away his good sense.

Darkness had crept into the city. Zawadi was nearby, and that should have put him at ease. Yet out of sight meant out of mind. As a child fears a closet at night, with a growing dread of dangers unseen, Dr. Corwin feared this lonely street a few thousand miles from home. Except the monsters *he* feared—the human monsters—were all too real.

No, not monsters, he thought. Monsters act without cause or purpose, and single-minded belief was the hallmark of his enemies. As twisted as he thought their logic was, he knew they felt the same about his own.

Only a handful of people, his inner circle, knew of the invention. He was letting his fears control him.

And yet. Best to take precautions.

He tried the imposing iron-studded wooden doors at the entrance to the lecture hall. Locked. Scanning the street revealed a corridor of limestone buildings, proud but graying, on either side of the pedestrian-only thoroughfare. In place of sidewalks, tunnels of high arched porticos formed ground-floor walkways that disappeared into the darkness. Bologna had miles and miles of these elegant shaded arcades. The signature of the city.

Though no one was in sight, a feeling of being watched overcame him. Was this a product of his imagination? Paranoia springing from the import of his invention?

In this part of the old city, a maze of towers and cobblestone courtyards that took naturally to the gloom, he could have blinked and imagined he was in Renaissance Europe. Dr. Corwin stood still for a moment and listened, leaning on one of the mauve pillars supporting the porticos. Nothing but distant laughter and the coo of a pigeon.

Just calm down, he told himself. *No one knows yet. I've barely tested it.*

He tried to call for a taxi but couldn't understand the dialect of the first operator who answered. The second told him it would be an hour wait. After promising himself to be more careful, Dr. Corwin limped forward on his cane, toward the city center. The libraries under Society protection were too far away. A half an hour walk at least. The closest place he knew to grab a taxi was near Tower Asinelli, at the other end of Via Zamboni. Maybe he should have downloaded Lyft or Uber like the younger generation, but as much as he embraced technology, some habits die hard.

A group of local men appeared in the distance, walking right toward him. They had a rough look about them, far too unkempt and dissolute to have been sent by *them.*

The stares of the men lingered as they passed. One, an emaciated man with crooked yellow teeth, offered him drugs. This area of Bologna was seedier at night than Dr. Corwin had realized. Though he did not fear common street thugs, he lowered his head and tried to walk faster, his joints and bad knee creaking.

The street emptied again. His isolation in the maturing darkness became a tangible thing. All of the ground-floor entrances—the gelato shops and *cicchetti* bars and university buildings—were shuttered. Canvas shades concealed the windows on the higher stories. The busy core of the city center, merely blocks away, felt like the other side of the Korean DMZ. If his legs were younger, he would have broken into a sprint.

Scolding himself again for his childish fears, he drew on his past for strength. James Gerald Corwin was no simple professor. Born into poverty, his mother had worked four jobs to put him through a Catholic school in Kingston, Jamaica. A gifted student from the start, James had scratched and clawed his way to an Oxford degree. His brilliance led to contact by the Society, and a lifetime of extraordinary adventures followed.

Though aging, his mind was as sharp as ever, and he was far from ready to embark on that final journey into the unknown. There were too many secrets to uncover, mysteries of the universe to solve. He was closer than ever to some—closer than he had even realized. If it would not have raised eyebrows at Duke, he would have canceled the Bologna trip. He yearned only to return home and pour every ounce of his energy into the project. It was meant to be a novelty, a testing ground, but the theorems had exceeded his wildest expectations.

A car door shut nearby, followed by footsteps slapping on stone, too swift for normal pedestrians. Dr. Corwin had just passed one of the gaps between porticos that signaled an alley, and he couldn't resist any longer. He took out his phone and tried the number he knew by heart.

It rang and rang.

Unease swept through him. Zawadi would answer at once if nearby.

Where is she?

Half a block away, he spied a narrow piazza in front of a brick basilica. Deciding not to take any chances, he hobbled forward as fast as he could, pushing through the pain, cursing his knee. The footsteps drew closer as he entered the courtyard. The mournful face of an ivory woman atop the church gazed down on him in the moonlight.

Parked cars filled the cobblestone piazza. Bicycles were chained to iron posts along the perimeter, and leftist political graffiti defaced the grimy stone walls. He decided to hide behind a blue Škoda, positioning himself with a view of Via Zamboni through the passenger mirror. An archway on the far side of the piazza led to a connecting side street.

Moments later, they came for him. A man and a woman. Locals, very attractive, dressed in smart evening clothes. They could be just a couple enjoying a night on the town—except for the way they veered purposefully off the street and right into the courtyard, their eyes in constant motion. The woman had a hand inside her purse; the man was gripping something in his pocket.

In that moment, Dr. Corwin knew someone had betrayed him, perhaps even Zawadi herself. *They* knew what he had made—and they had come for him.

Dr. Corwin reached inside his briefcase and grabbed the handle of his Taser. He had carefully hidden his invention, but no doubt they wanted to stash him in a safe house and try to extract information. He had taken precautions against that too.

The woman hurried forward, eyes focused on the distance. She was a tall and lithe blonde, almost as tall as Zawadi. She ran past without seeing him, then disappeared beneath the archway. The man stayed in the courtyard, checking behind the parked vehicles one by one. Dr. Corwin's knee screamed as he shifted to the balls of his feet. Determination alone allowed him to withstand the pain of his cramped position.

In the passenger mirror, beneath the reflection of the basilica, he watched the man draw closer and then disappear from view. Seconds later, he emerged less than ten feet from the driver's side of the Škoda. Dr. Corwin shuffled forward to position himself at the rear of the vehicle, leaning heavily on the cane. The Taser was a police-grade weapon that, if properly applied, might give him time to escape.

A whiff of expensive cologne drifted to his nostrils. Steady footsteps. The flap of bird wings on a roof.

As the man rounded the back of the Škoda, Dr. Corwin waited half a beat more, looking for a clear shot at the chest or thighs. Large muscle groups worked best for neuromuscular incapacitation. Before the man could draw his concealed weapon, Dr. Corwin aimed the laser sight and pressed the trigger. A crackle of electricity broke the silence as the pair of electrodes darted outward, striking the man in the chest.

Instead of freezing up and falling to the ground, incapacitated by the current, the man barely paused. Dr. Corwin's elation turned to dismay. His pursuer must have had protection under that thin blue shirt. Leather provides excellent defense from Tasers, he knew, but more advanced options were available. Bodysuits and chest wraps as thin as foil, made to counter electroshock weapons.

With a quick, arrogant smile, the man rushed forward, sure he was about to overpower the frail old man leaning on a cane. Yet his confidence worked against him. Dr. Corwin threw the useless Taser at the man's face, causing him to flinch, and then, using the technique Zawadi had taught him, the professor brought his cane up and swung it with all his strength, snapping his wrist.

Whether guided by skill or luck or providence, Dr. Corwin's strike was true. The heavy cane—reinforced with steel bands—struck the assailant in the temple. He slumped to the ground, unconscious.

The pain in his knee caused the professor to collapse against the car. With a grimace, he pushed off the vehicle and hobbled toward Via Zamboni.

Had the woman heard the scuffle? There was no help for it now. He pressed down the silent street, breathing in labored gasps, wincing with every step. The sounds of nightlife increased. After passing a church with a thirty-foot entrance, he at last entered the piazza housing two of Bologna's most beloved landmarks, Tower Asinelli and the crazily leaning Tower Garisenda.

Pedestrians, street hawkers, cars, and taxis whisked around the traffic circle. Trattorias were still serving dinner. As soon as Dr. Corwin was safely ensconced in a taxi, speeding toward his hotel, he took a deep breath and considered his next step.

For a moment, he debated heading for the nearest sanctuary, the library inside the Archiginnasio. He knew a secret entrance, and the library was well fortified. Still, after that brazen attack in the city center, he dared not risk another betrayal. Best to aim straight for his hotel, where he could lock himself in his room and request protection.

Yet to whom could he turn? That was the insidious nature of betrayal. The damage it did to the rest of one's relationships. Could it be Lars Friedman? Dr. Corwin would have bet his life otherwise. Anastasia? Xialong?

Or was it Zawadi after all? The thought of this—the most probable answer—caused him to feel as if he had aged another decade in the last hour. *What did they offer her? Or has she always been in their thrall?*

The hotel was minutes away. Bologna's exquisite old town—courtyard palaces and uneven cobblestone lanes and romantic balconies jutting over porticos—passed by in a blur. His thoughts turned to safeguarding his invention. The test run that had succeeded beyond his wildest dreams. This was no mere path to enlightenment through the tangled wood of history.

This was a door that had never been unlocked.

Even if he arrived safely back in Durham, all could still be lost. All could *already* be lost. He had to act fast, to protect what little chance remained. Letting his invention fall into the wrong hands could be catastrophic.

"*Signore!*" he said to the taxi driver.

"*Sì?*"

"I need a favor. A very important one," he said in fluent Italian. "And I'm willing to pay for it."

"*Buono,*" the cabbie said, hesitant.

"Tomorrow morning, as soon as you can, I need you to mail something for me."

The driver's face scrunched in confusion, but Dr. Corwin was already scribbling a note to Andie on a sheet of paper he had ripped from a Moleskine journal he carried in his briefcase. He hated to involve her but saw no other way. She was perhaps the only person on the planet he could trust without question, and who had no connection to the Society.

He left Andie's address on the piece of paper, gave the driver further instructions, and tipped him an extra one hundred euros in front of the hotel. As archaic as it seemed, snail mail sent by a random person was the best way to ensure the note arrived undetected. And if Andie did exactly as he said, no one should know of her involvement.

He hoped he was making the right decision.

Beaming, the driver shook Dr. Corwin's hand and sped off. If something happened to the professor before he reached the United States, the fate of his invention depended on the integrity of a single Bologna cabdriver.

Still reeling from the attack, his mind spinning with permutations, Dr. Corwin hurried toward the entrance to the Starhotels Excelsior, absorbing his surroundings with a glance. Plenty of cars still traversed the busy road that separated the old city from modern Bologna. A well-dressed couple who looked American had just exited the hotel, arm-in-arm. To his left, three Germans stumbled toward a late-night bar. Nearest to him, a homeless woman had just stepped onto the curb, approaching with a palm extended. The left side of her neck was distended by a grotesque tumor, covered in sores, slick with blood and pus. He hefted his briefcase and hobbled away from her, not trusting how quickly she had targeted him. Though the woman's wrinkled hands and soiled clothing appeared genuine, such a disguise would be child's play for the people searching for him.

As he limped away on his cane, she pressed closer beneath the sodium glow of the streetlamps, muttering in rural Italian as she jabbed at her tumor, demanding attention. He could smell the reek of her now, fetid and rotting. Feeling her hand brush his shirt, he glanced back in alarm and saw the truth in her eyes: The stench of this woman was the stench of death. It was no disguise.

The knowledge that she might have been used as a decoy chilled him, right as he turned to see the American woman unlock her arm from her companion's, exposing a tiny handgun concealed by her purse and pointed right at the professor. From the shadows to his right, a hooded shape darted out, also holding a gun. Yet the muzzle flash came from the woman's small pistol.

The force of the bullet jerked Dr. Corwin to the side like a marionette. He stumbled and fell, blood pouring from his shoulder, as the American couple drew back in feigned shock. Two porters from the hotel rushed right past them as the man in the dark hood grabbed Dr. Corwin's belongings and fled into the night.

A police siren cut through the pandemonium outside the hotel. Within moments, a *carabiniere* whipped into the street and parked right beside Dr. Corwin, blue lights strobing, followed by an ambulance. Both vehicles must have been right around the corner.

The pain was intense, but Dr. Corwin thought he would survive. As the paramedics inspected the wound, applied oxygen, and lifted him onto a stretcher, he tried to explain what had happened. No one would listen, and they kept telling him to calm down as the onlookers pointed the carabiniere in the direction the man in the dark hood had run off. Dr. Corwin looked around in vain as two paramedics loaded him into the ambulance, but the American couple had disappeared.

As the ambulance swept through Bologna, the paramedics cleaned and bandaged the professor's wound and sedated him with an intravenous drug. When the ambulance came to a stop, he realized something was wrong as soon as the rear doors opened and he saw crates stacked along the walls of a dingy warehouse. One of the paramedics held him down while the other took a scalpel and removed the skin from the underside of one of Dr. Corwin's thumbs. The sedative dulled the pain and drowned his feeble protestations. After bandaging that wound, they shoved a tight-fitting latex mask over his face. He panicked when he couldn't breathe, but then he heard a telltale beep—likely a handheld scanner—and they removed the mask.

All of this happened very quickly, and Dr. Corwin could only watch in horror as the paramedics hustled him out of the ambulance and lifted him into the trunk of a black sedan. Just before the trunk closed, he saw another man setting a plastic-wrapped corpse, similar in age and build to Dr. Corwin, into the back of the ambulance.

Durham, North Carolina

2

Andie Robertson woke bleary-eyed and stumbled to the bathroom of her rental home, a midcentury modern in dire need of renovation on the outskirts of Durham. The semester had ended, but she was helping Dr. Corwin with a textbook over the summer, and a folder full of source checks had kept her up half the night.

Though she would have helped him for free, because it was Dr. Corwin and because she loved the research, her mentor knew she needed the money. Andie was a PhD candidate in astrophysics at Duke. With her tuition scholarship, teaching duties, and the pittance she made as Dr. Corwin's research assistant, she was able to scrape by, but her lifestyle included copious amounts of coupon shopping, street food, and camping out at local coffee shops.

Though a state school was more Andie's speed, she had come to Duke because of Dr. Corwin. He was not just her faculty mentor; he was an old family friend. Twenty years ago, when Andie was a young girl in Princeton, New Jersey, Dr. Corwin had mentored Andie's mother, Samantha, in her own PhD studies. Samantha was his favorite student. Andie's father was a novelist who loved to cook. They often invited Dr. Corwin—a lifelong bachelor— over for dinner parties, or even by himself for a solid meal during the week. Andie and Dr. Corwin had spent many hours in the back yard, cataloguing the garden and studying the sky after dark, while her parents prepared dinner.

Over the years since her mother disappeared, Andie had continued her close relationship with Dr. Corwin, and considered him a second father.

Was my mother anything like me? Andie sometimes wondered. *Before she decided to abandon her family and go find herself in the Far East, traipsing through temples and ruins while her husband drank and flailed, leaving her daughter to grow up bitter and alone?*

No. We are nothing alike.

As always, Andie crushed thoughts of her mother as she would a roach scuttling across the floor.

She brushed her teeth and thought about more pleasant things, like her plans over the break. Late spring in Durham was glorious and green. She liked when the city emptied of students and the humidity pulsed and the cool dark interior of a coffee shop beckoned. Stargazing at night on her flagstone patio, watching a movie during the afternoon heat, day trips to Wrightsville Beach.

Andie finished brushing and leaned over the sink, splashing water on her face to wake up, running her fingers through short brown hair with cowlicks as stubborn as a rusty lock. She didn't do hairstyles, rarely bothered with makeup, and bit her nails to the quick.

Water dripped off her fingers, trickling down her narrow face. When she rubbed her eyes and looked up, the mirror had disappeared and she was floating inside a shadow world that surrounded her like the bottom of a dark lake, suffocating, all-consuming. Her surroundings still resembled her bathroom—the outlines of the objects and walls were intact, though transparent, revealing a hazy vista that resembled the gloom of a dusk sky. It was a place both familiar and surreal. Shapes of vaguely human forms, haunting and ominous, drifted through the murky substance of the void. A sensation of being watched overcame her, and of others seeking escape, and of glimpsing a small piece of a greater whole.

And, above all, a feeling of being hopelessly, terrifyingly lost.

The vision lasted only a moment, as it always did, winking out of existence as abruptly as it had arrived. Reeling, she thrust her palms onto the bathroom counter for support. She was dizzy and nauseated, panting, whipping her head around to make sure the room was real.

Dammit, when will this stop?

Andie had experienced similar visions countless times, for as long as she could remember. It was more than a dream, because she felt fully conscious. Yet it was not the real world either.

She had hoped it would end when she reached adulthood. Instead the visions had grown stronger. No doctor or psychiatrist had been able to help; she didn't even think they believed her. Stress and sudden bright lights seemed to be triggers, similar to epilepsy, though no drug had provided any relief. And sometimes it happened for no reason at all, as it just had. After a lifetime of searching for answers, from mysticism to traditional religion to scouring the annals of unexplained psychiatric phenomena, she now believed it was a glitch in her mind. Part of the great yawning mystery of the human brain and consciousness that science was barely at the tip of comprehending.

As with everything else, she wanted to blame her mother, but these flashes had predated her desertion. Unable to give voice to the experience as a child, Andie had never even told her.

After a minute, the dizziness passed, and she felt normal again. Or as normal as she ever felt. With a shuddering breath, she pulled a pair of summer jeans over her long legs, then shrugged into a green tank top that her pointy collarbone jutted out of in an annoying way. She didn't care. It was hot.

She ate a quick breakfast and finished dressing: a jade ring, a pair of leather bracelets dyed silver, and single-hued magenta knit sneakers—shoes were her one nod to fashion. Dr. Corwin was scheduled to return in two days, and she had a lot of work to finish.

But first, she had a different sort of obligation.

A child with a coffee-toned complexion in the front row waved her hand in the air, her mass of curly hair bouncing like copper springs. "Hey, are you really a teacher?"

From her podium atop the scuffed auditorium stage, Andie smirked and tapped the silver piercing in her left nostril. She had heard the children giggling about it. "Does this suggest I'm not?"

"It means you're different."

"Thanks for the compliment. Is that your only question?"

The girl, maybe eight years old, thought for a moment. "I know we've been to the moon, but I want to go to a star. Can I do that one day?"

"That's a great question. I'd love to go to a star one day too."

"So can we?"

"Hmm. Did you know the closest star to Earth is the sun?"

"The sun isn't a star. It's the *sun*."

The other children giggled at the little girl's brashness. Milky Way Monday had become one of Andie's favorite days of the month. She loved almost everything about her chosen field: the cutting-edge research, the nights spent gazing at the heavens, the heated debates about radical cosmological theories with her colleagues.

Yet modern astrophysics was an esoteric field that dealt with concepts and distances vaster than most people could imagine. Mathematical formulas so complex they resembled an alien language.

Andie found a visceral and very human satisfaction in talking about the cosmos to elementary school kids in daycare programs, especially in the poorer neighborhoods of East Durham. Not because the kids were any different—she found most children, in their own ways, amazing and insightful—but because of the chance to spark the imagination of kids who might not have the best opportunities in life.

How many geniuses had humanity lost over the years to poverty or circumstance?

How much further along might we be?

While Andie was a very driven woman now, she would have

fallen through the cracks herself without the intervention of Dr. Corwin at certain times in her life.

"I'm not sure you'd want to go to the sun," Andie said to the crowd of children. "It's a little bit hot up there."

"How hot?" challenged the same girl.

"The parts you can see are, oh, about five times hotter than lava."

"Hotter than *lava*?"

"You think that's hot?" Andie said. "The nuclear fusion at the core of the sun can reach temperatures of twenty-seven million degrees!"

This fact elicited a roomful of blank looks. Neither nuclear fusion nor million-degree temperatures were cool. *Lava* was cool.

"So you like volcanoes?" Andie asked, trying to recover. Children kept her much higher on her toes than a roomful of undergrads.

"Yeah! Yeah!"

"Did you know the planet Mars has a volcano three times as tall as Mount Everest? It's the tallest mountain in the whole solar system." After a few oohs and aahs, she turned to the curly-headed girl again. "Let's get back to your question. What's your name?"

The girl twirled a finger in her hair. "Kayla."

Using a laser pointer, Andie aimed at one of the stars displayed on the projector screen. "You want to go to one of these, right? Maybe that bright one right there?"

"Uh-huh."

"After the sun, this is the next-closest star to Earth. Its name is Proxima Centauri, and it's about four point three light-years away. Does anyone know what a light-year is?"

Silence.

"It's easy. A light-year is simply the amount of distance a beam of light can travel in a year. We even know how far that is: nearly six trillion miles."

The class started to fidget, and Andie thought about how to make it relevant.

"How many of your parents own a car?" Most hands shot up. "If you wanted to drive a car to Proxima Centauri, it would take you about forty million years to reach it."

"I don't wanna drive, yo," Kayla said. "I wanna *beam* up there, like on TV!"

The class tittered so much the teachers had to calm them down.

"We're working on that," Andie said after the riot had subsided. "I hope you can one day."

In the third row, a Latino boy with glasses and a gap between his front teeth meekly raised a hand. "How big is the universe?"

She always got this question, and it always provoked a soft smile. If these children couldn't even grasp the distance to the nearest star, how then to explain that our solar system alone, the region of space affected by the gravitational force of the sun, is more than twenty-three *trillion* miles in diameter? How to explain that our Milky Way galaxy is infinitely larger than our solar system, so big as to defy belief, and contains four hundred billion stars?

How to explain the estimates that the universe contains more than two trillion galaxies similar to our own and is ninety-three billion light-years across, a distance so unfathomably vast that no analogy Andie had ever heard could render it comprehensible?

And that was just the observable universe. Who knew how big it really was, or what else was out there?

"Even we scientists don't know for sure," she said. "It's bigger than you can possibly imagine. But just think about how much adventure is waiting in space! Maybe you'll all be astronauts one day, and you can tell *me* the answers."

This led to a series of rapid-fire questions, the polite raising of hands forgotten in the excitement.

"What do astronauts eat?"

"Are there aliens?"

"What's inside a black hole?"

Andie put her hands on the podium and leaned forward. "Do you want to know a couple of *really* cool facts?" As the children quieted, she pointed at the projector screen. "First, did you know that outer space is only fifty miles away? If a car could drive straight up, you'd be there in less than an hour."

That got her some more oohs and aahs. She pointed at Proxima Centauri again. "Remember when I said this star was about four light-years away? That means that when we see it in the night sky, we're not actually looking at the star itself. We're looking at light from the star that has traveled all the way through space for over *four years* to reach us. Some of the light in our night sky has been traveling for hundreds, thousands, and even millions of years. When you look at the stars, you're actually looking back in time."

"You mean like time travel?" Kayla asked.

"Not exactly. But you *are* looking at a snapshot of the past. Starlight is the history of the universe itself."

As their pliable young minds tried to grasp this, Andie felt her cell phone buzzing in her pocket. Normally she unplugged during these talks, but this time she had forgotten. Unable to resist checking to see if the guy she'd met last week was texting her back, she discreetly pulled out her iPhone behind the podium.

The message wasn't from the drummer in a local band who had chatted Andie up in a dive bar. It was from Lisa Cranton, one of her colleagues at Duke.

You've seen the news about Dr. Corwin? I'm so sorry.

No, Andie hadn't seen the news. Nothing had popped up in her email, and she hadn't had time to browse. But if there was important news, why wouldn't her mentor have told her himself? And more importantly, what was Lisa sorry about?

What news? she quickly texted back, feeling uneasy.

Her phone buzzed again within seconds. Not wanting to disrupt the lecture, but too curious to wait, Andie let her eyes slip downward as she spoke.

He was mugged and shot in Italy. He died on the way to the hospital. I can't believe it.

Andie lurched against the podium, dropping the laser pointer. Unable to find words, she ran out of the auditorium and into the nearest bathroom. She locked herself in a stall, pulled up her browser, and prayed there had been a mistake. But the awful truth was splattered like cheap paint all over the internet.

LEADING PHYSICIST KILLED IN BOLOGNA

She knew that Dr. Corwin, one of the top physicists in the world and an authority on quantum gravity and the geometry of spacetime, had gone to Italy to attend an international conference. It was a routine event for him.

So what in the hell had happened?

She scanned the online reports. The night before, after a lecture at the university of Bologna, Dr. Corwin was assaulted outside his hotel. It was a brazen attack, a senseless robbery. A hooded assailant had stolen his wallet and his watch, a midrange Swiss brand that Dr. Corwin favored.

A modest timepiece, 150 euros, and a few credit cards that had probably bought the mugger a tank of gas and a case of beer before the cards were flagged as stolen.

This was the price of a human life.

Andie leaned over the toilet and vomited.

After returning to the auditorium and apologizing to the kids, mumbling something about an emergency, Andie hurried to the cantankerous Buick Riviera convertible handed down from her father. She was glad the threat of an afternoon shower had convinced her to leave the top on. She didn't want to be visible.

Though a little eccentric, Dr. Corwin was a kind and thoughtful man who always had time for Andie, despite his brilliance and international renown.

Yet it went much deeper than that. Andie was never quite sure why, after her mother left, Dr. Corwin had taken Andie under his wing. He was not particularly close with her father. An affair with her mother was unlikely—Andie's pale skin and pointed nose spoke strongly against a Jamaican heritage. She knew only that Dr. Corwin and his mother had been close, he had no children of his own, and that for whatever reason, he had appointed himself Andie's guardian.

Maybe he had known more about her mother than he had told her. Maybe he had made her mother a promise.

Andie had never asked. She figured it was his story to tell.

During her undergrad years, Andie was an angry young woman who careened from crisis to crisis. Her father was an alcoholic writer with whom she barely talked. She resented her parents and the sorry state of the world and the fact that her car never started in the cold northern winters. Her reckless behavior culminated in a lost year: she dropped out of school, took a bus to California, and bummed a ride to Puerto Vallarta with some surfers. Telling herself she was searching for sunshine and good times, inspiration and meaning, she spent the year in a haze of wild parties and self-loathing. After ending up in a Mexican drunk tank for a night, the bottom of the bottom, terrified she was turning into her father, she knew she had to make a change. But then she was hit with a bogus fine, the equivalent of three thousand US dollars, and told if she didn't pay it she was going back to jail. Broke and staying in a hovel, she asked her father for money for the first and last time in her life.

And he refused. He simply didn't have it. A novelist who had published one semisuccessful book in his thirties, he had continued to chase a fading dream that took him further and further into poverty and depression. Andie had grown up on welfare checks and secondhand clothes.

The next day, Dr. Corwin—Andie assumed her father had told him—flew to Mexico himself, paid the fine, and put her on a plane home. Her father met her at the airport, reeking of liquor and sobbing with relief.

Andie walked right past him.

Somehow, she managed to graduate with a decent GPA in physics, and aced her GREs. Still, she didn't have the résumé for Duke. Dr. Corwin convinced her to apply anyway, and her acceptance came a month later. He never admitted to pulling strings, but it was the only explanation, and Andie had vowed not to let him down.

She had no siblings, no connection to an aunt or uncle or cousin, no living grandparents. After her father, Dr. Corwin was the closest thing to family she had left. He was her mentor, her benefactor, her only real compass in life.

This can't be real, she whispered to herself as the first drops of rain splashed against the windshield, bringing her back to the present.

This can't be real.

Christened by the shower, the leafy streets of Durham glistened with moisture as Andie drove home in a daze. She pulled into her long gravel drive, shaken, unable to order her thoughts. Everything felt surreal, the colors of late spring muted around her.

Andie's rental home was in a rural area fifteen minutes from campus, on a wooded lot that linked up to the Eno River trail. After sitting in the driveway with her hands gripping the wheel, lost in sadness, she left the car and went straight to the shed where she kept her heavy bag. A dedicated kickboxer during her undergrad years, she was too busy now to keep it up and had taken up running instead. Yet at times, when she was particularly stressed or angry, she let loose on the bag.

It was as hot as Hades inside the shed. She kicked until her thighs ached and sweat washed away the tears. When she was finished, panting and wobbly, she went inside for a cup of tea.

Though Andie had a few friends in the astrophysics department, she struggled to form lasting bonds. Her chosen profession was very demanding, and she knew she had trust issues. Her love life was a train wreck, or more precisely a *theoretical* train wreck.

With a pang in her chest, she realized that if anyone else close to her had died, she would have sought refuge with Dr. Corwin.

Numb to her surroundings, ignoring the intermittent buzz from her phone, she spent the afternoon on the couch, drowning in misery.

Needing some noise in the room, she ordered some moody electronic beats from the voice assistant. She let the music wash over her, though after a time it started to cloy, and she realized the sentiment wasn't right. Dr. Corwin was dead, murdered, and it wasn't fucking fair. Andie was sad, desperately sad, but above all, she was angry at the world for letting it happen. She needed something with an edge. A serrated one.

After considering a witch-house mix or some old-school Nine Inch Nails, she decided what she wanted. "Okay, Google, play Johnny Cash instead."

"Ring of Fire" came on, and Andie frowned. "No, not that. Play 'Hurt,' Google."

She raised the volume as a voice full of pain filled the room, a voice with too much knowledge of the world, a voice of loss and bitterness and love gone away. A voice filled with the quiet rage of the dying.

"That's better," she murmured, and replaced her tea with a bottle of whiskey.

The next morning, head throbbing, she started a pot of coffee and checked her email. One of the deans had left a heartfelt message about Dr. Corwin.

After breakfast, she stepped outside, breathing in the loamy smell of pine. There was a UPS Express envelope on the doorstep. To her surprise, the envelope was addressed to her given name, Andromeda Genesis Zephyr.

Zephyr was her mother's surname, which her father had taken when they married. A feminist and high-powered career woman, her mother had dominated her handsome but flighty husband. Or at least that had been Andie's young impression.

Whether from love or inertia, her father had never reverted to his own surname. But the day Andie turned eighteen, to further excise the memory of her mother, she had legally changed her last name to

Robertson, her father's family name.

Not many people knew her true name, and when she saw the return address on the UPS envelope, Andie's breath stuck in her throat.

Starhotels Excelsior in Bologna, Italy.

Sent by Dr. James Corwin.

With a melancholy smile at the name of the hotel, she opened the envelope, curiosity cutting through her grief, wondering why in the world he had sent her a snail-mail package. And UPS Express international? That must have cost a fortune.

Inside was a handwritten note, dated May 27, on a piece of paper ripped from a Moleskine journal. God, he had sent this right before his murder. As she read Dr. Corwin's distinctive scrawl—there was no doubt it was his—her pulse quickened, and a series of chills swept through her.

> *Dearest Andie,*
>
> *I apologize for the bizarre circumstance, but there's no one else I can trust. If this message reaches you before you hear from me, go immediately to Quasar CAM Labs in the Research Triangle, give the note to Dr. Lars Friedman, and tell him where the birthplace of <u>mathematics</u> is. Do not ask questions. Do not try to reach me <u>under any circumstances</u>. Do not call or send an email to Dr. Friedman—go in person, as soon as you get this.*
>
> *Should I fail to return from Italy, <u>trust no one</u> with this message besides Lars. Not the police. Not even your own family.*
>
> *No one.*

3

Feeling a sudden chill, Andie clutched the piece of paper and returned inside her house. She sat cross-legged on the love seat in her study, surrounded by piles of books and papers. The view of the forest outside the tall windows normally beckoned, but now the silent trees felt watchful, menacing. She wished she had curtains to draw.

She read the note again and again, trying to parse the message.

What had Dr. Corwin gotten himself into? And why had he come to her? If he knew he was in trouble, she would have expected him to go to someone on the faculty, or a family member. Dr. Corwin had never married, but he had siblings in London and Jamaica.

Do not ask questions. Trust no one. Not the police.

The implication of these words, and the use of regular mail—suggesting his phone and email might be tapped—unnerved her even further.

Andie rose to pace the room, gnawing on her thumbnail so hard it started to bleed. That was clearly no random mugging, and she realized the UPS package had been sent from Bologna the morning after his murder. He must have paid someone to send it, knowing he was in danger.

She had never heard of Quasar CAM Labs or Dr. Lars Friedman, but the reference to mathematics she understood. In his office, Dr. Corwin kept a framed photo of the Ishango bone: a baboon fibula unearthed in present-day Democratic Republic of the Congo. At least eighteen thousand years old, the clearly defined notches on the bone indicated an ancient counting device.

If asked, most people would point to an Egyptian papyrus or ancient Mesopotamian texts as the earliest evidence of human computation. But the Ishango bone—and other bones like it, less intact but far older—proved that Paleolithic tribes in central and southern Africa were using protomathematics more than fifteen thousand years before the pyramids.

It was the first known evidence of human calculation. The birthplace of mathematics.

Dr. Corwin knew she was familiar with the Ishango bone. But plenty of his colleagues would have understood the reference as well.

She put her head in her hands. None of this made any sense.

For a moment, she wondered if her mentor had started to unravel. Had his brilliant mind developed schizophrenia later in life? Or had he medicated in secret all these years, then stopped taking his drugs for some reason?

It was possible, though schizophrenia usually started at a young age. And he was so personable. Witty and cosmopolitan, schooled at the best universities, never exhibiting any of the antisocial or erratic behavior typically associated with advanced schizophrenia.

Even more compelling evidence that mental illness was the wrong line of inquiry: his murder had proven his fears correct.

Yet as she continued studying the note, the line that kept hitting her the hardest, the one that made her feel dizzy and unmoored, was the next-to-last one.

Not even your own family.

Andie didn't have a family. Just her estranged parents and some distant cousins. Dr. Corwin knew this. So what the hell did that mean?

She blew out a long breath. Her province was the realm of science, a cold and beautiful place where logic held sway. She loved mysteries, but had never done well with psychology and hidden meanings. At least not as they applied to human beings. That was the beauty of her field. The rules of the universe, as insanely complex as they might be, did not change once unraveled. They did not deceive.

She kept pacing and biting her nails, trying to decide what to do. A quick internet search revealed that Quasar CAM Labs specialized in quantum metallurgy. Though the company kept a low profile, she found a number of patents pending in obscure areas of materials science. Dr. Corwin was on the board of directors, but that did not surprise her. He was on a lot of boards.

The siren song of grief called out to her, urging her to lie in a dark place and close her eyes to the world. She wanted to succumb, but too many questions flooded her mind. Maybe Dr. Lars Friedman could shed some light on what had happened, and maybe not.

Yet all of that could wait. Her first decision was easy: she was going to carry out the dying wish of her beloved mentor.

Trees and more trees surrounded her Buick as it sped through Duke Forest, the ribbon of asphalt a blackened tongue flicking through the woods. The surrounding jaws of the forest opened briefly to expose the city and then snapped shut once more, spitting her out on a lonely road delving into the heart of the Research Triangle.

The Silicon Valley of the South, the Triangle was the largest science-and-technology park in the world, in terms of acreage. VC money poured in like water, and it was home to a surfeit of Fortune 100 satellite offices, start-ups, and lab facilities.

Yet none of this was obvious on a drive through the heavily forested park. Most of the office buildings and laboratories were hidden from view, set far back off the road. The Research Triangle had always creeped her out a little. The isolated location, miles from the surrounding cities, evoked images of secret labs and nefarious corporations, of a modern-day Dr. Frankenstein performing illicit research in the bowels of a gleaming glass fortress. As a scientist herself, she knew the feeling was unwarranted. Yet she couldn't shake it—especially when driving alone through the woods to a cutting-edge tech company in order to fulfill the bizarre edict of a murdered professor. She also had the unsettling thought that perhaps her vision the previous morning had been a reaction to her *impending* stress.

As if, in that place inside her head, time didn't exist in the same way.

The feeling of foreboding increased as she turned onto East Cornwallis Road, heard the whine of sirens, and saw black smoke billowing into the sky. Her hands tightened on the wheel as she turned left onto a smaller road, and the source of the fire drew closer. By the time she reached the gated entrance to Quasar Labs, the sirens had ceased, but a column of greasy smoke still emanated from inside the property.

Andie parked beside the guard shack and stepped out of her car. A bulky man in his forties, his mustache bristling beneath beady eyes, slid open a glass window.

"Can I help you?" he asked.

Andie started to take out her Duke ID, then thought better of it. "I work nearby. I saw the fire and wanted to check on someone who works here."

"They're not answering their phone?"

"No."

"I can't let you through without authorization. Sorry."

"How bad is it?" she asked.

"So far, just the one building. I think they've got it under control. Listen, who do you know? I might be able to check on them."

"Dr. Lars Friedman."

The guard's face twitched, and one of his hands dropped below the window. "How do you know Dr. Friedman?"

"He's a friend. Why? Is he okay?"

"What's your name?"

Wondering why the guard was acting so nervous, Andie gave him the name of the protagonist in a book she was reading.

The guard looked her up and down, then glanced at her scratched-up convertible. By the smirk that tugged at the corners of his lips, she guessed what conclusion he had drawn.

"I really need to see him," she pressed, not giving a damn.

He mashed his lips together, as if trying to make a decision. "Look. I can't let you in, but between you and me, no one's seen Dr. Friedman for a few days."

"What do you mean no one's seen him?"

"He didn't come in today. Or yesterday."

"Did he call in sick?"

"I can't give out that information."

Trying to conceal how much the guard's revelation disturbed her—Dr. Friedman had disappeared the same day as Dr. Corwin—she said, "What started the fire?"

"Hey, lady, are you a reporter?"

"I'm a friend. Like I said."

"Yeah, well, if you're his friend and you hear something, let us know, okay?"

"Sure," she said, backing away.

"Why don't you leave me your contact information, and I'll let you know if he shows up."

"That's okay. I'm sure he'll call me." As the guard continued to watch her, she couldn't resist a final question. "Was it Dr. Friedman's lab that burned?"

It took him a moment to answer, but she saw the truth in his eyes. "I can't give that information out."

She returned to her car, feeling the sudden urge to get as far away from Quasar Labs as possible. As she started the engine, a black SUV approached the gate from inside the compound. It stopped at the guard shack and then rolled past her. Right before the tinted window was raised, she glimpsed a strikingly attractive Middle Eastern woman in the back seat, her black hair caught in a bun. She was reading a document held up in her hands. Beside her, a pale man with glasses and an aquiline nose was talking on a cell phone. Both wore business suits and had a laser focus on their tasks. As the man continued his phone conversation, he turned his head toward Andie, holding his gaze as if cataloguing her features. She froze, unsure whether to look back or turn away, feeling dissected by his stare. The moment passed, and his attention returned to his call.

When Andie tried to get a look at the driver, she felt a prickle of gooseflesh rise along her arms. It was hard to tell through the tinted windows, but she noticed before the car pulled away that the driver's arms stayed locked on the steering wheel in the exact same position, eerily so, and that his head never seemed to move. Maybe it was her imagination, and she never got a look at his face, but his rigidity caused a dissonant reaction to his silhouette.

As if something about it wasn't quite right.

4

Omer Kveller approached the ticket scanner at gate C7 in Terminal 2 of the Raleigh-Durham International Airport. As the leggy blonde manning the scanner held out her hand for his documents, Omer drew to his full height, met her gaze, and flashed a warm smile. The blonde smiled back.

Omer was six foot two, dark-haired, blue-eyed, and blessed with the bone structure of a movie star.

They always smiled back.

His charm offensive did not stem from worry about the fictitious name on his passport. The more the technology surrounding legitimate documentation improved, the harder it became to detect the well-crafted false ones. Perfectly replicated laser perforations and intaglio printing were a bitch to expose.

Omer's fake ID was almost foolproof. He didn't need to play nice with the gate agent. He simply found that greasing wheels eased his passage through life.

And in his business, one used every advantage at one's disposal.

"Portuguese?" she commented, glancing at his passport. "I love Lisbon."

"It's beautiful," he agreed.

Omer possessed the sort of swarthy complexion that could pass for any number of nationalities. A former linguist for Israeli special forces, as well as the son of a diplomat, Omer had the worldliness and language skills to support his false identities.

Just before he placed his cell phone under the scanner, using his left hand so no one noticed the missing right pinky, a text made him draw the phone back. "Ah, one second," he said, stepping out of line. "I'm sorry."

"Boarding closes in five minutes," the gate agent chided, maintaining eye contact as he backed away. An unspoken promise. "Don't miss your plane."

"Understood. Thank you."

He needed to find a secure place to make the call. Unfortunately, that meant outside the airport. He waded through the crowd at the gate and slipped into the flow of people returning through the terminal. Near baggage claim, someone grabbed him from behind. On reflex, Omer spun, gripped the man by the underside of his right arm, and prepared to gouge out an eye or press a thumb into the man's windpipe.

Omer was scanning the crowd for more assailants when he realized the person who had bumped him was a husky college kid with ripped jeans and a goatee.

"Hey, man! Let me go!"

"Excuse me," Omer said, raising his palms in apology. The encounter had occurred in a heartbeat. "You startled me."

"Jesus, I just tripped."

"I apologize."

Though Omer's heart rate had remained steady during the encounter, recent events had him on high alert. The attack in Bologna, the fire, and the chaos that the unfinished business was sure to bring. The college kid could just as easily have been someone sent to kill him before he boarded his flight.

The kid was cradling his right arm, which had gone limp from the pressure applied to the ulnar nerve. "What'd you do to my arm?" he called out as Omer walked away.

"An accident. You'll be fine in a minute."

Once outside, Omer crossed over to the airport parking deck and took the elevator to the top floor. No clouds marred the hypnotic blue sky. The air felt thick and heavy. When he stood alone in a deserted portion of the deck, far from video surveillance and the threat of hidden microphones, he dug a different phone out of his calfskin duffel bag and called a familiar number.

"We are here," answered an anonymous robotic voice.

Omer continued to scan his surroundings. "I just got a text."

"Where are you?"

"At the airport."

"You need to stay a while longer."

"What if there's footage from the lab? Police could match it to the passport."

Omer was not worried about someone intercepting the communication. Names were never used on these calls, and the people on the other end of the line were using burner phones and a messaging app encrypted with a block-cipher algorithm.

The reason the call was filtered through a speech modifier, he knew, was to disguise the identity of the caller from Omer.

"Let us take care of that," the metallic voice droned. "Any troubling footage will be erased."

"Understood," Omer replied. "What do you need?"

"A young woman appeared at the lab and asked for Dr. Friedman. It was not his wife or any known associates."

"When?"

"This afternoon."

"Who was it? The Society?"

"We're running facial-recognition software and should know by the end of the day."

"Was there any sign of the device?" Omer asked.

"No. But she might have knowledge. Are you certain it's not in Durham? You checked the office and the home?"

"And left no trace. I know my job. But this woman—what's the protocol? Interrogation?"

"Deliver her," the voice replied, and the line went dead.

Half an hour later, after procuring a different rental car on a different false passport, Omer pulled into the parking lot of the Fairfield Inn & Suites near the airport. He bypassed the entrance and pulled his gray Nissan Armada deep into the back lot. After checking for surveillance cameras—hotels like this rarely had them in the rear—he parked and climbed into the middle row of the SUV.

He placed his duffel bag on the seat beside him, pausing to set his phone to a London-based classical music station. Next, he opened the bag and extracted a disassembled advanced-polymer firearm wrapped in pieces inside his clothing. He wasn't particularly worried about his target, but there were dangerous forces in play. A violinist in his youth, he hummed along to Stravinsky as he pieced together a zip gun invisible to airport metal detectors. The handgun resembled a flattened rectangle with a trigger and a snub-nose barrel. The last piece was an electric component that attached to the miniature scope, and synced to Omer's wristwatch. Among other tricks, the watch could fire the zip gun remotely, at a distance of ninety yards.

He loaded the weapon with sharpened polymer-coated rubber bullets. It was hardly the sort of piece he would carry into a war zone, but the zip gun was lethal at fifty feet or less. Next he removed his clothes and slipped into a skintight ballistic vest made of interlaced microfibers. He changed into lightweight slacks and a gray moisture-wicking shirt, then returned to the driver's seat to await further instructions. Exhausted by the last few days, he locked the doors and let his eyes close. Trained to wake at the slightest sound, he hoped the next thing he heard was the buzz of his smartphone.

As he began to doze, his last thought was of the protocol he had been given for the mission. He did not fully grasp the big picture. He knew the Ascendants were searching for a device of vital importance, something that involved a new technology, but he was not privy to the details. One day in the future, he hoped.

Omer had always felt that for people like himself, high achievers with natural gifts, a different path in life should be available. A higher ceiling. Yet not in his wildest dreams could he have imagined the turn his life would take. The extraordinary people he would find.

The lofty citadels of human potential available to those willing to work, to suffer—even to die—to reach them.

While the mission remained opaque, the protocol he understood perfectly well. Follow the Archon's orders exactly as they are given. Do not ask questions. Do not deviate.

Do anything it takes to deliver the target, find the device, or gain information about it.

Anything at all.

5

Stunned by the fire and the news of Dr. Friedman's disappearance, Andie made a snap decision as she drove back to Durham. Dr. Corwin had told her not to get involved, but she wasn't about to sit on her couch and start preparing an elegy. She was going to dig into Dr. Corwin's life and find out what the hell had really happened in Bologna. And the police . . .

Trust no one.

Instead of turning onto the downtown connector, she stayed on Cornwallis and headed north. Before she made any decisions, she was going to campus to see if she could figure out the meaning behind her mentor's mysterious message.

After clearing the visit with Dean Varen, head of the physics department, Andie stepped into Dr. Corwin's office and experienced a shock.

The framed photo of the Ishango bone was missing.

It used to hang on the wall across from his desk. She was sure of it. But now his Oxford diploma was hanging in its place.

Unsure what to do, she stood by herself in the middle of the office, remembering, absorbing, shuddering at the loss of the man who used to greet her so warmly from behind the desk. Eventually she turned to take in the contents of the room: globes, telescopes, bookshelves, more framed diplomas, his prized Fields Medal for mathematical research, and a detailed star map that glowed in the dark. A chalkboard covered one wall, filled with strings of numbers and formulas. In the corner, a hovering bonsai tree was supported with the clever use of magnets.

She approached Dr. Corwin's desk. Stacks of journals, notes, and research papers were arranged in neat piles around an iMac. Though much of a physicist's work took place on the computer now, Dr. Corwin liked to use his chalkboard. String theory and quantum gravity were still pen-and-paper theories, relying on creative insight more than computer programs. Like her mentor, Andie specialized in the intersection of theoretical physics and astronomy, though Dr. Corwin was a far better mathematician than she would ever be.

Still no sign of the Ishango photo.

A memory of Dr. Corwin's spicy aftershave, mingling with puffs of chalk dust as he scribbled on the wall, caused a fresh wave of emotion. She took a moment to gaze at the photos on his desk. Dr. Corwin hobnobbing with luminaries of his field. Feynman, Dirac, Hawking. A very old photo of Heisenberg in a lecture hall.

Her gaze lingered on a photo where she was standing next to Dr. Corwin outside a local restaurant named Foster's. To celebrate a finished project, he had taken his research assistants out to brunch on a bright spring morning. With his silver-gray hair and sharp blue blazer, Dr. Corwin looked as distinguished as always. Foster's was a casual place, more of a glorified coffee shop, and unlike the other assistants, Andie had shown up as she always did: her tall, lean frame clad in black jeans and an old leather jacket. No makeup, messy hair, and sleep-deprived eyes.

Beside Dr. Corwin, she looked like an overgrown street urchin, and she laughed at the memory.

The empty space on the desk beneath the monitor, where the laptop used to sit, drew her eyes. All of a sudden, she had the wild notion that Dr. Corwin might have been killed for his research.

As far as she knew, he had discovered nothing groundbreaking in recent years. But the idea caused her to close the office door and search his desk.

Nothing unusual in the top middle drawer: pens, sticky Post-it notes, an old graphing calculator he kept around for nostalgia, and a stack of business cards from colleagues around the world.

The drawers on the left side of the desk were filled with scientific papers, grouped into drop folders. She browsed some of the headers: LOOP QUANTUM GRAVITY. HIGH-ENERGY PARTICLES. THEORETICAL CONDENSED MATTER. DARK MATTER DETECTION. GAMMA-RAY BURSTS.

Again, nothing unexpected, except for the folder on condensed matter. She hadn't realized that was an interest of Dr. Corwin's, but it dovetailed with his connection to Quasar Labs. Curious.

On the other side of the desk, the top drawer was filled with blank notepads. The other drawers on the right were locked.

Locked? Why are these locked?

After staring at the desk for a few moments, indecisive, she rummaged around until she found a box of paper clips. She took two out and straightened them. After setting one down, she made a loop at the end of the other clip, bent it at a ninety-degree angle, and twisted the bottom end. Her tension wrench and rake. Andie had once dated a guy who had worked on motorcycles for a living. He had nice arms and could even talk literature. On their first date, after seeing a local band, he had broken into a nearby bar for kicks. He said he knew the owner, and Andie went along with it. At the time, she hadn't cared about much of anything. They poured themselves a drink, had a laugh, and made out behind the bar. After three more dates, she realized he was probably a part-time criminal and let him go. But he had taught her a few tricks, and those biceps . . .

Concentrate.

She inserted the tension wrench into the keyhole of the middle drawer, then jiggled the rake around beneath it. She hadn't practiced in a long time and was afraid she had lost her touch.

Every few seconds, she paused to listen, expecting footsteps in the hall. She kept fiddling until she got the lock to turn, and the drawer popped open.

The first thing she saw made her gasp.

It was a photo of Andie and her mother.

After biting her nails for a moment, she picked up the thin black frame. In the photo, her mother was walking along a city street, carrying Andie in a baby backpack. Andie didn't recognize the city. The people in the background were white but did not look American. The city had cobblestone streets and old stone buildings. *Where was this taken? Why have I never seen this photo?*

The sight of her young mother in the picture, gazing lovingly down at her daughter, brought a lump to her throat. Her mother had a similar build to her own but with long blond hair, a wider chin, and sharper cheekbones. A beautiful woman. Andie swallowed away her emotion. *If only your beauty were more than skin-deep.*

Why did Dr. Corwin have this? Was he once in love with her mother? Somehow, Andie didn't think this was the case. He had never talked about her or looked at Andie in a weird way, as if seeing her mother in her.

Still, the photo made her feel that she was missing an important piece of her past—and made her even more determined to find out what was going on.

With a deep breath, she set the photo aside and picked up the only other object in the drawer: a silvery nine-sided object the size of a softball. One of the sides had a touch screen that displayed the common representation of an atom: the orbital swirl of electrons around a nucleus. The only difference was a tiny black hole in the center, a disk of darkness surrounded by a spiral of colored gas.

At first she thought the object was a metal alloy, but as soon as she picked it up, she realized the entire thing was made of plastic, including the screen. She had the strong feeling it was a replica—but of what?

At various points on the device, a number of circular depressions were indented a quarter of an inch into the device. They resembled dimples, and she counted ten.

Odd.

On closer inspection, noticing a seam, she gently twisted the object. It separated into two hollow parts. With a shrug, she set it down. After listening for footsteps again, she picked the lock on the bottom drawer and found more research papers, also organized into drop folders. But these were a far cry from peer-reviewed scientific papers in Dr. Corwin's field. These folders concerned topics to which she never would imagine him giving a second thought, not to mention keeping under lock and key in his office.

ASTRAL PROJECTION. NEAR-DEATH EXPERIENCES. PALEO-ACOUSTICS. AFTERLIFE MYTHOLOGY. DREAM STATES. REALMS OF HIGHER CONSCIOUSNESS.

A glance inside the folders revealed a range of documentation, from quasi-academic papers to articles printed off the web to photocopies of handwritten accounts from old journals. Much of the research paralleled her own forays into these topics, in connection to her bizarre lifelong visions.

Why was Dr. Corwin interested in all of this?

She had a sudden thought: Did her mother suffer in the same way?

Yet the most profound shock of all lay inside a folder lying flat at the bottom of the drawer. Inside were a set of ink drawings with the same general image: a depiction of a shadowy realm, a darker version of reality, that made her hands clench against the paper. Though the actual location was vague, she recognized all too well the murky hues, the sense of drifting in a void the image captured, the other-worldly *feel* of the drawings.

It was the same place she went to in her visions. She was sure of it. As if a very talented artist had been inside her head, or seen one of her visions for himself.

Could Dr. Corwin possibly know about my affliction? If so, why did he never tell me?

There were about a dozen drawings, and she took the whole stack. On impulse, she took the photo of her mother as well, sticking everything inside an empty folder. She wanted to take the strange nine-sided plastic model but didn't want anyone to notice her carrying it out. Instead she put it together and replaced it, closed both drawers, and relocked them.

On her way out, still shaken, she stopped down the hall at the office of Dean Varen, an octogenarian once known for her beauty as much as her intellect and stern demeanor. Andie had always thought the dean disapproved of her, but to her surprise, Dean Varen came around her desk to give Andie a hug.

"I'm so sorry," the dean said. "I know how close you were."

Andie looked away. "Is there anything I can do? Help catalogue his research?"

"Perhaps when the dust clears. I just can't believe . . . Did you hear someone robbed his hotel room? They took his computer, passport, clothes—everything."

Andie grimaced. "Any idea why?"

"I assume it was a follow-up to the robbery. It sounds like something out of a movie, but James wasn't . . . It just doesn't make sense."

"None of this does," Andie murmured, trying to process it all. A murder, a robbery, and a missing scientist from Quasar Labs. She debated asking the dean if she knew Dr. Friedman, then decided against it.

Trust no one.

"What will happen to the contents of his office?" Andie asked. "Since he doesn't have a family?"

"I'll have to think about that."

"I was just in there and noticed his photo of the Ishango bone missing."

The dean's brow furrowed. As in, why was Andie talking about this?

"I know it's a strange thing to bring up," Andie said quickly. "I just noticed it for some reason. He must have taken it home."

How long before they rob his office and house in Durham too? Or what if someone's already been to his office and taken the photo—or they're on their way right now?

Dean Varen moved closer, lightly touching Andie's forearm. "Grief evokes peculiar responses. We want to grasp on to the familiar."

Andie shivered and rubbed her arms, then moved for the door. "Do let me know if I can help."

"I will. Oh, and Andie?"

She turned back.

"I think James moved the Ishango bone to the library recently. I remember seeing it in the Reading Room. If you like, I could put in a request for you to keep it." She finished with a soft, sad smile that Andie could have sworn had an undercurrent of . . . something. Perhaps suggestion?

Was Dean Varen trying to tell her something, or were her frayed nerves playing tricks on her mind?

"Thank you," Andie said, backing toward the door. "I'd like that."

Duke University's West Campus is a rambling collection of neo-Gothic stone buildings tucked into a densely wooded forest, connected by a leafy maze of side paths. Andie had to admit the campus was beautiful, but she had always felt out of place. She did not wear privilege well. It made her uncomfortable.

As she hurried through the main quad that evening, past ancient oaks and a lawn as smooth as a putting green, the panorama of stone towers and carved limestone was as invisible to her as the cosmic background radiation that permeated the universe. After entering the library through a side door, she paused to get her bearings. Overhead rose a ribbed and vaulted ceiling that would have fit right in at Oxford or Cambridge.

The dean could only have been referring to one place. A staircase on Andie's right took her to the second floor, and she hurried down the hall and through a door to the Gothic Reading Room, which everyone referred to as simply the Reading Room.

This was one of her favorite places on campus. Tall arched windows provided ample sunlight during the day, iron chandeliers with clever faux candles hung from the apex of the ceiling, and built-in wooden cabinets with glass doors housed a collection of old manuscripts. Andie walked the length of the room as a generator hummed softly in the background. Since the semester had ended and the library would close in half an hour, the room was almost empty.

The photo of the Ishango bone was nowhere in sight. Confused, she left the room and stood in the common space outside. Had the photo been moved again? Or had someone else found it already? That thought caused her to glance around uneasily and poke her head into the Reading Room once more. The few remaining students looked absorbed in their work.

On the walls of the common space, a pair of interactive monitors and a line of plaques commemorated the history of the university. Andie padded down the carpet to the end of the hallway, turned right, and found herself in a narrow seating area at the rear section of the floor. On the far wall, hanging between a pair of windows overlooking the main quad, was the framed photo of the Ishango bone. She recognized the distinctive metallic frame at once.

The seating area was tucked away in an isolated corner of the library. No one was around. No cameras in sight.

Andie approached the photo of the Ishango bone. The man-made notches on the baboon fibula, dating to at least 18,000 BCE, signified primitive calculations, such as addition, subtraction, prime numbers, multiplication, and even a lunar phase counter. The Lebombo bone, a similar find, was estimated to be more than *forty thousand* years old.

It was mind-blowing to think about the age of these artifacts. What else was out there, lost to the ravages of time? Had advanced cultures existed in the millions and millions of years of prehistory, the vestiges of their civilizations destroyed by an ice age or some other geologic event?

The longer Andie stared at the photo, the less she understood her mentor's cryptic message. What was she supposed to find? As advanced as the Ishango bone was for its age, there wasn't much to it. A baboon bone standing upright in a frame. She paced the room, studying the photo from different angles. The frame was dark bronze with a silver border, an inch wide on each side. On a whim, she tried to lift it off the wall, but it wouldn't budge.

That gave her pause.

Most frames were attached to hooks or some other type of hanging apparatus. Her father used to drag her to antique shops, and she knew the frames of heavy paintings were sometimes recessed into the wall and had to be pulled straight out. She doubted this was the case here, but she tried it anyway.

It felt glued to the wall.

There were no signs of nails or pins on the frame. So how was it attached? A strong adhesive would ruin the back. She tried to run her hands behind the metal edge, but it was so tight she couldn't even slip a fingernail around it. She applied a bit more pressure and still failed to budge it.

She heard a door open in the common space behind her, probably to the Reading Room. Andie hurried to gaze out the window, onto the darkening quad, until the footsteps receded. Choosing a different tactic, she took a deep breath, took hold of the bottom of the frame, and pushed upward, soft at first and then hard. Still nothing. She pushed even harder, then caught her breath as the entire frame slipped upward, enough to expose a thin strip of metal attached to the wall.

At first she was confused. Had she just broken the frame? Then she remembered the bonsai tree in her mentor's office, and put two and two together.

Dr. Corwin was fascinated by the phenomena of electricity, an elemental force which powered everything from the common light bulb to human life itself. The chief byproduct of electrical charges, the electromagnetic field, was brimming with mystery. Images

Andie had seen from the Fermi Gamma-Ray Space Telescope had revealed an entire world of cosmic light and energy, much of it from unknown sources, and nearly all of it invisible to the human eye. The entire universe, the air around us, was quite literally seething with unseen activity.

Now that she knew the secret, she gripped the underside of the frame and peeled it off the wall. It wasn't easy, but she kept pulling, exposing another magnetic strip at the top and two long ones down the sides. Once the framed photo was removed, she found herself staring at a wall safe.

Okay then.

Roughly a foot square, the steel door of the safe had a digital keypad in the center. She tried the handle, just to be sure. Locked. Curious, she turned the frame over and noticed a metal plate attached to the back. A magnet strong enough to discourage a casual discovery if anyone tried to move the photo.

But why had Dr. Corwin taken it to the library?

Because he knew his office—and his life—were at risk?

She could worry about that later. The library closed in a few minutes, and she had a decision to make. Should she try to open the safe now or come back later?

After peering around the corner, she set the photo against the wall and examined the keypad. It contained only numbers, beneath a five-digit code. Trying to guess the combination seemed like a fool's errand, and a safe like this was far beyond her rudimentary lock-picking skills.

Yet she worried its contents—if not already stolen—would be gone when she came back. She remembered the dean's eyes lingering on hers as she left. After giving the hallway behind her another nervous glance, she exhaled and returned to the safe.

Hardly anyone used a random passcode. She started trying every combination personal to Dr. Corwin she could think of, from his phone number to his birthday and zip code. After exhausting her knowledge of his personal life, she moved on to common mathematical figures. Dr. Corwin had always loved puzzles and number games, and had even designed a logic toy for children.

She tried the first five numbers of pi, a string of prime numbers, the start of the Fibonacci sequence. Still nothing.

Think, Andie.

She thought about the projects on which he was working. After running through them in her mind, she couldn't think of a particular theorem that would fit. There was also Dr. Corwin's career-long obsession with cracking the mathematical universe theory, or what he affectionately called MUT for short. MUT was an offshoot of what physicists call the theory of everything, a universal model that would unite the natural laws of the universe under one umbrella. So far, the two pillars of scientific theories governing the laws of physics at the macro and micro scales—general relativity and quantum mechanics—had proved incompatible.

Yet at their core, both theories were simply math. Mind-blowingly complex calculations, of course, and in the case of quantum mechanics, they weren't even truly understood.

But they worked.

Just math.

And if they were just math, then a unifying theory that linked them, well, that should just be math too. Maybe the universe *itself* was just math, Dr. Corwin had suggested to her once, after one too many cups of coffee.

She smiled. *Just math.*

The MUT was a hobby of his. A pet theory, little more than a distraction from his serious work. Or so she had thought.

Not long ago, he had asked Andie to perform a handful of calculations for him concerning speculative quantum effects on macroscopic objects. In theory, that would include human beings. It was an odd topic, though not unknown to researchers. He had never gotten around to telling her exactly why she was working on it, but hypothetical exercises to work out a sticky problem were commonplace.

She took the piece of paper out of the backpack and read it again.

I apologize for the bizarre circumstance, but there's no one else I can trust. If this message reaches you before you hear from me, go immediately to Quasar CAM Labs in the Research Triangle, give the note to Dr. Lars Friedman, and tell him where the birthplace of <u>mathematics</u> is. Do not ask questions. Do not try to reach me <u>under any circumstances</u>. Do not call or send an email to Dr. Friedman—go in person, as soon as you get this.

Should I fail to return from Italy, <u>trust no one</u> with this message besides Lars. Not the police. Not even your own family.

No one.

The underlined phrases had bothered her from the start. Dr. Corwin wasn't the sort to overemphasize his prose. She assumed he had done so in order to stress the urgent nature of the message, but she read it again.

Mathematics. Under any circumstances. Trust no one. It also struck her that if she had managed to pass on the note to Dr. Friedman, *he* would have had to know the combination to the safe as well.

Give this message to Dr. Lars Friedman.

Was Dr. Corwin trying to tell him something? Why had he wanted Andie to deliver the note itself? She assumed it was for proof of life, so to speak. A way to assure Lars the message came from Dr. Corwin.

But what if there was another reason?

She concentrated on the three phrases, wondering if there was a hidden meaning, perhaps a way to recombine the letters. Then it hit her. It was so simple. *Mathematics. Under. Trust.* The first three letters of each emphasized phrase.

MUT.

Dr. Corwin's pet theory, staring her in the face.

She snapped her fingers. The zip file in which he kept much of this research, and to which he had recently given her access, had a five-digit password. She rarely forgot a number that small, and she hadn't forgotten this one. She might as well give it a shot.

After clearing the keypad once again, she punched in the five-digit password to the MUT research folder. There was a short beep, and the door to the safe cracked open.

Los Angeles, California

6

Before every live show, Cal Miller performed an old-school security ritual. First he walked the perimeter of his matchbox LA bungalow, checking for footprints or miniature spyware. Inside the house, he tapped light bulbs and inspected air vents, secured the doors and windows, and armed the security system. Last and probably least, he made sure his elderly Rhodesian ridgeback, Leon, was awake and paying attention.

The new-school work had already been done. Installing the strongest virus scanner and full disk encryption on the market. Using a firewall and a highly complex password on his personal router. Covering the webcam on his Toshiba with black tape. Cal even disconnected his Xbox when not in use. Being hacked while playing a first-person shooter would be an embarrassing way to go down.

A die-hard Generation Xer, raised on Atari and Colecovision and the Commodore 64, Cal had even learned to program in Basic as a kid and considered himself part of the "video game" generation. That said, once he went off to college and became an investigative journalist, he had mostly lost touch with technology. The rapid advancements had passed him by as swiftly as a Canadian summer.

He loved his smartphone and the internet—who didn't?

But he didn't understand them. He didn't even understand his nonstick frying pan.

And all that crazy tech out there, far more complex and insidious than a magic kitchen utensil, scared the shit out of him. He shuddered to think what the world would look like in twenty, fifty, a hundred years.

By nature, Cal was not an overly suspicious person. In fact, he considered himself easygoing. He had never been obsessed with Big Brother or personal security—not until he had exposed a Bolivian black-site facility belonging to a global technology company, PanSphere Communications, through a source who had disappeared under mysterious circumstances right after the piece was published in the *LA Times*.

Cal had met with the source himself, but PanSphere didn't let it go. The company hired a powerful law firm to sue the *Times* for falsifying a lead, libel, and publication of an unverified story. The *Times* conducted their own investigation, but no record of the source could be found. It was as if the Bolivian scientist Cal had met in an empanada restaurant in La Paz had been a ghost.

Cal had *seen* the man. Held his ID badge.

How had they disappeared him so thoroughly?

In the end, the discredited piece got Cal fired and blackballed from major journalism. The whole affair creeped him the hell out, and left him with the constant nagging feeling that someone was always watching.

So he knew for a fact there were links out there, behind the scenes. Unexplained events. Hidden connections. Conspiracies to keep it all quiet that stretched back an untold number of years. Most of the hard-core stuff he couldn't talk about on the show. Not until he found the face behind the mask, a puppet master he suspected of pulling a fistful of strings.

Cal wanted his job back. His *life*. Right now, no employer would touch him, and the only way out of the maze was to prove his source was not false. That was the purpose of the show: to disguise his search for truth behind the guise of a conspiracy theorist, which allowed him to probe touchy angles without raising red flags.

The more followers he had, the more weapons of information he would wield.

Buried within every show was a personal research angle he wanted to crowdsource, a money trail or a face in a photo or conflicting accounts of a news story that didn't add up. Whoever these people were, he knew they were out there.

And he wanted them. Bad.

Focus, Cal. Three minutes until you're live.

He cast a final glance out the kitchen window, then carried a fresh thermos of coffee to the breakfast nook. Leon followed him in. The nook still had the original chrome Formica table, vinyl chairs, and black-and-white tiled floor. Not because Cal was retro-hip, but because he was too house-poor to renovate.

These days, after he was forced to go freelance, he was just poor in general.

Cal opened his laptop and plugged his Blue Yeti condenser microphone into the USB port. He logged on to an internet broadcasting app, Twitch, which allowed him to run a live online show with audience participation.

Again, some people might think he was tech-savvy, but he just used the stuff. He likened it to a rat using electronic sensors to open gates in a maze to reach its food.

Ten seconds . . . five . . . the soothing aroma of fresh coffee . . . God, he loved coffee . . . he was live.

"Welcome to another episode of *Seeker's Corner*, the live show formed in the spirit of legendary Hyde Park Corner in London. Everyone has a voice here, and our goal is to crowdsource the truth out of modern conspiracies. This is Doc Woodburn, coming to you from a kitchen table someplace in the known universe. You, my friends and listeners, are part of the revolution. Help me crack the codes and expose the world's darkest secrets to the light of day."

After the initial spiel he always gave, Cal took a sip of coffee, cracked his knuckles, and continued.

"Last time, we made some headway on Project Blue Beam and Malaysia Air. I heard from a couple of sources this week that turned those theories on their heads. I'll update you at the end of the episode, but before that, we'll talk about the main topic. How does a link between the Las Vegas shooter, a gorgeous Russian spy, and North Korea sound? Juicy, right?"

The comments started rolling in:

Hey Doc, is it the Phantom Time Hypothesis?

Planet Nibiru?

The Homo Capensis conspiracy?

He also saw the sort of random assertions that always cropped up during the show.

Did you know Stephen Hawking was a robot controlled by aliens who live in the hollow core of the moon?

Dinosaurs built the pyramids.

Stranger Things is based on fact, because my uncle worked at Hawkins Lab and saw everything.

There was even the requisite come-on squeezed into the responses:

I'm not wearing any panties under my sundress. Tell me where you're at and I'll fly to meet you. I promise I'm hot. You won't regret it.

"I see some responses already, but hang on. We'll get there. I need your help with something first, and I don't want to sit on this one." Cal rubbed Leon behind the ears as he let the tension build. "It's a modern-day secret society," he said finally, "and I think it's a deep one. Let's work through this together. Who out there tonight has heard of the Leap Year Society?"

He switched to some mood music and gave people time to respond. During the pause, someone wrote in:

Hi Doc, are you a sexy bald Latino midget? That would check all my boxes.

After chuckling, Cal thought maybe he should encourage that

persona. It would be a good cover. Though his skin had darkened a shade or two from living in LA, Cal was a corn-fed white boy from Indiana who couldn't dance and loved Tom Petty and A-Ha. He was also six foot one with perpetual stubble and a full head of short dark hair. *Sorry to disappoint you, lady. Or guy. Or whoever you are.*

Strangely, the chat line was quiet. Oh, the nutjobs were chiming in—as they always did—but during the half-minute break, which was usually all it took, no one had offered a serious response.

"The Leap Year Society," he repeated. "Anyone? I can't discuss how I learned of it yet, but I'm putting the call out to anyone who might be listening: if you have anything on the Leap Year Society, hit me up. Who knows, maybe they'll even be one of the good guys. You know, back in the day when the church and the state controlled everything—as opposed to big business and the state—the lodges of the secret societies, from Freemasons to the Oculists, were the tech incubators of their day. Those mumbo-jumbo handshakes and rituals were used to keep the identities of their members secret as they advanced democracy, science, and philosophy behind closed doors."

Toward the end of the show, he noticed a shadow at the edge of his vision, a vehicle passing across the kitchen window. It disappeared and returned less than a minute later, approaching from the other direction. He looked up to see a black van coming to rest on the curb outside his house.

What the hell?

Cal did not have commercial sponsors, because he did not want anyone to have access to his true identity. If the freelance gig ever dried up completely—which it often threatened to do—he might have to reconsider, but for now, he kept the show as anonymous as possible.

Which meant there were no true breaks on his live show. If he had a bad hangover or an urgent restroom need or, say, a mysterious black van parked outside his house, he played a little music or suffered through.

The van still hadn't moved. No one had exited.

Surely something he had just mentioned on the show couldn't lead to a personal visit this fast—could it?

It had to be unrelated.

Either way, he didn't like it one damn bit.

As he rehashed a story in the news about how philologists were using algorithms to crack ancient manuscripts, buying himself time to think, Cal picked up his computer and microphone and moved to the window. He eased back a corner of the frilly brown curtain he detested but had never bothered to replace.

The vehicle was standard SKV—serial-killer van. No distinguishing marks. If he wanted to see the plate, he would have to go outside.

It was probably just a neighbor. Or a teenage rock band smoking up before a show. He lived in South Hollywood, after all.

Except Cal's particular block was a residential neighborhood, bands had bumper stickers and window graphics, and he had never seen a van of any sort parked on his street before.

As he kept talking and glancing outside the window, he realized there was a distinct advantage to a live show that he had never had reason to consider.

"Slight change in programming, folks." After another pause for emphasis, he said quietly, "Things just got a little real over here."

Wondering if this was a very bad idea, Cal opened his front door and felt the cool night breeze caress his skin. He strode down his sidewalk until he could see the license plate on the van, half expecting the rear doors to burst open to expose a posse of men in ski masks who would shoot him up with a black-market barbiturate and stuff him in an underground bunker beneath the Arctic ice.

"Right this very moment—live on the air—there is an unmarked black van parked in front of my house. And I've never seen it before in my life."

As Cal drew closer and closer to the street, unsure how far he was prepared to go, the engine on the van revved up.

"If the people inside the van are listening," Cal said, "they know a few thousand of you are too. I'm going to walk right up to their door, knock on it, and broadcast the conversation live on the air."

He glanced down at his computer. The chat line was exploding.

None of his neighbors were outside. The street was quiet and dark and smelled of mimosa. It felt incredibly strange to be connected to thousands of listeners, yet physically alone as he approached the van. The disconnect of modern life played out in real time.

The heavy tint on the windows obstructed his vision. As he approached the driver's side to get a closer look, the van pulled away slowly, as if making a statement, before turning left at the end of the street and disappearing.

Swallowing a few times before he spoke, Cal told his listeners what had happened as he walked back to his house, glancing over his shoulder with every step.

Rome, Italy
⟶○ 1932 ○⟶

For once, life felt good to Ettore Majorana.

The sentiment had nothing to do with his surroundings, despite the immense charms of the Via del Corso, a narrow little street in the heart of Rome.

Nor did it have to do with the fact that Ettore had snagged the *gelateria*'s lone sidewalk table, or the creamy perfection of his cappuccino, or the aroma of his beloved Macedonia cigarettes, or the soft breeze caressing his skin on a sunny afternoon in late fall.

Though Ettore was not immune to sensory delights such as these, his mind, as often, was elsewhere. He knew the tragedy of his life was that he could not turn off his thoughts and simply live in the moment.

Oh, how he wished to cruise the streets of Rome without a care, perhaps in one of the new Alfa Romeo models with an open top his countrymen had a flair for designing. To stroll with a partner on a cobblestone lane, discovering a new fountain or statue along the way, stopping to hold hands and admire. To have the simple confidence to ask to join a game of football in the park.

But no.

Ettore's passion in life, theoretical physics, was also his prison. He could not turn off the equations, theorems, and speculations on the nature of the universe that danced in his mind. Even worse, he often felt as if he were the only inmate in this prison, since so few people could understand the places his mind could go.

When Ettore was a child, his mother liked to impress her visitors by asking him to multiply three-digit numbers in his head. Terrified of both public attention and disobeying his mother, Ettore would dart underneath a piece of furniture and shyly call out the answer, to the delight and astonishment of the crowd.

Ettore did not play marbles with the other children. He met with tutors, and explored the limits of calculus, and annihilated grown men at the chessboard in public squares.

Born into a wealthy family, Ettore was pushed toward the profitable field of engineering. Yet once he discovered the higher mysteries of physics, he never looked back. In 1928, at the age of twenty-two, he officially switched his field of study to physics at Sapienza University of Rome. A year later, he earned his doctorate.

It was a heady time to be a physicist. After shocking the world with special relativity, Einstein had given the world general relativity in 1916, explaining that gravity was not a purely intellectual concept but in fact arises from the actual curvature of space-time, like a warm body sinking into a cloth chair. Outer space itself has substance! And it bends!

At the opposite end of the spectrum, the study of subatomic particles, the bedrock of quantum mechanics had been formed by a number of prominent physicists, including Max Born, Paul Dirac, Werner Heisenberg, Wolfgang Pauli, and Erwin Schrödinger. Never before had such advancements been made so quickly and the secrets of the universe so exposed. Theoretical physics was no less than magic made real, Ettore knew. The codification into science of Mother Nature herself, or the mind of God, or whatever one wanted to call it.

A portion of the curtain had been pulled back. And what lay behind it was far more bizarre than anyone could have ever imagined.

Yet it was beautiful too. So beautiful that Ettore was spellbound. As much as he longed to live in the moment and experience the world around him, he yearned to solve the biggest questions of science even more.

At least with science he had a chance.

But the reason life felt so good at the moment was because Ettore had made a discovery. Something worthy of his own impossible standards. A few years earlier, Paul Dirac had published a paper on quantum theory. Barely older than Ettore and even more socially awkward and withdrawn, Dirac was already considered one of the world's foremost authorities in the field—if not *the* foremost.

Einstein's theory of special relativity had proved that when the speed of light is reached or even approached, strange things happen.

Time slows down.

Mass increases exponentially.

Acceleration becomes almost impossible.

Yet, maddeningly, otherwise universal truths did not seem to apply to objects smaller than an atom. So what exactly happens, Ettore and everyone else wanted to know, when the movement of *quantum* objects approaches the speed of light?

Dirac's paper sought to answer this very question and marry quantum theory with special relativity. Yet when he found an equation that worked, he was surprised to find the number of particles had doubled. A field of identical electrons with the same mass and spin but with *negative* energy.

The world of antimatter had been born.

The math behind Dirac's theory was beautiful, but so complicated that only a handful of people in the world could understand it. Ettore was one of these people—and he didn't like what Dirac had proposed one bit.

In fact, he thought it was dead wrong.

So Ettore developed a new theory. One that did not involve an ocean of fanciful new particles and negative energy that shouldn't exist.

Instead of matter and this theoretical antimatter, Ettore devised an equation describing the behavior of *all* particles in a single quantum-mechanical wave. The way he saw it, the behavior of these particles at vastly different levels of energy, such as when an electron approaches the speed of light, was simply two sides of the same coin.

No new particles popped into existence. The old particles just presented a new face.

Another magic trick.

Ettore knew it was his best work. It felt right, a universal quantum equation that satisfied the infinite-dimensional space requirements. And for once, he was ready for the world to bear witness.

"Ettore!"

He turned to find Enrico Fermi, the leader of the Via Panisperna boys, approaching the café with his wife, Laura.

Formed by a powerful senator in the late 1920s, the Physics Institute on Via Panisperna was a collection of Italy's brightest scientific minds, tasked with exploring the emerging field of atomic theory. The group's achievements had led to worldwide acclaim and national pride.

"Tsk, tsk," Fermi chided. "A cappuccino in the afternoon? Is Sicily no longer part of Italy?"

Ettore stubbed out his cigarette in response. Sheeplike adherence to cultural norms was a mark of unoriginal thought.

"Still, you have no idea how much it pleases me to see you enjoying the beautiful sunshine!" Fermi said. A lean man with a piercing gaze and a high receding hairline, he reminded Ettore of a talking bullet.

Fermi turned to his wife. "Ettore never stops to enjoy *la vita bella*, you know. He is always too busy making world-changing discoveries and correcting the feeble ideas of our group."

As usual, Fermi delivered his praise of the younger physicist with a dose of bitter sarcasm. Ettore said nothing, his gaze slipping to the bottom of his empty cappuccino. Laura's presence annoyed him. He had asked Fermi to meet him, not Laura. She would have no idea of the import of his discovery.

"Oh, I think he's doing just fine," Laura said. "Look at what he's reading—Schopenhauer!"

Fermi rolled his eyes. "Oh, Ettore's a philosophical man. Maybe even a metaphysical one."

"You see?" his wife said. "I've never seen you reading anything other than science."

"Bah. That's because everything else is a waste of time."

"You're impossible."

Fermi disappeared, returning with an espresso for himself and a sambuca *corretto* for his wife. "Have you two officially met?" he asked. "By that, I mean has Ettore ever actually spoken to you?"

Laura laughed away the comment and stuck out a delicate hand. "It's a pleasure to formally make your acquaintance again, signore."

Ettore briefly touched her hand.

"My dear Enrico speaks of you often. He tells me how you win races to solve a difficult math problem using only your mind, when the rest of the group works together on a chalkboard! And how you refuse to perform experiments to prove your theories, though they are always right. You even correct Enrico's own theories, don't you?"

The cutting remarks had the intended chilling effect on Fermi. Ettore mumbled a reply, aware of how much his casual accomplishments chipped away at the confidence of their group's hypercompetitive leader.

"Most of all," she continued, "Enrico tells me how you care nothing about publishing your discoveries, though you could be famous the world over. Is this true?"

"If the man exists who gazes not at his own reflection," Fermi said, "it's our Ettore."

"But that's why I've asked you here," Ettore said. "I've decided to publish a paper."

The older physicist carefully set his espresso down. "Don't fool with me, Ettore."

"What do you mean?"

"You're serious?"

Ettore blinked. "Of course."

With a whoop, the tension between them forgotten, Fermi

pulled Ettore to his feet and embraced him. "Buono, my good man! Buono! I couldn't have heard better news. Did you know, dear Laura, that our Ettore deduced the structural forces of the nuclei before even Heisenberg? Yet wouldn't let me discuss it in Paris? And the discovery of the neutron—don't even get me started! What kind of deranged person keeps such things to himself?"

Laura sipped her drink and watched the crowd stroll by. "Fascinating, darling."

With a shy smile, Ettore retook his seat and shook the last cigarette from his pack. "You must give me a preview," Fermi said. "Right now, on this beautiful afternoon."

With a shrug, Ettore held his unlit cigarette between his fingers and obliged. He launched into a brief, excited description of the content of his paper, including a set of complex equations scribbled on a napkin.

"I do say," Fermi said with a chuckle to his wife, stroking his chin as Ettore finished, "that's the most words I've ever heard Ettore utter in one day."

Laura ignored him.

"What do you think?" Ettore asked Fermi.

After taking the napkin and studying it for a long moment, Fermi gave his colleague a paternalistic clap on the back. "Dirac might not be pleased."

Ettore smirked. "I would think not."

"I'll have to study it further, but it's a great start, one which I'm sure will spark much debate. Most of all, I'm happy you've decided to share it with the world. Let's hope it's the dawn of a new era."

Slowly, Ettore reached for his lighter and lit his cigarette, hiding his emotions behind a cloud of smoke. His superior's reaction had made him feel hurt and confused and sad.

Fermi had not understood his theory, he realized. That or he did not find it persuasive. Perhaps both.

That was okay, he thought. *When I'm given the Nobel Prize, perhaps he'll understand his mistake.*

Ettore was not a vain man, saddled by visions of glory. He just believed in his new theory that much.

Yet he *wanted* Fermi to understand. Despite their fundamental difference in personality—Fermi didn't understand failure, and Ettore didn't understand success—Fermi was the most gifted physicist in Italy, after Ettore.

"I have to go," Ettore said, pushing to his feet.

"But we just arrived!" Fermi said.

"I'd like to read over my paper again," he said coldly.

Like many geniuses, in order to compensate for a lifelong failure to fit in, Ettore had learned to erect a shield of superiority at a moment's notice.

Before he left the table, Ettore crumpled his pack of cigarettes and left it in the ashtray. After a hesitation, Fermi reached for it and brushed off the ashes.

"What are you doing?" his wife asked.

"Ettore sometimes leaves theories on his cigarette packs that could win an international prize," Fermi said with a sheepish smile.

Laura gave a soft laugh in reply.

Ettore walked away and didn't deny it.

Later that year, Ettore's fortunes continued to improve, culminating with the news that he had been awarded a grant from the National Research Council to study in Leipzig. He was to help the great Werner Heisenberg himself expand his theory of the nucleus.

For once, Ettore's cloud of depression seemed to lift. His health was good. The upcoming trip to Germany was exciting. The world's greatest physicists had read his paper, and it had been well received. While no one was sure whether Dirac or Ettore had gotten it right, they were all paying attention. Ettore's old professors were now quoting *him*.

It looked to be a period of great promise. A new country, a new era. Perhaps he would unlock the mysteries of the nucleus itself.

As he prepared for his journey, never one for politics, he ignored the nationalistic ranting of Adolf Hitler. How could anyone with a rational mind listen to such drivel, let alone give it a platform?

Ettore left for Leipzig in January of 1933.

A week after he arrived, Adolf Hitler was declared chancellor of Germany.

While the elevation of the future führer would affect Ettore in many ways in the days to come, it was but a portent of the terrible darkness that would soon befall the young physicist.

Durham

7

Angling her back toward the library hallway to shield her actions from view, Andie peered inside the open wall safe concealed behind the framed photo of the Ishango bone. Inside were two objects: a cell phone and a thick Moleskine journal.

The sleek phone appeared to be a newer-generation smart-phone, with the deep-silver sheen of an aluminum or titanium alloy. Curious but wary, she touched the surface lightly with a finger, as if it might shock her. When nothing happened, she pulled it out, along with the journal.

The phone had no brand name or other identifying marker, except for a small black star on the back. Puzzled, she flipped through the journal and saw that it was filled with notes in Dr. Corwin's handwriting.

For a moment, she stood there staring dumbly at the empty safe. Was it coincidence that she knew the password? Maybe Dr. Corwin had been pressed for time to write the note, and the password to the MUT folder was the best thing that came to mind.

Or maybe he had wanted her to know.

After a final glance down the hallway, she pocketed the phone and stuck the Moleskine journal in the folder she had taken from Dr. Corwin's office. She closed the safe and replaced the framed photo.

On her way out, she slipped through the back door of the library and angled behind Duke Chapel, keeping to the heavy darkness at the base of its walls as she hurried toward the lot where she had parked.

Sweat was trickling down her neck by the time she reached her car. Her hands shook as she locked the doors and she set the bulging manila folder in the passenger seat. Assuming the cell phone and the journal were important, she understood why Dr. Corwin had stashed them somewhere outside his office or his home.

Yet how had he installed a safe in the library without anyone knowing? Had it been there for years, for a different purpose? Covered by a different piece of art?

She logged on to the Duke faculty website and navigated to the home page of the library. To her surprise—he had never told her about this—she discovered Dr. Corwin was the current chair of the Library Council.

He was also an ex officio member with an unlimited term.

She scanned the names of the other members, but no one jumped out at her. Dean Varen was not listed.

On impulse, she called information and asked for the number for Dr. Lars Friedman in the Raleigh-Durham area. Surprisingly, there was a home listing, and Andie chose the automatic connection.

"Yes?" A woman with a pleasant voice answered, on the third ring.

"Is Dr. Friedman home?"

A long silence. "Who is this?"

"A colleague."

"What's your name?"

As Andie hesitated, unwilling to give out her information and trying to decide if she should use another false name, the woman's voice turned desperate. "I haven't seen my husband in two days. Please, if you know where he is, if you know anything at all, you have to tell me. *Please.*"

"I don't know anything about that. I'm sorry."

"Are you with him right now?"

"What? No, of course not." She wanted to say she was a friend of Dr. Corwin's, but that was information she was unwilling to divulge.

"Then who are you? How did you get this number? Why did you call?" The woman's voice choked off into a sob. "Do you know if he survived the fire?"

"I'm very sorry," Andie whispered again, and ended the call.

By the time Andie returned home, darkness had sealed the surrounding forest like the closing of a tomb. A large animal of some kind, a fox or a bobcat, slunk into the trees as her headlights illuminated the long gravel drive.

She parked her car and stepped out, feeling dazed. Her entire world had just turned on a new axis, spinning in a completely different direction. Needing to calm her nerves, she poured a whiskey and sat on her secondhand sofa with the folder she had taken from Dr. Corwin's office.

She emptied the contents beside her. A cell phone, the black Moleskine journal, the drawings of her visions, and the photo of her mother.

The ink drawings pulled in her gaze like the bottom of a whirlpool, dark and hypnotic. She still couldn't believe what she was seeing. Who had drawn these? Dr. Corwin? A sudden, terrifying thought occurred to her. Had she and her mother been subjected to some kind of experiment? If so, had that contributed to her mother's decision to leave? What if Dr. Corwin had been trying to help her?

Andie set the drawings aside. She wanted so very much to buy into that line of reasoning. But she would need far more proof than this.

Next, she picked up the cell phone. There was an old-school camera eye, but no battery access she could find. Nor did she see an outlet jack, a microphone, or volume control. There was a single long button on the underside of the phone. When she pressed it, the LCD display lit up, revealing an image that materialized to fill the center of the screen: a bust of Democritus, the ancient Greek philosopher who had first conceived of the atom. She recognized him at once.

Just below the image of Democritus was a line of nine cursor spaces. A flashing prompt appeared on the first space, as if awaiting an entry.

Below that, at the bottom of the screen, was the symbol of a keyboard. She touched the image of Democritus, but nothing happened. There seemed to be no way to manipulate the image. When she pressed the symbol of the keyboard, however, the image switched to a screen containing numbers, letters, and symbols. The nine cursor spaces remained, as did the keyboard symbol, which allowed her to toggle back and forth.

Besides the typical array of numbers and letters on the keyboard, she found mathematical symbols, astronomical figures, characters in foreign languages, periodic table symbols, and a few icons she didn't recognize. There were no emojis, apps, or even a text or call button.

What the hell was this thing?

Setting it aside for the moment, she turned to the Moleskine journal. A quote from Nikola Tesla graced the inside cover:

"My brain is only a receiver, in the universe there is a core from which we obtain knowledge, strength and inspiration. I have not penetrated into the secrets of this core, but I know that it exists."

Due to his interest in electromagnetism, Dr. Corwin had studied Tesla's work extensively. Andie wondered at the meaning behind the quote as she flipped through the beginning pages of the journal and found a host of complicated theorems and proofs. Musings on string theory and quantum gravity. The effects of electromagnetic radiation near black holes. Nothing too unusual for Dr. Corwin.

Then it got weird.

Speculation on whether a human being can be converted into living energy and back again. Quantum time calculations she had never seen before. Musings on what sort of theoretical super weapons a solution to MUT might unleash. An outline of the major theories debating the existence of other dimensions and universes, and what sort of formula might unlock a door to them.

Where was all this coming from?

Near the middle of the journal, she found a series of sketches of the nine-sided plastic model she had found in his office. In the journal, Dr. Corwin referred to the device as the Enneagon. Just after that, over the next twenty pages or so, were lines and lines of theorems that made no sense to her. It wasn't that she couldn't handle the math; the symbols and formulas were nonsensical.

As if they had been encoded.

Was this a real device, that Dr. Corwin had collaborated with Dr. Friedman of Quasar Labs to build? If so, what did it do?

Every now and then, she spied a mysterious reference in the margin that caught her eye. *Who are the Unknown Nine?* She wondered. *The Leap Year Society? Someone named Zawadi? The Ascendants? And what in the world is a Majorana Tower?*

The only Majorana she knew of was an Italian physicist who had disappeared under mysterious circumstances in the early twentieth century. Dr. Corwin had mentioned him in his lectures, and she knew of his work on the neutrino. But he was a minor figure, and she didn't remember a tower of any sort.

Further along in the journal, she found a sketch of the device with the strange keyboard that was sitting right beside her. It was neatly labeled *Star Phone*. A drawing of a staircase with nine steps filled the opposite page. Just beneath the staircase, Dr. Corwin had written *Star Phone*. Across the top, with similar care, he had written *Enneagon*. Beside the staircase, an arrow pointed from top to bottom, from the Star Phone to the Enneagon, along with a string of nonsensical symbols along the arrow.

The only other notes on either page were on the first step of the staircase, where two words were written, in capital letters: *DEMO-CRITUS ARCHE.*

The second word was unfamiliar to her, but it only took a moment of searching to uncover the language—Greek—and the translation.

Arche. The beginning.

Most of the rest of the journal was filled with encoded text. She set it down, picked up the Star Phone, and let it rest in her hand, studying the image of Democritus. *The beginning of what?*

Nine steps on the staircase. Nine cursor spaces. The implication, she supposed, was that the Star Phone led to the Enneagon in some way.

It was late. Her head was starting to pound. Feeling the need for some fresh air, she stepped into a pair of sneakers and wrapped herself in a light shawl she had picked up on a research trip to the APEX Observatory in Santiago. Carrying the journal, she walked through a set of French doors to a crumbling flagstone patio open to the night sky.

After turning off the outdoor light, she sat cross-legged in the center of the patio. Those stares she had garnered at Quasar Labs, along with everything else that had happened, made her feel nervous and exposed. She was only a PhD student, but she was Dr. Corwin's mentee.

What if they came for her next? It seemed absurd to consider, but maybe she should leave town for a while.

In an effort to relax, she leaned back and let the vastness of the night sky absorb her. It was a delicious evening. The smell of honeysuckle and pine, the soothing drone of crickets. Andie had always been a city girl—still was—but the view of the stars and the cheap rent had swayed her. The trails behind her house, which extended for miles and miles, were a boon as well. Andie was an avid, borderline obsessive runner. She'd completed a dozen marathons and was training for a fifty-mile ultra in the fall. Vigorous exercise, exhausting herself to the bone, was the one thing that calmed her mind.

God, the sky was beautiful. Those inky depths that went on forever. A trillion suns and their planets waiting to be discovered, supernovae that outshone galaxies, the glow of nanodiamond dust around newly formed stars. On another night, she would have wheeled out her home telescope, a Celestron NexStar she had scrimped over the years to buy, and which on a dark night could spot the mesmeric cloud bands on Jupiter, Martian ice caps, and the unearthly blue of Neptune.

To Andie, her chosen field was not just about cataloguing the galaxies and studying the mechanics of interstellar physics. Her job was to imagine other worlds, to peer into the hidden corners of space and time. She felt as if she and her colleagues were participants in the greatest detective story of all time, the quest to unlock the secrets of the universe.

As her thoughts turned yet again to the circumstances of Dr. Corwin's death—she couldn't shake the image of him lying in a pool of blood on some anonymous Italian street—the hum of an engine in the distance broke the silence.

A flash of light appeared. Andie flinched as she realized that headlights were cutting through the trees. Tires crunched on loose stone as they turned onto her gravel drive.

She jumped to her feet and rushed inside. Out the kitchen window, she watched a gray Nissan Armada park right behind her Buick, as if wedging it in. A dark-haired man in a lightweight green jacket stepped out. The vehicle's dome light revealed a strikingly handsome face with a fine-boned, almost aristocratic structure. Only the missing pinky on his right hand—an image frozen in her mind as the door snapped shut—marred his appearance.

The property was too remote for uninvited visitors, especially at night.

She was getting the hell out of there.

Inside a ceramic jar in the kitchen marked FLOUR, she kept a tiny canister of mace, as well as a few valuables. She scooped up the mace, her passport, and a wad of emergency cash from the jar, then dashed to the couch and grabbed the Moleskine journal, the Star Phone, the photo of her mother, and the ink drawings.

As the man knocked on the door, she grabbed a backpack off a chair and stuffed everything except the mace inside, then raced through the open French doors to the patio. Trying to move as quietly as she could, she fled across her muddy backyard to where the path in the woods began. She got twenty feet into the trees before stopping, afraid to move any farther after spotting the man creeping around the side of the house, erasing any doubt as to the purpose of his visit.

The man stepped onto the patio, peering inside windows as he went. Though composed and unhurried, his eyes were active, sweeping the house and the property. Feeling his gaze pass over her raised the gooseflesh on her arms.

He tried the patio door and found it unlocked—thank God she had closed it behind her. Expecting him to go inside, allowing her to get away, she tensed when he turned to scan the backyard again. There was no chance he could see her. She was too deep inside the darkened woods, concealed behind a tree.

Yet instead of turning back to the house, he flicked on a tiny flashlight and aimed it at the ground. After studying the backyard, he began walking right in her direction, with the light trained at his feet.

Oh my God, she thought as fear flooded through her. *He sees my footprints in the mud.*

Los Angeles

—o 8 o—

LA's Industrial District passed by in a sun-drenched haze of abandoned buildings, barbed-wire fencing, tent cities for the homeless, and graffiti-covered brick walls. Home to Skid Row, the treeless streets stood out like a scar on the city's otherwise verdant topography.

Ever since his firing, over two years before, Cal had often experienced the feeling of being watched. Eyes on his back in a public square, a car following him for too long on the freeway.

To steal an old song lyric, this time it was more than a feeling.

He parked his geriatric Popsicle-red Jeep Cherokee on the curb near the edge of the rough neighborhood, a few streets west of the Arts District. He gave his trusty steed a fifty-fifty chance of being stolen. Across the street loomed a warehouse with a fading brick facade and a fresh coat of lime-green paint on the door. A sign above the door read DC CAFÉ AND WORKSPACE.

Along with the handful of cars and electric scooters parked outside, the café was the only sign of life on the block. Cal scanned the street and scurried through the green door. Inside was an artisanal coffee shop with a glass wall that opened onto a warehouse converted into a shared workspace.

Behind the counter, a heavily tattooed Samoan woman pushing three hundred pounds, most of it muscle, was arranging a line of pastries and sweets in the display case. Her name was Sefa, and she was rumored to have an IQ over 140.

"Calvin!" she said. "Good to see you."

"Right back at you. Is Dane in?"

"Let me see if he's busy. Coffee?"

Sefa's pour-overs were legendary, but they cost about three times as much as Cal was willing to pay. "Nope."

With a frown, she disappeared through the door in the rear of the café, emerging soon after. "You're good."

"Thanks."

She swiped an ID card through the slot beside the glass door, granting access to the workspace. On Cal's way through, she gifted him with a friendly slap on the back that almost knocked him over.

At just over two hundred pounds, Cal was not used to being pushed around like a toddler. *That woman needs to be in the NFL instead of serving coffee.*

Past the door was an open warehouse with three tiers of loftlike workstations. Cords and wires ran along the floor, draped over movable stands, and looped through hooks in the rafters. A drill press and a 3-D printer took up space in the center. Here and there, the maniacal grin of the Joker—the patron saint of the café—leered from a movie poster, coffee mugs, and other memorabilia.

Though available to anyone to rent, the workspace attracted a hard-core tech crowd and served as a meeting spot for a hacker group. Cal was a little unclear as to how it all fit together: café, hackerspace, urban collective, tech-oriented coworking space. He supposed it was a millennial thing.

What he did know was that a man named Dane owned the building and probably ran the hacker group. Dane was also known as Priest—as in, the high priest of technology—and he was an in-demand IT consultant and systems engineer, in addition to having the reputation as one of the city's best hackers. Cal had worked with him a number of times in the past, stretching back to his journalism career.

Most of the diverse crowd was hunched over laptops glowing in the dim light. Cal walked to the back and entered a hallway that dead-ended at Dane's office. A pair of video monitors marked his presence. For once, the cameras felt reassuring.

He pressed the intercom button. "It's Cal."

A buzzer sounded, and the heavy door swung open. Cal stepped into a room with metal paneling and five monitors mounted above a corner desk. The only decor was a series of framed Batman comics on the wall. Cal had once asked if DC Café was a reference to the comic book publisher, but Dane had told him it stood for "deterministic chaos theory."

Which was Cal's second choice.

The desk chair swiveled, revealing a thick-necked man in his late thirties. A bushy red beard concealed his face, and a mane of wavy, pumpkin-colored hair fell past shoulders as wide as a coffee table. Though not quite as large as Sefa, the scarily intense owner of the DC Café also shattered the hacker stereotype of a misanthropic weakling.

Or at least the weakling part.

Dane was dressed in a pair of black work boots, jeans, and a gray hoodie with a symbol on the front: a white circle with eight arrows sticking out in all directions.

Two deep-set blue eyes drilled into Cal. "You said you needed to find someone."

Dane spoke with a clipped nasal voice that did not match his appearance. His expression rarely changed, and hyperaware eyes blinked too much from screen fatigue.

"Good to see you too, old buddy."

Dane said nothing.

"You might want to talk to Sefa," Cal continued. "She almost broke my back again. Maybe some employee sensitivity training?"

"She only greets people she likes."

"Lucky me," Cal said.

The café owner frowned and checked his watch. Cal sighed. He knew Dane did not suffer fools and was all business, but over the years Cal kept expecting him to loosen up.

"A few nights ago," Cal continued, "someone showed up outside my house in a black van during a show. When I walked outside to confront them, they took off."

He finally got a reaction: the computer expert's eyebrows arched a fraction of an inch. "I assume you don't know who they are?"

"That's why I'm here. I got a plate number."

"Don't you have contacts?"

"Yeah. LAPD and DMV. According to both, that plate doesn't exist. It's freaking me out."

"Cali plates?"

"Yep."

"What is it?"

Cal told him.

"Sounds like a typical plate," he said, steepling his fingers in his lap. "Intriguing."

"Can you help?"

"*Can* I? Probably. *Will* I? That depends."

"On what?"

Dane paused a beat before he spoke. "I find it hard to believe you have no idea who's following you."

"You know my background. I've pissed off a lot of people over the years. It's more a matter of *which one*. But I never said I had no idea."

Dane spread his hands, acknowledging the point.

Cal pointed at a chair in the corner. "Do you mind?" After a grunted response from Dane, Cal wheeled the chair closer and took a seat. "During the show, I was discussing a group called the Leap Year Society."

Dane gave him a blank stare.

"It's an organization I ran across. They're like a ghost, and I think they might be players. Thirty minutes after I mentioned them on the show—for the first time ever—this black van rolls up right outside my window. I don't know if they're related, but—"

"Did it have a Polybius sticker?"

"A what?" Cal asked, then rolled his eyes when he remembered the reference. Polybius was an urban legend about a fictitious and highly addictive arcade game planted around the country to data-mine psychological information, serviced by government agents dressed in black. "So you do have a sense of humor."

"Thirty minutes?" Dane repeated, unmoved by the comment.

"Can they track me that fast?"

"If they've got a bot looking out for their name, it will take them straight to the source. They either know the admin or they hacked your show—are you using a proxy?"

"Uh, not that I know of."

Dane rolled his eyes. "Then they meta-track the IP address by comparing it to email accounts or social media, cookies if they're a bit smarter, Tor or VPN accounts if we're dealing with a real expert."

"Speak English, Tonto."

"Yes, they can track an unsecured amateur broadcast like yours. Fast. Maybe speed-of-light fast. But the house visit means they have a physical presence in LA."

"That, or they can teleport."

"That, or they were watching you already."

After cracking his knuckles, Cal crossed his arms and leaned back in his chair. He had thought of that, and it made him queasy.

"How do you know about them?" Dane asked.

"Sorry?"

"The Leap Year Society. If it's like a ghost, then how did you hear about them?"

Cal hesitated, debating how much to spill. He knew Dane considered himself a modern-day Robin Hood, redistributing information instead of money. Like the coffeehouses of old-world Europe, many of the hacker collectives worked toward enlightenment and social reform through the spread of knowledge banned by the elites.

A noble goal. Telecomix, a Swedish hacker group, had helped foster communication in Middle Eastern countries where the internet was suppressed.

Yet Dane was a private and very intelligent man. Cal didn't know his ultimate aims or allegiances.

"No names," Cal said. "But I can tell you a story."

Dane reached into a minifridge beneath the desk and cracked a Club-Mate energy drink. He took a giant swig, belched, and held out a palm.

"I assume you're familiar with Cicada 3301?" Cal began.

Dane answered with a smirk.

The mystery known as Cicada 3301 started as an enigmatic message posted on internet chat boards around the world. It featured the image of a cicada on a black background and the number 3301. A note above the image read: Hello. We are looking for highly intelligent individuals. To find them, we have devised a test. There is a message hidden in this image.

To those who could crack the first clue, which involved a line of code buried inside a Caesar cipher, a rabbit hole awaited: a series of cryptic puzzles, involving everything from data security to steganography, linguistics, alternate reality games, Mayan numerology, bootable Linux CDs, MIDI files, physical objects, and even references to famous paintings and novels.

The internet was abuzz. Speculation ran rampant among the techie elite as to the identity of the group, and conspiracy nuts around the globe proffered all kinds of theories. Was Cicada 3301 a cyber mercenary group? A recruitment tool for the NSA, the CIA, MI6? Some unknown government organization? Aliens searching for the best and brightest to take to their home world? The Freemasons, the Illuminati, Skull and Bones? Some type of online cult?

A handful of people claimed to have solved the series of brainteasers. Some of the solutions were even posted on YouTube. According to one person, passing the final test granted access to a private forum on the dark web where members discussed ways to advance online privacy and freedom of information.

"Cicada never verified the claims the puzzle had been solved," Cal said.

"Maybe because the bored teens in the basement wanted to preserve the illusion of mystery?"

"Maybe. And maybe not."

"That silly dark-web chat room is real," Dane said. "I've been there."

"And?"

Dane caught his meaning. "Sure. I get it. Maybe the chat room was a publicity stunt and there's another level. It's all speculation. Why are we talking about this?"

"About a month ago, I had a conversation with a woman on my own chat board. Or at least she said she was a woman. We know how that goes. Anyway, she claimed her boyfriend found an Easter egg buried on Cicada 3301."

"Why does that surprise you?" Dane said. "They probably have dozens."

"She said this one led to the Leap Year Society."

Dane took a long drink. "Go on."

"It gets weird. I won't give you her online identity—"

"Why not? Maybe I could trace her."

"Journalistic integrity, my man."

"Really?"

"Really."

Dane waved a hand, and Cal continued. "She said her boyfriend—let's call him Bill—found an Easter egg that led to a whole new set of puzzles on the dark web."

"What was the egg?"

"I don't know. I don't even think she did. But Bill claimed this mysterious side path was even more difficult than the original, with all kinds of insanely hard clues. He said he got to the end of it too. Guess what he found when he did?"

"The Leap Year Society?"

"Give this man a cookie."

"Okay," Dane said. "We'll assume it's real for the moment. So what does she know about it?"

"Nothing. Bill claimed the end of the route was an anonymous webpage with Leap Year Society displayed in the center. After a few seconds, the web page disappeared, and he couldn't find it again. Or so he said."

"Sounds like a prank."

"She thought so too. Except three days after her boyfriend told her—about six weeks ago, according to her—he quit his job and disappeared. And she hasn't seen him since."

Dane tilted back in his chair. "Maybe she's lying. Or maybe he lied to her. Dude probably had a mistress in Argentina, and didn't want to tell her."

"Helluva way to leave a bad relationship."

"What did Bill do for a living?"

"A mathematician and systems integration engineer. Serious creds—MIT and Princeton."

"And he's still gone? He just up and left his job? Have you tried to verify this?"

"She's anonymous, he's anonymous, they could have logged in from anywhere. I could go old-school, but where do I look? Private companies all over the world? Professors? The government?"

"We can do better," Dane said, "but back up. Have you talked to her again?"

"She hasn't been back. During our chat, she sounded genuinely worried and said she even went to the police. I dug around for everything I could find on the Leap Year Society and came up empty. I finally decided to go public. You know what happened next."

"His leaving could be a coincidence."

"*Anything* could be a coincidence." Cal wagged a finger. "I have two theories. The first is that, as people have thought all along, Cicada is a recruitment tool for highly gifted people who share a similar ideal. Maybe the Leap Year Society is their real name and they set it all up, and the Easter egg is the way in."

"To some supersecret hacker group even I've never heard of?" Dane crushed his energy-drink, and just missed his toss at the trash can. "It's not really our style. Hidden from the world at large, sure. But not other hackers. Recognition for genius is kind of the point."

"Agreed. So here's my theory. What if the Leap Year Society noticed Cicada 3301 and decided to subvert it? Use it as a tool for their *own* recruitment?"

"A piggybacking Easter egg? That's devious."

"Cicada is world-famous. I'd wager a good number of the world's best hackers and computer geniuses have taken a shot. If the Leap Year Society is ultrasecret yet also wanted to attract top tech talent, that would be a great way to do it. What if they hacked the hackers?"

"Someone in Cicada would find out."

"Then maybe they got an invite—or the Leap Year Society had a mole inside."

Dane crossed his thick arms and regarded Cal in silence. A wolfish gleam entered the computer expert's deep-set blue eyes, and he swiveled to face one of the keyboards. "Give me a sec."

"Sure."

As the minutes ticked by, Cal eyed the monitors in the room. He saw a ticker tape of the world's financial markets, a replay of an Australian rules football game, a video game called *Rocket League*, a thread about beer brewing techniques on 4chan, and a screen saver depicting a half-naked anime woman wielding a glowing sword.

One would think, Cal mused as he watched Dane work, that all the new technology and information in the world would be useful for unlocking secrets and exposing conspiracies. And it was. Yet it was also a hindrance: the forms of encryption had grown increasingly sophisticated, and there was an overwhelming amount of information to process. E-books, the internet, entertainment media, podcasts, blogs, VR, AR.

There was simply too much noise. These days, one could hide in plain sight.

Cal asked for a beverage and got another grunted reply. Half expecting Dane to bite his head off, Cal reached into the fridge and pulled out a can of Coke. He sighed in pleasure with the first sip. He was a simple man.

A printer fired up, and the café owner swiveled to face him. "Why do you do what you do?"

"Excuse me?"

Dane walked over to grab a sheet of paper off the printer. "We've worked together before. Minor stuff." He looked down at the paper. "I don't know where this leads."

"Isn't that why we do this?"

"I know why *I* do this."

Cal snorted. "To fight the good fight, man. Take down the oppressive governments and all that. You're right, privacy and data-flow isn't my thing, but outing the new world order very much is."

"Okay. I'll ask again: *Why?*"

"Does there have to be an answer to that question?"

Dane folded the piece of paper in half, swiveled again, and started playing *Rocket League*.

Cal threw up his hands. "I'm terrified of North Korea? *1984* wasn't just a book? Nazis are bad, and it'd be better if that sort of thing never happened again?"

When Dane still didn't turn around, Cal said quietly, "It started with my father."

The café owner finally paused the game.

"I'm from Indiana. Dad was an airline mechanic, a real company guy. He lost his job, and then his pension, when the company went belly-up and shed all its debt to right itself. He died broke and bitter, and I never forgot the lesson. I've never trusted big business, or big anything, since."

Dane turned to face him, lips pursed. "Better," he said, and handed Dane the piece of paper.

"Thanks. What do I owe you?"

"A Coke."

Cal squeezed his soda can, stepped back, and shot a fadeaway. He nailed it.

"Used to play?" Dane asked.

"Yup."

"Still a fan?"

"Clippers all the way."

"Really, man? The Clips?"

"Even in the old days." As he backed toward the door, Cal waved a hand in dismissal. "By the way, the story's true, but my dad was a prick. I guess I just like a good underdog."

Durham

9

Andie clutched the canister of mace like a lifeline and took off through the woods, into the pressing darkness of the trees, down a footpath she had taken a thousand times on her trail runs. A glance over her shoulder told her the dark-haired man had heard her and was sprinting across the lawn.

The footpath was straight and narrow. She knew it joined up with a larger trail in about a quarter mile, then branched out. One of the forks led to the river, another doubled back to the main road.

She glanced at her phone—no signal—before taking off at full speed down the path. The darkness and the woods were her allies, and Andie had all of the major obstacles memorized on this part of the trail. Twice she heard him grunting behind her, no doubt tripping on one of the many rocks and roots that littered the path.

When she reached the fork, a powerful beam from a flashlight sliced through the foliage to her left. She hesitated for the briefest of moments at the split, wanting more than anything to head toward the main road and flag down a car. Yet the half-mile stretch of trail to the highway was straight and level. The dark-haired man looked very athletic. She might be able to outlast him, but there was a good chance he would beat her in a sprint.

Flooded with adrenaline, she headed for the river instead, pumping out a swift but steady pace, breathing in through her nose and out through her mouth to keep the oxygen flowing. There was just enough moonlight to view the path.

A hundred yards farther, she paused to listen, wondering if he had turned back. The forest seemed to swallow her whole, suffocating, pregnant with danger.

Footsteps in the distance. He was still coming. A fresh wave of fear washed over her. Should she leave the trail and hide? Find a log or a boulder, or just crouch somewhere off the path?

No.

She already knew he had tracking skills. The risk of discovery was too great. Her best bet was to use her knowledge of the forest and run for her life.

She summoned a mental image of the trails as she ran. The Eno River was another quarter mile away, and the path paralleled it for some time. That would be a bad place to run, too straight and exposed. On the other side of the river, the trail system was much more built-out.

Soon the gurgle of the river rose above the crickets, giving her a surge of energy. As the trail curved to the left, running alongside the river, she followed it for another fifty yards, glanced back to make sure the dark-haired man was not in sight, then left the trail and stepped into the water.

She stifled a gasp as the cold shocked her legs. The Eno was not a large river, maybe fifty feet across at this point. Would the water rise over her head? She doubted it, but didn't know for sure. She rarely dipped into the water.

Either way, she had chosen her path. She waded through the thigh-high river, losing her balance again and again on the smooth rocks underfoot, each time managing to right herself before she fell. Every few feet she glanced back at the woods. As the water reached her waist, she grew nervous he would catch her exposed in the middle. She debated sinking to eye level in the river, then ducking underwater until she caught a glimpse of him, with the hope he would pass by.

Too risky. Stick to the plan and get across.

The water level kept rising, forcing her to remove her backpack and hold it above her head. Halfway across, she heard him running hard in the woods behind her and saw the beam from his flashlight strobing through the trees.

As she neared the far shore, her foot slipped off a rock again, and this time she plunged into the river. Gasping from the cold, she managed to hold the backpack out of the water, yet when she righted herself, she heard a soft splash and saw the Moleskine journal floating away. She made a grab for it, but the current carried it out of her grasp.

Her pursuer emerged from the woods, spotting her at once. He raced for the riverbank as Andie stumbled onshore and dove into the underbrush. She scrabbled through the thick weeds, pushing through thorns and vines and God knew what else, until she reached the wide trail she knew ran along that side of the shore.

A splash came from behind. He must have entered the water. Andie took off, this time at a dead sprint, knowing this was her chance. As she ran, she checked the backpack, realizing she had not fully closed the zipper in her haste to flee the house. The Star Phone and the other items were safe, but the journal was a grave loss.

A few hundred feet in, the trail split again. She could still hear him splashing through the river. She turned inland, legs churning, her breath coming in labored gasps. A quarter of a mile later, there were no sounds of pursuit, and the path split again, and again, and again. Andie slowed to a fast jog to conserve her energy, her skin crawling with fear as the trees loomed thick and silent all around.

Behind the canopy of trees, the stars were hidden from view, as if they had abandoned her to her fate.

Andie slowed and held her sides as she emerged at West Point on the Eno, a Durham city park near her house. Sometime during the nightmarish run, she had doubled back to the path by the river and followed it south.

The sight of a streetlamp in the distance, glowing like the birth of a universe, gave her a shudder of relief. Wet and shivering, her arms covered in scratches, she exited the park on North Roxboro Street, a few miles from downtown Durham.

Everything felt surreal. As if these terrible events were happening to someone else. She debated going to the police, but that line in Dr. Corwin's email kept repeating in her mind.

Trust no one.

Even if she went to the authorities, she knew they wouldn't provide around-the-clock protection from whoever was chasing her.

She tried to think things through. Someone must know she had opened the safe and had taken the Star Phone. Judging by what she had read in the journal, the phone led to some kind of secret technology, this thing called the Enneagon. That had to be the reason Dr. Corwin was murdered. Even if she turned over the Star Phone—and she wasn't about to give something that belonged to Dr. Corwin to these people—she doubted they would just let her go.

How many people had they killed already?

She needed time to think. A safe place.

Her own phone still worked, despite her plunge into the river. She had two hundred in cash. After Googling the address of a nearby motel, she changed her mind. Too obvious.

She brought up the Uber app, then paused again. What if they had bugged her email or phone?

At some point, she knew she had to take a chance. For now, just in case, she walked down Roxboro and hailed a cab by hand.

The driver was an Indian man with graying temples. His eyes widened at her bedraggled appearance, and she gave him a lopsided smile. "I was on a night run and fell in the river."

He hesitated, looking her up and down as if searching for a weapon.

"I'm a student," she said, flashing her Duke ID just long enough for him to glimpse it.

"Okay," he said. "Where to?"

She jumped in the cab before he could change his mind. "Hillsborough."

"What address?"

"Do you know a hotel there?"

He gave her a suspicious look in the rearview mirror.

"My phone got wet," she said. "Can you find one for me?"

After another pause, he said, "There's a Holiday Inn Express."

"Perfect. And I need to use the nearest ATM."

"Okay."

When he reached to start the meter, she added, "And fifty bucks extra if you keep this off the books."

Nestled among rolling green hills, filled with quaint local shops, Hillsborough was a small town twenty minutes northwest of Durham. On the cab ride over, Andie had withdrawn the maximum daily amount from her bank card. She paid up front for her ground-floor hotel room and left a cash deposit for incidentals. After taking a long hot shower, she collapsed into bed.

The next morning, she set her shoes outside to dry, closed the blinds and brewed a cup of coffee, then sat cross-legged in a chair. She set the Star Phone on the table beside her, pushing away her grief and fear and anger. Succumbing to her emotions would get her nowhere.

Below the image of Democritus, the first cursor space was still flashing.

Arche. The beginning.

Was there a code she was supposed to enter?

Democritus was one of Dr. Corwin's favorite historical figures. At the last department Christmas party, a white elephant affair, Dr. Corwin had given her a paperweight replica of the same bust. Unfortunately, she had dropped it, cracked the porcelain, and thrown the pieces away.

Some quick research told her the depiction of the ancient philosopher on both the Star Phone and the paperweight replica was a specific one: an original bust that sits in the Victoria and Albert Museum in London. The coincidences kept mounting, and she could only assume that her Christmas gift had possessed a greater significance.

She spent half the day trying to enter every combination of numbers and symbols she could think of into the nine cursor spaces on the device. As before, she racked her brain for mathematical formulas, theorems, and information personal to Dr. Corwin. Every time, after she entered the ninth number or symbol, all of the cursor spaces would empty, leaving the first one winking at her again, as if laughing at a silent joke. She kept expecting the screen to lock from her repeated attempts, but it never did.

All of these insane developments, the enigmas and encoded messages, made her think some type of cult or secret society was involved. She wanted to scoff it away. Except for being a genius, Dr. Corwin was a regular guy. He loved English pubs, Indian food, solving puzzles of all sorts, and watching hours of golf and cricket on the television to wind down. As vanilla as they come.

Or so she had thought.

Finally she had to admit defeat. A nine-digit code was impossible to crack by guesswork. After ordering a pizza to her room, she turned her attention to the actual murder. Andie spoke almost no Italian, but she finally got someone on the phone in the Bologna police station who spoke English, only to be told they couldn't give out details about the crime. She realized she would have to hire a lawyer in Italy or, at the very least, plead her case in person. Even then, she wondered how much that would accomplish—and she would be revealing her identity in the same city where the murder took place.

Frustrated, she poured a cup of coffee and paced the room.

What were her choices?

She knew very little, almost nothing, about what was really going on. Impossibly, it seemed as if her strange visions and even her mother might be involved in some way.

No matter what she chose to do, if her pursuers found her, she had to assume they would kidnap and then kill her. That alone was enough for her to put her mind to solving the mysteries gathering around her like a cloud of dangerous radiation.

But it went beyond that.

Someone had been taken from her, murdered, who she loved very much. Someone irreplaceable.

And Andie wasn't going to sit around and do nothing.

She owed Dr. Corwin more than that, so much more, but it was a start. She couldn't believe she had lost the journal, but she did have the Star Phone. It was up to her to figure out how to use that to her benefit. Maybe she could get her hands on the Enneagon itself, and use it to lure Dr. Corwin's murderer out of the shadows.

The idea of putting an ocean between herself and her pursuers appealed to her, as did laying eyes on the original bust of Democritus. Despite Dr. Corwin's warning, she needed information more than anything, and there was someone in London, an Oxford classmate of Dr. Corwin's named Philip Rickman, whom she thought she could trust. Dr. Rickman was also a physicist and a former cricket player, and the two men had stayed extremely close over the years.

Maybe, just maybe, Dr. Rickman could fill in some of the blanks about her mentor.

As she made the decision to go to England, she realized she was not just trying to solve a murder, but the enigma of Dr. Corwin himself.

What sort of research was her mentor involved in?

Who was he, really?

Yet she knew the answer to that final question, while vexing, had no effect on her decision. She didn't care who Dr. Corwin had been to anyone else, not even to her own mother.

Because Andie knew exactly who he had been to her.

Deep into the night, Andie dreamed of walking alone through the halls of Duke Chapel, her footsteps echoing in the gloom of the

Gothic cathedral, feeling as if an ominous presence lurked amid the shadows of the alcoves. Then she was trapped alone at the bottom of a crater on the moon, choking on the lack of oxygen, the stars glittering like diamonds on a tyrant queen's tiara far above, haughty, unreachable, mocking. Then she was racing through the forest again, only this time the woods belonged to the eerie world of her visions. Lost souls roamed the spaces between the trees, the branches reached out to grasp her, and always there was a dark-haired man running behind her, pressing closer—

When she woke midmorning, her back damp with sweat, she downed a glass of water and hovered over the coffee maker as it brewed. Feeling unsteady, knowing she had to keep moving, she took a shower and grabbed her backpack. On the way to the Raleigh-Durham airport, Andie paid the cabdriver to stop at a Marshalls off the interstate. She picked up a pair of lightweight stretch jeans, a gray baseball cap, socks and underwear, a pair of long-sleeve T-shirts, and a thin black windbreaker. The weather would be cooler in London. She also bought basic toiletries and a green nylon daypack, then threw the old one in a dumpster.

At the airport, thankful beyond words she had grabbed her passport, she bought a changeable round-trip ticket to London. The flight left that evening, and the price was eye-popping. Forced to use her credit card, she reasoned she had already displayed her passport. If her pursuers could hack an airline's computer system, so be it. Or maybe they were watching the airport and had already spotted her. She probably should have driven to Charlotte or DC for her flight.

She put a hand to her temple. All of the subterfuge was exhausting.

Yet if these people caught her, she didn't want to think about what might happen. For now, she had to stay focused and do the best she could to resolve the mounting questions.

Would the nine-digit cipher on the Star Phone lead to the Enneagon?

What *was* the Enneagon? Did it have anything to do with the ink drawings of her visions, her mother, or the reams of research on occult and metaphysical speculations she had found in Dr. Corwin's desk?

Most important of all, who had killed Dr. Corwin and was chasing her?

Was it someone at Quasar Labs? A rival corporation? A foreign government?

The wait for her 6 p.m. flight felt interminable. She managed to choke down a bacon-and- avocado sandwich, then hunkered down in a corner until the time came to board. Andie took her seat at the rear of the plane and studied the face of every single passenger she could. No sign of the dark-haired man, but that was little relief, since she doubted he was acting alone.

Her seat was situated between an elderly British woman and a trim blond man wearing horn-rimmed glassed and a pin-striped suit. Andie thought his palms looked too calloused for a businessman's.

After she sat, he turned to her and said, in a mild German accent, "I guess we're stuck together for a while."

"I guess so."

"Flying to London, or on to somewhere else?"

"Somewhere else."

"Ah."

"Rome," she added, so it wouldn't look suspicious.

"Been there before?"

"Yeah."

"Business or pleasure this time?"

"Both."

Maybe he was fishing for information, or maybe he was just chatty. Either way, she had to cut it off. Before he could ask another question, she pulled the airline magazine out of the seat pocket and began reading it. He got the hint and fell silent, though she felt like he was watching her out of the corner of his eye.

They taxied for almost an hour. When the plane lurched into the air, triumphing over gravity with a mighty roar, she gripped the armrest and vowed not to let her guard down.

Leipzig, Germany
──○ 1933 ○──

Germany was a breath of fresh air to Ettore.

Maybe Italy itself had b a contributor to his lifelong depression. As he strolled the streets of Leipzig, he decided a creeping aura of decay had beset the psyche of his home country ever since the collapse of the Roman Empire. Just like Ettore, Italy needed a new start. Something to be proud of. And not the petty nationalism trotted out by that buffoon Mussolini.

After a month in Leipzig, despite the troubling political events unfolding in Germany—particularly the appointment of Adolf Hitler as chancellor—everything about the new city felt invigorating.

The cold weather and the heaps of pristine snow. The handsome, refined populace who had emerged from their postwar shell. The wide boulevards and grand display of Gründerzeit and art nouveau architecture that sparkled in comparison to Italy's clogged streets and grime.

One evening, after a long day at the research foundation where Ettore worked, Werner Heisenberg invited him to a beer hall with a few colleagues. Still in his early thirties, Werner was already famous for his uncertainty principle, which held that observation itself has an effect on the behavior of particles at the quantum level. This made them inherently uncertain, and impossible to precisely measure.

Like it or not, it appeared that chaos reigned in the quantum world.

Ettore readily accepted Werner's invitation. He rather idolized the leader of the physics institute, who along with being a brilliant scientist, was also a hard-drinking ladies' man who could play the piano, dance, and ski.

Like most extreme introverts, Ettore was able to relax whenever Werner's larger-than-life presence filled the room. Werner even seemed to genuinely enjoy his company, and they shared a fierce mutual respect for each other's intellect.

The beer hall was a raucous place, full of stein-pounding Germans squeezed side by side on long wooden benches. As the strapping Werner waded into the crowd, Ettore scurried in his wake like a foal clinging to its mother. They found some seats and ordered foaming mugs of the local pilsner.

"Did you hear about the decree?" Werner shouted to Ettore, once they had beers in hand. Two of their colleagues had taken seats across the table and could not be heard above the din.

"What decree?"

Werner's broad face tightened. "Surely you know about the fire?"

"But of course."

The day before, an unknown arsonist had burned down the Reichstag, the German parliament building. The Nazis were blaming the Communists, stirring up populist fervor.

"Hitler has asked our weak-kneed president for an emergency order, and I'm sad to say he granted it. Most of our civil liberties have been suspended, Ettore. Overnight. It's fascist." He scowled into his beer. "It's obvious to everyone what is happening, but Hindenburg is too afraid of Hitler to refuse him."

"Why do people listen to him?" Ettore asked, feeling lost in the huge room. "He's such an ugly little man."

"Because men like to follow other men. Especially leaders who tell them they are special and better than everyone else."

"What will it mean for the institute?"

"It depends on how things evolve. I'll tell you one thing, though." His scowl deepened. "I worry for our Jewish colleagues. The rhetoric against them grows worse by the day. I've heard calls for resignation. Philipp Lenard has gone so far as to denigrate relativity as 'Jewish science.' Can you believe that swill? And himself a Nobel laureate!"

"What do you think will happen?"

Werner lifted a palm. "Albert, of course, will be fine. Some of the others may have a harder time. I'll talk with them privately, urge them to consider reassignment."

Ettore gave an absent nod, unable to feel much in the abstract for people he did not know.

Werner noticed. "These days, it isn't enough to focus on science and shut out the rest of the world. If quantum mechanics has taught us anything, it's that we're all connected in mysterious ways, *ja*?"

"But as you yourself proved, it also taught us that everything is uncertain. So why bother?"

He laughed. "Don't obfuscate, Ettore. We live in the real world, not in the world of abstract physics."

Ettore failed to understand the difference, since the "real world" was composed of protons and electrons and other particles. But he didn't wish to debate the point and upset Werner. "Speaking of inde-terminacy, have you and Albert corresponded recently?"

Werner belched. "Bah. He stands firm in his opposition. 'God does not play dice,' he says. Yet what does Albert know of either the casino or an omnipotent deity? He avoids them both like a bout of syphilis."

"What if God does play dice," Ettore said, thoughtful, "but knows all the outcomes beforehand?"

"That's theology, not science."

"Is it? What do we know of the mind of God, or the universe, or whatever one wishes to call it?"

"Good Christ, have you been following along? We know quite a bit!"

"Do we?" Ettore said quietly. "We once thought the Earth was the center of the universe, that light was a single uniform substance, that a stone dropped off the edge of the planet would fall forever. We think we're enlightened, but how will humanity view our positions one hundred years from now? One *thousand*?"

Werner started to speak, then took a long drink. "I will grant you that, my friend. But it is my firm belief that humanity will one day understand the physical laws of the universe."

"I don't disagree. And I think you and Albert both have it right. There is great beauty in the chaos. Structure."

"You agree with Albert then."

"I agree that what we know right now—what we *think* we know—tells but a fraction of the story."

"Bohr has spoken to that, as you surely know," Werner said. "Our problem is merely one of observation. If we could see the quantum world from all the right angles, the chaos would disappear."

"And what if more layers of reality lie beneath the quantum world?"

Werner laughed. "What a mind you have! What are these new layers of which you speak? I take it you've considered this already?"

Ettore gave a small smile and fell silent, not yet ready to discuss these thoughts in public.

Werner raised his glass in a toast. "Good man, Ettore. I appreciate discretion. That fellow Dirac cares not a whit for experimental truth, as long as his math works out."

Ettore clinked his glass and fell silent. He had risked everything by publishing his paper in opposition to Dirac's theory, and hoped with every fiber of his being that his own position would prove to be the correct one. In a rare display of pride, Ettore had even taken to trumpeting his theory in Leipzig, and casting aspersions on Dirac's model.

Werner's eyes had turned glassy from the alcohol. When he leaned closer to Ettore, bending so that their heads lightly brushed, the leathery musk of his cologne tickled Ettore's nose.

"I have a confession," Werner said. "I've been approached by the Nazis."

Ettore swallowed and waited for him to continue.

"They wish for me to join them. Become their top scientist."

"Surely you desisted?"

Werner looked amused. "Are you yourself not a member of your country's Fascist Party?"

Ettore sniffed and waved a hand. "A formality. I didn't even sign the papers myself."

"Well, I fear it's a little more serious over here."

"So what will you do?"

After turning to scan the crowd, the German leaned even closer, draping his hand across Ettore's narrow shoulders. "I put them off for now, but I fear for the future. I won't abandon my country, you know. I'm a patriot. Yet I can't align myself with that madman. I . . . don't know what I will do."

It was a rare moment of weakness for the charismatic man. Ettore disengaged and patted him awkwardly on the back, not knowing what to say or how to comfort him. In response, Werner gripped his hand, causing a tingle of warmth to spread through him.

Ettore walked home alone, his breath fogging the air. He passed through Leipzig's handsome market square and then strode down lively Brühl Street, passing near to where the home of Wagner once stood.

Eventually, his thoughts turned to his friend, as they often did these days. Ettore did not know how to categorize his feelings for Werner. He did not think it was a sexual response, though he did not really know. Were love and friendship and sexual relations inextricably intertwined? Ettore's knowledge of math and physics was in inverse proportion to his knowledge of the human heart. He knew only that he had never enjoyed anyone's company as much as he did Werner Heisenberg's.

Yet Ettore was fiercely independent, and terrified of removing his armor of isolation. It made him want to pull away from Werner.

Intimacy was too dangerous a thing.

After crossing a footbridge with a decorative iron railing, he entered a quieter, more residential part of the city. The glow of the street lanterns faded as Ettore passed alongside the cemetery that marked the start of his neighborhood. There was a shortcut through the somber stone tombs, though after nightfall he preferred to keep to the street. Thieves were not unknown in Leipzig. And while Ettore was not a superstitious man, he could admit to an atavistic fear of the dark. Unlike most of his colleagues, he did not scoff at this. Recent discoveries had proved the universe strange beyond all imagining. Early man was afraid of the spirits haunting the night sky, and who was to say they were wrong? Ettore did not believe in spirits in the traditional sense, but matter and energy were interchangeable and always conserved. What happened to human consciousness after death? And this mysterious field of corporeal energy that so fascinated Tesla—what if ghosts were real, just not yet understood by science?

What if they were a *product* of science?

As usual, Ettore's speculations distracted him from his surroundings. When he looked up, a gang of unkempt youths in dark coats were slipping out of the darkness of the cemetery like oiled eels. They hopped the low wall and approached the street, boots crunching on dried leaves.

Walking right toward Ettore.

There were half a dozen of them brandishing knives and clubs, their confident grins splitting tobacco-stained teeth.

Ettore shrank back as the largest of them stepped forward. Perhaps twenty, he was a hulking young man with bright-red hair and a high-necked coat an inch short in the sleeves.

"*Guten Abend,*" he said.

"Good evening," Ettore tried to reply, but his voice cracked too much.

"It's past curfew, you know."

Ettore, whose German was far from perfect, thought he had misheard him. "Curfew?"

"That's right," he said, smacking his cudgel into the palm of his hand, over and over. "Because of the Reichstag fire."

"Oh. I didn't know."

"Maybe you should pay attention to the local news, *Ausländer.*"

Ausländer meant "foreigner." Ettore shuffled his feet and looked down.

"There's a fine, you know."

"A fine?" Ettore whispered. "But I'm a scientist."

"The fine is all of your money paid to me. Right now."

"I don't have—"

The thug lunged forward, grabbing Ettore by his collar and jerking him up on his toes.

"You're in my territory is what you are."

Ettore struggled to speak. His own collar was choking him. "I—I have very little. I'm only here on a grant—"

"*Give it.*"

Ettore fumbled to reach the coins in his pockets, but his hands were shaking too much. He gasped and tried to explain, but the street thug tripped him to the ground, sticking the cudgel painfully into his chest. He snarled and said, "Take off your watch."

A warm trickle of urine escaped Ettore's bladder. He couldn't seem to make his muscles obey. His neurons had scrambled, overcome by fear, no longer his to command.

His failure to respond enraged the brute. As the others jeered, he kicked Ettore in the ribs, then reached down and jerked the watch that Ettore's favorite uncle had given him off his wrist.

"Take his clothes, Dirk!" one of the others crowed.

"And his shoes!"

"Look at his dark skin! He's probably a pathetic little Jew!"

As Ettore trembled, wondering if they were going to kill him, a loud crack rang out, causing his assailant to jerk away.

"Stand back!" a voice commanded from the street behind Ettore.

He risked turning his head and saw a tall man with a lean, craggy face and cropped blond hair walking toward them with a raised pistol. A woolen peacoat fell to the top of his boots, accompanied by gray gloves and a matching scarf.

When the thug standing over Ettore hesitated, the man fired his pistol in the air again, above his head. "Was I unclear? Now!"

Dirk backed away. He and his friends started to slink off into the night, but the newcomer called out again.

"Stop moving."

It was not a shout, yet something in his voice, an assumed tone of command of which the most experienced field general would be proud, caused the gang to stand still and face him.

"Return the watch."

Dirk muttered something under his breath but tossed the watch to Ettore. He fumbled the catch, and the watch fell to the street. Thankfully the face didn't crack.

"You're lucky," the new man said to the youths, "that I have other business tonight. Else I would drag you all to jail by your collars. As it stands, if I ever catch you approaching this man or any other on the street, the penalty will be harsh and swift. Am I clear?"

"But look at him!" one of them said, pointing at Ettore. "He doesn't belong here! He's not a German!"

"Look at you," the man replied. "A pack of dirty thieves who *are*."

The gang members looked away or down at their feet, their weapons having disappeared into their coats.

The newcomer fired right at Dirk's feet, causing him to leap back. "Am I clear?"

"Yes," Dirk said, his voice shaky. "Clear."

"Clear, *Sergeant Major*," the man corrected, tapping the gun against a red-and-white heraldic eagle on his sleeve.

After Dirk meekly repeated the words, he and the others hurried down the street, swallowed by the night.

"Thank you," Ettore croaked, brushing the dust of the street off his jacket.

"You're welcome."

"I was fortunate you were nearby. If not—"

"It was more than fortune, Ettore Majorana."

Ettore started, his heart still pounding from the encounter. "How do you know my name?"

"Because I've been watching you. This route isn't safe after dark, you know. You should choose another."

"Watching me? But why? Who are you?"

In the ensuing pause, Ettore glanced down, relieved the urine stain on his thigh was not visible beneath his double-breasted coat.

"Shall we walk?" the man said. "I'll accompany you home. I'm sure the experience was a traumatic one."

"Thank you. Yes. I've . . . never been robbed before."

"You have my utmost apology that this ugliness occurred in my country." As they continued past the cemetery, he said, "My name is Stefan Kraus. I'm a sergeant major in the German army, as well as a senior leader in the Schutzstaffel."

Ettore twitched at the mention of the Schutzstaffel, which everyone referred to as the SS.

Stefan flashed a rueful smile. "At times, a man is forced to adopt a mantle he does not truly wear, ja? I am not acting on official business tonight. Or at least not *that* official business."

Ettore was so grateful to him for saving his life that he did not really care about his other motives.

"I represent a very special organization, Ettore. One that is very aware of—and impressed by—your work."

"Are you with one of the prize organizations?"

The man laughed. "No, I'm afraid not. Though you deserve that and more. Still, those types of awards are not really important to you, are they?"

"I suppose not," Ettore agreed.

"Why is it that you almost never publish your research?"

"But how do you know that?"

"Please answer."

The command was softly given, almost a suggestion, yet Ettore felt as if he had no choice but to obey. "Because I don't find it important," he said finally.

"Yet your recent paper on particle theory is different, ja? You believe strongly in this one."

"You've read it?" Ettore said, incredulous.

"Of course."

"And understood it?"

The corners of Stefan's lips turned up. "Not only that, we believe in it. And in your potential for even greater things."

"We? Who *are* you?" he asked again.

Instead of answering, Stefan launched into a spirited discussion of the latest theories circulating among the elite theoretical physicists of the day. He was even fluent in quantum electrodynamics, Ettore's favorite subfield.

"Surely you are a working scientist," Ettore said in amazement after they had talked for some time on the street in front of his lodging.

"I once was, yes. Among other things. Now I serve a higher calling."

Ettore sniffed, failing to hide his disdain. "You mean your political party?"

"No, Ettore. The group I mentioned earlier." Stefan reached into his coat and opened his palm to reveal a large black coin etched with an elaborate series of numbers and symbols in silver ink around the edges.

Ettore could make no sense of the inscription. In the center of the coin, three prominent capital letters, inscribed in silver, demanded attention.

LYS

Ettore looked at him blankly. "I don't recognize any of this. Is it supposed to be a theorem of some sort?"

"Not a theorem. A cipher."

"I don't understand."

"Nor should you. Not yet."

"Is the coin made of stone?"

"It's an alloy."

Ettore frowned. "Of what type?"

Stefan returned the coin to the pocket of his coat. "We'd like you to join us, Ettore. We extend an invitation to an extremely few number of people, but I believe you would be an excellent addition."

"An addition to what? What does 'LYS' mean?"

Stefan regarded him in silence for a moment. "Do you wish to probe the outer limits of science, Ettore? Reach to the stars and beyond? Unlock the potential of mankind?"

"I'm a theoretical physicist. Of course I do."

Another small smile. "Of course."

"Surely you know I work at the physics institute," Ettore said, growing annoyed. "Some of the best work in the world is undertaken there."

"Yet you are limited by certain boundaries, are you not? The extent of your grant, the resources of your institution or government, the aptitude of your colleagues?"

"I work directly with Werner Heisenberg," Ettore said stiffly. "One of the greatest living scientists. Why have you not asked him?"

"Haven't we?"

As Ettore stuttered, Stefan laughed and clapped him on the shoulder. "Werner is undeniably brilliant, yet he adores the lights of the stage far too much."

"There are plenty of other physicists."

"No, Ettore." Stefan shook his head. "There are not. How many others at the institute does the great Werner Heisenberg address as an equal? We have attended the conferences, heard the talks. Does Heisenberg not sometimes start his sentences on nuclear theory with 'According to Majorana' and 'As Majorana has stressed'?"

Ettore could not deny it. In fact, it embarrassed him very much.

"I understand your reticence. We have just met, and my claims are bold. Yet I know you sense that mankind is on the cusp of discovering even greater knowledge." He took a step closer, palms upturned. "Do you really think the discoveries in the headlines tell the whole story? That the world's bloated governments and profit-hungry corporations are the only players in the game? That your scientific institutions alone work to wrest the truth out of Mother Nature? There are more things in heaven and earth, my dear Ettore, than are dreamt of in your philosophy."

As he repurposed the words of Shakespeare, the German officer's stare bored into Ettore, pulling in the physicist's gaze like a pendulum dangled by a master mesmerist. "Meet with us. See who we are."

Just like Werner—perhaps even more so—the German officer had an undeniable charisma that drew Ettore like a moth to a flame.

He had to admit he was curious. The thought of hidden knowledge had always intrigued him. In any event, what could it hurt to see?

"Where do I find you?" Ettore asked.

Stefan stuffed his hands in the pockets of his coat as he backed away, his parting smile as mysterious as the Sphinx. "I'll let you know."

# PART TWO

London, England

10

The heavy Boeing jet roared away from Raleigh-Durham International Airport, soaring high above the geometric loop and tangle of roadway, the emerald pastures and office parks, the spiderweb of creeks and rivers.

The higher the plane rose, the more a pattern materialized out of the chaos below, reminding Andie of zoomed-out shots of Earth, the solar system, and the Milky Way. She suspected the whole universe was like that, a pattern made of patterns, mimesis on a cosmic scale, everything a matter of perspective.

Turtles all the way up, down, and in between. Turtles hurtling through space and time.

She had a layover in Toronto, descending into the Canadian city as the horizon drew a line of fire above shadowed earth. Despite her frayed nerves and her promise to stay awake, she fell asleep during the red-eye to England.

As soon as the plane landed at Heathrow, she squeezed past her German seatmate without a word and hurried to customs. The line was horrendous. By the time she made it through, still blinking the sleep away, jet lag making everything fuzzy, it was 3 p.m. London time. She grabbed a cappuccino and an egg sandwich at Costa, hunkered down at a table, and debated what to do. Just to be safe, she kept her phone off and purchased a burner with a prepaid internet plan at the airport.

The crush of people passing through Heathrow was dizzying. Andie had been to London before and loved it, but this time, the incessant flow of bodies and babble of foreign languages made her feel vulnerable.

Had someone watched her deplane? Followed her through customs?

A quick search told her the Victoria and Albert Museum closed at a quarter to six. By the time she could get there, it would be well after five. She didn't want to rush her visit, and decided to wait until morning.

A year ago, after a presentation by Dr. Corwin at Imperial College, she had accompanied him on a visit to Professor Rickman's third-floor flat near the Thames in Central London. She still remembered how to get there. As she finished her sandwich and tossed the wrapper into a futuristic recycling bin, she decided not to call him beforehand, and to do her absolute best to make sure she wasn't followed.

The Temple station was the closest tube stop to the professor's flat. A straight shot east from Heathrow on the Piccadilly line to Earl's Court, then a change to the District line. Yet as the underground train bulleted past the rows of granite chimneys squatting grimly among the forests of glass and steel, she studied the wall map of the subway lines and made a snap decision to take a detour. Professor Rickman might not even be home yet, and she could further cover her tracks.

At Leicester Square, she changed for the Northern line, taking it five stops north to Camden Town. She exited with a pack of Londoners and tourists into a cauldron of grungy humanity. The smell of leather and incense and street kebabs. Tattoos of every type imaginable. Ripped clothing, piercings, hair dyes across the visible spectrum.

Andie felt right at home.

She knew CCTV was omnipresent in London. The question was whether the people pursuing her had access. Either way, she felt better as she ducked in and out of the maze of shops and crowded street stalls, winding her way toward the canal. She stopped to buy a British flag T-shirt, a lightweight green field jacket, a pocketknife, and a pair of sunglasses, then changed into the new outfit. She stuffed the knife in her pocket, and her other clothes in the backpack.

After grabbing a Cornish pasty for fuel, she decided it was time to get going. On the way to Professor Rickman's flat, she changed tube lines three more times, hopping onto trains at the last second. Maybe she was being overcautious, but by the time she emerged into the city at the Temple station, she was reasonably certain she had managed to arrive unobserved.

The mercurial weather, which seemed to change block to block, had turned cooler, and the twilight sky began to spit rain. The gray sweep of the Thames was just across the street. Following her phone, she walked a block up to Fleet Street, where tall, handsome residential buildings with ground-floor commerce lined both sides of the avenue, punctuated here and there by a massive stone landmark. The crowd was whiter and far more conservative than in Camden Town. She walked a few blocks down Fleet, to a cobblestone lane squeezed between the buildings. Directly ahead loomed the dome of Saint Paul's Cathedral.

After passing beneath an overpass and winding alongside an ancient pub, the little byway opened into a courtyard ringed by three and four-story brick flats. A tree with white blossoms twisted out of the ground in the center of the courtyard. She approached the first building on the left, unlatched a waist-high iron gate, and pressed the buzzer for Dr. Rickman's apartment.

As she waited, she recalled what she knew about him. A tenured professor in Imperial College's prestigious theoretical physics department, specializing in black holes and other condensed matter, Dr. Philip Rickman was a Welshman who had studied and taught in the United States for much of his career. He had been at Princeton at the same time as Dr. Corwin and Andie's mother. In addition to his love of cricket, she knew him to be a cellist and an accomplished chef who dabbled in molecular gastronomy.

She wasn't sure how well he would remember her, if at all, but when he opened the door, he blinked and then greeted her with a hug.

"Andie Robertson? What in the devil are you doing here?"

She gave the courtyard a quick, nervous glance. "Can I come in?"

He blinked a few more times, perplexed, then ushered her up a flight of stairs and into his sitting room. The flat was small but well appointed, with a view of Saint Paul's through the window.

A portly man an inch or two shorter than Andie, the professor had an owlish face and a trimmed beard that had grayed considerably since their last meeting. "I didn't realize you were in London. I figured you would be . . ."

"Attending a funeral?" she said quietly.

"Yes. Yes, I suppose that's right." His face crumbled as he sank into a leather armchair facing a wall of bookshelves. "I can't believe he's dead."

"Me either."

"I'm sorry—may I offer you a drink? When did you arrive? Why didn't you call?"

She took a seat in another armchair. "A glass of water would be nice."

When she failed to explain further, he walked to the kitchen, returning with a glass of cold water.

"Is everything all right?" he asked gently. "I assume grief alone did not bring you across the Atlantic."

Andie drank half the glass in one swallow and closed her eyes. "I'm not sure where to begin."

"Begin with what, dear?"

After setting the glass down, she steepled her fingers against her mouth and summarized the events of the last few days, leaving out the discovery of the Star Phone, Dr. Corwin's journal, and the bizarre items she had found in his desk.

Professor Rickman's pasty face turned even whiter, his blinking now incessant. When she finished, he rose to pour himself a Laphroaig single malt. "Would you care for one?"

"I think I will."

He splashed more Scotch into a cut-glass tumbler. "I can't believe someone tried to kill you."

"Just so you know, I have no reason to think anyone followed me to London, and I took every precaution coming here."

"Thank you. I'm glad you came. But isn't it time to involve the authorities?"

"Dr. Corwin said not to trust anyone," she said, leveling her stare at him.

After a moment, he said quietly, "Then why me?"

"You're his closest friend. I need answers, or at least some insight."

Instead of taking a seat again, he moved to stand by the window, pensive as he sipped his Scotch. "I'm afraid I don't know what to say. Do you have any idea what he might have gotten himself into?"

"I came here to ask you the same question."

"This project with Quasar Labs . . . he never mentioned it?"

"Never."

"Nor to me. I suppose we didn't know James as well as we thought we did."

Her gaze slipped downward, stung by the truth of his words and frustrated by his lack of knowledge.

"If you're not going to the authorities with this," he said, "what are you planning to do?"

She looked up, eyes flashing. "I'm going to find out who killed him. Then I'll go to the police."

"Andie, I don't think that's—"

"I didn't come to ask permission. I came for information. Promise me you'll keep this between us for now, until I figure out what's going on."

He gave a slow nod. "If that's your wish. Though I'm not sure what to say, or how I can help."

"You have no idea about a secret project he might have been working on?"

"My guess is you would know before I would."

That surprised her. "Why would you say that?"

"Because he thought very, very highly of you, my dear."

Andie buried her face in her glass, breathing in the peat, until she had control of her emotions. "But you knew him on a different level. You were peers."

He hesitated, gently clinking his ice cubes.

"Dr. Rickman?"

"It's probably nothing, just a strange conversation we had recently. I'm not sure I should break confidence and bring it up, but given the circumstances . . ."

"Please. Anything could help."

"Well . . . you're familiar with his pet project, the mathematical universe theory?"

She gave a soft smile. "He called it MUT."

"That's right. Quite frankly, I don't give it much credence."

"I think he saw it as a way to tie all the other theories together."

"Of course, of course. I understand James's mind-set. The theory of quantum physics, as we know it, is either incomplete or inconsistent. How can the observable universe consist of underlying particles that cannot even be measured until observed? Who did the initial observing? Where is the line drawn? And yet while we don't understand *why* quantum theory functions as it does, we know the wave functions that describe these particles *do* work."

"Wave functions are just math," Andie said, "but if they work, then they must be real on some fundamental level."

He rubbed his thumb against the glass. "In our last conversation, James postulated that reality, at the most basic level, might not just be described by mathematics—it might *be* mathematics."

"He mentioned that to me before."

"Maybe he was being metaphorical. But I don't think he was that concerned with the answer."

"I'm not sure what you're saying."

"We know our basic reality consists of four-dimensional space-time and the subatomic particles that underlie it. Setting aside the theoretical multiple dimensions of superstring theory, mainstream science acknowledges a deeper level, the place where the wave functions defining these quantum particles live."

"Hilbert space," she said.

"That's right. An infinite-dimensional geometric construct that, again, we don't really understand, but we use to describe the spaces in between. Just like with quantum physics, James thought there might be a way to utilize the infinite-dimensional formulas without really understanding them."

"Hilbert space has been extensively studied."

"Of course, my dear. Yet as far as I know"—he tipped his head and chuckled, as if whatever he was about to say did not bear much weight—"no one has tried to *reach* it."

It was Andie's turn to blink. "I don't understand."

"In our last conversation, James asked me quite earnestly what I thought would happen if we found a way to access Hilbert space."

"Access it how? With a microscopy device? We're nowhere close."

Dr. Rickman returned to his seat and finished his Scotch with one swallow. "With our minds."

"With our—that sounds like nonsense."

"I thought the same," he said quietly.

"And if it isn't?" she said, taking a moment to digest his words. "What would that even mean?"

"Quite frankly, I've no idea."

"Did he tell you more about it? Why he thought this was possible? What he thought it would accomplish?"

"I asked the same questions, and he laughed them off, saying it was just a wild theory, and wouldn't it be neat if we could peer behind the curtain?"

"Yeah, sure," Andie said. "That would be *neat*."

They both fell silent, and when Dr. Rickman rose to refill their glasses, Andie waved him off. She had to think clearly.

"Does the name Zawadi mean anything to you?" she asked. To her surprise, his eyes glanced quickly to the side, and she saw him swallow ever so slightly.

"I'm afraid not. Why?"

"The Unknown Nine? LYS? The Ascendants?"

"I've never heard of any of those."

Why is he lying about Zawadi? Or isn't he?

"I found a drawer in Dr. Corwin's desk," she said, thinking furiously about how much she was prepared to reveal. "It contained research on unexplained phenomena. Things like astral travel, ESP, and near-death experiences. I also saw the names I just mentioned."

"I've never heard him talk about these things."

"Me either. What about a Majorana Tower?"

"As in Ettore Majorana?"

She held a palm up.

He continued shaking his head. "The only field of speculative research I knew to interest James was electromagnetism. He'd go out on a limb there."

"I know he revered Tesla and Faraday."

"He was also intrigued by the mathematical concepts involved in consciousness, and their relation to the electromagnetic field surrounding the human body." He rose and started to pace. "I'm shooting in the dark here, but what if he was working on a way to tap into the body's energy field with a device of some kind? The establishment would laugh, which is why he'd keep it secret."

Andie began to gnaw on a thumbnail. She wanted to ask him about the Enneagon and the Star Phone but knew she couldn't trust him completely.

"If James broke new ground in the quantum arena," he said, "then you must understand how important this could be. We've all been waiting for the next leap. Whatever it is, the value to science—and commercial interests—will be incalculable. If someone even *thinks* Dr. Corwin developed something groundbreaking . . ."

"A man with a gun just chased me five miles through the woods in the middle of the night. I think I'm aware of the seriousness of the situation."

"Yes, yes, of course you are." The professor's eyes flicked nervously to the window, and he stood in the center of the room, looking very lost. "What can I do, Andie? How can I help?"

"If you think of anything else that might be relevant, shoot me an email."

"That's it?"

"For now, yeah. I can't put anyone else in danger." As she rose to leave, she kept thinking about that glimmer of recognition when she had mentioned Zawadi. She wasn't sure what it meant, but there was too much at stake to let it go, too many unanswered questions.

"Who's Zawadi?" she said, staring right at him.

"What? I already told you—"

"That folder I mentioned, in Dr. Corwin's desk? Your name was listed right beside hers."

Her lie made an impact. Dr. Rickman started to say something in response, thought better of it, then walked to the window and turned his back to her. The long silence spoke for itself. Still facing the window, he said, "Come back tomorrow night, at eight p.m. I have a function after work but will come home straightaway."

"Why can't you tell me now?"

"Eight p.m. And I can't make any promises."

"Promises about what?"

"I have to . . . talk to someone. I won't mention your name. I promise."

"Talk to who?"

"You'll have to trust me."

"Why should I?"

When he turned back around, a strange light had entered his eyes, shrewd and troubled. Somehow, he seemed taller than before, his posture more erect, his demeanor more confident.

"Because James did," he said.

That caused her to pause, torn between her desire for answers and her wariness at his sudden change in behavior.

"I'll meet you," she said, reasoning she could always change her mind. "But not here."

"Where?"

She thought for a moment. "The pub outside the courtyard. Come alone."

"Fair enough. You don't have to worry, Andie. At least not about coming here."

"I hope not."

Her face tucked inside the hood of her green field jacket, Andie hurried away from the professor's flat, keeping to the shadows. Night had fallen, and she had to make a decision about where to sleep. Reaching into her memories of the city, the best option she could think of was Victoria Station, which had plenty of cheap hotels and access to transportation. It was also close to the V&A Museum.

Just to be safe, she took another circuitous route on the tube, thinking through all that had happened. She had never felt so out of her depth.

It was obvious Professor Rickman knew more than he had told her—but how much?

And who was this Zawadi person?

Despite his caginess, Andie felt like the professor was on her side. Still, not trusting the situation—which might be out of his control—she was relieved he had agreed to meet in a public place. She also reasoned, should her instincts about him be wrong, that he would be less willing to cause a scene in a pub right outside his flat. And it was a busy part of London, easy to get away if needed.

In her mind, the meeting was worth the risk. But she felt as if she were flying blind in the darkness, rushing into unknown peril with no copilot and no radar.

Tomorrow night I might have some answers.
One day at a time.

Starving and wired, she surfaced at Covent Garden to grab a bite to eat. All of the expensive shops were closed, leaving an assortment of flower vendors, pubs, sidewalk cafés, and street performers to entertain the tourists still clogging the main arcade. After grabbing fish-and-chips from a street vendor, she spied a side street that made her pause. Along the street was a line of stalls draped in black cloth and colorful silks. She drew closer and noticed a preponderance of body piercings, tattoos with occult symbology, and crystal jewelry.

Andie recognized the vibe from the old days, when she was still searching for an arcane answer to her visions. She had tried them all over the years: Wicca gatherings, faith healers, magic conventions, New Age festivals, ESP demonstrations.

The red-bearded man behind the first stall—a neodruid dressed in a black kilt and bronze wrist bands inscribed with runes—told her the market was a monthly gathering of the London Occult Society. On a whim, she took out one of the ink drawings she had found in Dr. Corwin's desk and showed it to him. He had no idea what it was, but she started showing it around, asking if anyone had ever seen or heard of such a place.

The practitioners ran the gamut: theosophists, witches, clairvoyants, fortune-tellers, MK Ultra survivors turned remote viewers, tarot readers, the Society of the Inner Light. As with her past inquiries, no one had anything credible to offer. A hoodoo practitioner with dreadlocks hanging to her knees told Andie that for a small fee, she would throw the bones and see what they had to say. A LaVeyan Satanist leaned over a candle flame and professed that the drawing represented the prison of Andie's own mind. She more or less agreed with that assessment.

Behind the next-to-last stall, a teenage girl with spiky green hair, dressed all in black and wearing purple lipstick, watched insouciantly as Andie approached. Her stall displayed a stack of books about the life of Aleister Crowley, pamphlets for the Ordo Templi Orientis, and sample instructions for the Gnostic Mass.

The girl lifted a cigarette out of an ornate silver case. The head of a ram was tattooed on her neck. "You selling something?"

"No," Andie said. "Why?"

She lit up, releasing an odor of cloves. "I saw you asking around."

The teenager had a Caribbean accent, and the lighter shadows in the background of the ink drawing matched the color of her skin. After debating walking away, Andie decided she might as well show her the drawing. "Have you ever seen anything like this?"

The girl took the drawing and peered closer. "I think so."

"You have?" Andie took a step forward, leaning over the stall. "Where? When?"

"*Silent Hill.*"

"What's that?"

"A video game."

Andie yanked the drawing back.

"No, really," the girl said. "What is it?"

"It's not a game is what it is," Andie snapped.

"C'mon. I was just winding you up."

"Not what I need right now."

"Look, I might know someone who could help, if I knew what it was."

Andie put a hand to her temple in frustration. "I have visions sometimes. They look like this place. That's all."

The girl took a long drag and blew smoke out of the side of her mouth. "I'm just watching the stall for Mum. All this"—she waved a hand—"is for tourists."

"Of course it is."

"Then why bother? No offense, yeah, but it sounds like you need a good psychologist."

Andie shook her head and started to walk away.

"I work at a bookstore a few nights a week," the girl called out. "It specializes in religion and mysticism. The real stuff."

Andie turned back, her voice mocking. "The *real* stuff?"

"Hey, I'm just into the music and the games. But the old white guy who owns it, all kinds of people come to see him. Mum says he's *the* expert in London." She took out a card from behind the stall. "In case you want it. And, hey, cool ring. Where'd you get it?"

Andie took the card and glanced down at the circular jade band entwined with silver on her left ring finger, feeling a twinge of long-buried pain. "It was my mother's."

As she walked away, she took off the ring and pocketed it, realizing it might be picked up on camera. Without much interest, she slipped the card the girl had given her into the same pocket. Andie had never seen anything come of her inquiries over the years, and doubted anything would change.

Even at night, a swarm of people choked the streets around Victoria Station. Tourists and commuters and off-duty laborers packed the dizzying array of pizzerias, kebab stands, bars, and street-side patios. The area was one of Andie's least favorite in London, but at least she felt anonymous.

A plethora of cheap hotels in grungy Victorian buildings ringed the transport hub. She chose one at random and paid cash for two nights. Her room was cramped and musty, but she collapsed on the sagging bed, thankful to escape the beggars on the corners, the obnoxious tourists, and the claustrophobic streets reeking of garbage and stale beer.

Her mind was too piqued to sleep. In the madness of the last few days, she had not had time to research any of the weirdness she had found in Dr. Corwin's journal. With nothing else to do, she lay on her side and did a little searching on her burner phone.

She learned that Zawadi was a feminine name in Swahili that meant "gift." It was also a hotel in Zanzibar. She supposed it could refer to a meeting place involving her mentor, though judging from the conversation with Professor Rickman, she felt like it referred to a specific person.

Besides a few pop culture references, she found nothing useful on the Ascendants.

A search for "the Unknown Nine" was also unproductive. However, *The Nine Unknown* was a novel by an English-born American writer named Talbot Mundy. The title referred to a mythical secret society founded in ancient India to preserve and develop books of hidden knowledge.

A symbolic reference perhaps?

Googling "Leap Year Society" turned up nothing except for some innocuous groups formed by people born on February 29. Frustrated, she kept searching, scrolling through pages and pages of useless data. She paused when she found a Yahoo! Answers question posed by someone called DocWoodburn.

Anyone out there know anything about the Leap Year Society?
DocWoodburn Ÿ 9 days ago

The recent date caught her eye. So far, there were no responses to the inquiry.

Interestingly, she found the same question posed with the same username on Reddit, 4chan, and a number of other chat forums. The 4chan posting—which was mocked mercilessly by a few responders—asked anyone with knowledge of the Leap Year Society to contact DocWoodburn at *Seeker's Corner* on Twitch.

Andie was familiar with Twitch. Gamers gravitated to it, but it attracted all sorts of people looking for a voice online. Curious, she created a new user ID, Mercuri999, based on her favorite scientist. She logged on and discovered a weekly broadcast billing itself as a live show crowdsourcing the truth out of modern conspiracies. The host was someone with the handle of DocWoodburn. The show was mildly popular, closing in on ten thousand followers. She listened to the most recent episode—which had occurred during the last week—and heard the host describe how a black van had pulled up right outside his residence, just after he mentioned the Leap Year Society.

Andie sucked in a breath. Before the last few days, she might have written that off as a publicity stunt. She did not do conspiracy theories, pseudoscience, or alien sightings. The host sounded like a kook. But if he knew something about the Leap Year Society . . .

She noticed DocWoodburn was online right that very moment, or at least had left his Twitch account open. She chewed on a thumbnail as she debated whether to contact him. Putting herself out there in any form was hazardous, but she was using a burner phone in an anonymous hotel room in London. In her mind, just like contacting Professor Rickman, acquiring information outweighed the risk of discovery.

She thought hard about what to say, then fired off a query.

Hey Doc r u there?

I am big fan and want discuss Atlantis New Hypothesis

Let's see how smart DocWoodburn is.

She made the assumption that whoever had sent the black van to his house had a bot on the internet searching for mention of the Leap Year Society. She also had to assume that another bot, perhaps even a live user, was monitoring his Twitch account.

Ten minutes passed with no response. She figured he must be offline, or had failed to understand the reference. She left the account open, just in case, and resumed her other searches. Half an hour later, a response to her message appeared.

Aloha Mercuri! Do you mean a new theory about Atlantis?

No. I mean Atlantis New Hypothesis. A-N-H. Do you know it?

Inspired by the code Dr. Corwin had used on the Moleskine note, Andie had created a simple alphabetic cipher to disguise the name of the Leap Year Society, counting out the same number of letters between the initials. Thirteen letters separated *L* from *Y*, and counting backward, six from *Y* and *S*.

LYS = ANH. Atlantis New Hypothesis.

To connect the dots further, she had done all this in response to his post about the Leap Year Society.

Had he understood?

Sorry I am Latvia girl my English is not so great, she wrote.

It's OK I understand <u>completely</u>

Thank you.

What's the theory? I'd be very surprised to hear anything new about Atlantis.

Could Atlantis not we early taken alien life kreatures? She quickly corrected her purposeful typo: Very sorry *be* not *we.*

Andie bit her nails harder as she waited for his response. She had just sent him another encoded message, using the first letters of each word. *Could Atlantis not we early taken alien life kreatures?*

Can we talk?

She hoped the line was strange enough to catch his attention, and that he was clever enough to figure it out. For all she knew, her first veiled message had passed right by him, and he was simply humoring a foreign fan.

Half an hour later, she got a response.

You're making me laugh, Mercuri. Do you mean could the people of Atlantis have been taken away in pre-history by alien life forms?

Yes!

Anything's possible, but I've heard that one a thousand times. Sorry. Thanks for listening to the show

☹ welcome

DocWoodburn logged off of Twitch. She left her account open and paced the room, wondering if he had understood.

Twenty minutes later, she had a friend request from a user named Rhodies4ever351! The subject of the message was "Who Are You?"

A little thrill passed through her.

Just to be sure, she rattled off a quick response after she accepted the friend request.

Is this a house call by the doctor?

At your service. Though I usually only call on the last day of February.

Exactly what I wanted.

Your English seems to have markedly improved. Especially your alphabet.

Paranoia affects my speech patterns.

You too?

100%

Who are you?

A friend. Maybe.

Why maybe?

I don't know you.

I don't know you either. But I want to talk about "Atlantis."

Me too.

It's not safe here.

Where is safe?

Let me think about it and contact you.

Here?

For now yes.

When?

Soon.

OK.

Stay tuned and be smart. I think they are very dangerous.

Andie typed with a vengeance. I know they are.

How do you know?

Read the news about the physicist killed in Italy.

After that last message went through, Andie shut it down. She had gone as far as she was prepared to go, at least for the night. After checking the window and drawing the lone curtain tight, she put on some ambient electronica and curled into bed.

The next morning, Andie took a tepid shower and stuffed her belongings into her backpack, in case she wasn't coming back. Relieved to see the Star Phone still worked, she wondered if it was solar-powered. She had heard Dr. Corwin speak of a theoretical electromagnetic battery that utilized quick sips of power and could last months at a time. Maybe Quasar Labs had developed the idea.

After a takeaway coffee and croissant near the hotel, she took the Circle line two stops west to South Kensington. A five-minute walk down busy Cromwell Road brought her to the doorstep of the Victoria and Albert Museum.

She paused on the marble steps as tourists flowed like ants in and out of the monolithic arched entrance. The random chatter made her feel both invisible and all-knowing, as if everyone around her were actors in a play of which only she—and the shadowy people chasing her—were aware. A metareality she had stumbled onto and could not escape.

Pushing away thoughts of her impending meeting with Professor Rickman, she gripped the Star Phone in her pocket and stepped beneath the carved muses of Knowledge and Inspiration overlooking the twin doors of the museum.

11

As soon as Omer cleared customs in London, he taxied to a safe house in the West End, using a key to unlock the dead bolt on the outer door. The ivy-covered three-story brick townhome blended right in with the other residences in the posh Knightsbridge neighborhood.

The inner door, built into a customized foyer, was crafted from African blackwood with a reinforced steel core. The keypad restricted entry with a nine-digit code, as well as a biometric hand-geometry reader. Once inside, Omer climbed to the second floor as he gave a series of commands to an AI voice assistant programmed especially for the safe houses. Coded to Omer's preferences, the AI turned on the lights, ran through the nightly menu options, and pumped a selection of modern violin concertos through hidden wireless speakers.

Though he had not slept more than a few hours over the last three days, and had remained alert during the flight, he did not succumb to exhaustion. Especially not after the escape of the target in Durham. Omer had given up everything for his ambition: family, home, even his true identity. But the Ascendants had recruited him to complete specific missions. They did not tolerate failure.

So instead of collapsing, he stripped down and stepped into a glass enclosure for a freezing-cold shower. Because he was conditioned to withstand extremes of temperature, the twenty-minute shower melted away the stiffness, and after toweling off he performed his breathing exercises on a Persian rug in the bedroom.

Omer was a faithful adherent of hormetism, the practice of subjecting oneself to low doses of substances or activities that in larger amounts were harmful—even fatal—to the human body. The biological phenomenon of hormesis was similar to homeopathy, yet not unknown to traditional science, which had learned that organic systems generally respond in a positive manner to negative stimuli, as long as they are given time to adapt. Alcohol, caffeine, and trace amounts of metals can all have beneficial effects but are toxic in the extreme. An athlete lifting weights, a yogi, a long-distance runner: every time muscles are broken down, the body rebuilds them stronger. The flu vaccine works on the same principle. Same with allergen immunotherapy.

The old adage was true: that which doesn't kill you makes you stronger.

While the Mossad had trained him well, the race to acquire the world's top technologies was a ruthless game, played out across the globe by governments, multinational corporations, and a rogue's list of shadowy organizations. To gain an upper hand, Omer had embraced hormesis. If the practice worked for some things, he hypothesized, why not for others? Why not for *all* things?

Dioxin, a cousin to Agent Orange, had benefits at low doses. So did heat shock. Calorie restriction. Hyper-gravity and anti-gravity. Poisons. Suffocation. Viruses. Not only had Omer developed resistance or immunity to a laundry list of harmful agents, but he had developed an amount of control over physical processes that modern science would scarcely believe. He could regulate his body's production of hormones, such as adrenaline and serotonin and, with enough time for meditation, could even influence his nervous and immune systems.

He slipped into a silk robe and checked his phone. No word yet. He entered the kitchen and downed one of the drug cocktail packets: combinations of vitamins, minerals, and performance enhancers with which all the safe houses were stocked. For dinner, he devoured a grass-fed rib eye, sautéed duck livers, and a side of broccolini, all washed down with a glass of Argentinian malbec.

If only Juma were in town! The very thought of her perfect breasts and lips like crushed velvet made him wonder if the principles of hormetism could somehow be applied to intense sexual behavior.

He was sure that it could . . .

After sinking into the king-size bed, secure within the safe house, Omer slept until dawn. He took another cold shower, dressed, stuck his zip gun into a concealed holster, and strapped a high-carbon full-tang fixed blade into his boot sheath.

The text he was dreading came during breakfast.

Call us.

After a swallow of coffee, he stared down at his smoked salmon, knowing his superiors were not pleased. Trying to imagine their response was tormenting him. The punishment for dereliction of duty in the organization was not death, but something just as final.

Abandonment.

Omer did as he was told. A digitized voice answered the call on the second ring. "Contact has been initiated."

Omer sat up straight. "Where is she?" They gave him an address for a hotel near Victoria Station. "Should I take her now?"

"Rest. See where she goes today. We have others in place."

"Understood."

There was a long pause. "When the time is right, we trust she won't escape this time? The Archon was not pleased."

A flicker of fear swept through Omer, despite his mental training. *Archon* simply meant "ruler" or "lord" in ancient Greek, and the secrecy around the head of his order was so great that not even a given name was known. It was not just that the Archon could snuff Omer's path to Ascension—or his life—with a whispered command to the others. There were strange stories, tales of secret knowledge at their leader's disposal. Stories of prisoners who had killed themselves rather than face prolonged interrogation.

He took a deep breath to bring his apprehension under control. Caution was healthy, normal. There would always be people more dangerous than he.

Fear, on the other hand, was a distractor. A mental weakness that, like any other, can and should be controlled.

Omer spoke quietly into the phone. "I'll do better."

"We hope so. You should know the protocol has changed as well."

"To what?"

"Elotisum."

The line went dead without further explanation, leaving Omer to figure out the rest. With a little shudder, he began adjusting his preparations, thinking through how to proceed. Elotisum was a special, elevated version of the deliverance protocol. An edict of the highest importance.

Elotisum meant the Archon wanted to conduct the interrogation.

Los Angeles

12

Beverly Hills isn't even a real place, Cal thought as he drove down a commercial avenue lined with expansive gold-framed windows displaying an endless parade of luxury goods, shuttered for the night but still gleaming in the aura of the streetlamps. Meant to emulate the finest old-world Europe had to offer, the architecture instead smacked of new wealth, nothing subtle or refined about it.

Porsches, Range Rovers, and Bentleys were as common as minivans in a suburb. A Lamborghini Aventador had just roared by. Cal's battle-worn Jeep Cherokee felt like an old Yugo sputtering down the Moscow Ring Road on the way to a vehicular nursing home.

The destination was the Mandrake Hotel, a limestone tower right in the diamond-studded, silicone-laced heart of the neighborhood. If Dane's info was any good—and it always was—then the company that owned the black van was in turn owned by a man, Elias Holt, who frequented a secret club called the Infinity Lounge on the thirteenth floor of the Mandrake on select nights of the month.

Tonight was just such a night. Not wanting to be seen when he arrived—or rolling up in a pedestrian ride sure to raise eyebrows—Cal parked two streets over from the hotel. He grabbed a peak-lapel tuxedo jacket from the back seat and threw it over a silk gray T-shirt and his lone pair of designer jeans. The outfit had served him well over the years, when he needed to mingle. He had splurged on the tux for a friend's wedding over a decade ago and was pleased it still fit. A frugal lifestyle was good for the waistline.

Carefully trimmed stubble, a pair of slip-on loafers, and Cal felt right at home. His real disguise was the bleach-blond wig, horn-rimmed tinted glasses, pencil mustache, and zirconium stud earring, all of which he had taken from his props chest. Following the advice an actor friend had given him long ago, Cal changed his walk to an arrogant swagger, a peacock's strut. Observers keyed on body language as much as appearance.

He knew he was taking a risk, but Cal wanted to lay eyes on Elias. Besides, they already knew where he lived, so what changed if they spotted him in a public place?

He tried not to think too hard about the potential answer to that question. His strange Twitch chat with Mercuri999 had left him even more convinced he was on the trail of something important, and perhaps very dangerous. Whoever she was, unless Cal's guess was way off, Mercuri knew about the Leap Year Society. He had gotten chills when, following her tip, he read about the physicist gunned down in Bologna. The news report said it was a robbery gone wrong, but an American professor shot to death outside a nice hotel in a sleepy part of western Europe, by some random guy in a hoodie?

Unh-uh.

Halfway down the block, Cal cut through a narrow lane with immaculate paving stones, its line of dumpsters tucked discreetly behind tiled walls and potted palms. *Goddamn, even the alleys are nice.*

Dane had provided an identity and the name of the club. Cal's own research had uncovered that Elias Holt was the founder of a business, Aegis International, which specialized in security for technology companies. Cal dug a little deeper and uncovered a number of employees with backgrounds in intelligence and private defense firms. He had investigated enough of those types to know that, except for deep undercover ops, people with those backgrounds did not conceal their former employers. They simply didn't disclose the nature of their work. "Overthrew a foreign government" or "expertise in persuasive interrogation" was never a good look on a résumé. Unless, he mused, you were searching for a job in sales.

Onyx sculptures of faceless human figures, chandeliers hanging from a thirty-foot ceiling, and a polychromatic waterfall fountain greeted Cal in the lobby of the Mandrake Hotel. After walking in like he owned the place, he nodded to the concierge, took a wrong turn into the restroom, then doubled back and discovered the elevators were situated behind the sheet-thin flow of the waterfall.

Like many hotels, in a nod to triskaidekaphobia, the Mandrake did not have a thirteenth floor. Cal viewed the avoidance of the number 13 as a ridiculous practice—but one that he followed himself, if it didn't put him out too much.

He was fully aware that humanity had a long history of succumbing to ignorant beliefs based on primitive superstition. On the other hand, the world was teeming with unexplained mysteries. There was usually some fact behind the fiction, and as the old adage went, sometimes the truth was the strangest thing of all.

After exiting on the fourteenth floor, Cal found a staircase and descended one flight to a landing, where a door led back into the hotel. A thirteenth floor *did* exist—it just wasn't for guests.

That was about all Cal knew in advance, except the cover charge was a cool hundred dollars, and two grand for table service.

What a load of LA bullshit.

The door opened onto a hallway with Moroccan-patterned carpeting and blue velvet walls, dead-ending at a red lacquer door. From behind him came the echo of a set of footsteps on the stairs. Another potential patron, he hoped.

But maybe not.

Notes of remixed electro pop floated down the hallway. When he opened the door, he caught a clubby aroma of musk and cedar. The muscular Japanese doorman standing just inside, with his earpiece and fancy vest, looked on loan from the yakuza.

As Cal was being frisked, he heard the door to the stairwell open. He glanced back and saw with relief that it was just a leggy brunette wearing high heels and an iridescent cocktail dress. She shimmered with the sort of almost-movie-star good looks that were as common in LA as traffic jams.

The Infinity Lounge had plenty of open space and a funky ret-ro-future vibe. Lots of neon streaks under dim lighting, silver ban-quettes, cocktails served in geometric blown glass and smoking with liquid nitrogen. Most of the people were dressed in getups from the Roaring Twenties, gangsters and molls and Gatsby clones.

All in all, a very LA speakeasy. Cal didn't quite understand the theme. But he never really did.

He sidled to a portion of the bar next to a fish tank lit with psy-chedelic coral. Along the far wall, downtown glittered through a line of pinched windows. He ordered a fancy bourbon cocktail, the first on the menu, and scanned the room.

It took a minute of casual observation before he noticed Elias sitting in a semicircular banquette, dressed in a chocolate-brown four-button suit with a vest. He was performing a card trick, to the delight of the small crowd surrounding him. The back of the playing cards depicted a rocket shooting into outer space.

Cal moved closer. Elias had changed so much from his online photo that at first Cal didn't recognize him. Instead of the awkward young genius whose gaming start-up was gobbled up by Sony—the only picture of him online—the sandy-haired, cleft-chinned CEO holding court at the silver banquette was as suave and attractive as the aspiring actors in the room. Though still thin, his face was firm-jawed, his tanned skin flawless. Sharp cerulean eyes demanded attention. White teeth gleamed. When the trick was finished, Elias stood and spun the cards through his fingers so fast it was hard to fol-low. He built a multilayered pyramid in seconds, right in the center of the table. Mesmerized, the crowd clapped when it was over, and Elias graced them with a bow.

According to Cal's research, Elias had graduated at the top of his class from Stanford, obtaining dual degrees in math and computer science. He was on the chess team, a member of the Magicians Club, and had won an award for a published journal article on machine learning, a rare feat for an undergrad. After graduation, he designed some apps and then helmed a virtual reality start-up. In an interview with *Wired* magazine, Elias—wearing thick glasses and clothing that looked secondhand—had referred to himself as a computer nerd and talked about his love of video games, as well as his struggles to relate to others throughout his life.

After selling his first company, as far as Cal could tell, Elias had fallen off the radar. There was no mention of him in any press release or public forum, except for his listing as CEO of the security company with the California Secretary of State, a required financial reporting. But Aegis was formed nearly ten years after Elias sold his first company.

Where had he gone? What had he done?

Cal never forgot a face. That was Elias Holt; he was sure of it. Yet as he watched him flirt with the knockout redhead beside him, he wondered what had caused such a radical transformation.

It was almost as if, somewhere along the way, Elias had become a completely different person.

Cal snapped some photos of Elias and his admirers by palming his cell phone against his thigh. When a seat at the adjoining banquette opened up, Cal sidled over.

Elias had switched from card tricks to mentalism. He began by "reading the minds" of the people around him, and then took a slow walk around the detached banquette, lifting jewelry off of a burly Latino man without him noticing. When pressed for his secrets, Elias spouted psychobabble about how the human brain can process only so many things at one time, and how magic is simply another form of technology that appears supernatural to those who do not understand it. Quantum physics labs around the world, he claimed, were performing feats that would appear "magical" to nonscientists.

Cal had no beef with that.

When the crowd around Elias dwindled, Cal left the hotel, retrieved his Cherokee, and idled down the street in front of a sushi restaurant with a view of the entrance to the Mandrake. He ignored his hunger pangs as the night went on. Cal loved sushi. He wished he could still afford it.

An hour later, Elias stepped out with a pair of women, followed by two men in dark suits. After the entourage climbed into a custom Lincoln Navigator, Cal used binoculars to catch the plate, then followed the Lincoln from a safe distance as it turned onto Santa Monica and later into a flat, manicured, palm-lined neighborhood. Once they began to climb into the landscaped hills, where the true wealth resided, Cal grew nervous about the lack of traffic. He had to fall back or risk being spotted.

After rounding a curve and encountering an empty road, he spotted the lights of the Navigator disappearing down a driveway accessed by an ornamental iron gate. Cal kept driving so as not to raise suspicion. He caught the house number but could see only the flat-topped roof of the mansion above a Mexican-tile wall that surrounded the property. He also noticed security cameras atop the gate.

After cruising up the hill, he parked as far away from Elias's house as he could while keeping the gate in view. Unsure what to do next, he debated trying to order a pizza to a parked car when a pair of headlights swung into view. He gripped the steering wheel as a black van sped up the hill, the gate to the mansion opened, and the van disappeared inside.

Thank God I parked near the top.

Worried a neighbor might get nervous and alert the cops, Cal left and took a different route home. He reheated a plate of pasta as he scratched Leon's ears, cracked a beer, and ate on his patio, deep in thought.

Halfway through his second beer, he returned inside and fired off a text to Dane.

I need help. Call me.

To his surprise, Dane called him back within minutes. He sounded as alert as ever, despite the fact that it was 2 a.m. "Help with what?"

"The name you gave me," Cal said.

"What kind of help?"

"I'm not sure."

"Okay . . . Why don't you tell me more. As in everything."

"I can't pay you," Cal said. "At least not yet. I had to give up cable this month."

"It's not all about money."

"Then what?"

"Is it my imagination," Dane said, "or did you not text me five minutes ago asking for my help?"

"What I have in mind could get very real. Just like you, I prefer to work with transparent motives."

"This coming from a man whose former job description included the art of disguise and false entry? Let's just say I'm intrigued, had too much caffeine today, and that Aegis International and I have very different philosophies on how the world should work. I'm afraid that's all the motive you're going to get. Take it or leave it."

Cal debated how far to trust him. The man had his faults, for sure. In a room full of people, Dane would probably piss off 99 percent of them. Also, despite his gruff exterior, he was an idealist. Cal didn't trust idealists. When push came to shove, he feared Dane would put his ideologies ahead of Cal's interests, and maybe even his safety.

On the other hand, Cal was also a bit of an idealist, and if he wanted to take this further, he needed the sort of help Dane could give.

Seeing little alternative, Cal told him about his research on Aegis and Elias Holt, and everything he had witnessed that evening. "I need to get inside that house," he finished.

After a long pause, Dane gave him a new cell phone number to look out for. "I'll be in touch."

As noon rolled around, while Cal was scrambling to meet a deadline for an internet news site in Australia, a piece on transcontinental political conspiracies during the Vietnam War, he received a text from the number Dane had given him.

Gates open at 3 p.m. No guards on-site.

No owner?

Spa appt.

How do you know?

Unimportant.

Unless it's false info.

There was no response to that, so Cal shook his head and added, Anything else?

Check your mailbox, and use only this number.

After hurrying down his front walkway, Cal found an anonymous package wrapped in brown paper inside the mailbox. After returning inside, he opened the package and found a USB flash drive.

He set it on the kitchen table and exhaled a deep breath. He knew what Dane wanted, and he wasn't playing around.

The afternoon appointment did not surprise him. Security was tighter at night in most places.

So let's do this.

He had already thought through the scenario. After renting a van for the day, he finished the conspiracy piece and fired it off, then paced his living room to steel up his nerve. He was afraid of these people and how deep in the shadows they lived. Whoever they were, he got the sense they played for keeps. Mercuri999 seemed to think so too.

But one did not succeed as an investigative journalist without learning to deal with fear.

And one most certainly did not get one's life back without taking a few risks.

Just before 3 p.m., under a blazing midday sun, Cal turned his white rental van onto Elias Holt's street. An hour earlier, after leaving the house dressed in jeans and a blue work polo with a SUNSHINE

PLUMBERS logo, he had picked up the rental and plastered a matching decal on the side.

Years before, Cal had ordered the uniform and the car decal for just this sort of situation. None of the neighbors would look twice. The question was whether Dane could deliver what he had promised.

Just as Cal reached the driveway, the high iron gate hummed and began to part. He caught his breath and prayed Dane was right about the lack of on-site bodyguards. If not, Cal was about to be stuffed into a black van and disappeared.

The gate closed behind him as soon as he pulled through. The driveway led up a hill lined with manicured cypress. He assumed Dane had overridden the security cameras, and hoped the hacker was keeping an eye on him.

Cal parked as close to the modern trilevel mansion as he could get. Up close, the gleaming white villa was a stunner, an elegant jigsaw puzzle of glass and marble. The patio was a whisper of slender pillars and billowing canvas sheets that opened onto an infinity pool overlooking the golden-brown hillside. The Mexican-tile wall and lush landscaping ensured complete privacy.

Cal had no idea how much the place was worth, but there was no time to dwell on the lives of the rich and famous. He hurried to the front door, flinching at the presence of another camera. Before his hand reached the doorknob, the keypad lock whirred and the door opened on its own. He guessed the entire house was wired to the security system. Very safe and convenient—until someone like Dane decided to hack it.

Inside, Cal took a moment to orient himself, knowing he had very limited time to find a computer and hoping Elias had not carried his laptop to the spa. The bottom floor of the mansion was full of gadgets, fancy appliances, and sleek white furniture that looked about as comfortable as a church pew. A circular robot whirred into the living room, startling him. He assumed it was picking up dust and ignored it.

Just because there was no security didn't mean there were no visitors. Could Dane see into all the rooms? He took a moment to text him.

I'm in.

The reply came swiftly: I know.

U sure I'm alone?

Reasonably.

Cal swore and hurried through the kitchen, dining room, living room, piano room, and guest suite. No sign of a computer.

He took the stairs two at a time, ears cocked for an approaching vehicle. All of the doors on the second floor had been removed, and the rooms were full of mixed-media paintings and objets d'art on elaborate stands. The art was of the modern ilk—abstract and bizarre—and sported a theme: the transformation of mankind and planet Earth by technology. Much of the work resembled a digital fever dream of people and places warped into pixelated images. Papier-mâché figures made of bytes, emerging out of caves in the bushveld. Pop-art tapestries of classic cars driving into outer space. One entire room had been cleverly painted to induce a three-dimensional feeling of stepping into a futuristic cityscape.

On the third floor—the living quarters—Cal worried someone would pop out of one of the doors in the long, silent hallway. Yet no one did, and he grew excited when he found a Lenovo desktop in the study attached to the master bedroom. He didn't bother trying to figure out how to unlock the screen; he inserted the flash drive and texted Dane.

We're on.

The computer expert repeated his earlier reply.

I know.

Cal rolled his eyes and paced the room. The paneled study had a private elevator and vintage wooden furniture. The decor was an ode to the art of stage magic: enameled decks of playing cards; handcuffs and wands and other props displayed in glass cabinets; framed photos of Houdini. A floor-to-ceiling bookshelf was stocked with historical tomes on illusions, escapes, mentalism, and other tricks.

The blend of magic and technology in the house, reminiscent of the Infinity Lounge, made Cal wonder if Elias sponsored the private club himself.

Or what if the club had another purpose? A gateway into the Leap Year Society for a select few, like the online puzzle?

He probably started it to get laid.

Not that he would need it.

When the desktop unlocked, Cal rushed over to take a look. The background image was a grayish circle that filled most of the screen, blurred at the edges to lend it a mysterious, otherworldly aura. Two words were inscribed in fancy font along the bottom, though Cal had to move some folders and app icons around to read them.

Ascensio Infinitus

After rearranging the desktop a bit more, he gripped the mouse when he saw a large *L* filling the left side of the background image, and an *S* on the right. The *Y* in the middle stretched artfully across the entire diameter of the circle.

LYS

Cal's eyes whisked hungrily across the screen, scanning the names of the folders. Most of them appeared to pertain to Aegis, and he knew he didn't have time to sort through them all. He thought Dane would have taken control of the cursor, but the USB drive was flashing, so the big man must be content with a remote data transfer.

The names of the folders drew Cal's attention. Nootropics. Paleoacoustics. Ocular Nanotech. Compelling stuff, but there was an itch he wanted to scratch. After pulling up the search bar on the start menu, he typed in his own name, not really expecting a result.

To his surprise, there was a hit: a zip file nested in an archived folder titled *Closed Marks*. A hollow feeling started to expand inside him when he saw his name in alphabetical order among a long string of others. When he clicked on his name, he saw his entire life laid out before him, in a series of Word docs and PDF files.

Birth Certificate and Social Security. Education. Credit History. Curriculum Vitae. Persons of Interest. Addresses. Personal Information.

Opening the Personal Information file revealed a list of his hobbies, haunts, favorite restaurants, daily routine, dog walk routes, everything. Chills swept through him as he checked the dates on the folders and the zip file. As best he could tell, they had started a file on him the same day he had published the piece on PanSphere's black-site lab.

The last entry was the day he was fired.

He stared at the file in disbelief. *These are the people. These are the bastards who ruined my life.* With a shaky hand, feeling in his bones that somewhere in the zip file was proof that his source had been authentic and the evidence against him falsified, he started to move the file onto the USB drive, just to be sure it got on, when the screen flashed twice and went blank.

Stunned, he started pressing keys at random, trying to unlock the screen. A buzz from his phone caused him to look down. It was Dane again.

Get out. Now. Run.

Cal pounded on the keyboard. *"No, goddammit!"*

But he knew it was useless. He jumped to his feet, wanting to take the entire desktop and instead grabbing the USB drive. The desktop was too heavy to run with, it might have a tracker, and it was surely now compromised. After stepping toward the elevator and deciding that entering an automated coffin was a bad idea, he dashed into the hallway and raced to the stairs.

A floor-to-ceiling window on his left provided a view of the street below Elias's house. At the edge of his line of sight, he saw a black van turn onto the street.

I'm never going to make it.

By the time he fled down the stairs and out the front door, he could hear the van's engine roaring up the hill. Dane had left the gate open, and Cal raced for his rental, trying to judge whether he could reach the gate before the van blocked him in. He doubted it. But he didn't see another option.

As he sprinted away from the house, a familiar electronic whir caused his stomach to lurch. He reached the driveway and confirmed his suspicion: they were closing the gate on him. The black van didn't even have to beat him to the house. They could just trap him inside.

In a panic, he thought about where he could hide, and debated ramming the gate with the rental van. He discarded both ideas, turned, and sprinted for the wall behind the house. It was out of view of the driveway. If he cleared it quickly enough, he might have a small window to escape. The problem was the height of the wall. Nine feet at least. In high school, Cal could dunk a basketball, but that was twenty years and thirty pounds ago.

Already huffing from the run, he jumped for the top of the wall, managed to grip it with both hands, and hung on for dear life. His toes slipped through the ivy as he scrabbled for a foothold. Shouts came from the driveway as his forearms burned with the effort. At last he found a notch in the stone, dug in with his left foot, and threw an elbow atop the wall. He risked a glance back and saw two armed men in dark suits slipping through the gate just before it closed. With a heave that brought him the rest of the way up, unsure if the men had seen him, Cal threw himself over the wall and onto the scrub-covered hillside below.

London

13

Cautiously hopeful the bust of Democritus held a secret connected to the location of the Enneagon, or would help her solve Dr. Corwin's murder in some way, Andie stepped through a set of double doors that granted access to an entrance hall supported by marble pillars.

Admission was free to the renowned gallery, which boasted the world's largest collection of decorative art and design. Millions of paintings, ceramics, costumes, textiles, and other objects filled the museum, spanning over five millennia of human history. Inside a vast hall to her right was a reconstructed Roman villa, replete with life-size statues, fountains, and carved Ionic columns. The ceiling rose up through the higher floors and set the tone for the grandeur of the museum.

After checking her backpack and passing through security, she took a moment to orient herself. She had studied the map online but wanted to be aware of her surroundings in person, especially the exits. She observed the other visitors as well. No one jumped out at her as suspicious, but there were so many people it was impossible to keep an eye on everyone. She would just have to get on with it.

With over seven miles of galleries, the museum resembled a gigantic square doughnut, four massive wings on four main floors surrounding an open-air green space in the middle. Before leaving

Durham, she had called to verify the bust of Democritus was on display, and after asking for directions at the information desk, she walked through the gift shop toward the central courtyard, where dozens of visitors were basking on the lawn or dipping their toes in the shallow basin of the fountain. Just before entering the courtyard, she ascended a wide staircase to the third story—in British parlance, the second floor.

Halfway down a hallway covered in frescoes and mosaics, she turned down a wide corridor with a line of glass display cases in the center. More cases were attached to the wall on her right. To her left, a balcony overlooked the Roman villa.

According to the information desk, this hallway was home to the Democritus bust.

Dozens of small objects filled the glass cases: statues, masks, pottery, metalwork. Andie walked the room once, didn't see the bust, and then returned more slowly, eyeing each and every piece. She finally spotted it in a display case in the center, about halfway down the hall. The carving was made of beige soapstone and much smaller than she had expected, not even six inches high. The bust portrayed Democritus with a beard and a sharp nose, dressed in the classic robes of a Greek philosopher. The head was turned slightly to the right, covered by a tight-fitting hat similar to a skullcap. A sly grin suggested the wily old scholar was in possession of a secret.

Let's see about that.

As a steady stream of tourists wandered through the hallway, Andie bent to study the bust. Unlike the larger pieces in the museum, the knickknacks in the display case had no descriptive placards. She stared at the bust for some time, unsure what to do, and felt eyes on her back. Trying not to overreact, she turned and saw a smiling woman with cropped gray hair limping toward her, a museum badge pinned to her chest.

"Can I help with anything?" the woman asked.

"Just browsing."

"Of course."

"Actually—do you have any more information on this bust of Democritus?"

The worker pointed at a tiny crystal cube in the display case, placed between Democritus and the next piece over. "That tells you where to look in the information booklet." Her finger moved to a corner of the room, where a binder dangled from a chain attached to one of the cases.

Andie leaned in. She had noticed the crystal, but not the number 32 lightly engraved on the surface. What an odd way to provide information. Maybe it was meant for the staff.

"They called him the Laughing Philosopher," the woman said, "because of the way he mocked human folly."

"We're a pretty easy target."

"The sad chap next to him is Heraclitus, the weeper. They were often paired together in eighteenth-century sculpture. The stone is steatite, you know. It's quite rare."

She wandered off, leaving Andie questioning why she had spoken to her and no one else. Was she being paranoid? Or was it a message of some sort?

What if the woman was about to go report her presence to someone?

A glance at the binder revealed the artist, Johann von Lücke, and the date, 1757. The woman had conveyed the rest of the pertinent information.

Andie grew nervous about standing in the hallway for so long. A heavyset Indian man with glasses, chapped lips, and hair curling out of his ears had entered not long after Andie. He was still there, perusing one of the cases near the far end, wearing a puffy gray jacket that seemed too warm for the season.

Was she missing something? What was she supposed to do? Or was the image of Democritus on the Star Phone a red herring, a simple screen saver? Was all of this a product of her twisted imagination, like her visions probably were?

Forcing away her doubts, she recalled what she knew about the ancient philosopher. Why had Dr. Corwin chosen Democritus instead of Heraclitus, the old man sitting right beside him?

Was it a statement? Laughter over tears? Or was someone laughing at *her*?

Born around 460 BCE, Democritus was a pre-Socratic Greek philosopher who made a startling array of contributions. Though none of his writings survived, his works were quoted and referenced by plenty of ancient writers. He had penned lengthy treatises on subjects as wide-ranging as epistemology, aesthetics, literary critique, ethics, language, politics, anthropology, biology, mathematics, and cosmology. Democritus had believed in a spherical Earth and the existence of multiple worlds, and posited that the Milky Way was a dense mass of stars.

Knowledge far, far ahead of its time.

Yet the reason many—including Dr. Corwin—considered Democritus "the father of modern science" was his work on atomism. Democritus had argued—shocking Andie when she had discovered it—that all matter is composed, at the basic level, of tiny invisible atoms; that these atoms are always in motion and are indestructible; and that a void exists around and among these atoms.

Before Andie began studying science, she had never even heard of Democritus. In college, she would have pegged the Enlightenment—at the earliest—as the genesis of atomic theory. And to some extent, she would have been right. Plato fought to bury Democritus's ideas. Aristotle respected him but rejected his ideas on the atom. Due to conflicting philosophies and other factors—chiefly the suppression of scientific theory by the church—atomic theory would not be revived until Descartes and Boyle in the seventeenth century.

Incredibly, Democritus had hypothesized the invisible building blocks of reality two thousand years before the West threw off the shackles of Aristotelian physics.

In reality, we know nothing, since truth is in the depths.

A saying attributed to Democritus. Andie gave a little shiver thinking about how far humanity might have progressed had his ideas caught on.

While she bowed to his intellect, she identified with sadness more than laughter as representative of the human condition. The ancient philosopher had urged his followers to strive for a state of ultimate good or cheerfulness, in which the soul lives in tranquility. That was something Andie couldn't get behind. Democritus was a trust fund baby who had traveled the ancient world on his parents' dime. How hard was it to have a sunny disposition when loafing around the agora or strolling through the Hanging Gardens of Babylon?

She stared hard at the bust. Those parted lips seemed to mock her. After glancing around and noticing the Indian man bent over a different glass case, she took the Star Phone out of her pocket. If he or anyone else was watching, they must already know she had it.

Or maybe not. Maybe no one but she knew what Dr. Corwin had kept inside that safe.

In any event, she didn't know if she would have another chance at this. Feeling rather foolish, she waved the Star Phone around the room, then aimed it at the bust of Democritus. When nothing happened, she peered through the camera eye and got the same disappointing result.

Maybe the appearance of the old woman—where had she disappeared to?—had significance. She had led Andie to the information booklet, yet before that, she had pointed out the tiny crystal cube beside the steatite bust. Pretending to snap a photo, Andie aimed the Star Phone directly at the cube. No effect. She pressed the device to her face and peered into the camera eye, and then the room started to spin.

Reeling, Andie lurched backward and stumbled into someone, thinking she was having another of her visions. But no shadowy realm appeared, and the room stabilized as soon as she looked away from the Star Phone.

After apologizing to the startled teenager behind her, realizing the device must have caused the effect in some way, Andie exhaled and tried a second time, doing her best to look innocuous. As soon as she focused on the crystal cube, the room spun again. This time, she held on as the cube expanded into a life-size image of Democritus, similar to looking through an augmented reality lens. She guessed the cube must have some sort of embedded code aligned to the Star Phone, maybe RFID or a block cipher.

But how in the world had Dr. Corwin managed to attach it inside a glass case in a world-famous museum?

She could worry about that later. The enlarged image of the philosopher, still dressed in flowing robes and a skullcap, was moving like a GIF: every few seconds, the old philosopher shook with laughter, and the gnarled hands clasped at his belly spread apart to reveal a nine-digit code string of numbers, letters, and symbols. Excited, Andie memorized the sequence and then examined the rest of the image, aware how vulnerable she was.

The only other deviations in the augmented image were two symbols in the top corners. On the right was the same marking she had seen on the replica Enneagon: the representation of an atom with a black hole in the nucleus. In the top left loomed a white circle inscribed by a black border, with *infinitus* written along the bottom. An elongated *Y* filled the center of the circle, set between an *L* and an *S*.

She caught her breath. LYS. Leap Year Society.

Three shapes hovered in the white space above the *Y*: a hollow square, a sun, and a lemniscate—commonly known as the infinity symbol. She had no idea what it all meant.

When Andie finally looked away from the phone, the Indian man was gone. That made her nervous. Had he left to seek help?

As much as she wanted to try the new code in the Star Phone, she decided it was time to get the hell out.

Taking a different route, she passed through a section filled with silverwork and jewelry, then hurried down a set of stairs in the opposite wing, which led to the cafeteria. She merged with the crowd and inhaled the aroma of fresh pastry. The cafeteria spilled into the courtyard, and she squinted in the bright sun. When she reached the gift shop, she almost collided with the thick-bodied Indian man. It took all of her self-control not to react. Though he gave no sign of recognition, she didn't like the way his red-rimmed eyes lingered a moment too long on hers.

After retrieving her backpack and checking to ensure everything was in place, she slipped into a hallway to the left of the main entrance, aiming for an elevator. With constant glances over her shoulder, she slipped inside and shut the doors. The elevator opened onto a subterranean tunnel that Andie had scouted online. To her right, a sign pointed her toward the Science Museum. A much-longer tunnel on her left led to the South Kensington underground station.

Reasoning that anyone following her would guess she was aiming for the tube station, she hurried down the shorter tunnel and made the turn for the Science Museum. So far, no one had exited the V&A behind her.

Once inside the Science Museum—another gigantic and free exhibit—she hurried to the restroom and locked herself inside a stall. Excited, she took out the Star Phone and input the nine-digit code.

Instead of disappearing, the code locked into place, backlit by a sapphire light. The image of Democritus dematerialized, and a new image appeared: a gray scroll with a white ribbon tied around it. Displayed below the scroll was a short sequence of numbers and letters.

stt38

Andie frowned. She had no idea what to do with that.

The nine-digit code disappeared, reverting to a single blank cursor.

For the rest of the day, she avoided the outside world by wandering through the comforting exhibits of the Science Museum, pretending to study the displays while she chewed on her nails and pondered the new clue.

By 7 p.m., Andie was tucked into a secluded table at the Gryphon's Beak, the pub outside Professor Rickman's flat. According to a plaque by the door, the establishment was the former guesthouse of a monastery, converted to a tavern in 1538, and rebuilt after the Great Fire of 1666. Frequented by Charles Dickens and Samuel Johnson, it was one of those atmospheric English pubs that fulfilled the fantasy of every weary traveler: a mahogany-walled common room lit by wall sconces, scuffed wooden floors, cozy booths with red upholstery, taps stocked with real English ale, the aroma of bitters and shepherd's pie, a stone hearth ready to warm the patrons in colder months.

Yet the pub had hidden depths. A set of creaky wooden steps, with a ceiling so low Andie had to duck as she descended, led past a warren of alcoves tucked behind iron-barred posterns, as if the place had once been a dungeon. All the posterns were open, and candlelit tables for two occupied the recesses of the alcoves. It could have been 1712, she thought, as a passage at the bottom of the stairs spilled into a basement bar with plaster peeling off the brick walls and dusty casks of sherry along the perimeter. Besides the bartender, she was the only person down there. The quietude both relieved and unnerved her.

After padding across the sticky cement floor, she ordered a pub burger and took a seat at a secluded wooden table in one of the alcoves. As she ate, she pondered the new image unveiled by the Laughing Philosopher.

If the Star Phone led to the Enneagon in some way, as Dr. Corwin's journal had intimated, then the bust of Democritus was a bit of a gimme. Though not obvious at first glance—and, granted, it did require travel to London—it was not that difficult to research the location of that particular piece, find it in the V&A, and point the Star Phone at the crystal cube.

She remembered the note in the journal on the first step of the staircase. *Arche.* The beginning.

There were nine steps on the staircase. What if the journey had just begun? The thought made her queasy, though it did seem like the sort of intellectual puzzle Dr. Corwin would devise.

But why?

A waiter brought her food. She devoured her burger and fries but made no progress with the string of letters and numbers displayed on the Star Phone. Google didn't help. Neither did her training in mathematics and astronomy. The figures must be a cipher of some kind, but if so, she had no idea how to go about solving it.

She focused on the scroll icon. There was nothing to distinguish it from any other depiction of rolled parchment. She assumed the scroll and the alphanumeric code tied together in some way, but again, she was at a loss.

Eight o'clock came and went with no sign of Professor Rickman. That was fine; he had said he might be late. Just in case, she ordered a half pint of Samuel Smith and took it upstairs, to an upholstered pew that overlooked the alley and the courtyard. If she leaned far enough to her left, she could see the entrance to Professor Rickman's flat.

At eight thirty, she noticed movement out of the corner of her eye. Turning to the window, she saw a tall and athletic black woman, taller even than herself, closing the door to Professor Rickman's flat. The woman's face was smooth and sculpted, as if carved from obsidian, and she moved with intent, stepping lightly through the gate and hurrying down the alleyway toward Fleet Street.

The woman looked too young and statuesque to be Professor's Rickman's mistress. She could be a friend or colleague, though how many casual acquaintances had access to his flat? And why had she hurried away so quickly?

A name came to mind, based on her ethnicity. A name with Swahili origins written in Dr. Corwin's journal, and which had caused Professor Rickman to pause when Andie had mentioned it.

Zawadi.

By the time nine o'clock rolled around, Andie decided she had to check on the professor. After closing out the tab, she slipped on her backpack and left the pub. The faint smell of diesel laced the air, with a trace of wild roses. Except for a shout or two drifting over from Fleet Street, the courtyard was silent and empty.

She buzzed the door to Professor Rickman's flat, then buzzed again when there was no response. All the curtains were drawn.

Glancing over her shoulder, nervous the woman might return, Andie tried the front door. Unlocked. That was strange. She stepped inside, closed the door, and stared down a dark hallway with jackets and umbrellas hanging on the wall to her left.

"Professor Rickman?" she called out.

No answer.

Not liking the situation one bit, she opened her knife before creeping up the stairs to the second story, where a landing opened onto a short hallway with a pair of closed doors. After calling his name again, she eased the door to the sitting room open and saw him lying on his back in a pool of blood on the polished wood floor. His arms were akimbo, wrists slashed vertically halfway to his elbow. Sightless eyes stared in mute accusation at the ceiling.

The visceral, metallic odor of fresh blood cut the air as she rushed over to check his pulse. No trace of a heartbeat. Fear coursed through her, and then anger, and then guilt at waiting so long to knock on the door. She was certain he was dead, but in case there was a chance of saving him, she called emergency services on her way out.

A voice in the back of her mind implored her to search his flat, but she couldn't risk explaining her presence to the police, and she worried someone else might wander in.

Or maybe the killer was watching her right now.

It seemed clear the tall woman had killed the professor. Andie envisioned her breaking into his flat earlier in the day and waiting for him to return. Maybe the professor had stopped by home to use the restroom, or for some other reason, on his way to meet Andie. The woman had constrained him and slit his wrists, arranged the body to look like a suicide, and probably searched his flat before leaving.

What if he had met with me first? Would we both be dead?

As Andie hurried into the courtyard, trying to appear calm but clenching her hands in rage and fear, she wasn't sure which scenario was more disturbing: another murder of a scientist connected to whatever madness she was involved in, or Professor Rickman committing suicide on the very night he was supposed to meet her.

The sight of his pale corpse stained with blood made her think of Dr. Corwin, crowding her mind's eye as she retraced her steps through the alley. Feeling sick to her stomach, blinking away tears, she emerged on Fleet and turned toward the tube station—then stopped as if jerked by a rope.

A hundred feet away, clearly illuminated on the well-lit street, was the dark-haired man who had chased her through the woods in Durham. He was passing a flower seller and walking right toward her.

They noticed each other almost at the same time. He stilled, just as surprised as she was, then began sprinting in her direction.

For a split second, Andie felt rooted to the ground, too terrified to move. Then her adrenaline kicked in, and she fled back down the cobblestone lane, worried the tall woman might be waiting for her if she ran down Fleet. She remembered that the alley continued on the far side of the courtyard, and she would have to take her chances.

As she ran past the pub, drawing stares from the patrons by the window, she yearned with all of her being to return inside and shout for help. But she didn't trust that would save her. Maybe her pursuer wouldn't kill her in front of a dozen witnesses—and maybe he would—but he could easily create chaos by shooting out a window or pulling a fire alarm, then drag her away during the confusion.

No. She couldn't put herself at his mercy. She was better off running.

The cobblestone alley led to a deserted cul-de-sac. After a moment of panic, thinking it was a dead end, she saw a couple emerge arm in arm from a footpath between two of the flats. Andie put a finger to her lips as she sped past them, hoping they would get the hint and stay quiet. The footpath led to another courtyard ringed by buildings. A vine-covered trellis gave access to a cement-walled corridor that wound through a web of modern glass buildings. A commuter byway of some sort. Surely, she thought, it had to lead to a road, where she could flag a police officer or jump into a cab.

Except for the ominous sound of footsteps pounding the pavement behind her, it was eerily quiet as she sprinted through the corridor. When she entered an office park with no apparent exit and glass and brick soaring above her on both sides, an urban Greek labyrinth, she began to wish she had taken her chances with Fleet Street.

She tried a few of the doors. All rear entrances, and all locked. She scampered among the buildings until she stumbled onto a landscaped terrace facing a building with living walls, fronted by a brick walkway exiting the park in both directions.

The footsteps drew closer. She had to choose. Gasping for breath from the sprint, noticing more light to her right, she ran across the brick walkway, finally emerging on the sidewalk of a busy street. Relief poured through her as she ran forward, scanning for a taxi, but the predominance of residential apartments made her curse. She had ended up in one of the least touristy sections of Central London.

Several taxis passed by, but no one stopped when she waved. At the edge of a neighborhood park, she glanced back and saw the dark-haired man exiting from the same corridor as she had. They locked eyes again, and he ran straight for her as she cut into the park.

A gravel path meandered through the gnarled trees. She raced right through the middle of the park, leaping over rocks and benches, debating whether to hide in one of the dense copses of bamboo. Too obvious, she decided.

A rock in the middle of the path caused her to trip. She fell hard, scraping her arms on the gravel. Swallowing her cry of pain, she picked herself up and kept running, thankful not to have sprained an ankle and wondering how much longer she could last at this pace.

On the other side of the park, she scrambled over a fence and noticed, not too far away, a castle-like structure with high stone walls and a parapet rising above the other buildings. After looking to both sides—still quiet and residential—she dashed across the street and down a lane that tunneled between the buildings. Her heart dropped when it dead-ended at an eight-foot brick wall with a gated entrance and a card swipe for property owners. To her left was a Thai restaurant with a sign overhanging the street. Without pause, she stepped up on the ground-floor windowsill, clambered from there to the sign, jumped, and clung to the top of the wall. Her pursuer entered the narrow lane just before she dropped to the other side and sprinted into the residential complex.

Running beside a high brick wall, she made her way to a lush courtyard on the other side of the gated community. She slammed into the iron door granting access to the street, furiously twisting the knob. As she burst through to the sidewalk, she saw the fortress she had noticed, looming just across the street and protected by a high stone wall topped by spikes, like something out of Harry Potter. A thought came to her, based on where she had started, that it was probably one of the Inns of Court, a collection of ancient buildings housing London's legal society.

When she looked to her left, she saw a blue sedan whipping onto the street, threatening to hem her in. Her heart pounding with terror, Andie ran straight for the nearest entrance to the castle, looking frantically for a way inside. The walls and iron gate were too high for her to climb. A camera overlooked the entrance, and she waved and shouted for help, in case someone was watching in real time.

A shuttered, flat-topped guard tower extended three feet above the wall. She dashed around to the other side and noticed a terra-cotta drainpipe reinforced with circular notches. Breathing heavily, she grabbed the pipe and started climbing, praying it would hold. The notches, set a foot apart and just wide enough for a toe, held fast as she climbed to the edge of the roof. She scrambled atop the guardhouse and risked a quick glance back. The blue sedan had come to a stop near the gate, disgorging a short-haired blond woman and the heavyset Indian man from the museum. Andie caught a glimpse of a handgun holster inside the woman's coat. The dark-haired man caught up to them, and they all noticed Andie perched atop the guardhouse.

"We just want to talk!" the dark-haired man called out, right before Andie dropped down on the other side of the wall and kept running.

Talk, my ass.

Her only question was why they hadn't shot her, and she had to assume they wanted to take her alive and interrogate her. Or maybe the cameras had stayed their hand.

All around her, fortresses of stone rose from the darkness, stentorian guardians lit by the occasional glow from a lamppost. There was no one in sight, and the sounds of pursuit—scrabbling on the drainpipe—faded as she ran. The solitude bore weight, suffocating, and she pushed herself to the limit as she wound through the ageless buildings, racing through parking lots and courtyards and jumping over hedges. Her new fear was that the stone wall encircled the entire complex and she wouldn't be able to escape.

That worry faded when she found a green space that backed onto a public street. Another iron fence separated the park from the road, but the overhanging branch of an old yew provided an easy escape route. Unable to sprint any longer, Andie cleared the fence and continued as fast as she could down a quiet side street, following the noise and lights until she emerged onto a busy thoroughfare. Her lungs burned as she raced, waving her arms, for a red double-decker bus just as it was pulling away. Tires screeched in the distance. She knew she had moments before her pursuers saw her.

The bus didn't slow.

Andie dug deep. Chest heaving, she caught up to the front of the bus and paced alongside it, holding up her bloodied arms as she mouthed for help. Still the driver refused to turn his head.

She wanted to scream and beat on the door in anger. Instead, as the bus started to accelerate, she swallowed her pride and put her hands together in a praying motion, keeping up with the bus for as long as she could, pleading with her eyes until the driver finally looked over.

Just as she began to fall back, the bus decelerated a fraction and the door popped open. Andie used the last of her reserves to catch up and leap onto the steps. She gave the driver a five-pound note and collapsed in an open seat in the rear, soaking in sweat, not daring to look out the window but saddled with the stabbing fear that the people chasing her had seen her board.

Copenhagen, Denmark
——○ 1933 ○——

During the Easter break, Ettore's grant took him to Copenhagen to conduct research at the Niels Bohr Institute. He would soon return to Leipzig, but for a month he would work alongside Bohr himself, a Nobel Prize winner as well as a friend and mentor to Werner Heisenberg.

Ettore had mixed feelings about the trip. It was good for his career, true. And Germany had become a political pressure cooker. Yet he was sad to part ways with Werner, even for a short time, and the trip also drew him away from Stefan.

Though Ettore had met with the charismatic sergeant major half a dozen more times in Leipzig, always on a walk in the city that ended up outside Ettore's apartment, Stefan had not yet introduced him to the mysterious Leap Year Society.

Was it all a farce? Was Ettore the butt of some cruel joke, as had been the case throughout his schooling?

He *wanted* to believe the Society was real. He wanted to believe there was more to the world than meets the eye, to join the secret club. In the past, he would never have believed there were people in the world who possessed more knowledge or performed more cutting-edge work than Ettore and his colleagues. Now he wasn't so sure. Stefan's range of knowledge, including his scientific acumen, was astounding. And it was true that governmental institutions were limited by funds, ethical considerations, the political climate, and the visions of their founders. Even if the Leap Year Society was just a collection of like-minded people searching for greater truths, if they were as smart and engaging as Stefan, then Ettore wanted to be a part.

But he had come to doubt their existence. As far as he could tell, there was not a single mention of this organization in the historical record. He had come to suspect it might be a covert group of Nazis who wanted to subvert Ettore to their cause. That, or Stefan was a paranoid schizophrenic who had drawn Ettore into his web of self-delusion and lies.

Oh well, he thought with a sigh as he sipped his coffee in the flagstone courtyard of his hotel on a quiet Saturday morning, enjoying a rare bout of Scandinavian sunshine. *I must forget about Stefan and concentrate on my work. New breakthroughs are occurring in the quantum world on a daily basis. This is where I must focus, not on some ridiculous covert society that is likely a figment of a troubled imagination.*

The temperature was surprisingly mild for March in Copenhagen. Frost still clung to the bushes and windows, but Ettore was able to sit outside in his peacoat without a frigid wind cutting him to the bone. He had seen nothing but gray clouds and gloom since his arrival, but today a hint of spring was in the air. To celebrate, he decided to walk to the royal observatory, which he had been meaning to visit since his arrival.

After finishing his coffee, he strolled past the line of bicycles in front of his hotel, heading toward the city center. He cut through the busy train station and walked east on Vesterbrogade, past the whimsical arched entryway to the Tivoli amusement park. The pleasure ground was legendary throughout Europe, and as the cries of delighted children floated to his ears, it brought a wave of nostalgia for his own childhood, as well as a stab of regret for not having wed.

How very human we are, he mused. *My heart lies with science, yet the cry of joy of a single child, flying through the air from a Ferris wheel, makes me reconsider my entire life in an instant.*

Copenhagen was a flat, immensely walkable city. Quite different from Rome and Leipzig, the Danish capital managed to be both cosmopolitan and bohemian, progressive yet laced with tradition. The contradictions fascinated Ettore. He also liked that the city did not take itself too seriously, smug with the superiority of its own culture, as Germany and Italy were.

Ettore did not consult a map but let himself wander through the cobblestone streets. He felt bewildered by the crush of people on Strøget, the main pedestrian artery through town, yet once he entered the narrow lanes veering off in every direction, he became lost in the ivy-covered walls and courtyards, enjoying the street musicians and jugglers, the spray of fountains and the aroma of fresh pastries, the stiff but reviving breeze that carried the tang of sea air, the parks and quiet cafés. The lack of tall buildings imparted a rare feeling of intimacy for a European capital.

After passing through the university district, he made his way toward a cylindrical brick tower jutting above the city like a giant thimble. This was the Rundetaarn, or Round Tower, the beloved landmark that everyone told Ettore he simply must visit. Not one to dwell on historical facts, he knew little about the seventeenth-century edifice except that it boasted great views of the city and housed one of Europe's oldest observatories.

Inside, a ramp of inlaid brick—broad enough for a motor vehicle—spiraled upward around the whitewashed core. There were no stairs in sight. It was quite a unique building. As he set foot on the walkway, someone touched him on the shoulder from behind, startling him. His surprise turned to shock when he turned to find Stefan's piercing blue eyes glittering with amusement from beneath a tweed cap.

"A fine morning for a walk, ja?"

A familiar double-breasted woolen coat wrapped the German's tall and lean figure, all the way to the tops of his black boots. Ettore noticed the military insignia was nowhere in sight, and wondered if Stefan had removed it or owned more than one coat.

"I admit it is, but what are you doing here?"

Stefan studied him for a moment. "This is your first time to the tower?"

"Yes."

"Then come. Let us talk above the city."

As the German officer led the way into the higher reaches of the observatory, Ettore followed behind, drawn as always by the man's hypnotic charisma.

I wonder if some human beings exert more gravitational pull than others. Or perhaps the source is not gravity, but the mysterious body of energy that surrounds us all, repelling and attracting the spirit rather than the corporeal body. How else to explain the ability of men like Adolf Hitler to bend a nation to their will?

The slope on the long and winding ramp was quite gentle. Along the way, windows recessed into oval archways provided excellent viewing points, as well as nooks that sheltered delighted children hiding from their parents. Halfway up the tower, Ettore and Stefan passed an open door that led to a connecting corridor.

Ettore stopped to peer inside. Displayed in glass cases were a variety of historical objects: a sextant, an old copper globe, a collection of antique telescopes, and a set of crossed stone keys. A star map on the wall connected the constellations with dotted yellow lines.

"When the tower complex was first built," Stefan said, "this corridor led to a library, which housed the entire collection of the university. The width of the ramp allowed a horse and carriage to transport books to the library, as well as instruments to the observatory."

"Remarkable," Ettore said, though he was not that interested.

"Do you believe public libraries should provide access to all books, Ettore?"

When he glanced over at Stefan, surprised by the non sequitur, he found the German affixing him with an intense stare. "Why wouldn't I?" Ettore said.

"Perhaps because you have never thought deeply about the question."

"Oh," he said, flustered. "Do you not agree?"

"Is some knowledge not unfit for public consumption?"

"I don't believe banning literature is beneficial to society. I've heard it rumored that the Nazis"—Ettore couldn't help glancing with distaste at the sleeve where Stefan normally bore his military rank—"wish to make a bonfire of literature that conflicts with their myopic worldview."

Stefan caught the downward glance. "Yes, of course that's an affront, a buffoon's attempt to silence his critics. An easy target. But what of morally reprehensive books that might offend the sensibilities of women and children? Books illustrating the sexual practices of various cultures or discussing in detail the perversions of man? Books containing explicit descriptions of violence?"

"Yes, I suppose you're right. There should be some limits."

"Do not simply agree with me, Ettore. You should think long and hard about this question. It is one of the most important mankind has to answer."

"Is that so?" Ettore said, unable to keep the sarcasm out of his voice.

There was a knowing light in Stefan's eyes, as if he had anticipated Ettore's rebuff. "You are more aware than most of the incredible advances of science in recent years. Every day, we unlock more and more of Mother Nature's secrets. I ask you: Should a library contain the recipes for deadly poisons and chemical weapons that can be manufactured in the home? The blueprints for every single detail of our capital cities? What if someone were to prepare a vat of phosgene and mustard gas and unleash it in a subway in Rome or London or New York City?"

"What a horrible thought! But, yes, I . . . I suppose you have a point there."

"And what of your own field of study?" Stefan's lips parted in a grim, humorless smile. "Tell me, Ettore: Should we teach every man and woman on the street how to split the atom?"

"That is an impossible task, outside of a handful of institutions."

"Is it?" he said calmly, which took Ettore aback. "But that doesn't answer my question. We both know the technology will one day be far more accessible. The query remains: *Should* we teach such a thing? Do we make all knowledge accessible to the general public?"

"Perhaps not every form," Ettore mumbled.

"Oh, no? Who are you to judge! Why should you become a censor and not Adolf Hitler, or a farmer from Lower Saxony, or a bushman from an indigenous culture in the Amazon jungle?"

The German's rebuke confused Ettore. He had never met anyone so unpredictable. "Because I have experience with these technologies. I understand the awesome potential of their power," Ettore said.

"And?"

"I'm sorry?"

"Are you so arrogant to think the ramifications of this awesome 'power' cannot be explained to others? Did you yourself create the atom? Why should your position as a scientist give you the moral high ground? Should not the public decide? The church? The state? A body of international observers? A committee of farmers and bushmen? Who, Ettore?"

Ettore opened his hands, flustered, but said nothing. Stefan chuckled and clapped him on the shoulder. "I was not seeking an answer, my friend. At least not today." His penetrating gaze locked Ettore in place, making him feel as if he were the most important person in the world. "I ask only that you consider the implications of these questions for yourself," he said gravely, "as you go about your work. Agreed?"

Ettore shrugged. "Agreed."

"Good."

They continued upward, stopping to peer inside the planetarium before accessing the observation deck via a claustrophobic stone staircase at the top of the tower. Ettore appreciated the metaphor of the long walk up the ramp to the observatory, spiraling into the heart of the cosmos.

As they exited onto an open-air viewing platform surrounded

by a wrought-iron lattice and buffeted by the wind, they saw below them the city unveiled: its canals and palaces and green copper spires, chimneys and sloping red roofs, the gossamer blue table of the sea. Stefan pointed to the east. "Over there is the tip of Sweden. This morning is a rare treat."

Ettore squinted into the haze, wrinkling his nose as the wind carried a whiff of cloying perfume from a trio of older women. "I didn't realize it was that close."

"Ja, only a few kilometers." After absorbing the view for a while, Stefan continued, "How are you finding the institute?"

"It's adequate. Niels is a bit tiresome, to be honest."

"Isn't he considered one of the founding fathers of quantum mechanics?"

"I suppose, if one's father is rather senile, drinks beer like a dockworker, and is grumpier than a babushka."

Stefan gave a hearty laugh and led him across the wooden planking to a more isolated section of the deck. Quietly, out of earshot of any listeners, he said, "We need your help, Ettore."

"Who does?" he said absently.

"The Leap Year Society."

A hiccup of disbelief escaped Ettore, until he looked over at Stefan and saw how very serious he was. "Help with what?"

"With an important mission."

"I don't understand. What kind of mission?"

"Do you trust me, Ettore?"

"I don't really know, to be honest."

"That's fair. You need validation. Something to prove I am not simply a master of spirited rhetoric, or perhaps even insane."

It's as if he can read my thoughts. "I suppose, yes," Ettore said faintly.

Stefan gripped the railing as he stared out at the city. "You have asked me before how I can wear the uniform of an SS officer. I can tell you now—I had to learn to trust you as well—that our society is working to subvert the Nazis from within. The elections in Germany were rigged, and Hitler has seized full power. He is a cancer that must be stopped. There are things happening in my country—depravities—of which the public does not yet know. Corruptions you would not believe attributable to the mind of man. The Nazis *must* be deterred, Ettore."

"I cannot disagree. But what can I possibly do?"

"Right now, a small but important task. Everyone who seeks justice has a role of some kind to play—never forget that."

"What sort of task?"

"Help us with this, and I promise you will be granted membership to the Leap Year Society. Not in some indeterminate future, but before you leave Copenhagen."

"What—the Society is here too?"

Stefan's eyes gleamed in the rising sun.

That evening, according to Stefan's instructions, Ettore stepped out to meet a black coupe de ville with curved fenders that pulled in front of his hotel at precisely ten.

Tonight, Ettore thought, *we shall see if he is mad or not.*

When the rear passenger door opened, he saw Stefan waving him in, clad in a pair of wool trousers and a crisp white shirt, his overcoat folded across his lap. The driver was invisible through a partition of smoky glass separating him from the passenger section. Ettore found that odd—he had never seen such a thing before—but said nothing.

Stefan offered him port and a cigar, which Ettore declined. After a few minutes of small talk, the German was uncharacteristically quiet as he puffed on his cigar and sipped from a fluted glass. When questioned about their destination, he said it was better to wait, and that all would be revealed in due course.

Highly curious and more than a little uneasy, Ettore consigned himself to riding in silence as the car left Copenhagen and entered the Danish countryside. The towns and road signs grew sparse, the road turned rough and narrow. A gibbous moon revealed glimmers of flat grasslands dotted with lakes and forests, as well as the occasional church steeple marking the presence of some shuttered village.

Judging by the long drive and the direction they had left Copenhagen, Ettore's limited geographical knowledge of the region told him they must be nearing the southern tip of Zealand, the main island. Where in God's name was Stefan taking him? Was he about to be kidnapped and ferried across the border, held hostage in Berlin while forced to develop advanced weaponry for the Nazis?

Just before midnight, Ettore thought he was dreaming when they pulled into a long, paved drive that led to a fairy-tale castle backlit by a starry sky. He blinked twice. The castle was still there.

Though small, the fortification was quite fetching, tall and elegant and graced with a forest of spires and conical towers. Instead of taking the bridge across the moat, the driver veered down a service road, parking beside a high wall covered in ivy. Stefan exited the vehicle, switched on a brass flashlight, and beckoned for Ettore to follow. The driver waited inside, still unseen.

After passing through an iron gate set farther down the wall, they entered a landscaped portion of the castle grounds marked by fountains, dormant flower beds, and rows of cypress. The smell of damp soil settled in Ettore's nostrils. Stefan led them to the far side of the gardens, where they passed through another iron gate and entered a passage lined on both sides with a hedge of sharp holly, which rose well above their heads. As the passage twisted and turned and split off in multiple directions, Ettore realized they were inside a hedge maze.

"It's designed on sacred geometry," Stefan said in a low voice as they walked.

"What is sacred about geometry?"

"Do you not find order in the grand design? What is *not* sacred about geometry?"

"I suppose it depends on your meaning of 'sacred.'"

"I'll allow that 'sacred' means different things to different people, but it doesn't change the nature of the word. Whatever one believes, the incredible repetition of certain shapes and proportions is a fact of nature. The plants in this very garden are brimming with the Fibonacci sequence. The shells of the snails that eat the plants reflect the spiral arms of the galaxies. Repeating patterns are the law of the natural world, of the universe itself. Infinite symmetry. You should know this better than I, Ettore."

Ettore smiled to himself. He knew a very great deal about such things. He was only being contrary and had wanted to hear what Stefan had to say. "Is there a particular geometric inspiration for the design of this garden?

"The vortex," Stefan said softly, after a moment.

"And why is that?"

But the German never answered.

They probed the maze for at least half an hour. Despite the confidence with which Stefan guided them, Ettore began to wonder if they were lost. As he grew more and more nervous, realizing he had yet to see another human being in close proximity to Stefan besides the thugs in Leipzig, not even the face of their driver, Ettore was relieved when they rounded a corner and saw two middle-aged men conversing by the light of a kerosene lamp hanging from the hedge. The passage dead-ended where the men were standing.

"One thing," Stefan whispered as he and Ettore approached the men. "Do not mention the Leap Year Society."

"Why not? Are they not part—"

Stefan silenced him with a finger. "They are. But you are not. Just follow my lead, please."

Feeling rather like a devoted beagle, Ettore shadowed Stefan as he entered the clearing and greeted the two men. Ettore caught his breath when Stefan introduced the taller of the two—a spindly, dark-haired man with kind eyes and a widow's peak that formed a narrow isthmus down his forehead—as a member of the Danish royal family. A prince, no less, whose face Ettore remembered from a portrait at the Copenhagen institute. He was very respected among the Danes, and his presence lent gravitas to the midnight meeting, as well as raising Ettore's estimation of Stefan.

The German soldier bowed to the prince and shook hands with the other man, whom he introduced by title instead of name: a senior member of the US State Department. Despite their prestigious positions, both men seemed to hold Stefan in high regard.

When Ettore himself was introduced, the two men shook his hand with respect, nodding gravely as Stefan summarized his scientific accomplishments.

"It's an honor," the prince said, causing Ettore to blush in the shadows of the kerosene lamp. "I'm the scientific liaison to the crown and am kept well apprised of the institute. Niels speaks very highly of you."

"He does?"

Stefan blew on his hands as he studied the high walls of the maze. "I trust there is no possibility of interference?"

"The castle is nearly empty this weekend," the prince said, "and this corner of the maze was designed expressly for this purpose. No other passages are within reach of eyes or ears."

"I've checked for listening devices myself," the American added. He was much more businesslike than the prince.

As Stefan nodded in satisfaction, the prince bent to pick up a padlocked leather attaché case. "The documents are in order," he said, then shocked Ettore by holding it out to him. Unsure what to do, Ettore sensed Stefan's stare boring into him and felt he had no choice but to take the attaché case.

"Thank you," Stefan said to the prince. "It will reach its destination safely."

The prince addressed Ettore. "Your assistance in this matter is greatly appreciated. You're doing the crown—and the people of Denmark—a great favor."

Ettore had no idea what they were talking about but sensed that Stefan wanted him to play along. "It's my pleasure," he murmured.

After a round of handshakes, the meeting adjourned, and Ettore found himself returning through the hedge maze with his friend, fraught with questions. Once they were settled in the car again, on the way back to Copenhagen, Stefan calmly lit another cigar and cracked the window to expel the thick smoke as he puffed.

Ettore could contain himself no longer. "What in the world is this about? What am I supposed to do?"

Once the cigar was fully lit, Stefan said, "We need you to deliver this briefcase to my counterpart within the Society in Malmö, Sweden—the city just across the strait from Copenhagen. As part of his many duties, the prince assists with military defense and diplomacy, and needs to ensure these documents arrive safely in the hands of the Swedes."

"What's inside?"

"Trust me, it's better if you're not familiar with the contents."

"But I don't understand. Why me? What does this have to do with science?"

Stefan's smile was wolfish. "Not a thing. German spies are everywhere now. The borders are not secure. But you're an outsider, unknown to the intelligence services."

"What if they search the briefcase?"

"You work at the institute, with an impeccable international reputation. No one will dare touch you."

"I don't know about this," Ettore said, trying to stem a rising tide of panic. "I could lose my position, or worse."

The German patted Ettore's knee. His voice was paternal, warm with understanding. "I cannot assure you there will be no risk. I can only say that I would not ask you to do anything I did not have full confidence you could accomplish. Dark days are upon us, Ettore. The world needs its heroes."

"I'm hardly a hero."

"As I said, every man plays his part."

"I haven't even agreed yet."

"Yet I believe in you. Will you aid us, my friend? Will you join us in our cause and help fan the flames of democracy?"

Despite his misgivings, despite the surreal nature of the evening and the gravity of the request, Ettore found himself once again soothed by Stefan's confident demeanor, lulled into a sense of security and desiring only to please the German soldier.

"I will help you," Ettore said, so softly he could barely hear his own voice.

Los Angeles

——o 14 o——

After twisting up a serpentine road into the parched hills above Hollywood, high above the iconic sign, Cal stepped off the DASH bus with a crush of other tourists at the entrance to Griffith Observatory.

Perched atop the south-facing slope of Mount Hollywood, resembling a cross between the White House and a mosque, the observatory's trio of copper domes overlooked all of central Los Angeles yet stood a world away from the smog and busy streets. The beloved attraction was free to wander through, and hosted a busy calendar of exhibits, astronomical viewings, and presentations on the cosmos. *The city planners got this one right.*

It was four in the afternoon, hot and windy. In one hour, if nothing suspicious drove him away, Cal was scheduled to meet the anonymous source who had first brought the Leap Year Society to his attention. The public exposure made him jumpy, but he was excited by the prospect of gaining more ammunition in his newly declared war on the enigmatic organization that had ruined his life.

The rendezvous at the observatory was happening at his request. The lone road to the top of the hill made it hard to trail someone unobserved, and after exiting the bus, he stood on one of the terraces for the next half hour and watched every single person who arrived by bus or hiked up from one of the public parking lots. Even if the communications with his source had somehow been intercepted, the observatory was swarming with schoolchildren and visitors from around the world, and he couldn't imagine anyone making a play in such a crowded place. Especially people who lived in the shadows.

As he watched and waited, Clippers hat pulled low and hands tucked nervously into his jeans, he reflected on the events of the last twenty-four hours. After scrabbling down the dusty hillside behind Elias Holt's mansion, terrified he would get shot in the back, tripping over rocks and ripping his clothes and skin on the cacti and thorny underbrush, he had stumbled into a ravine that led to the bottom of the hill. No one came after him. He assumed they hadn't seen him climb the wall and had instead searched the mansion. Once Cal found a road, he jumped into a taxi and sped away.

But he had crossed a line by leaving the rental van—procured in his own name—parked at the mansion. He had to go dark and figure out what to do.

When Cal arrived at his house, he asked the taxi driver to wait while Cal inspected his Jeep. The glove box and all the compartments had already been emptied.

Trying not to panic, fearing they were still in the house, Cal waited in the taxi while he called 911 to report a burglary. When the police arrived, Cal told them he had seen someone in the house through the kitchen window, rummaging around as the taxi pulled up. The police snooped around long enough for Cal to grab what he needed: his dog, Leon; his passport and cash, hidden under a floorboard; and spare clothes. Most of the drawers had been upended, but he kept his laptop in a secret desk drawer and was relieved to find the chalk dust on the lock had not been disturbed. They simply had not had time.

He stuffed everything in a backpack and hurried to the Jeep as soon as the cops left. No doubt they had planted a tracking device, so Cal ditched the Jeep in a public lot and called in a favor. He asked an old pickup basketball buddy who lived in the desert, Brett Stellis, to take Leon for a while. They met at a busy fountain at The Grove, a ritzy outdoor shopping center, and Brett took Leon without question, knowing the risks of Cal's profession.

Feeling very alone without Leon, Cal did his best to lose himself in the crowds as he wove his way on foot to La Brea. He paid cash for a cheap motel, grabbed some cold peanut noodles at a Vietnamese place next door, then holed up in his room and tried to get a handle on the disturbing turn of events.

He had just seen, with his own two eyes, evidence the Leap Year Society was real and connected to Elias Holt. Far more important, they had opened a file on Cal at the same time he had run the story connecting the CIA and a handful of prominent defense contractors to the black-site lab of a global technology company.

Cal's source—a Bolivian scientist working at PanSphere's black-site lab—had blown the whistle on forbidden research into genetic engineering, nanotech chemical agents, and other highly regulated technologies conducted on-site and sold to various players. Bizarrely, his source had also claimed an unknown entity was siphoning off the best research and leaving the scraps to the CIA and corporate defense firms, right under their noses. Unfortunately, the scientist had gone dark—or been disappeared—before he could flesh out this part of his story.

Four things had gotten Cal fired: the sudden desertion of his source, the outright denial of the Bolivian government of the existence of the lab, the miraculous appearance of falsified evidence that contradicted Cal's claims in his article, and the lawsuit against the *Times*.

The CIA, or even one of the defense contractors, could have pulled all of that off. But Cal had always suspected his mention of this elusive metaconspiracy was the real trigger.

And now he had proof.

Who *were* these people?

The knowledge that such an organization existed—hidden in plain sight—terrified him. But it did not surprise him. No one had a handle on anything anymore. Technology was too complex, spiraling further out of control every day, metastasizing like some cancerous AI overlord. It took a genius to fully understand one little part of the puzzle, like microchip components or modern programming languages. Everyone was so specialized that no one had a handle on the big picture.

He didn't have the choice to walk away anymore. He had pulled on the dragon's tail—twice—and been caught. It was publish or perish in the most literal sense.

When he had plugged the USB drive with the stolen data into a computer at the public library, he had found nothing but encrypted gibberish. He needed Dane, but the computer guru was not taking his calls or responding to his emails. Though frustrated, Cal couldn't blame him.

In desperation, he had reached out to his original source, the one who had turned him on to the LYS in the first place.

To his surprise, she had responded to his chat request with a simple but chilling message.

My bo*fr*end came back. And he isn't the same.

After a hard swallow, Cal had replied immediately. What do you mean?

I . . . saw something. Someone should know.

What is it?

I'm not sure email is safe.

Are you in danger?

I don't think so but he might be.

Cal knew he had to play it cool. What do you suggest?

I don't know.

I'm a former reporter. I might be able to help.

How?

Where are you located?

Thinking he had pushed too far, too fast, he released a huge sigh of relief when she finally replied.

San Diego area.

Her response thrilled him, but it also put up his guard. Then again, the Golden State had forty million people and bred conspiracy theorists like minks. He suspected quite a number of his listeners lived nearby.

I'm in LA.

Really?

20 years and counting. Maybe we could meet?

Her response was again slow to arrive. I don't know.

I'll come to you and take every precaution.

I think it's better if I come up there. Less chance he follows me.

OK

When?

Cal told her the truth. Sooner is always better.

It would have to be public.

Of course.

Let me think about it.

She emailed him three hours later and agreed. After considering his options, Cal asked her to meet him at Griffith Observatory during daylight hours.

The situation made him wary. It was a little too convenient. But he had talked to enough potential and anonymous sources to know her responses felt natural.

Even if she was compromised or one of them was followed, the sheer popularity of the planetarium should protect him. He had taken another precaution as well: taking a cue from Dane, he had purchased a burner phone so he could text the actual location right before they met. He also texted Dane about the meeting, though he had not received a response. With a sigh, Cal supposed he would have to figure out something else to do with the USB drive.

A bang in the crowd snapped him back to the present. Thinking it was a gunshot, he whipped around to find a parent scolding a child holding a bag of those small white poppers Cal had loved as a kid.

Get a hold of yourself, buddy. You're a pro. Act like it.

With twenty minutes to go, he moved inside, scanning the crowd as he walked past the exhibits in the Central Rotunda and the Hall of the Eye. Crackling, bullet-like strikes of contained lightning awed a crowd watching a demonstration of the Tesla coil. Cal kept moving until he reached the edge of the giant Foucault pendulum, pretending to watch the mesmeric swing of the bronze ball suspended from the ceiling while he sent an email to his source that contained the number of his burner phone. Even if someone was watching, no way they could track a burner phone that fast.

Moments later, she texted him.

Are you here?

Yes.

Me too.

Meet me at 5:00 Event Horizon show. Back left row, two seats by the aisle. I'll save you one.

Do I need a ticket?

No.

K.

Tingly with anticipation, he made his way to the main elevator. The show in the Event Horizon, a presentation theater on the lower level, would be less crowded than the show at the wildly popular Oschin Planetarium. Easier for him to procure seats and ensure his instructions were followed.

He was fifth in line when the doors opened. He hurried to the back left of the tiered auditorium and draped an arm over the seat next to him, discouraging other visitors.

As the minutes ticked by, the auditorium filled to half capacity, but no one sat anywhere near him. Almost everyone had crowded into the bottom half, close to the giant screen. He wondered what had happened to his source when five o'clock arrived and the lights faded to black, casting the theater into darkness.

Had she changed her mind? Been intercepted?

Growing nervous, he decided to call it off as a booming musical score heralded the arrival of an exploding star on the presentation screen. He recoiled as someone brushed against his shoulder, then realized a woman with long hair had slipped into the seat next to him. He sank back down, relieved, as the camera zoomed into a vast cluster of stars so dense and iridescent it took his breath away.

How to start the conversation? He had to build as much trust as possible during the brief show. He guessed she would want to leave before it was over, escaping in darkness as she had arrived.

A floral sweetness in her perfume reminded him of running through a childhood meadow, the sultry summer air laced with honeysuckle. As he leaned over to speak in her ear, the theater screen panned to an image of a black hole, the classical score soared even louder, and someone shoved a foul-smelling cloth over his mouth.

The smell of vinegar washed over him. He shook his head back and forth, trying not to inhale the toxic substance as two pairs of hands lifted him out of his chair and carried him away in the darkness. Cal's muffled shouts for help were drowned by the rag over his mouth and the thunderous music.

A crack of light appeared. They carried him through a door, either in the back of the theater or in the hallway, that opened onto a gray, dimly lit stairwell. He struggled to free himself, but his limbs had started to numb, and the men holding him were strong.

By jerking his head from side to side, he caught glimpses of two large men hustling him down a flight of steps. One was blond and pale, the other a balding black man with a keloid scar on the side of his neck. Both were dressed in shorts and polo shirts. They could have been tourists visiting the observatory with their families. At the bottom of the stairs, they took him through an unmarked door and into a long hallway lit by a faint glow at the far end.

This is it, he thought. *This is where I get stuffed in the back of a van.*

As they passed a series of closed doors in the hallway, Cal's lassitude increased until he felt almost weightless. He was about to pass out, his shouts for help dying before they left his throat. Another closed door loomed at the end of the hallway. The stocky blond man hurried ahead to open it, revealing a blue Kia Sedona idling in the sunlight. Behind the vehicle was a small paved area and a dumpster squeezed against the side of the hill. The shouts of children drifted down from the main entrance, but no one else was in sight.

When he saw the waiting vehicle, Cal's adrenaline spiked, giving him a burst of energy for one last struggle. The man carrying him like he was a recalcitrant child held him tighter, and Cal failed to break free. The rag was still pressed against his face. The brief exertion had sapped the last of his energy. His limbs felt like water.

The blond man held the door for his partner as the side of the minivan slid open, exposing a retrofitted cage cordoning off the front of the vehicle. The shadow of someone very large was visible in the driver's seat. As Cal was carried outside, he noticed a blur of movement from behind the planetarium door as it closed. A hulking figure stepped into view, and before anyone could react, the figure stiff-armed the blond-haired man across the neck so hard his eyes rolled back before he hit the ground.

Dane's broad face was twisted with anger, his long hair framing his face like a Viking raider. Elation shot through Cal, but his heart sank when he realized the café owner had arrived barehanded.

The man holding Cal released him, and Cal fell coughing to the ground, without the strength to keep his feet. As his captor reached for a weapon, Cal heard the pump of a shotgun, and a familiar calm voice calling out from inside the van.

"That would be unwise."

The passenger window had lowered to reveal the double-barreled snout of a shotgun pointing at the remaining captor, who stood very still with his hands raised. Sefa's enormous head leaned over from the driver's seat as Dane pounced on the second assailant, knocking him out with a heavy elbow to the temple.

Dane looked shaken as he checked to make sure both men were unconscious, then dragged them toward the back of the van. The rear door lifted automatically, and Sefa hurried over to help lift the two men. Cal could see the unmoving legs of a third man, presumably the driver, already inside.

After shutting the door, Sefa hustled to the driver's seat as Dane helped Cal up. "Can you walk?"

"Not yet." Though his voice was barely a whisper, he could feel his strength returning.

"You need a doc?"

"Don't think so. Just go."

The big man stuck him in the front seat, awkwardly straddling the console between him and Sefa. Cal looked back and saw a padlock on the cage separating the rest of the van. The rear door had no handle.

A prison meant for him.

Sefa circled back to the top of the planetarium on a service drive, headed back down the hill, and parked in the public lot at the bottom, along with hundreds of other vehicles. After lifting each of their captives' wallets and taking photos of their faces, Dane and Sefa locked the Kia, threw the keys into the woods, and helped Cal limp across the parking lot to a silver Toyota Prius.

Cal managed to croak, "Whose car is this?"

"Mine," Sefa said, as the two of them helped Cal into the back seat, then lowered their heads as they scrunched into the front.

"Do you realize how ridiculous you two look in this car?"

Sefa looked wounded. "Just trying to help the planet, man."

After a moment, Cal said, "It could have been me back there. *Would* have been. I thought you'd written me off."

"I wasn't sure where I stood," Dane said. "Not sure I do now. The way they intercepted my hack at the mansion and sent it back at me so quickly . . . These people are the real fucking deal."

"How'd you know about the meeting?"

"We got your message and decided to follow you off the radar. Stay in the shadows and see what happened. But when that Kia swung around the building after you went inside, we didn't like the look of it, so we tracked it down the service drive." Dane popped an energy drink. "Thirsty?"

"Like a dog in the desert."

The big man handed him the can, popped another, and took a sip. "After the two men who grabbed you went inside, I ran the plate on the van. It belongs to a man in Topeka, Kansas."

"Who?"

"Someone named Frank Lietzer. He died two years ago."

Cal gazed out the window as they entered the frenetic, palm-lined streets of Hollywood. He had the sense they had just poked a grizzly bear in the eye in its own den.

"I don't think that van was going back into the corporate fleet," Dane continued. "I think it was going off a cliff with you in it. My advice is to back the hell off this thing."

"When you can do nothing," Sefa added, "what can you do?"

"Thanks for the Zen," Cal muttered. He lowered his window and took deep draughts of air, the caffeine and the fresh oxygen helping to rid his system of toxins. "Where'd you learn to fight?" he asked Dane.

The big man chuckled. "That was a combination of martial arts movies, Australian rules football, and me being bigger than the next guy."

Cal put a hand to his temple. "Goddammit, thanks for saving me, but these people are killers. We got extremely lucky back there, and they won't make the same mistake twice."

The two of them exchanged a glance. "Which is why we're holing up at the café from now on," Dane said.

"That's a good idea."

"And you're banned from coming in."

"I'd never put you at risk like that."

Dane turned to level his intense stare at him. "Tell me you're skipping town for a while."

Cal considered the question, realizing his throat was still very dry. "Got any more liquid poison?" After Dane tossed him another can, Cal took a long drink and said, "That's probably the best idea."

"You might need some help with that, depending on where you're going."

"I can't put you in danger."

Dane belched and crushed his can. "I researched your dad. He was fired from the airline and lost his pension, just like you said."

"I never said I lied about that. Just that he was a dick."

"I don't get it."

"That's because while you may be a tech genius, you suck at understanding people."

After a moment, Dane said, "I won't intervene again. Not in person. But I might be able to help in other ways."

"I said I don't want to—"

"I'm not doing it for you, kemosabe. I have my reasons too. You're a fool if you don't back off, but . . ." He held out a palm, not to shake hands, but as if requesting an offering. "I'll help where I can."

Cal regarded the outstretched hand. "Do you want something?"

"The USB drive."

Dane had surmised that someone had hacked Cal's email, intercepted his communications with his source, and catfished Cal into going to the observatory. On the way downtown, they stopped at a random café while Dane cleansed Cal's computer and gave him a different USB drive loaded with internet-anonymizing software, to help defend against surveillance. Dane also gave him a dark web onion address to log into in case they needed to talk. Cal planned on involving him as little as possible, but it helped to know he was out there.

Three hours after dropping Cal at a rattrap hotel near Skid Row, Dane had called to inform that the USB drive Cal had inserted into Elias Holt's computer was absolutely worthless. Cal hadn't understood all the jargon, but the gist was that Elias's desktop had extremely complicated antivirus software installed, designed to derail just such an attempt.

Cal supposed he should have expected nothing less from the CEO of an internet security company. But that was okay. As much as it hurt to lose the physical proof on that computer, Cal had seen the evidence for himself.

Evidence that could set him free.

He knew he had to go underground to fight these people—and not just online. As Dane said, it was time to leave LA.

The knowledge pained him. He didn't like being driven from his home. He also wasn't sure how he would survive. His mortgage was upside down, his emergency savings dangerously low. He might have enough on his single remaining credit card for a couple of plane tickets and a few weeks of bare-bones living, and that was about it.

For all of these reasons, his voice was grave later that night when he sat with his laptop on the frayed bedspread, logged on to Twitch, and addressed his listeners for what could be his final broadcast. He skipped the intro and went straight to his prepared speech.

"Tonight's episode will be a very short one. In fact, it isn't an episode at all. It's a warning. You may not hear from me for some time, and if things go poorly, perhaps never again." Cal paused for a sip of bad coffee as he let that sink in. "I have no doubt tonight's broadcast will be erased from the internet. Wiped from the collective digital memory. But no one, no matter how powerful, can take away what we hear and see for ourselves. They can try to subvert, and confuse, and manipulate, but they cannot erase our minds. For those of you who are listening right now, *you* will hear. *You* will be awake. I know for a fact the Leap Year Society is real and very dangerous. I don't know what it is yet, or how far it reaches. I do know Elias Holt and Aegis International are involved, and that they're trying to silence me. I suspect that if I survive long enough to find out more, one of the world's most powerful conspiracies will be exposed. A new world order that is trying to control our information networks and silence opposing voices and determine the course of history. So far, I've seen precious little. The tip of a dirt-encrusted fingernail reaching out from a grave in a forgotten cemetery, hidden from the world at large for years untold. But now I've seen the evidence with my own eyes. They exist."

As Cal paused to catch his breath and consider his final words, a moment of emotion overcame him, rage and fear and a confusing stab of melancholy for a lost innocence, a way of life that could never be recovered—both his own and society as a whole.

No, the world was not all right.

"We're lab rats, friends. Everything we eat, everything we hear in the news, everything we think we know about history and the nature of our world and the universe—everything is filtered down to us from someone, somewhere, something. We are born into ignorance, and so we remain. Enough, I say. We may never know the whole truth—I believe that as human beings we are damned to exist in a middle ground of self-aware ignorance. And I know we all have our unassailable belief systems, our political views, our religions. Our battlefields we draw from reading the same things we have always read and listening to the same voices we have always heard. It's far too easy for those in the shadows to hold us in thrall, especially those of us with warm beds and full stomachs, those who enjoy worldly success, those in the First World who cling to belief systems and societal structures that preserve the status quo. But for those of you who yearn to know as much of the truth as possible, who desire to take the red pill, who desire to wake from that long, dark sleep and drop the scales from your eyes and stare deep into the abyss of reality, then I implore you to never stop searching. Never stop believing in a better world. Stay alert, stay aware, stay focused. And never forget what I've told you tonight, for it may be the only record of an essential truth."

The chat line was exploding. Cal logged out of Twitch, shut his computer down, shoved a chair in front of the door, and closed his eyes to get some long overdue rest.

He had a feeling he would need it.

London
15

As far as Andie could tell, no one had followed the double-decker bus as it wound its way through the jam-packed streets of London. Eventually, she moved to the top and hunkered near the enormous front window, hood pulled low, catching a chill from the sweat clinging to the back of her T-shirt, her jumbled emotions reflected in the ceaseless urban tableau unfolding in Piccadilly Circus.

The river of time might flow in one direction, at least in human perception, but the current very much matters. Hunter-gatherers migrating across ancient lands to an emerald isle in the Atlantic, war, empire, colonization, art, ideology, religion, plague, industrialization, technological change: a few thousand years of history had resulted in this one neon-strobed night, trillions of neurons on a single street corner sparking hopes and fears and dreams, a cauldron of quarks and leptons bubbling away in a sea of consciousness, the very fact that any of it exists at all a wondrous and terrible and unbelievable thing.

With no idea where to go, she was content to ride on the bus as she considered her options. Thinking of Professor Rickman made her tremble with fear and rage. Was the woman she had seen leaving his apartment Zawadi, and had she known about the meeting? If so, why kill the professor and not Andie? To stop him from talking?

But if that was the case, why had the dark-haired man been so surprised to see Andie on the street? Maybe they *hadn't* known about the meeting.

Before she and Professor Rickman had parted the previous evening, he had said he was going to talk to someone about . . . what exactly?

Had that conversation gotten him killed?

She shivered, racked with guilt and uncertainty, as she considered the implications.

More in the dark than ever, all she really knew was at least three people were hunting her, and probably Zawadi as well. London had its advantages to someone on the run, but it was also teeming with people and CCTV cameras. Andie felt a desperate need to leave the city, but she didn't know where to go or who to trust.

She was committed to following the clue on the Star Phone, but how? The scroll and the string of alphanumeric digits—*stt38*—had stumped her. Her only real theory was that it was a GPS code or some other type of coordinates. It had that look about it. But no matter how she turned and twisted the cipher, trying to transform it into a location, it got her nowhere.

She had an idea for a place where she could make some inquiries in the morning. She liked the idea of consulting someone in person, to avoid leaving a digital footprint as much as possible.

First she needed to sleep.

Going back to her old hotel was out of the question. It would be easier, and safer, to stay on the bus and drift until morning. What would happen if she did?

She decided to find out.

Curling deeper into her seat, she put her backpack against the side window and leaned her head against it. The soporific drone of the engine, even the wheeze of the brakes and the creak of the doors opening and closing, lulled her quickly to sleep.

Deep into the night, a chorus of raucous shouts from the lower level of the bus awakened her, followed by the sound of someone retching. The clubs must have closed. She returned to sleep until the bus stopped moving and a well-mannered robotic voice called out over the loudspeaker.

"This bus terminates here, please take all of your belongings with you as you leave."

Andie sat up and blinked, disoriented. She peered through the window and saw a cityscape of lamplit streets and tall gray buildings with shuttered shops on the ground floor. She could be anywhere in London.

"Hey. You must get off."

The heavily accented voice, young and feminine, had come from her right. Andie turned to see a young Muslim woman standing in the aisle. The woman's beige hijab framed a pretty but tired face with no makeup, thin eyebrows, and sunken cheeks.

"Thanks," Andie said.

The woman hesitated. "You are homeless?"

"I am tonight."

"We can't stay. The driver walks through."

"Okay."

"Follow me. It will be better together."

Andie looked back and saw a handful of men in grubby clothing shuffling toward the stairs. One of them stared at Andie with a hungry look in his eyes. With a grim expression meant to ward them off, she slipped on her backpack and followed the Muslim woman onto the street, then to another bus stop three blocks away.

"This one runs for two more hours," the woman said. She was carrying a large drawstring bag full of clothes. "One more after that and the sun will rise. Do you have enough fare?"

"I do. Thank you."

"It's okay. Safety in numbers."

When the bus came, Andie paid for both of them, causing the woman to grip her hand in gratitude. They found an empty pair of seats on top and sat across from each other. They had not even exchanged names. As Andie drifted to sleep again, she felt buoyed by the silent companionship, the spark of light in the darkness.

Soon after a feeble morning sun teased Andie awake, the final bus of the night pulled into a cavernous central station. Her companion was still with her. As they exited together, Andie said, "You don't have an extra hijab, do you?"

"I have several."

"I'll pay you for one."

"You are Muslim?"

Andie shook her head. "It would be helpful," she said quietly.

The woman bit her lip as her eyes slipped downward in understanding. She dug into her bag and pulled out an olive-green scarf. "This is okay?"

"Perfect. I can't thank you enough. For this and last night."

"Do you know how to tie it?"

"No clue."

Gently, the woman wrapped the silky material around Andie's head, gathered the folds under her chin, and inserted a pin to hold it in place. Explaining as she went, she took the longer side of the hijab and wrapped it around Andie's head, pinning it again near the temple. Finally she tucked the shorter length of material under the neck, completing the process.

Andie had no idea how much a hijab cost, but she took out three twenties. The woman refused her, but Andie pressed them into her palm and closed her hand over it.

"*Allah yusallmak*," the woman whispered.

Pulling the hijab even lower on her forehead, Andie slipped on her oversize sunglasses as she walked away, feeling confident her face was hidden. London awoke around her as she got her bearings at an intersection, realizing with a start the bus had terminated at Victoria Station, a block from her old hotel. She hurried away, passing through Saint James's Park on the way to Covent Garden. The lush gardens, beautiful in the morning light, smelled of lavender and rose and made her think of Duke Gardens. Commuters on foot and bicycles hurried past in both directions.

Deciding to avoid Piccadilly, she walked a bit farther north, into the maze of streets and shops in Soho. She chose a nice-smelling bakery and sat as far from the door as she could, tucked into a drafty corner for a coffee and a pastry, perusing a daily paper as she waited for the map shop to open.

Professor Rickman had made the front page.

The death was ruled a suicide.

Andie knew she needed help of some sort, sooner rather than later, or she was going to get herself killed. Before she made any major decisions, she had decided to follow this hunch and see where it took her. London was huge, she liked her disguise, and with any luck the people chasing her would presume she had fled the city instead of returning to its beating heart.

After another cup of coffee, she walked into Covent Garden again and down a different side street radiating out from the main arcade. Squeezed into the high-end retail was a shop called Stanfords, which had stuck in her memory. It billed itself as having the world's largest collection of maps and travel books, and as far as she could tell, it was not a false boast.

Along with the eye-popping collection of maps and guidebooks, Stanfords sold globes and atlases, travel literature, travel games, compasses and other navigational aids, maritime and constellation guides, and travel accessories of all sorts. Even some of the walls and floors were giant maps. The place was catnip for anyone who had ever had an itch to put on walking shoes and explore a foreign shore.

As soon as the register was free of customers, she approached a pasty-faced clerk with a double chin and asked him if the store carried anything on GPS coordinates.

"What do you mean exactly?"

"I don't know, books, coordinates, maps?"

"Hmm . . . you might do better online."

Along with the retail selection, one of the reasons Andie had chosen to visit Stanfords was the promise of "travel specialists who aid our customers."

"Really?" she said. "You want me to shop at Amazon?"

"I just thought it might be—"

"I've tried online. That's why I came here."

"Well, can you be more specific?"

"Can you see if you have anything?"

Looking flustered, he consulted a computer, then turned it around to show her the results. There were various GPS guides for walkers, one for boaters, a coordinate map, a road atlas, and a logbook.

"Where do I find these?" she asked.

"Most are on the bottom level, along the far wall. Let me know if I can be of further assistance."

Further assistance? Maybe switching to a career in data entry would help.

Stanfords had three levels, all of them sizeable. She took the stairs to the basement and made her way to the scant section of GPS-related titles. After an hour of flipping through the books, she considered the historical tidbits she had learned.

GPS had originated in the Sputnik era, when American scientists learned they could track the Russian satellite using its radio signal. During the Cold War, the Department of Defense refined the technology for military purposes—wasn't that always the case?

The first GPS system was called Navstar, and the first official satellite launched in 1978. The modern iteration employs dozens of satellites that use trilateration to pinpoint a location anywhere on Earth within three meters. The standard positioning service is available to anyone worldwide, and found in everything from cars to mobile phones to GPS shoes.

There were limitations, such as dense forests, canyon walls, and underground spaces. But it was remarkable to think that for about fifty bucks, anyone could buy a GPS device—or simply download an app to one's phone—that accessed a space-based navigation system with a built-in atomic clock for time correction, utilizing radio waves traveling at the speed of light.

Technology was insane.

Something that had caught her interest was geocaching, a high-tech treasure hunt played all over the world. Basic geocaching seemed too trite for the Star Phone. But what if the concept—GPS and embedded QR codes and the like—had inspired the new clue in some way? This line of thinking brought to mind the Star Phone and whatever technology connected it to the bust of Democritus.

A uniformed store clerk wandered over. He was an older man with kind, crinkly eyes and a scraggly gray beard. "Can I 'elp you?"

She said, "Do you know anything about GPS positioning?"

"Quite a bit, actually. My grandson's fourteen—going on thirty, mind you—and it's our common ground. I'm a letterboxer, and he loves Pokémon Go and Ingress, but we bond over waymarking."

She had to work to understand his strong Cockney accent, and his low smoker's growl didn't help.

"I'd reckon 'im and me, we've hiked half of Britain together," he said proudly. "What's your question?"

What do I have to lose? She told him the five-digit code. He scratched his chin and asked her to repeat it.

"Hold on a bit," he said, pulling out a smartphone with a green rubber case. His gnarled fingers pecked clumsily at the touch screen. After a short search, a slow grin spread across his face. "Thought so."

Andie caught her breath. "What is it?"

"I'm curious where you got this."

"I'm on a scavenger hunt."

"Ah," he said wisely. "Okay. Take a look-see."

The image on his phone revealed a list she recognized at once as GPS coordinates. "I don't understand—are these related? How did you get them?"

"Let me back up," he said, taking the phone back. "Are you familiar with geohashing? Not *cach*ing—*hash*ing?"

She shook her head.

"I've used it now and again, but it's a lot more obscure." He showed her the phone, which displayed a satellite map and a trio of text boxes at the top labeled LONGITUDE/LATITUDE, PRECISION, and GEOHASH. "It's just a different way of getting coordinates," he said. "That's about all I know. I think it's pretty complicated. We can reverse engineer it, though."

He typed the Star Phone code "stt38" into the geohash box. Out popped a set of coordinates. The satellite map zoomed in, outlining a specific area in a transparent blue box. The location was Alexandria, Egypt, and Andie's palm pressed into her thigh when she saw the name of the building in the lower portion of the outlined area, written in both Arabic and Latin script.

BIBLIOTHECA ALEXANDRINA

She understood the import at once.

Taken together, the geohash code and the scroll on the Star Phone had to be referring to the Library of Alexandria, the legendary storehouse of ancient knowledge.

"Thank you," she murmured.

"Of course. Anything else I can help you with?"

"Not right now."

"Right then. Good luck with the scavenger hunt."

"I'll need it," she muttered as he wandered off.

After Googling "geohash," she was even more convinced she was on the right path. An obscure geocoding technique invented by Gustavo Niemeyer, the system worked by subdividing the world into a spatial data structure, assigning numeric values, and expressing the location with an alphanumeric string. Instead of pinpointing a location on a grid, as with longitude and latitude, geohashing coordinates were expressed in bounding boxes that could be narrowed or expanded by altering the number of binary digits.

In effect, a geohash reduced a geographic region to numerical data. Expressing the world as mathematics.

How very James Corwin.

If her guess was correct, his use of geohashing instead of basic GPS coordinates was another subtle clue. Although the original Library of Alexandria had been destroyed two thousand years ago, the Egyptian government had erected a modern library on the suspected site of the original building. They had even renamed it the Library of Alexandria.

If desired, Dr. Corwin could have given her exact GPS coordinates for the new building. Yet he hadn't. Instead he had given her a bounding box, a grid, which encompassed a larger portion of the city.

Why?

Her gut told her the image on the Star Phone—the ancient scroll and the geohash—referred to the original Library of Alexandria in some way. Yet how or why or what it all meant, she had absolutely no idea.

Malmö, Sweden
⎯⎯o 1933 o⎯⎯

On the journey to Malmö, a quick ferry ride across the narrow strait separating Denmark from the southern tip of Sweden, the events of the previous night seemed far away, fuzzy in Ettore's memory. The long drive into the countryside, the moonlit walk through the hedge maze, the clandestine meeting with the prince and the American diplomat: Had all of that really happened?

Sometimes, when Ettore was not working out a complex mathematical problem or dwelling on the structure of the universe, it felt as if the world was a little bit less than real. Where was the line between dream and reality, consciousness and oblivion, quantum probability and the collapse of the wave function?

And yet, as another rare bout of sunshine sparked the tips of the waves, Ettore could not deny the presence of the mahogany-brown leather attaché case sitting on his lap on the ferry bench, or the Swedish border agent making his way down the aisle as the rocky shoreline of Sweden drew nearer outside the window.

The agent was checking documents and inspecting luggage in a diligent manner. This made Ettore very nervous.

What if the agent asked him to open his briefcase and Ettore had to tell him he didn't even know the code to the lock? Would they confiscate it? Uncover the evidence of espionage it most certainly contained? Was it still too late to—

A stern voice interrupted his reverie. When Ettore failed to respond, the agent repeated the request in German. "Passport, please."

Ettore looked up, blinked, and then fumbled in the pocket of his coat. "Here," he said, handing over the passport.

"You're Italian?" the border agent asked, flipping through the stiff pages.

"I'm in Denmark on a research grant. With the Niels Bohr Institute." Ettore's voice cracked on the last word, as if he were a child on the verge of a breakdown. Disgusted with himself, he willed his fingers to stop trembling as he held up a copy of the grant papers and his identification badge with the institute.

"Your purpose in Sweden?"

"I've never been before. It's such a short trip, I thought I would spend the day in Malmö. I would like to visit the castle and Saint Peter's Church, in particular."

Why am I going on like this? Ettore wondered. *All I have to say is that I'm a tourist.* He was especially mortified that he had mentioned Saint Peter's Church—the location of his covert meeting with Stefan's contact—to the border patrol.

Could he be any more inept?

After the agent studied his documents, he gave the briefcase a long glance while Ettore quivered in his seat, sure he was about to be arrested.

"Do you always bring a briefcase on your sightseeing trips?"

Ettore chuckled, trying to play it off, cringing at the disingenuous sound of his own laughter. "Yes, it's quite tragic. I'm afraid I have some work to finish today. I'm hoping to find a nice café in town."

The agent's eyes lingered on the briefcase for another moment. After glancing at the clock on the wall, he stamped Ettore's passport and returned it. "Enjoy your visit."

As Ettore wandered through central Malmö, the sky a deep bruise streaked with haze, his thoughts turned once again to the contents of the leather attaché case.

He had no reason to doubt the veracity of anything he had heard in the hedge maze. On the contrary, the presence of such luminary figures as a prince and a United States diplomat made him trust Stefan all the more. The other two men even seemed to defer to his German friend. Did this have something to do with the hierarchy of the Leap Year Society? Did Stefan's position in the organization transcend titles and importance in the world at large?

Yet why had Stefan not let Ettore mention the Society's name? Because of some bizarre code that forbade nonmembers from speaking of it—or because it didn't exist?

Or a third option: Perhaps the Society existed but Stefan had no intention of ever including Ettore. Had he been grooming him for some ulterior purpose? Perhaps for this very trip?

It seemed a little far-fetched to go to all that trouble just to deliver a single briefcase to Malmö. And Stefan's knowledge of theoretical physics was very real. Thinking it through, Ettore truly believed the German held him in high esteem and wanted him to join their organization. Yet why the delays and the subterfuge?

On the other hand, serious events were taking place on the world stage. Events that transcended other interests. He could understand the caution. And if Ettore could play a role in slowing the rise of the fanatics in charge of Germany and his own country, the ugly nationalism threatening the fabric of democracy, he should be happy to do so. Delivering a briefcase seemed a terribly small contribution.

Buoyed by this line of reasoning, he enjoyed himself as he bundled up in his wool coat and scarf to absorb the sights of Malmö, waiting for the appointed hour. Though he knew nothing of intelligence matters—he had never even read a spy novel—he thought it sounded like a good idea to arrive early and not run straight to the contact. Besides, it was true Ettore had never been to Sweden. He might as well see a few sights.

He found Malmö to be quite different from Copenhagen, much more orderly and reserved. No one crossed the wide cobblestone streets when they were not supposed to. No children waved as they passed him on their bicycles.

Still, he enjoyed gazing upon the city's timber-framed guildhalls and its Baroque squares lined with handsome rust-colored buildings topped with the curlicue facades of the Dutch Renaissance style. There was a fine castle in the center of town and plenty of cozy cafés to enjoy warm cinnamon buns and coffee. He suspected half of his pleasure derived from the anticipatory thrill of adventure as the meeting drew near. Never in his life had he done anything remotely like this.

As the fleeting March sun began to descend, Ettore approached Saint Peter's Church, a hulking Gothic edifice right in the center of town. It was a very stern building, which aligned with his impression of the Swedes. Ettore circled the perimeter, his step slowing as he approached the intersection of Själbodgatan and Göran Olsgatan, looking over his shoulder at every turn, palms sweating inside the thick gloves he had brought to ward against the cold.

Then he saw it, just as Stefan had said it would be: a single wooden bench pressed up against the side of the cathedral, situated between two flying buttresses, barely visible through a thicket of evergreen shrubs. It was positioned just off a gravel footpath that encircled the grounds of the cathedral.

Sitting alone on the bench—again aligning with Stefan's story— was a man in a gray coat and a matching bowler hat, a blanket across his lap for extra warmth, reading a newspaper and sipping out of a disposable cup. The full cheeks and ash-blond stubble marked him as a Swedish man about Ettore's age.

The man never looked up as Ettore approached on the gravel footpath. As instructed, Ettore set the briefcase on the bench beside the man and kept walking, as if out for a stroll around the church. The man gave him a murmur of thanks, right before two gunshots exploded from very close by, causing Ettore to lurch to the side, cringing as the retort rang in his ears.

Unsure where the gunshots had originated, he spun in a circle—and saw the contact slumped on the wooden bench with a crater in the side of his head, a spray of dark blood blotting the cathedral wall behind him.

Horrified, Ettore stumbled away, his adrenaline spiking so sharply he couldn't think straight. He knew only his life was in danger and he had to get away as fast as possible. After regaining his equilibrium, he started to run when a familiar authoritative voice called out from the foliage to his right.

"Stop running. Keep walking around the church."

"Stefan!" Ettore said, as his friend stepped into view from behind a chestnut tree. "Did you see—"

"Keep walking," Stefan repeated, more firmly this time.

It was then that Ettore noticed the smell of gunpowder in the air, caught a glimpse of steel as Stefan calmly buttoned his double-breasted wool coat, and put two and two together. Ettore's words came out as a strangled whisper. "You killed him—"

Stefan gripped him by the arm and led him down the gravel path, around the corner of the cathedral. "Quickly now," he said, "before the authorities arrive."

Ettore felt as if he couldn't breathe. He was shaking all over, his heart pounding against his chest as if trying to smash through. "Are you going to kill me?"

"What? Of course not."

"Where are we going?"

"Back to the ferry. Our work is done."

"I don't understand," Ettore said as Stefan guided him off the path and toward an intersection on the far side of the church. Voices shouted from somewhere across the street, cut off from view by a dense clump of evergreen bushes. A woman screamed, and Ettore knew someone had found the body. "What about the mission? Was it all a lie?"

"That *was* the mission," Stefan said, intent on scanning the streets as they walked.

"The mission?" Ettore repeated in a daze.

After they had walked a bit farther, Stefan relaxed a fraction and said, "I apologize for the subterfuge. It had to seem real. Not just to you, but to the others with whom we met. We have a mole in our organization, Ettore, a Nazi sympathizer who would destroy everything we have worked for and place the world in grave peril. You have just helped to draw him out."

"I have?" he said, still trembling like a frightened puppy. "That . . . man you just shot?"

"He was but a foot soldier. The one we sought was a much greater threat. Now that we know for sure, our people will deal with him as soon as I send word."

Ettore thought it through. "Is it one of the men we met with?"

As Stefan gave a curt nod of acknowledgment, the ferry dock came into view, causing Ettore to press forward. He was terrified the authorities would apprehend them while still in Sweden, or that one of the slain man's associates would appear, to take revenge.

Stefan placed a hand on his elbow to slow him. The German had two tickets in hand as they approached the terminal, and looked as calm as someone taking a morning stroll in his garden.

"What was in the briefcase?" Ettore asked as they headed down the metal ramp to board the ferry.

"Newspapers."

As Ettore stopped walking, stunned, Stefan grinned and slipped an arm across his shoulders. "I would not have put you in peril. It was a test, Ettore, and you passed with ease. You're brave, loyal, and resourceful."

Am I? Ettore wondered. He just felt terrified, and sickened by the bloodshed in which he had played a role. On church grounds, no less.

A blond woman with severe lips and erect posture took their tickets, and then the two men were safely aboard the passenger ferry, on their way back to Denmark. It was a large and crowded boat, and they found seats near the middle. Ettore's adrenaline ebbed during the return journey. Stefan sat quietly beside him, reading a thin volume of philosophical essays he had produced from the pocket of his coat. When the Danish border agent walked through, he gave their passports a cursory glance and stamped them.

Outside the ferry terminal in Copenhagen, once they had separated from the crowd, Stefan faced him and said, "I know what you saw was shocking to you, but in times like these, hard choices must be made." When Ettore didn't answer, Stefan continued. "I can't disclose details, but you should know you've probably just saved an untold number of lives. A bullet from a gun kills one person at a time, Ettore, but a man in a position of power can kill thousands, tens of thousands, with the stroke of a pen."

Ettore shuffled his feet, struggling to relate to this abstract thing. Was that what it meant to be brave? The ability to feel great empathy for people he didn't even know?

Though he could not get the awful image of the corpse and the blood-spattered wall out of his head, he did feel strangely proud about his part in the mission and was happy to have pleased Stefan. "What happens now?"

"I trust you're still eager to join the Society?"

Ettore compressed his lips and considered the question. Part of him wanted to walk away and forget he had ever met this man of action, to ensure the sick thrill of danger never again ripped through his gut like a swallowed bag of razor blades.

Yet part of him had never felt so alive.

But more than any of that, Ettore's curiosity about the enigmatic Leap Year Society, his yearning for hidden knowledge, had risen to a fever pitch.

"I am," he said.

Stefan slipped on a pair of black leather gloves. "Then we are ready to receive you."

"When?"

"Two nights hence. I'll send another car."

Ettore swallowed. *That soon?* "Okay."

"Oh, and Ettore?" Stefan said as he backed away.

"Yes?"

"Your induction will not occur at a regular meeting of the Society, but during a very special one. I have an important announcement to make."

"Which is?"

A hard but knowing glint had entered Stefan's eyes. "You'll have to wait and see."

London
16

Shielded from the bright afternoon rays by her sunglasses, still wearing her hijab, Andie stood in the courtyard plaza at the entrance to the British Library, gazing at the mélange of glass, steel, and brick thrown together in a jarring mix of modernist and traditional design. The awkward angles of the multitiered edifice reminded her of a half-crushed termite mound. In the background rose the handsome red brick towers and spires of Saint Pancras station, in her mind a far superior example of architectural beauty.

Something about the library bothered her, and not just the insipid design. A vague feeling of uneasiness had lingered ever since Dean Varen had directed her to the Reading Room at Duke.

Maybe *uneasiness* was the wrong word. Andie couldn't categorize the feeling as good or bad. It was more a sensation of being watched.

She didn't think the feeling was particular to her. More that someone, or multiple people, were watching the library. As if the public institution itself, and maybe others, were pieces on some unseen board, part of a very serious game with rules all its own.

A ridiculous sentiment, she knew. The sort of reaction that belonged to paranoia and superstition. Yet she couldn't shake it.

Did she really need to go inside? At Stanfords earlier in the day, she had taken the time to peruse a couple of guidebooks on Egypt, each of which provided a cursory overview of the history of the Library of Alexandria.

Established around 300 BCE by King Ptolemy I at the suggestion of Demetrius, a disciple of Aristotle, the lofty goal of the Great Library was to possess a copy of every book in the world. Ptolemy pursued an aggressive acquisition strategy: searching every ship that came into harbor, confiscating scrolls from travelers, and sending out agents around the world—the world's first literary scouts—to search for written knowledge in everything from bazaars to royal libraries. At its height, the library was reported to hold a million titles or more.

Most of the priceless collection consisted of scrolls, chiefly papyrus or leather, kept in pigeonholes with titles inscribed on wooden tags. Contrary to popular conception, the library was not destroyed in one great conflagration, but by a series of fires and thefts during the Roman period, which gradually depleted the collection. Despite the loss, the library had established Alexandria as the intellectual capital of the ancient world, providing an example for similar institutions to follow.

All the books said the same things. So did the internet, after Andie had taken a risk and hunkered down in the café at Stanfords to conduct more research. She did find conflicting theories concerning the dates and motives behind the library's demise, and there was plenty of dispute as to the contents of the collection. But everyone agreed the Great Library had been utterly destroyed.

She wondered how much more there was, if anything, to uncover in the British Library. Oh, she was sure to find more details about the dismantling, and all sorts of scholarly speculation on the collection itself.

But would she find anything useful? Was it worth the risk of exposure? If the people pursuing her knew about the Star Phone, might they not be watching the entrance to England's largest storehouse of public information?

She believed the message on the Star Phone was clear. In some way, she was supposed to visit the Library of Alexandria. Whether that meant a physical visit to the rebuilt library, or a location within the geohash boundary box displayed on the Star Phone, or some other type of visit, she didn't know. But she felt sure the next part of the puzzle lay in Egypt and not England. Alexandria had libraries and museums too—and she was betting they held more information on the city's past.

She turned on her heel, having made her decision. It was the smarter and safer choice—*if* she could get to Egypt unseen.

And for that, she knew she needed help.

So she made another decision, one that had marinated in her mind ever since her exchange with DocWoodburn.

The British Library put out a strong Wi-Fi signal, but just to be safe, she chose a random Costa and purchased another coffee. After logging in to Twitch, she sent a message to DocWoodburn's other handle, Rhodies4ever351!.

While she awaited a response, she browsed an online travel guide to start familiarizing herself with modern Alexandria. An hour later, she received a reply.

Hi Mercuri. Sorry, I needed my beauty sleep. What time zone are u in?

Probably a very different one from you.

You don't trust me. That's smart. I don't trust you either.

Why not?

I was just tricked by Atlantis into meeting an anonymous source. It almost got me killed.

Really?

Really.

Andie took a deep breath. So it wasn't just her. Why take the chance now?

I've had a security upgrade.

Are you really a former investigative journalist?

I am.

I need to trust someone.

Me too.

How do we get there?

Good question. Any ideas?

You said it wasn't safe to talk here.

It's not.

Where is?

Still working on that.

Andie bit down on a nail. I need to leave the city I'm in.

That makes two of us.

I'm not sure how.

Maybe I can help with that.

How?

There was a long pause before his response. What about a pa**port?

Andie felt a tingle of hope, then admonished herself to be cautious. Why would you do that?

I need allies. And information.

That would be helpful.

To establish trust?

Yes but I would have to trust you in the first place.

Yeah. I suppose so. Are my good looks and charm not enough?

At least I know you're not a bot. Or are you? Atlantis seems handy with technology.

Trust me—I'm the anti-bot. I looked into the Italian physicist. Did you know him?

Andie didn't reply, though after a few moments, she realized her silence *was* a reply. She had probably made a mistake by giving out that reference. You should check out Quasar Labs too.

I'll do that. I have a feeling you're scared, Mercuri, and on the run. So am I. Maybe I can help.

Why do you want to?

When we trust each other, I'll tell you.

OK.

I do need a location for the pa**port.

Of course he does. Andie went back and forth with herself, trying to decide what to do. After another long pause, she was stunned by his next message.

My real name is Cal Miller. Look me up.

Why did you tell me that?

More trust. Atlantis already knows who I am.

In the end, she decided to tell him her location for the same reason he had given her his name: the people after her already knew where she was.

London.

Thank you. That helps. I have a contact there.

Andie took a deep breath. She wanted very much to trust someone. Especially someone who understood this madness she had entered, and could maybe even help her. But she was going to need more. Much more. I want fast answers. What was the first article you published?

As a beat reporter?

Investigative.

Corruption in Los Angeles County prisons.

His replies were coming as soon as she posed the questions. Name of your pet?

Leon. Rhodesian Ridgeback. He's as old as Moses.

She grinned at the connection to his Twitch handle. Any distinguishing marks you or the vet would know?

Leon broke his leg two years ago.

I'm sorry.

Hit by a car right in front of me. Audi convertible. Bastards took off.

She regarded his responses. They were specific, verifiable. He added more.

My favorite ice cream is Breyers with real strawberry chunks. Coffee with two creams. Pepperoni and onion pizza. Mole on my left shoulder blade.

That's pretty personal.

Condensed story: Atlantis got me fired and ruined my reputation.

I want my life back. They want the opposite.

So you trust me already?

I think we're both desperate. I've given you nothing besides info you can verify. Once you trust me, and if I'm convinced you're legit, then maybe we can help each other.

I know I'm legit. Not sure I can give you more.

One step at a time. Check out my info while I work on the document. Stay tuned.

How long?

Very soon. Today I hope.

OK.

Verifying Cal's answers to her questions would go a long way toward establishing trust. But she would have to make phone calls, enter personal information into databases, and who knew what else. It would expose her too much.

While stopping for a green curry at a hole-in-the-wall Laotian restaurant in Soho, scrunched into a red booth with sticky seats, she thought of a potential middle ground. After Googling nearby private investigators, she finished eating and walked to the office of the first investigator who had time for her that day. City Investigators, on Southampton Row.

In a cramped office full of metal shelving jammed with file folders, Andie hired Adelaide Warfield, registered member of the Association of British Investigators, to conduct research on Cal Miller.

A muscular auburn-haired woman with a brusque manner, Adelaide claimed she had just finished a big case and was having a light week. She brushed off the request as an easy one. Andie paid for three hours of work up front, gave away nothing of herself, and said she would call back at the end of the day. Adelaide took the money, unperturbed by the clandestine nature of the request.

After leaving the PI's office, as shadows from the declining sun crept down the buildings of Central London, Andie checked the time and thought about where to sleep. She saw little choice but to stay in London for another night. That made her nervous, as did walking around in the open. No doubt the dark-haired man and Zawadi were scouring the city for her.

With no decision on where to board for the night, she fingered the business card the girl at the occult fair had given her, and couldn't help herself from taking a short walk to visit the expert on mysticism. She found the bookstore just off busy Leicester Square, on a narrow lane lined with Victorian townhomes.

Evocative of a London from another era, the pedestrian-only byway was made of worn paving stones, and a row of wrought-iron lampposts in the center of the street had just begun to glow in the mauve twilight. The gently lit interiors of the shops on the ground floor, nestled behind glass windows outlined in handsome green trim, added to the ambience.

She caught the store just before closing time. To her surprise, there were no displays of healing crystals or incense candles in the windows, no exotic herbs or animal skulls or tarot cards. Just a discreet sign jutting over the street that read FRANKLIN'S BOOKS, and a bronze placard declaring it THE OLDEST OCCULT BOOKSHOP IN THE WORLD. Situated between an art gallery and a print shop, and across the street from a pair of high-end antique stores, the very location lent credibility in Andie's eyes.

A bell tinkled as she entered. The crowded bookshelves, dour carpeting, and dusty hardbacks with gilt lettering resembled a typical antiquarian bookstore. Behind the counter was a sinewy older man, perhaps sixty-five, with a hawkish nose and a crown of white hair clinging on for dear life. The sleeves of his dress shirt were rolled to the elbows. Faint ink stains on the pockets.

As he reached for a sport coat hanging behind him, Andie set the business card on the counter. He peered down at it.

"I know you're closing," she said, "but I'm trying to reach the owner. Is he still in?"

"He is."

"Could I speak to him?"

He leveled a kind but piercing gaze at her. "You already are. I'm Harold Franklin."

"I . . . was wondering if you could take a look at something for me."

"What sort of something might that be?"

"A drawing of a place I'm trying to identify. It should just take a moment."

"Do you have it with you?"

She set down her backpack, took out the collection of ink drawings, and spread them on the counter. He shrugged on his jacket, picked up one of the drawings, and examined it with his full attention.

When he at last looked up, he said, "Do you mind if I lock up first?"

Her hands clenched at her sides. "You recognize it?"

"I'd like to show you a few things."

She hesitated, her eyes flicking out the window and then back at the proprietor. "Sure."

He gave a quick nod, walked over to set the dead bolt on the front door, and switched the sign to CLOSED.

"I've never seen an occult bookstore like this," she said.

"You've been to many?"

"I have, actually."

"Why?"

He posed it not in a challenging manner, but as a genuine question.

"For a long time, I was searching for something. I suppose I still am. I just grew disenchanted with the process."

He held up one of the ink drawings. "Searching for this?"

She pursed her lips and nodded.

"Give me a minute." He set the drawing down and headed into the stacks. "'Occult' has come to signify many things," he called out, as she followed behind. "For the vast majority of people, the term brings to mind magic, the supernatural, Aleister Crowley and his ilk. I prefer the original meaning: 'That which is mysterious, beyond the range of ordinary knowledge or understanding. Something hidden to the outside world.'"

"I prefer that definition too."

"What's your profession?"

"I'm an astrophysicist."

"Then you understand me."

She gave a small smile. "Yes."

After pulling out a thin volume with a frayed green spine, he moved two rows over to pluck a larger book from the top shelf with the aid of a stepping stool. He rummaged around in a locked drawer for a leather-bound notebook that fit in the palm of his hand, so old the title had faded away, then returned to the front and set the manuscripts on the counter.

Harold opened the larger tome, a collection of translated verse from a twelfth-century Sufi mystic. He took some time to find the right page, then read a passage that so closely mirrored the experience of Andie's visions that she gripped the edge of the wooden counter in disbelief. It was all there—the feeling of falling into a waking dream, drifting through an endless void that reflected reality through a distorted lens, the uneasy sensation of being watched, the bout of dizziness and nausea that followed.

"I've never heard of this book," she said. "What was the—"

A raised finger from the bookseller cut her off. He turned to the leather-bound notebook, took a second to find the right page, and read a shorter passage in a far more prosaic style. Nevertheless, the description bore an unmistakable correlation to the first passage, and to Andie's visions.

She was white-faced by the time he finished. "Who wrote that?"

"The notebook was compiled by a fourteenth-century Venetian nobleman, a contemporary of Marco Polo whose interests were more anthropological than commercial. That particular passage sets forth the nobleman's description of his dreamwalking session with a

Mongol shaman in central Asia. The shaman was Tungusic, I believe."

"A dreamwalking session . . ."

"There are more. A passage in an obscure Ovid text describing a visit to Pythia, the Delphic oracle. A Gnostic gospel that never gained credibility. The Yamabushi of Japan. This place, or one very much like it, has been described by a wide array of mystics, visionaries, and seers. They all specifically speak of a 'shadowy realm' that is 'like our world but isn't.'"

Andie took a deep breath, trying to process what she was hearing. "If it's so widespread, why isn't it more well-known?"

He wagged a finger, thoughtful. "Yes, you're right. 'Wide array' is the wrong terminology. In fact, it's exceedingly rare. A multitude of sources were consulted over many years to collect these references. Perhaps a better word is 'pancultural.' A very rare thing in the occult world—and one which, quite frankly, gives the accounts the ring of truth."

"What is your . . . What do you think of it?"

"Another peculiarity to these accounts is that they seem to bear no relation to popularized descriptions of other such places: limbo, purgatory, dream worlds, after-death experiences, and the like. My opinion? Though I have no idea how or why, I believe the world has produced a handful of truly gifted seers, throughout history and across all cultures, and that the best way to find them is by matching the contents of their visions. Why bother with a mystic who cannot seem to escape the clichés of his own milieu? Think about it—would true scrying into a realm beyond our own not uncover a universal truth? A place described in similar fashion by seers from vastly different eras and geographies? A place like"—he looked down at the ink drawing—"this place?"

Working hard not to appear overly excited, she said, "But how do you know of it? Why search for it in the first place? What else do you know?"

He set his palms on the counter. "Those are the right questions. As for the last, I'm afraid my answer will disappoint you. I've no idea what this place is, what it signifies, or whether it even exists outside of the dream state and mental visions described in the literature. Perhaps it's a mental glitch. The interior psychology of the true seer. A realm we don't yet understand. As to how I came across it . . . I once knew a chap named, well, we'll call him Jack. He was a regular customer of mine, and a very clever scientist. A physicist, like you."

Andie swallowed.

"We lost touch for a few years, but about a decade back I ran into him again, in a pub in Charing Cross. He didn't look too well. Unbalanced, slightly deranged. We caught up for a bit, and after one too many pints, or maybe five too many, he confided he was searching for a group of people he believed were in possession of secret knowledge."

Her voice barely rose above a whisper. "What do you mean?"

"I don't really know, except he described a place exactly like the one in your drawings."

Andie rocked back on her heels, overcome by a wave of emotions.

I'm not insane. This place is real, and it exists. But what is it? Or maybe this Jack person, all these other people throughout history, maybe we're all losing our minds. Maybe the shadow realm is the face of insanity.

"These people . . . did he find them?"

"I don't know. But it was Jack who led me to the passages I showed you. He compiled them some years ago." The proprietor tapped the counter. "I found these three after a long search. I gave it up after a while."

"How could you give it up?"

He gave her a thin smile. "Do you think your ink drawings are the only inexplicable mystery I've uncovered in my work?"

Her eyes lowered, lost in the murky hues and spectral imagery of the drawings spread out on the counter. "What did your friend think? Did he have any theories?"

"Jack thought the shadow place was some kind of higher plane, or a different reality. He wouldn't tell me anything about the people he was searching for, or even how he heard about them. To be honest, I assumed that part of the story was a flight of fancy." He looked down at the drawings. "How did *you* come across them?"

"I found them in an estate sale. I was just curious." Andie gathered the drawings and returned them to the backpack, trying to disguise how much the next question meant to her. "You don't have any idea where Jack is now, do you? Is there a way I can contact him?"

"I'm afraid that after that night, I never saw him again."

After leaving the bookstore, disturbed by what she had learned, Andie ducked into a café and logged in to Twitch. A message from Cal was waiting.

Beauty salon across from Sainsbury's in Kingsland Shopping Centre. Go in the morning or before 10 tonight. Paid in full.

It was nine o'clock. A quick search on Google told her she could just make it to Sainsbury's by ten on public transport. Slower by car.

Andie put a hand to her temple. She could be walking right into the lion's den.

Conflicted, yet not wanting to wait until the morning, she tried the number for the private eye as she walked toward the underground. It surprised her when Adelaide answered.

"Glad you called. I finished a while ago."

"You're working late," Andie said.

"I'm a PI, not a banker. I'm tailing a cheating husband around the West End tonight."

"Did you find anything on Cal Miller?"

"I did. And I wouldn't trust the wanker."

Andie stopped walking, her stomach sinking. "Why not?"

"Yeah, his story checked out. Former reporter with the *LA Times*, the piece on prison reform, his dog's name, the broken leg: it's all kosher. I even found a credit card receipt with Breyers strawberry, a stack of DiGiornos, and Folgers coffee."

"Then what's the problem?"

"The guy's broke as hell. His credit cards are almost maxed, and

I can promise you he won't get another anytime soon, because he keeps missing payments. It's not just his cards either. Delinquent student loans, cable, phone bill. Did he tell you he was fired from the *Times* for falsifying a source? It was a big scandal. The guy hasn't had a steady job in two years. I assume you've been together a little while, something smells fishy, and you're trying to get a read on him?"

"Something like that."

"Let me guess: he told you about the house in Hollywood, promised to move you in, described a future with rainbows and unicorns and dollar bills falling out of his arse. That about the size of it? He probably told you he's still a full-time reporter, didn't he?"

A grim smile crept to Andie's lips. "I guess he's a deadbeat after all," she said. *A deadbeat whose life was ruined by the Leap Year Society.* "That's too bad. He's a rock star in bed."

"Huh. Aren't they all?"

After taking the Piccadilly line to Green Park, Andie changed to the Victoria line, rode five stops to Highbury & Islington, then switched to the London Overground. It was a relief to leave the claustrophobic subway for a cleaner, less crowded train. Two stops to the east, after passing a sea of bleak council housing punctuated by the odd granite steeple, she exited at Dalston Kingsland.

The city felt different here. Working-class and incredibly diverse. It was edgier than Central London, more alive with energy after dark. Bags of trash were piled on the curb for pickup. There were no tourist shops or world-class monuments in sight. Hip restaurants and cafés swarmed the streets around the station, but as she walked east on Ridley Road, the smell of shish kebabs and frying grease wrinkling her nose, she saw a good number of secondhand shops, sandwich wrappers and fruit rinds on the sidewalks, imitation goods piled on blankets, music from a dozen cultures blaring from the shops.

Soon she cut right, into an indoor shopping center. All the shops had closed except for the Sainsbury's grocery at the far end. Just across the hall, she spied a shuttered hair-and-nail salon. One of the cashiers at Sainsbury's seemed to have an eye on her, but no one else was around. With a shrug, Andie pressed the buzzer beside the door.

Long seconds passed. She buzzed again. Finally a tall, athletic, and very attractive black man walked through the darkened salon to let her in. He was wearing white designer jeans, leather sandals, and a Tottenham Hotspur track jacket with no shirt underneath. The top of the jacket was unzipped, exposing a slender silver chain resting atop a muscular torso.

"Yeah?" he said.

"I was told to come here."

"By who?"

"Cal Miller."

"What's your name, dove?"

She hesitated. "Mercury."

A broad smile revealed a set of perfect white teeth that gleamed in the darkness. "Yeah, you are. I'm Puck. Let's go to the back."

He locked up behind her, then led her through a door in the rear of the salon. Inside was a drab office that reeked of marijuana, with smocks and razors hanging on the wall, an aging computer atop a desk, brooms in a corner, and a pair of beige filing cabinets.

When they entered, a blond woman with a wide-boned Slavic face was buttoning her jeans. She had a flushed look, her lipstick was smeared, and a lacy bra exposed the nipples of her flat chest. A matrix of faint scars covered her forearms.

Puck grabbed a shirt off the desk and threw it at the woman. "Hurry up," he said. The woman caught the shirt and scurried into the corner. Puck leaned against the desk, crossed his ankles, and smirked at Andie. "Came for a trip bip, huh?"

Andie was stunned, and seething, at his treatment of the woman. "What?"

"A passport."

"Oh. Yeah."

"Where you going?"

"That's my business."

He spread his hands and gave the hijab a long look. "If you're running from something, why not stay with me awhile? I can protect you. Put you to work."

"I'll have to decline that gracious offer."

"I treat my girls well."

"I can tell."

He tapped a hand against the top of his chest, his smirk widening. "Bang-up benefits, yeah?"

She grimaced. "The passport?"

With a chuckle, Puck opened a drawer and took out a camera. "Let's see those pearly whites. And the scarf has to go." Andie removed the hijab and faced the camera. After taking a few photos, he asked, "Are you a Lucy or a Sloane?"

"I'm not a Lucy."

"I figured," he said, then told her to wait and disappeared through a different door.

As she waited, Andie replaced the hijab, set her backpack on the floor, and crossed her arms against her chest. The woman in the corner had sunk to a squat, hands crossed over her knees.

The pungent smell and the stress of the situation made Andie feel a little nauseated, and her head began to spin. She closed her eyes, trying to regain her equilibrium, but when she opened them again she was inside the shadow world of her visions. The dark and spectral gloaming of her new environment throbbed with silence, oppression, and the familiar sense of drifting in a void, of being watched by unseen eyes.

Only this time it was different. Instead of disappearing in a flash, the vision remained in place, and Andie found herself able to move. Stunned, she took a tentative step forward, though the sensation felt more like drifting through low gravity than walking. The outline of her clothes was barely distinguishable from the penumbra of her shadow limbs, as if her jeans and jacket had merged with her corporeal form. When she put her hand to her face, it passed slowly into her head, which horrified her and made her feel like some sort of apparition. She looked around and, with a start, realized that someone else was inside the vision with her.

In the very same room.

After a moment of terror swept through her, she recognized the blond woman huddled in the corner. Or at least she thought it was her. It was hard to see clearly in the gloom, but the figure had the same build as the woman and was squatting in the same position.

This had never happened before. No one from the real world had ever appeared in a vision. Drawing a sharp breath, forcing her terror aside and wondering how long it would last—what if she was stuck in here forever?—Andie walked toward the woman and tried to speak. She opened her mouth, but no one words came out, at least not that she could hear. When Andie reached out with a hand, the woman finally looked up, exposing two flat silver-gray disks instead of eyes, floating in the opaque darkness of her face. As Andie stared in horror, the blackness began to twist and writhe where the woman's mouth should be, as if something inside were trying to break free. A silvery mouth formed and opened, releasing a scream that pulsated like an echolocation, reverberating inside Andie's head, stabbing into her temples, driving her downward—

And then it all disappeared and she was back in the real world, slumped in Puck's strong arms, inhaling his musky but not unpleasant odor. Andie took a long shuddering breath, feeling even more nauseated than before, disoriented by the scream still fading inside her head. She jerked her head toward the corner. The blond woman was leaning against the wall with a disinterested expression, as if nothing had happened.

Puck set Andie on her feet and held her by the arms, far too comfortably for her liking. "You okay, dove?"

As the urge to vomit passed, Andie's right leg tensed, readying for a snap kick to the groin. She wanted very much to give Puck a lesson on how to treat women, and to get as far away from him as possible.

Instead she pulled away, swallowing to control her nausea. "Just a dizzy spell."

Puck regarded her in silence, then handed her a crisp new United States passport. She inspected it, though she had no way of knowing how authentic it was. It looked as good as any. Beneath the photo of Andie was the name Sloane Beatrice Reynolds, and a birthdate within two years of her own.

"You're all good," he said.

"How much did Cal pay you?" she asked. "I'd like to pay him back."

"Not a pound. I owed him."

"For what?"

Puck looked taken aback by the question, shrugged, and said, "My sister lives in LA and got into a bit of a jam. Cal and I, we did business once. Information. He knew a copper who went easy on her."

Still unsteady from her vision, reeling from the questions it raised, Andie pocketed the passport and retrieved her backpack.

Puck spread his hands. "Anything else you need? Endo? Bills? A shoota? Puck's got you covered."

As eager as she was to get out of there, Andie realized she would need far more cash than she had to buy a ticket to Egypt, unless she wanted to use a credit card. And that seemed like a really bad idea.

"I could use some cash. But I don't have anything to sell."

His wide smile flashed again. "You sure about that?"

"Don't even think about it."

"You bring your old passport?"

The thought of selling her identity, especially to Puck, revolted her. Still, he was right. At the moment, she didn't need it, and staying alive had to take precedence. "How much?"

"Valid US?"

"That's right."

"Three grand."

That sounded low to Andie. "Make it five."

"Four and—"

"Five."

"Okay, dove, okay. You're the boss."

She hesitated. "Can I pawn it to you? Give me a month to return for it?"

He mulled over the question. "For Cal, I'll make it happen. One month, and a grand for my trouble either way."

"Fair enough."

After he took her old passport and disappeared again, Andie tried to engage the woman by asking her if she knew anything about the vision, or had experienced it herself. The only reply she got was an annoyed, disbelieving stare. When Andie asked if she needed help in any way, the woman glared at her and said nothing.

When Puck returned, Andie abandoned her attempts to talk to the woman. She was unable to believe someone could have a similar experience and remain so disaffected.

But why had the woman been in the vision? Why had it lasted longer than the others? Why had Andie been able to move and hear the scream? Was her condition getting worse?

Despite what she had learned at the bookstore, as always, the fear remained that it was all a projection of Andie's broken mind. Had her spirit rebelled at seeing this poor woman living in such wretched conditions? Had Andie internalized that pain in her vision?

With a snarl of frustration, she stuck the bag of cash in her backpack and walked out, relieved to be out of sight of that vile man, more determined than ever to find out what the hell was wrong with her.

The area around Dalston Kingsland station came alive at night, filled with a startling array of languages and skin tones and fashion styles, everyone dressed to the nines as they mingled on the street or headed toward the bars, clubs, and late-night restaurants. As she debated her next move, Andie holed up in a shisha bar with beaded curtains, rife with apple-spiced incense. She ordered a coffee and a hummus plate and then searched for flights to Egypt.

To her surprise, she found an affordable flight that left the next morning from London City Airport. A quick search told her the airport was in East London, not far from where she was, a quick trip on the Overground. She might have to pay double by not buying the ticket online, but if she wanted to avoid using a credit card, there was no alternative.

After hurrying through her meal, she took the Overground to the airport and bought a jacked-up ticket with three layovers just before the counter closed. She was relieved beyond measure when her new passport went through without a hitch.

Score one for trusting strange people on the internet.

She took her boarding passes and found a secluded corner of the airport, away from any cameras, to stretch out. She had slept in worse places. If the current trend continued, London City Airport might be a palace compared to her next destination.

Lying on her back on the cold floor, surrounded by fluorescent lighting and the hum of a generator, Andie felt an aching need for a human connection. Running on her own was taking its toll. Yet even if she could take the risk to contact a friend, what would she say? *How's it going? Oh, me? I'm running for my life and sleeping on an airport floor. It's cool, though. How's the weather?*

The only person who might commiserate—who might be in the same insane predicament as she—was Cal Miller. He was quickly earning her trust, and she wanted to contact him again. She started to reach for her burner phone, which she planned to ditch before the flight—then decided against it.

Not yet.

No one knew where she was headed, and she was going to keep it that way. If she reached Egypt unharmed—if the false passport held up—then maybe she would reach out to him again.

With a sigh, using her backpack as a pillow, she closed her eyes and did her best to get some rest. Some time later, a beeping noise woke her, akin to the chirp a fire alarm makes when the battery is dying. She realized it was coming from her pocket.

Thinking it was the burner phone, she was surprised to find the sound emanating from the Star Phone. It had never made a noise before. She was even more stunned when she took it out of her pocket and found the image of the scroll and the cipher had disappeared, replaced by a message slowly typing itself across the face of the device.

HELP. THIS IS JGC. THEY HAVE ME IN A

All of a sudden, the beeping stopped and the Star Phone flashed and went blank. Before she could react, the image of the scroll and the geohash code reappeared, as if nothing had ever happened. Stunned, Andie sat upright and tried to send a return message. As always, whenever she reached the end of the nine cursor spaces, the message would disappear and the cursor spaces would go blank.

Nothing else she attempted had any impact on the device. Whatever anomaly had occurred was finished.

Andie felt blood rushing to her head. *Ohmygod.* JGC—James Gerald Corwin—Dr. Corwin's full name—was it possible?

Had her mentor just tried to contact her through the Star Phone from some remote location? If so, how? Far more important: *Was he still alive?*

Of course, she had no way of knowing who was on the other end of that message. But why would someone impersonate Dr. Corwin in such a bizarre manner? If entrapment was the purpose, why not say more? Try to draw her out somehow?

She was more confused than ever, unsure whether to grieve or hope. Dwelling on why the message on the Star Phone had cut off so abruptly felt like trying to breathe through a wet cloth. If Dr. Corwin had sent that message—and she felt in her gut that he had—then what sort of terrible danger was he in? Who had cut him off? Were they torturing him right that very second?

Shaking with adrenaline, the prospect of sleep as remote as another galaxy, Andie spent one of the longest nights in her life in

London City Airport, pacing and thinking and agonizing, checking the digital clock on the flight board every five minutes, willing the sun to breach the horizon.

# PART THREE

London
17

As a drizzle of rain moistened the brick walkway at his feet, Omer worked hard to keep his emotions in check. He was standing outside the entrance to the safe house, trying for the third time to fit his key into the dead-bolt lock of the outer door. Was he that distracted by the escape of the target? Had he used the wrong key or failed to fully insert it?

His heart knew the truth. He was preoccupied, yes.

But Omer did not make mistakes with simple locks, no matter how distracted. In a profession such as his, where the tiniest of details could be a matter of life and death, there was no room for error.

Just in case, he tried once again.

Same result. The key didn't fit.

Earlier, he had walked to a pub for an English breakfast, and, in less than an hour, someone had changed the locks. He knew that even if he cut through the dead bolt, the biometrics and the code to the steel door would be altered as well.

Two doors down, a white-haired man in a suit approached a neighboring townhome, casting a sidelong glance at Omer, no doubt wondering why he was fiddling with a lock in such a posh neighborhood.

A chill worked its way down Omer's spine, all the way to the tips of his toes and fingers, followed by a flash of rage.

All these years of loyal service . . . of doing whatever it takes for the cause . . . They can't just cut me off! I've given them everything!

Yet he knew the penalty for failure. The target was not even a high-level operative or a clever scientist from the Society, someone who might know to take evasive measures.

She was a novice. A nobody.

The first time, though he still blamed himself, could have happened to anyone. No one would have expected a graduate student to run for miles at a high pace through the woods, navigating a maze of trails in the dark of night.

And the second time—it was a complete surprise to find her on the street walking right toward him, long before she was expected. Someone had fed him false information. And the target had proved her resourcefulness once again by escaping through the streets of London with very little head start. Yes, his hands were tied by the protocol—he could easily have killed her—and luck favored the bold, and his associates had been a step too slow, and she had disappeared like a ghost that night, and she was Dr. Corwin's protégé, and Omer suspected she was getting help from the Society.

But all of those things were excuses—none of which mattered to those above him.

Elotisum. The Archon had issued an edict, and Omer had failed to carry it out. It was as simple as that.

And they had banished him for it.

He would never receive another edict, never meet with another disciple, never attend another veiled meeting in a sanctum sanctorum.

A sentence of execution was reserved for traitors. Omer did not fear for his life, yet he knew that among many cultures, banishment was considered a fate worse than death. Until this moment, this was something he had never understood. Could one not simply start a new life elsewhere, even if on a different continent? Find a new family, learn a new trade, join a new cause?

Yet in a flash, in the simple failure of a piece of cut metal to engage the cylinder of a lock, an act that had destroyed his life's ambition, he understood the sheer horror of exile.

He had given up his career, his family, his entire old life in his quest to join the Ascendants. *The knowledge, the secrets, the power . . .* With a snarl, Omer jerked on the doorknob and then walked away in a daze, shuffling down the sidewalk of the quiet street, his rage persisting but subsumed by a disappointment so visceral it felt as if an actual weight pressed down on his back, shoving him toward the ground to crawl like a worm, whispering to him to put his gun in his mouth and pull the trigger so the feeling would go away.

Once, as a teenager, Omer's heart had been broken by a beautiful Swiss girl with eyes of sapphire and hair like spun gold. Her rejection was the closest thing to what he now felt. Except even as a young man, he had known that once the pain subsided, plenty of women existed for him to desire. That even love, while a powerful thing, was not unique to one person.

The Ascendants were different. There was no group on Earth like them. A steel curtain would stand between him and reality, and he would know that everything he could discover on his own was a lie at worst, and at best a shot of whiskey diluted with a bucket of ice water.

He clenched his fists as he hurried down the street. Omer was not a person who let things happen to him in life. He was a lion, not a gazelle. Yet forcing his way into the Ascendants was not an option. This they would never allow.

Even so, as long as he could draw a breath, he could still prove his worth. He could still make them see.

They would send someone else to find her, a team this time. Yet if Omer could reach her before they did . . .

Yes, he decided. He would find the girl first, take out anyone who stood in his way, and drag her by the hair to his own safe house. Then he would cut a deal and demand he be reinstated before turning over the target to the Archon. He knew enough about them to know they would understand the motive behind his actions. Not just understand: they would *approve.*

By whatever means necessary, Omer would claw his way back inside.

The first call he made was to Juma. A Saudi national, she was a former intelligence operative like himself, also recruited away. Sworn enemies in their past lives, they shared a common goal of joining the Ascendants, and had become lovers. They even had burner phones to be used only for each other, in case they wanted to rendezvous without anyone knowing.

Juma answered on the first ring. He heard the tension in her voice at once, glad she had not tried to hide it. "Omer. Where are you?"

"I'd rather not say."

"I'm so very sorry," she said quietly.

"So you've heard."

"Your name is already in circulation as a cautionary tale."

Bitterness flooded his voice. "Is that so?"

"I've been told not to consort with you."

"And will you heed that order?"

When she responded, her voice was almost a whisper. "Wouldn't you?"

He hesitated. "I suppose so."

"I will miss you. I want you to know that."

"Do you know who replaced me?"

"I don't."

"It isn't you?"

"No," she said without pause. Her relief was evident, and he believed her.

Though he also knew Juma was an expert liar.

He said, "Have they found her yet?"

"Would you really ask that of me?"

"It's all I need to know. A simple yes or no."

A touch of cold crept into her voice. "No."

"Thank you."

"Goodbye, Omer. I wish you well. I'm sorry that . . . things cannot be otherwise."

"Don't be so sure," he said softly, right before he hung up.

He wasn't sure how far to trust her—as she implied, had the roles been reversed, he would not have helped her either. But he had gotten what he wanted. Why lie if the target had already been found? It suited no purpose he could envision.

After a deep breath that helped expunge his lingering desire for Juma, as well as ignite the flames of his new mission, he pondered the situation. The girl had arrived in London on her own passport, making it easy for them to track her. He did not think she would do so again. Not after finding Professor Rickman murdered in his flat, and being chased through the city.

He wondered for the thousandth time how much she knew. What was the connection between her and Dr. Corwin? It had to be more than a simple professor-and-student relationship, no matter how bright she was. There was too much at stake. Was she a lover, despite the age difference? Or already an initiate?

He would have guessed the latter, except why remain in the open? Why take the risks she was taking? None of it made sense, unless she was operating on her own.

Which meant she was vulnerable, and he had a very small window before whoever had replaced him tracked her down.

Where would she go? Would she run or hide? Leave the country, return to the United States, go farther abroad?

Using a low-dosage amphetamine, Omer stayed awake the rest of the night and all through the next day attempting to answer those questions. He would no longer receive the benefit of the organization's network of information technology and human intelligence. He would not have access to CCTV networks and high-ranking public officials.

That was fine. He had his own network and methods, cultivated over a lifetime of clandestine work.

Most amateurs in similar situations would try to get as far away from danger as they could, as fast as possible. Most—if they had the means—would obtain a false passport and go to a different country.

Add to that the nature of his quarry. Along with visiting the museum, Andie had made contact with Professor Rickman. Was she trying to offload the device? Seek his counsel? Or was something else going on, to which Omer was not privy? He sensed a greater game being played.

All of these factors pointed to a high probability that London was a stopover. He had to act fast, and decided to hang his hat on her seeking a false passport. If that didn't pan out, he could reconfigure.

Due to the influx of migrants, the number of false passports had risen steeply in western Europe in recent years. Hundreds of illegal-passport vendors existed in London alone. Even with help, it could take him weeks to interrogate them all.

Yet Omer saw one great advantage to the situation. He did not have to concern himself with the forgeries and "look-alike" stolen passports that served the migrant population and the criminal underworld. How many false credentials were procured by a single white woman on a weekly basis in the city? Not counting sex-trafficking documents, which would of course still be requested by men?

His guess was not very many at all.

Most weeks, he might even say only one.

Using his network of underground resources, each in turn with their connections, a pyramid of black-market information that stretched to the gutters of the city, Omer spent the night compiling a list of known passport forgers. Once he had the names of the major players, he made phone calls and in-person visits, asking on the sly about a young American woman seeking to leave the country.

Forty-eight hours since he had lost her. After interviewing a dozen vendors in Central London, he moved to the East End and the boroughs of Hackney, Tower Hamlets, and Newham. While gentrification had given rise to boutique markets and hip cafés, it had also provided a bounty of easy marks, and the local criminals were still entrenched.

Omer dressed down for the hunt: ripped jeans and a black hoodie, a wool cap pulled low. His next destination was a small-time gangster who ran his operation out of a hair-and-nail salon in a pedestrian shopping mall. Puck, the transplant from Brixton who owned the place, specialized in pimping and human trafficking, of which passports were a natural accessory.

After exiting Dalston Kingsland station with a swarm of people, Omer made his way quickly to the mall. Though all the shops were shuttered, the street-side entrance was still open, and he walked through the empty shopping center until he reached the salon. No one else was in sight. It took a prolonged bout of buzzer pressing before a very large man covered in jewelry and tattoos opened and closed a door in the rear of the salon, walked through the darkened interior, looked Omer up and down, and cracked the glass door.

"You got a death wish, ace?"

"Is Puck inside?" Omer asked.

"Who wants to know?"

"I have a business proposition."

"Come by tomorrow. Salon's closed."

"Not that kind of business."

"You got stuffin' in your ears? I said *tomorrow*."

As the man moved to close the door, Omer stepped forward and, quick as a heron's strike, jabbed the stiffened fingers of his right hand into the hollow space below the man's Adam's apple. The man gagged and clutched his throat. Omer kicked the door open and whipped the man's right arm around his back, shoving it up until he was standing on his toes in pain. Omer jerked a pistol out of the man's pants, set it on a table, and pushed him forward while maintaining the shoulder lock. Unable to talk through his damaged throat or think through the pain in his arm, the man could only serve as a human shield as Omer walked into the back room and surveyed the situation, his free hand on the gun tucked into his jeans.

A man who fit the description of Puck was snorting a line of coke off the desk to Omer's left. A topless blond woman was curled in his lap. Puck jerked to his feet, dumping the undernourished woman to the floor. "What the fook!"

As Puck reached for a desk drawer, Omer struck his captive on the temple with the butt of his gun, letting him slump unconscious to the floor.

Omer pointed the gun at the salon owner.

"Okay, man, okay," Puck said, slowly raising his arms. "I don't keep cash on-site." He looked down at the coke. "Take a bump and go, and I'll forget this ever happened. You know who I am?"

The blond woman had scuttled to the corner and stayed there, shivering in her panties and pink socks. A sad sight but not a safety concern.

"Puck?" Omer asked.

The salon owner forced a broad, confident smile as he adjusted a gold watch poking out from the sleeve of his tracksuit. "The one and only."

"Come over here."

"Let's talk this—"

Omer leveled the gun at his head. "Now."

After sniffing and wiping his nose, Puck eased out from behind the desk. "What's your angle, cuz? The Lightey boys send you?"

"I need a simple piece of information. Have you processed a passport in the last two days for a young American woman?"

"Passport? I dunno what you're talking about."

With his free hand, Omer extracted a ballpoint pen from his pocket. He pressed the top, releasing a tiny blade as sharp as an X-Acto knife. "Tell me what I need, and this goes better for you. Do you understand?"

Palms out, Puck started walking slowly toward him. "Yo, man, we don't need to go there. Just relax."

Omer cocked the pistol. *Do you understand?*

"Sure, I understand," Puck said meekly, lowering his head in submission just before a four-inch fixed blade slipped out of his sleeve and sprang into his hand. He ducked his head and made a diagonal lunge, off-line from the gun, forward and to the right, trying to slip his blade into Omer's side before he could react.

Puck moved as fast as a professional athlete, strong and sure with the blade, but Omer read his intentions as clearly as if he had announced them from a podium. As Puck lunged, Omer calmly stepped to the side and sliced the underside of the wrist holding the knife, causing Puck to drop the blade as blood spewed from the vein.

Without pause, Omer pivoted, raised his leg, and kicked out the back of Puck's legs, dropping him on his back on the linoleum floor. Omer leaned down to place a knee on the other man's chest, pinning him down as he placed the tip of the penknife on the underside of Puck's chin.

Omer turned to the young woman in the corner. "You should leave now." When she failed to move, her lowered eyes glancing at Puck as if terrified to disobey him, Omer firmed his voice. "Go. Now. Out of the city. He won't follow you, I promise. You never saw my face."

Shivering as if it were twenty below, the woman grabbed her clothes and fled out the back door. She could identify him, but someone like her would never go to the authorities, or have any credibility if she did. Letting her go was a minor risk, but Omer was a professional, not a monster.

Moments later, another door slammed in the distance, and Omer increased the pressure of the knife under Puck's chin. "What happens next depends on you."

Puck grew very still except for his gaze, which roved from side to side until it rested on Omer's missing pinky. A bead of sweat trickled down the top of the salon owner's muscular torso. "Okay," he whispered.

Omer lowered the blade a fraction, and Puck started speaking very fast. After Omer got the information he was seeking, he said, "Close your eyes."

"Why?"

"Do it."

"You said it depends on me—I told you everything!"

"And so I will kill you quickly."

"I'll fooking look right at you."

"So be it." With a twist of his wrist, Omer turned the penknife horizontal and slid it deep across Puck's jugular. As the salon owner bled out, Omer did the same to the bodyguard before locking the doors and strolling back through the shopping mall. He did not like to take human life without good cause, but if he could trace the target's route through these men so easily, then so could the others.

On the cab ride back to Central London, Omer mulled over the situation. Obtaining the false name on the target's passport was a huge step, but he still had work to do. He again tried to put himself in Andie's shoes. He imagined she would want to escape the city as soon as possible, and London City was the closest airport by a long shot. Flight manifests were closely guarded by the airlines, hard even for law enforcement to obtain. The organization had ways to access them, but Omer did not—at least not on short notice.

But he saw another way. He possessed a local contact unrelated to the Society: an officer named Ian Bartelow who worked with London's Counter Terrorism Command. Omer had collaborated with Ian on numerous occasions when Omer still worked for the Mossad. They had prevented more than one attack together, and had become friends over the years.

As far as Ian needed to know, Omer still worked for a special Israeli deep-cover unit. Ian might not grab the flight manifest for him, but he had access to CCTV and might be willing to look up some footage. Omer didn't need to steal state secrets; he just needed to get his hands on a simple piece of information. He would let Ian believe he was helping track down a recently converted terrorist who might return to London with a bomb in her suitcase.

Now that he knew the target's false name, Omer just needed to search for a tall and athletic American woman with short hair and intense green eyes, likely wearing a hijab, who had probably arrived at London City Airport shortly after midnight two days prior.

Again: How many of those could there be?

Alexandria, Egypt
──o 18 o──

Despite a twenty-hour odyssey that included a brutal layover in Istanbul, Andie felt reasonably well rested when she arrived at Borg El Arab International Airport on the outskirts of Alexandria. After barely sleeping for days, she had decided a little rest was more important than constant vigilance on the airplane, and she let herself crash during the flights. Yet her wariness returned the moment she left the airport and hired a taxi to drive her to the modern version of the Library of Alexandria.

The highway into town snaked through the desert sands like a desiccated black tongue. Soon the skyline of the city appeared, a dense cluster of minarets, skyscrapers, and whitewashed apartment buildings pressed tight against the Mediterranean. The city looked more and more decrepit the closer they drew, yet in a romantic way, she thought, a decaying idol on the edge of the palm-lined sea, brimming with the mystique of a bygone era.

During the layover in Istanbul, Andie had sent emails to Dr. Corwin at both his work and home addresses. She used a brand-new account and an old-school internet café to ensure she remained anonymous. At the Alexandria airport, she had purchased a SIM card with twenty gigabytes of data for a ridiculously low price, and on the drive into town she logged into the new email account, praying for a reply from her mentor.

Crickets.

She wanted to verify his corpse was in the morgue, but a little research told her it took five to seven days to repatriate a body from abroad under normal circumstances—and much longer in the case of murder. She did not dare contact the Italian police again, and doubted they would help her in any case.

The taxi entered Alexandria from the south and cleaved right through the heart of the city. As Andie stared out the window, the minarets and crumbling white apartment buildings evoked a strong childhood memory. She had visited Egypt once before, the only overseas trip her family had taken, splurging on the advance for her father's novel. After absorbing the sights of Cairo, they had cruised the Nile, visiting the Valley of the Kings and Abu Simbel. Andie was eight. It was a big deal for the family, but mostly she remembered getting sick from the street food, listening to her parents argue about money, and smelling alcohol on her father's breath every morning.

Yet one happy memory stood out. She remembered her mother as someone who vacillated between periods of intense concentration and absentminded, almost vacant stares, as if her mind were somewhere else even when she wasn't working. Still, Andie had loved her mother very much, worshipped her even, and she remembered their time together fondly: visiting science museums and planetariums, dining at Mexican restaurants at the beginning of the month, elaborate bedtime stories on the nights when her mother's research did not consume her. Her mother had especially loved Madeleine L'Engle's Time Quintet, though Andie remembered being confused and a little scared by those books as a child.

The day they arrived in Cairo, despite the jet lag and exhaustion from the journey, her mother insisted they take a night tour of the pyramids. Right that very moment.

Andie's father kicked his shoes off, declared he was not moving an inch, and cracked a beer from the minifridge. Her mother glared at him but gave her daughter no choice: after a quick change of clothes, Andie was shepherded out the door and down to the lobby, her mother's eyes bright with anticipation. She had chosen a hotel in Giza, on the outskirts of Cairo, for this very reason.

Outside, after an exchange of money took place with a short Egyptian man with a funny conical hat and a mustache, he ushered them into the back seat of a brown Opel with a huge dent in the side. Even at that age, it was clear to Andie the man was not a real guide, and this was a dicey situation her mother had arranged on the fly.

It didn't matter. As soon as those monolithic testaments to human achievement came into view, far larger than Andie had expected, far larger than *anything*, her mother's eyes gleamed with an inner light, a feverish excitement Andie had never before witnessed.

Though access to the pyramids was limited after dark, her mother used the cold authoritative voice she sometimes deployed to make the driver get as near as they could, then commanded him to pull over and wait. Her mother took Andie by the hand and walked straight into the thin sands at the edge of the road, parallel to the barricade, stopping only when they had an unobstructed view. Andie still remembered the kiss of cool night air on her skin, the dry smell of the desert, the silence between passing cars that enveloped her like a warm blanket.

And there they were, even more immense than before. A trio of shadowy sentinels rising proudly out of the desert as if they belonged to some other world, backlit by a crescent moon and a surreal view of the Milky Way, timeless, hulking, eternal. Andie felt a strange lump in her throat at the sight, overcome by an emotion she couldn't name, her first feeling of numinous awe at the sight of something so much greater than herself.

Her mother had wrapped Andie in her arms from behind and whispered in her ear. Usually Andie pushed the painful memories away, but this time, only hours away from where she had once sat cross-legged with her mother on the beige sands, she gave in.

"*Magical, isn't it?*" her mother said.

Andie nodded.

"The Great Pyramid—that's the one on the right—stood as the tallest human-made structure for almost four thousand years. That's most of recorded history. The ancient Egyptians called it Ikhet, which means 'glorious light.' When it was built, the Egyptians covered it with a casing of polished limestone that reflected sunlight, causing the pyramid to sparkle like a diamond. It shone so bright it could have been seen from the moon. Imagine, Andie. A jewel that's visible from outer space."

"Why did they build them?" Andie asked.

"No one knows for sure. They're almost certainly tombs for Egyptian pharaohs, but some people think they serve other purposes as well. Perhaps a signal to somewhere very far away, or a message to the gods."

"What do you think?"

When her mother didn't answer, Andie turned and caught a small, distracted smile lifting the corners of her lips. "The Great Pyramid is located exactly where the extended lines of latitude and longitude intersect," her mother said softly. "Do you understand what that means?"

"Not really."

"It means it's located at the exact center of the Earth's landmass, even though it was built long before longitude and latitude were invented, at a time when this sort of knowledge was believed to be thousands of years in the future."

"They must have been really smart."

"Maybe smarter than we will ever understand. We still even don't know how they built them. The number of stones in these three pyramids alone could build a wall around France, and each block weighed as much as a small elephant."

"An elephant!"

"The crazy thing is, Andie, not very long before they built the pyramids, the Egyptians were still piling mud bricks together in twenty-foot-high burial structures called 'mastabas.' How did they go from dirt mounds to building stairways to the stars, in such a short amount of time?"

Andie felt a little lost by this idea.

"We think we're so superior to our ancestors, but that's not the case at all." She laughed as she squeezed her daughter's shoulder. "I'm sure one day you'll think you know everything and I don't know anything."

"I already do."

"Well, you just remember the pyramids, Little Mouse. Let me tell you a few more things. The Great Pyramid—the one on the right—has air shafts angled in correspondence to objects in outer space. The three pyramids together are aligned precisely with the stars of Orion's belt—Alnitak, Alnilam, and Mintaka—as they would have appeared to the ancient Egyptians, with the Nile in the position of the Milky Way. And the pyramids point north, to within five-hundredths of a degree of the magnetic pole. Not even the Royal Observatory in Greenwich is that precise!"

"What about my question?" Andie said distractedly, not sharing her mother's delight in these random facts.

"What's that, lovie?"

"Why do you think they built them?"

Her mother moved closer, holding her hand as they gazed together at the beauty and mystery of the night. "The Egyptians believed the afterlife was a mirror of the living world. Isn't that a nice thought?" Her mother's voice was almost a whisper. "That after death we might go someplace like our world, only different."

"Would we be together there, Mommy? You and me and Daddy?"

Her mother tilted her head to rest it on Andie's shoulder, her hair tickling the back of Andie's neck. "Of course, Little Mouse. Of course we will."

Hating how weak her memories made her feel, disturbed by her mother's long-ago answer to her question, Andie stared out the window of the taxi as a chasm opened deep inside her and threatened to swallow her whole.

By the time Andie arrived at the Bibliotheca Alexandrina, her romance with the city's nostalgic charms had faded. She felt drained

by the interminable journey, beaten down by the crowds and pollu-
tion and cement eyesores, the endless urban sprawl. It did not help
that her taxi's air-conditioning had given out halfway, forcing her
to keep her window lowered and endure the cacophony of blaring
horns and the soiled air of the inner city, a demonic intermingling of
smog and fried offal mixed with whiffs of sewage.

Yet the closer they drew to the harbor, the calmer the city grew,
as if the languid waters of the Mediterranean lapping against its
shores exerted a hypnotic effect. Though the ancient city had long
ago disappeared, shoved into the sea by earthquakes and burned
to the ground during wars and religious purges, it had experienced
periods of revival over the centuries, and Andie caught glimpses of
forgotten glory on the shabby streets: palm-fronted colonial buildings, the occasional statue, mosques and synagogues and Coptic
churches, glimpses of dusty white ruins scattered about the city like
the discarded bones of bygone civilizations.

To reach the entrance of the Bibliotheca Alexandrina, the driver
had to circle around on a busy freeway that cut off the city proper
from the narrow beaches along the coastline. The modern iteration
of the famous library resembled an enormous white discus sticking
out of the ground at an angle, sloping down to the sea. Surrounded
by a puzzle box of dated apartment buildings withering in the sun,
the gleaming library looked like an alien ship that had crash-landed
in the middle of the city.

Just to the north, perched on a spit of land extending into the
mouth of the harbor, was a handsome citadel that bore a marked
resemblance to an enormous sandcastle. The driver startled Andie—
he had not spoken since the airport—by pointing at the fort and
declaring it the former site of the Pharos lighthouse, one of the Seven
Wonders of the World. She envisioned this urban monster of a city as
the beacon of progress it once had been, home to queens and emper-
ors and an honor roll of the world's great philosophers, a wonderland
of palaces and gardens and architectural novelties.

Knowing she might not have much time before someone figured

out her location, she left the taxi and hustled to the entrance of the library, the balmy air perfuming the breeze. A familiar feeling of being watched overcame her as she purchased a ticket and approached the glass-walled entrance beneath an elevated walkway. Her step slowed as she crossed the handsome paving stones, until she stopped ten feet from the door, frozen in place, searching every face in sight.

Why am I so paranoid around libraries?

Or is someone waiting for me inside?

The granite wall supporting the rear of the disk was carved with letters and characters from the world's known alphabets. During her layover, she had read how the architects intended the circular diaphragm of the library, which extended four levels below ground and seven above, to symbolize the cyclical nature of knowledge as it ebbs and flows through time. All in all, it was a very impressive site, a fitting ode to past glory and an archetype for a new era.

On a whim, still balking at entering, she took out the Star Phone and pretended to be a tourist snapping photos. When she peered at the high glass wall above the entrance, she gasped as the image seen through the viewing lens blurred, again inducing the disorienting sensation of movement in her mind. Her vision stabilized to reveal a familiar motif carved in stone, a legendary creature with the head of a human and the body of a lion.

Though adopted by the Greeks and other cultures, she knew the sphinx was derived from Egypt, a powerful symbol of a watchful presence. A guardian, a protector.

Unlike the laughing image of Democritus, the three-dimensional sphinx superimposed on the library did not move, but overlooked the entrance in solemn repose. The admonition of this warder of temples and tombs was clear: beware to any who defiled this shrine, this repository of sacred knowledge.

Andie lowered the Star Phone. Nothing had changed on the face of the device. She returned it to her pocket and let out a deep breath. The presence of the sphinx gave her confidence she was on the right track, as well as a sense of calm.

Someone, she felt, was watching over the library.

But who?

Was it the ghost of scholars past? Someone from this mysterious society to which Dr. Corwin belonged? Someone aligned with the people who wanted to kill her?

She knew she was taking a risk by entering—but she had taken a risk from the moment she embarked on this path and opened the safe behind the Ishango bone. Her objectives had not changed, and she would just have to weigh the dangers as they arose.

If someone was watching, so be it.

The main section of the library was a cavernous space with eight terraces, each focused on a different sphere of knowledge. Famed as the largest reading room in the world, it was sunlit and beautiful, supported by slender columns that soared to a domed ceiling. The shelves and carousels spaced throughout the room matched the color of the light-grain wood floor.

Andie knew the library contained millions of volumes and felt overwhelmed by the sheer size of it. Now that she was here, what was she supposed to do? Was there some hidden meaning she was missing?

Legions of people milled about, most of them young Egyptians browsing the shelves or poring over books at the carousels. She tried a grand sweep of the room with the Star Phone, to no effect. After that, she wandered through the other sections of the library. Scattered about were lost artifacts from the ancient city, including pieces of the great lighthouse and stone blocks covered in hieroglyphs, unearthed by archaeologists in the waters offshore. Yet the Star Phone revealed nothing new until she found another sphinx embedded at the entrance to a hallway leading to the city archives section.

The smaller room inside had a flat, low ceiling more reminiscent of a typical library. The archives contained books and multimedia on the history of Alexandria. Was there a particular book or microfiche she was supposed to find? Another sphinx? A secret doorway?

A thorough sweep with the Star Phone revealed nothing. To the stacks then. With a deep breath, she decided to start with some research on the original library and see if she uncovered anything unique to the collection. She ignored the constant nagging feeling of being observed, even in this quiet little room, and forced herself to focus.

She soon discovered the loss of the original library was far greater than she had even realized. The world had known other great centers of learning. Mesopotamian, Aksumite, Sumerian, Assyrian. Timbuktu. The House of Wisdom in Baghdad. But none as ambitious as the ground on which she was standing. Ptolemy I, who studied under Aristotle as a boy, alongside Alexander the Great, had founded both the library and the adjoining Shrine of the Muses—the origin of the term *museum*. The fame of the library had ushered in a golden age of knowledge, a kingdom of the mind. By the middle of the third century BCE, Eratosthenes had calculated the circumference and diameter of Earth—believing it was round—within an accuracy of fifty miles. Others mapped the stars and catalogued the constellations. Aristarchus developed a heliocentric model of the solar system *two millennia* before Copernicus.

In the adjoining museum, the vivisection of condemned criminals had led to the discovery of the central nervous system and the hypothesis that the brain, and not the heart, sheltered the mind. Euclid penned his *Elements* at Alexandria, perhaps the most influential work in the history of mathematics.

The advancements had flowed out of the library and transformed the city itself. Andie was awed by the accounts of the beauty and sophistication of ancient Alexandria. Powered by running water, mechanical birds whistled from within gardens and fountains, and statues played instruments or lifted wineskins to their lips. The clever use of pneumatics allowed temple doors to open and close as if by magic, and enabled automatic streetlamps to light the wide central avenue. The mathematician Hero, the greatest engineer of antiquity, developed a play performed by rope-and-axle-controlled automata—perhaps the world's first robots. He also invented a coin-operated drink dispenser for the city, and a revolving sphere powered by a pressurized container of water.

Good God, she thought. *The world's first steam turbine engine, invented sixteen centuries before the Industrial Revolution.*

Recovered fragments from the library's catalogue system hinted at massive collections of rhetoric, law, lyric poetry, medicine, natural sciences, and other disciplines. Written accounts of the Egyptians, Greeks, Babylonians, and countless other cultures swept away by history. Scrolls of Zoroaster. Buddhist writings. Unknown plays by Homer and Sophocles. Early translations of the Pentateuch and the Septuagint.

Her mind reeled at the possibilities. It was as if only a fraction of Shakespeare's plays had survived, or just one of Einstein's theories.

She kept researching the demise of the library, to illuminate it in more detail. Julius Caesar had unwittingly destroyed much of the library when he was under siege inside the city and set fire to the enemy fleet. The fire spread from the harbor to the buildings along the waterfront, including the library. Presumably some of the collection was preserved, but no one knows for certain.

The next mention—perhaps apocryphal—related to an incident in the fifth century AD, after the surviving works were said to have moved to the Serapeum, a Greco-Egyptian temple dedicated to a deity manufactured by the ruling dynasty to appease both factions. Religious zealots razed the temple to the ground and dragged Hypatia, the last true keeper of the library, outside the city walls. It was said they scraped off her skin with oyster shells, tore her limb from limb, and burned her remains as a penalty for participating in the work of the devil.

From this point forward, the library disappeared from the historical record. A rather insane thought entered Andie's mind: *What if some remnant of the actual library* had *survived?*

What if it was still here, and what if she was supposed to find it?
A nervous chuckle escaped her. *Don't be ridiculous.*

Yet she couldn't shake the thought, and she turned her research in a different direction, toward any and all theories that a piece of the ancient library might have endured.

Unsurprisingly, the new direction opened a Pandora's box of speculation. There were alien conspiracy theories, Freemason theories, Cleopatra theories, Atlantis theories. She became overwhelmed by the storm of nonsense and was about to give it up when something caught her eye: a reference to a place called the Hall of Records.

According to legend, an ancient library—even older than the one at Alexandria—had once been kept in a secret underground chamber beneath the Great Sphinx of Giza. The persistence of the legend had spurred the Egyptian government, a little over twenty years ago, to excavate. To everyone's astonishment, they discovered a set of tunnels leading to a cave system hidden beneath the sphinx. Though no artifacts were ever found, there were signs of previous excavations, and even an underground river.

Even more recently, a British explorer claimed to have discovered a separate complex of caves, tunnels, and chambers beneath the Giza pyramid field. Beset by venomous spiders and colonies of bats—something straight out of Indiana Jones—the explorer was convinced the subterranean complex was tens of thousands of years old, or even older, and harbored secrets of an ancient civilization that might have inspired or communicated with the builders of the pyramids.

Inexplicably, the Egyptian government blocked further investigation, driving conspiracy theorists into a frenzy.

Andie did not like unconfirmed finds or baseless theories. No serious archaeologist gave any credence to the Hall of Records or an antediluvian city hidden below the pyramids. Yet the Star Phone had led her to the library, and twice revealed a sphinx. Could the myth possibly relate to the puzzle in some way? While intriguing, she was about to move on when a realization caused a sharp intake of breath.

The second sphinx the Star Phone had revealed was located above the entrance to a hallway that led to the city archives room.

Archives, of course, was synonymous with *records*.

A hall of records.

A little thrill passed through her. Surely this meant something.

Yet a feverish bout of research on the mythical hall only muddied the waters. She learned nothing useful and felt as if she were falling down a rabbit hole. Perhaps, she thought, she needed a suitably irrational guide.

When she checked the time, she couldn't believe her eyes. It was almost 7 p.m. The library was about to close.

She had spent the entire day inside.

Outside, Andie felt lost in the vastness of the city. She had some decisions to make, but she was starving and needed food to think clearly.

After considering a walk along the Corniche, the waterfront promenade that ran the length of the Eastern Harbour, she decided she would feel more secure in a less exposed neighborhood. As the sun dipped beneath the horizon, softening the decay and urban grime, she headed for the warren of streets southwest of the library, the core of the old city. While keeping an eye out for a place to eat, she used her SIM card to make a call on her burner phone.

It was a call she didn't want to make but knew she could no longer avoid. Word of her disappearance must have spread by now, and she had to let her father know she was okay.

He answered with the usual alcohol-induced slur to his speech. She couldn't remember the last time he had answered the phone sober.

"Andie! Thank God you're all right! I've tried to call, email . . . Where are you?"

"Rio," she said, in case anyone was listening.

"Brazil?"

"I needed to get away, Dad. Just for a few nights."

"Okay, I guess . . . Listen, dear, I heard about James. I just can't believe it."

"It still doesn't seem real."

"You must be torn-up. I know how much he meant to you. Andie, I . . . I'd love to see you. When you get back from Rio, I mean."

"You know where I live. You haven't visited since I moved to Durham."

"I'm sorry, but you know how it is, with the writing and the money . . ."

"Yeah," she said, not even trying to hide the bitterness. "I know."

"Now Andie, let's not—"

"I don't want to talk about that."

Despite her father's inebriation, hearing a familiar voice while on the run in a foreign city felt more comforting than she had thought it would. Still, she wasn't about to let her emotional state change the past. That ship had sailed long ago. She loved her father, she always would—and that was all she could say.

"I can't help if the books aren't selling, Andie. I'm a writer. It's who I am."

But did you ever think about who I am? And how your choices affect me? "Don't worry, Dad. I know exactly who you are."

"You didn't have to leave, you know. Go so far away."

"And what should I have done? Stay at home and wait tables to pay your bills?" *Calm down, Andie. Deep breaths. You do this every time.* "Listen, I called to tell you I'm okay, but there's something I need to ask you. And I don't want you to get all emotional or start an argument."

After a long pause, he said, "Okay."

"Why did Mom leave?"

This time, he took even longer to respond. She imagined he was taking a long drink from whatever bottle was at hand. "You know why she left. To join the ashram."

"Was that the real reason? Or did something else happen?"

"I don't know what you mean. Listen, I thought we promised never to discuss—"

"Please, Dad. It's really important right now. I can't tell you why. You'll just have to trust me. Were you and Mom just not getting along, or was there an affair, or . . . something else?"

"We hadn't been getting along for some time," he said quietly, more sober than he had seemed before.

"Why not?"

"Your mother had . . . different ambitions in life."

"Like what?"

"To tell you the truth, I never really knew. I just knew I couldn't satisfy them. She wanted something more, Andie. She wanted to travel the globe. Study every subject and try every food, have every experience, drink in everything the world has to offer. I mean, who doesn't? But more than *things*, I wanted a family and stability. The success of my first book was great and kept us together. I was able to give her some of what she wanted. But when the success went away . . . she did too. I loved her anyway, though. I really did. I never even blamed her—we can't change who we are. If she wasn't happy, then she wasn't happy."

Andie flinched at the sting in her father's voice, the pain of rejection after all these years. *I know the feeling. But I sure as hell blame her.*

"So that was it? You two just weren't right for each other? There wasn't anything between . . . her and Dr. Corwin?"

Her father seemed genuinely surprised. "That's what you—No, not that I know of. They were very close, but I don't . . . I would have noticed, don't you think?"

"Maybe. Maybe not."

"She took a number of trips with him, for research, but I never got the sense there was anything romantic. He was just a professor, not yet well-known . . . Even if it was a Machiavellian choice, it's hardly an upgrade from a best-selling writer. At least at the time," he muttered.

I'm not so sure about that. I'm beginning to think we don't know very much about Dr. Corwin at all.

The question is: How much did my mother know?

"So she went to the ashram," Andie said, "and just never came back?"

The silence stretched for so long that Andie knew something was wrong. She had entered a commercial sector of town, and the noise from sidewalk merchants and the hordes of pedestrians grew so loud she was forced to duck down a well-lit side street.

"Dad?"

"She never joined an ashram," he said quietly.

Andie stopped walking. "What do you mean? You've told me she went off to India to join an ashram my entire life."

"I'm sorry, honey. Samantha came up with the story and made me agree to it. She liked the thought of you believing she went somewhere to better herself. I suppose I agreed with her."

"Better herself."

"She loved you very much, Andie."

"So much that I never heard from her again?"

"I can't explain that. But the way she looked at you from the moment you were born, held you, read to you . . . that love was real. I'd bet my life on it."

"Then why did she leave?" Andie said, almost in a whisper.

"Everything else I've told you is true. She was looking for something in life I couldn't give her. A few months before she left for the ashram—I mean, you know what I mean—she took a trip to Asia."

"I remember. To a university in Tokyo for research."

"It wasn't for research, and it wasn't in Japan. We told you that so you wouldn't worry. It was over the summer—school was out—and she left for a month. She called me twice—once from Vietnam and once from India—to check in on you."

"What was she doing, if it had nothing to do with school?"

"She said she needed to see a few places for herself, packed her bags, and left. I know. It's strange. What's even stranger was her behavior when she returned."

Andie swallowed. "What do you mean?"

"She was never the same. What was once a restless and vague ambition seemed more focused. From the moment she got back until she left for good, she was distant, as if we barely knew each other. Judging from her behavior, I had to assume she'd met someone overseas and left me for him."

"What did Dr. Corwin say about it?"

"He was quite upset. But he didn't have any more insight than I did."

You sure about that?

"Was he gone during any of that time?" she asked.

"I don't think so."

Andie tried to process this information. "Why tell me this now?"

"You're asking these questions—really asking—for the first time. You're an adult. I think you deserve to know."

"So if it wasn't the ashram, where did Mom go?"

"I have no clue."

"What do you mean, you have no clue?"

Another pause. "Maybe she started a new life in Asia and left us for a new family. Maybe she wanted to leave but got in trouble. I just don't know—and it wasn't for lack of trying. I spent years, the last of our savings, hiring people to try to find out where she went."

"Didn't she tell you *anything*?"

His prolonged sigh was thick with emotion. "The day before she left, she said she was quitting her job and leaving the country to 'connect with her true self.' We had a huge argument, as you can imagine. The next night, she stayed by your side for a long time while you slept. At midnight she kissed your forehead, got in a taxi with her suitcase, and rode away. I never heard from her again."

Copenhagen
——○ 1933 ○——

As the appointed hour approached, Ettore paced back and forth in the courtyard of his hotel, his breath fogging the air. Walled in by the surrounding apartment buildings, listening to shouts from the street as candles warmed the windows above him, he was tired of staring at the peeling yellow paint and the line of bicycles along the courtyard wall, alone with the sweet pungent smell of the city and the faint reek of spilled beer worn into the flagstones.

Will Stefan come for me? he wondered.

Or would the German string Ettore along once again, forcing him to participate in another crazed, life-threatening situation?

No, not forced, Ettore had to admit. He was making his own choices, though he wasn't entirely sure why.

He was set to return to Leipzig in two days. He made a vow that, if Stefan failed to introduce him to the Leap Year Society by then—in fact, on this very night—then he would never speak to the man again. Ettore was an important physicist. He did not need this . . . *thing.*

The cold was bracing as a light snow began to fall. Still Ettore paced. He did not feel like being holed up in his room, or at the hotel bar listening to the prattle of strangers.

To his surprise, just as a bell tower chimed the stroke of midnight, a bellhop stuck his head out of the door leading to the hotel and informed Ettore that a car had arrived for him. Ettore started to rush inside, then slowed, dusting the snow off his wool coat and trying to appear collected as he walked through the hotel and saw a familiar black car idling by the curb.

Stefan looked amused as Ettore opened the door and slid into the soft leather seat. "You look flustered, my friend."

"I'm . . . I don't know what you mean."

Stefan's mirth faded, and he leveled his intense stare at the younger man, peeling back the layers of self-protection. "Are you nervous perhaps?"

"Of course not."

"Wary of what awaits? Terrified, even?"

"I'm quite fine, thank you," Ettore said crossly.

After locking eyes, Stefan laughed and clapped him on the shoulder. "My dear Ettore, the anticipation is written all over your face. Relax, my good man. With a little luck, you might even survive the night."

Ettore could not tell if he was joking.

Expecting another jaunt into the countryside—Ettore would not have been surprised if Stefan had hustled him on a plane and flew him to Africa—he was relieved when, instead of veering toward the highway leading out of town, they took Vesterbrogade into the heart of the city. The snow continued to fall, softening the rough edges, transforming the stately old buildings and cobblestone streets into a wintry utopia.

Soon they pulled up to the gate of a neoclassical mansion on the edge of the city center, the most impressive residence in a neighborhood full of historic homes. Four soaring columns spanned the width of the mansion, and the entire facade was crafted from a pale-blue shade of marble. A spiked iron gate backed by a towering hedge shielded the rest of the property from view.

The gate came almost to the edge of the sidewalk, flanked by copper lampposts. A clock tower on the corner of the street, topped by a miniature version of the city's distinctive green spires, added storybook charm. Both the street and the house appeared quiet, sedate. The entire scene was nothing like Ettore had imagined.

Where was everyone?

After the driver exchanged words with a pair of guards, the gate opened and they pulled inside, approaching a fountain at the end of the driveway. Greco-Roman statues graced the lawn, ethereal in the snow, as if the ivory-hued figures had coalesced from the flakes themselves.

The driver let them out. Instead of using the main entrance, Stefan hustled Ettore down a pebbled path beside the house. "We'll enter from the rear," he said.

"Why? Is that normal?"

"Nothing about your induction is normal."

"What do you mean?" Ettore asked as Stefan guided them inside an old servants' quarters attached to the house, now converted to a posh guest bedroom. Before they entered, Ettore caught glimpses of sizeable rear grounds enclosed within the hedge: a labyrinth of topiary, greenhouses, and curious domed structures that resembled walled-in stone rotundas.

"As you may have surmised," Stefan said as they passed into a shadowy vestibule inside the main house, "I'm the leader of our faction, and you were handpicked by me."

"Faction? Of the Society?"

Inside, the mansion was still and hushed, exuding a solemn grace. Ettore grew more nervous as Stefan closed the door to the guest suite, leaving them in darkness.

"We are at a crossroads, Ettore. There has been unrest among the factions, irreconcilable differences, for some time."

"I don't understand. And where are the lights?"

"Nor should you understand. Not yet. I can only say that those who support me have a radically different view of what must be done. Humanity is in grave peril."

"You're talking about the Nazis?"

"They are the immediate threat. But who will come next? Look at the world around you. As humanity continues to transform itself, becoming something closer to a god than an animal, wielding the power to destroy the very world in which we live, then hard choices must be made."

Stefan took him by the elbow and led him through the darkness like a lost lamb. Ettore's shoulder brushed against a doorframe. He felt a carpet or rug beneath his feet, then caught a pleasant floral scent. Moments later, Stefan flicked on a light, and Ettore was ushered into an enormous hall, with oil paintings adorning walls that soared to a gilded ceiling. Oriental rugs accented the polished wood floors, and soft light emanated from a succession of diamond chandeliers interspersed along the hundred-foot gallery. Ettore had never seen a chandelier with electric lights before.

"Do you believe we live in the best of all possible worlds?" Stefan asked.

"Whatever do you mean?"

The German stopped to admire a painting of the Garden of Eden. Ettore would have sworn it was a Michelangelo. "As you know better than most," Stefan continued, "the human race is on the cusp of creating technologies that men like Adolf Hitler, if given the chance, will use to enslave or consume the planet. Evil triumphs when good is silent, Ettore. Knowledge is power. These simple aphorisms possess great truth, but what is more complex is the philosophy that underpins them."

Stefan stepped closer, his eyes lit by an internal fire that burned more brightly than in any man Ettore had ever known. "Our brethren believe that wisdom must accompany the acquisition of knowledge. We do not disagree. Yet the world has changed, Ettore. It is no longer prudent to let humanity plot its own course. *We* believe knowledge must be acquired aggressively, at all costs, by a select few with a shared ideal and purpose, in order to save us all from destruction. Only then—in a future when these technologies are controlled and better understood—should they be shared with the world at large."

Ettore absorbed what the other man was saying, working to fit it inside his worldview. "I don't necessarily disagree. Though I would need to ponder it further, and consider each situation as it arose."

"As you should," Stefan murmured. "Come, I wish to show you something."

"What?"

Instead of answering, Stefan led him down the long hallway, and Ettore saw a succession of rooms that displayed more wealth than he had ever witnessed in person. Paintings and sculptures and *objets d'art* from around the world, vases, urns, velvet drapes and brocaded chairs, glimpses of bedrooms fit for royalty. The style of the furnishings was very modern, in keeping with Copenhagen's reputation as a progressive city, and the latest technologies were on display. This included an aluminum robot, standing as tall as a man, in a corner of the kitchen. Stefan stopped to issue a voice command, causing the automaton to wave its arms and waddle across the tile floor. It opened a freestanding metal box sitting on the counter beside a self-contained electric refrigerator, and began unloading pots and pans.

Ettore gawked at the display. He had never seen such an advanced model before, and certainly not in someone's home. "But how . . ." he began, only to see Stefan smile and continue down a shorter hall, which ended at a closed door. A plum tree laden with fruit was carved and painted in exquisite detail on the polished wood.

"To become a dedicated seeker of truth," Stefan said, "one must doubt, as deeply as one can, the nature of all things."

After that cryptic statement, he opened the door to reveal a study lined with floor-to-ceiling bookshelves, and a marble fireplace on the opposite side of the room. Besides the hardbound books and a leather armchair by the fireplace, the only object in the room was a standing globe just inside the door.

"Who owns this house?" Ettore asked.

"We do, of course."

"You mean the Society? But where is everyone? I thought I would be meeting others."

Stefan approached the globe and placed his hands on the painted porcelain surface. "As you shall see, we keep many secrets in this house, and in our other residences. I'd like to show you one tonight." He pushed with his fingers, causing two small, irregular pieces to depress on the face of the globe. The workmanship was so clever that Ettore had not noticed the interlocking pieces. Playing it like a piano, Stefan moved his hands and depressed another pair, and then another, causing a section of the bookshelves to hinge open, just wide enough for a person to slip through.

Stefan led him through the hidden doorway and into a darkened alcove. He flicked on a light to reveal a semitranslucent orb resting on a glass stand in the center of the room. About the size of a cantaloupe, the bauble was made of a rough bluish-green material, resembling quartz sprinkled with crumbled seashells.

Ettore stared curiously at the object. "What is that?"

"Our scientists believe," Stefan said, giving the strange bauble a hungry look, "that this is a glass-blown object at least three thousand years old."

"Three *thousand*?" Ettore drew closer to inspect the surface. He would not have guessed it was glass until Stefan told him. "But how?"

"Sophisticated glasswork was not unknown at the time. I'd like you to stay exactly where you are, and observe the object."

The German closed the door and cast the alcove into darkness. Moments later, a garish purple light bathed the room, emanating from a trio of glowing tubes embedded in the room's ceiling. Ettore had never seen a light so unusual. Fluorescent lamps, he knew, created illumination by sending an electrical current through tubes of mercury vapor. The mercury atoms exuded light photons rendered visible to the human eye by phosphor coatings, and he wondered if the glowing tubes on these lamps contained a different type of phosphor, one that allowed a shorter wavelength of light to pass.

The electric light may have been a novelty, but the inside of the glass ball made him gasp. Displayed within that ancient sphere, he saw the very room in which they very standing, reflected in varying hues of gray. He knew this because he recognized his own stooped posture and Stefan's tall erect form standing by the wall. Ettore waved a hand and saw the gesture reflected within the shadowy world mirrored inside the bauble.

"I . . . don't understand. Smoke particles will eventually settle. A vapor will dissipate over time . . . Perhaps two inert gases . . . But thermal equilibrium would not allow such a display to endure over any length of time."

"All true."

"How then? Is it a trick?"

"No trick, I assure you."

"A mirror coated in phosphors?"

Stefan nodded in approval. "That is our best guess."

"But how would a primitive culture understand the concept of a radioluminescent material that persists for so long, or the reaction of a phosphor to a specialized electric light?"

"We've no idea. It seems impossible, unless there is some type of special property to the glass or some unseen material inside that we do not understand. Perhaps breaking the glass would provide insight, or perhaps it would . . . break the spell, if you'll forgive the pun. As I've said before, I believe we've only scratched the surface of what our forebears were able to accomplish."

Stefan stepped away from the wall, clasped his hands behind his back, and began to pace. "I mentioned secrets, Ettore, and this is one of many. But the greatest of all—the cornerstone, in many ways, of our Society—is an enigma to which I am not yet privy." His voice turned bitter. "Those anachronistic fools believe decades should pass before a single meek step is taken, a babe crawling on hands and knees toward a curious light. The world will burn around us while they await their precious enlightenment!"

Ettore pulled his gaze away from the glass stand. "Greatest secret?"

"There is a place . . . a higher reality, another dimension. We don't know exactly what it is. We call it the Fold. I know only what has been whispered in the corridors of the sanctums, the lore they give us as scraps. Yet a few within the Society have seen it, Ettore. I *know* they have."

"Another dimension?" Ettore said in a daze. He couldn't seem to stop repeating Stefan's words. "What . . . How do you know this?"

"We only know that it's there, and reflects our reality in some way. Or perhaps our reality reflects *it*." He walked slowly toward the center of the room, his gaze locked on the glass ball. "What I do know is that it looks similar to this."

"In what manner?"

"A shadowy gray-hued world, an abnormal but deeper reflection of our own, with different physical properties. What if this three-thousand-year-old glass sphere was the original inspiration for the crystal ball? What if an ancient seer once peered into its depths to explore the Fold? Where do the boundaries of myth and legend intersect with reality? Superstition with science? We have reason to believe humankind has known about the existence of this place through dreams and other phenomena since the dawn of recorded history. No one understands it, but we all agree the Fold exists—and can be reached. Some believe metaphysics is the route to take—and perhaps it is—but I firmly believe we can reach it through *science*."

As outlandish as Stefan's claim might seem, Ettore had no problem conceiving of other dimensions and levels of reality that existed right next door to our own. In fact, they were part and parcel of his profession. What was quantum physics but proof that such miracles not only existed, but formed the bedrock of our physical universe? Of our very *reality*?

For some time, Ettore had harbored the sneaking suspicion that twentieth-century science, as advanced as it seemed, had only discovered the frothy silver tips of the waves skimming the ocean, leaving fathoms of dark water unseen.

He had to know more. "What do you mean it can be reached?"

Stefan spun on his heel to face him. "This is the reason I recruited you. Help me locate the Fold and probe its secrets before it's too late. Imagine what might occur if a scientist in the employ of Adolf Hitler arrives first, or someone else like him."

"I have so many questions. How does the Society know about this place? How do you know it's real? What do you want me to do?"

Stefan strode to the wall, turned off the strange violet light, and reopened the door to the study. "Excellent questions all. Yet before I provide answers, you must officially become one of us. Due to the rapid progression of world events, and because of who you are, I've convinced the others to allow you to circumvent our traditional trials. You're welcome here, Ettore. But even you must undergo our symbolic rite of entry."

When Ettore moved to follow him across the room, Stefan told him to wait by the wall. Ettore obeyed as Stefan returned to the globe and pressed his fingers into the porcelain surface, again manipulating panels. "Sometimes we have to descend into darkness before we can see the light. Please undress, Ettore."

"What?"

"Do it," Stefan said softly, yet in a voice so firm and commanding that Ettore felt as if he had no choice but to obey. Feeling vulnerable and rather foolish, Ettore stripped down to his socks and underpants, then removed those as well when Stefan ordered him to finish.

"What's going on?" Ettore asked, covering his privates with his hands. "Please, Stefan—"

"Take a deep breath and hold it."

"Why should—" Ettore began, right before the floor dropped away.

Enveloped by a sudden darkness, Ettore did not even have time to call out before he plunged feetfirst into a well of cold water. His toes never touched bottom, and he kicked blindly to reach the surface. He doubted he had dropped farther than ten feet. Working hard not to panic, he thrust with his legs to propel himself upward, and banged his head straight into a glass wall.

Dazed, Ettore tried to regain his equilibrium as he flailed in the water. *How could that be?*

He thrust a palm over and over against the barrier, then swam side to side, hoping it would end but finding that it extended all the way to walls on both sides, perhaps two dozen feet across.

Now he panicked. Had Stefan brought him here to die? Was he a true Nazi after all, sent to assassinate the scientists of rival nations?

Ettore forced himself to quell his terror as he groped blindly along the walls, searching for an opening as his oxygen seeped away. He recalled Stefan's last words before the plunge.

Sometimes we have to descend into darkness before we see the light.

He had assumed the cryptic words were metaphorical, but what if he was imparting a literal clue?

Though swimming deeper into the hole—descending into darkness—seemed counterintuitive, he realized it was the only place he had not explored. Corkscrewing his body in the water, Ettore dove into the enclosure, this time keeping his arms extended so he would not crack his head. Within three full strokes, he encountered a metal bar affixed in place. He groped around and felt another rail a few feet away, connected by shorter metal bars between them.

The horizontal iron ladder extended in only one direction. Left with no choice, Ettore propelled himself from bar to bar as fast as he could, his chest starting to spasm from lack of air. As the pressure inside his lungs mounted, the iron bars turned upward, and he spied a faint orange glow. A burst of adrenaline carried him the final dozen feet and through a hole at the top of the ladder. He groaned as precious oxygen coursed through his airways and filled his lungs with a narcotic pleasure.

Ettore climbed out of the hole with shaking hands, his teeth chattering from the cold, only to find himself staring down a constricted stone-walled passage. The golden glow he had seen was emanating from the floor of the passage, which, as far as Ettore could tell, was composed of hot coals.

The air inside the chamber was as hot and humid as a tropical jungle. He turned to face a solid wall behind him. There was only one way to go.

Across the passage of fire.

How long Ettore remained beside the top of the watery hole, naked and dripping and confused, he could not say. Debating whether to wait right there for as long as it took for someone to save him, Ettore took a tentative step forward, onto the coals. He jerked his foot back in pain. After another probe, he realized that, while the coals were hot to the touch, they did not burn as much as he would have thought. He peered closer and discovered they were synthetic, made of some unknown material. A clever illusion aided by the darkness cloaking the chamber.

Though terrified, his rational mind told him that Stefan and his people were not trying to kill him, and that this was another test.

No, not a test. What had Stefan called it? A "symbolic rite of entry."

Surprising himself, he stopped thinking through every possible angle for once in his life and rushed across the glowing surface. The heat became unbearable very quickly, and Ettore howled in pain as he raced over the wobbly stones, working hard to keep his balance. Soon he spied the end of the tunnel a hundred feet away. So very far! The pain was excruciating. He wondered how he would survive, and how in the world he had come to this place in his life, and where that dark hole at the end of the tunnel would lead—

And then he was through, standing on a stone floor at the edge of a patch of blackness. He sank to the floor and inspected the blisters that had begun to form. After a time, he pushed to his feet and stared into the maw of the tunnel.

Feeling oddly calm, Ettore led with his hands and walked into the unknown. Almost at once, a fierce wind poured into the chamber, buffeting him from all sides. He moved carefully, afraid the floor would drop away again, but he never faltered in the face of the gale, knowing it was part of the process and symbolic of something he could ponder at a later date. The faint glow behind him disappeared, and he walked for twenty paces through utter darkness, disoriented, the wind and lack of vision spinning his senses. He did his best to move in a straight line, staggering forward like a drunkard. Soon another glow—this one silver—appeared ahead of him, and as the wind died another sound picked up, a faint and dissonant whisper that increased the closer he drew to the light. He recoiled as he walked into an invisible wall made of some filmy substance, and then he was clawing his way through a viscous veil that clung to him like the strands of a spider's web. Ettore pushed forward, flailing, both determined and afraid, ripping at the barrier until he emerged into the freezing Copenhagen night, realizing he must have been walking on an upward slope and grateful beyond measure when he saw the moon and stars above.

Another passage stretched out before him, this one a long, snaking corridor of masked men and women dressed in evening clothes, each holding a single flameless candle that, together, emitted the silver glow he had witnessed. Stunned, Ettore estimated several hundred people awaited him, their identities obscured by beige masks covered in red markings that resembled hieroglyphs or runes of some sort.

The whispering had grown louder, emanating from behind the masks, low susurrations whose words he could not understand. A chant in an unfamiliar language, or perhaps in many languages. He looked around and recognized the domed stone huts he had seen earlier in the rear grounds of the mansion.

Lying on the snow-covered grass at his feet was a belted cotton robe. He gratefully slipped it on. The inside was dry, and standing barefoot atop the freezing ground gave relief to his blistered soles.

Ettore exhaled a frozen breath. Shoulders straight, trying not to look as bewildered as he felt, he strode down the tunnel of people. As he passed, each and every person tossed a handful of loose soil on his robe. The wet dirt stained the material and collected in his wake, marking the passage.

A lone figure, also masked, stood facing Ettore at the end of the corridor. As Ettore drew closer, the figure removed his mask, and Ettore was unsurprised by the identity of the lean and hawkish man awaiting him.

"Welcome," Stefan said, signaling with a hand for Ettore to stop when he was ten feet away. Before Ettore could croak out a reply, the German raised his voice to address the crowd. Ettore glanced back and noticed the tunnel had collapsed as the other people, still wearing their masks and holding their candles, gathered behind him.

"Before we complete the rite of entry," Stefan continued, "I have an announcement to make. For some time, as we all know, a schism of belief has ruptured the Society we hold so dear. We've attempted to coexist. Yet world events and the aggression of others have made clear the impossibility of this task." He paused to sweep his gaze across the crowd. "As the voice of those gathered tonight, I hereby declare the Ascendants the only true faction of the Leap Year Society."

Enthusiastic clapping erupted from the crowd, but Stefan quieted the noise with an outstretched palm. "We must pledge at all costs," he continued, "to seek through knowledge the ascendancy of humankind over the basest, most bestial aspects of our nature, and thereby save the world from itself. Though it pains me as no wound ever has, we must also declare war with our former brethren and continue our mission as we see fit. All of us know what this will mean. The trials that lie ahead." After another pause, in which not a single person stirred, Stefan thrust his mask high in the air. "A new future awaits, and it will be up to us, each and every one present, to determine its course. History has been thrust upon us!"

This time the applause was thunderous, followed by a scream. At first Ettore thought the shriek was one of wild abandon, approval for the new direction of the organization, but then another followed, and he saw Stefan go rigid. When Ettore spun to look, he noticed, all throughout the courtyard, men and women throwing off their masks and clashing with their neighbors, stabbing with knives or staving off attacks with bare hands. There was movement to his left, and he spun again to see a burly red-haired man, no longer masked, step out of the front row and lunge at Stefan with a long knife. The German officer twisted to the side to avoid the attack, at the same time snatching his attacker's wrist. As the red-haired man fought to free himself, Stefan stuck his left hand into his double-breasted over-coat, whipped out a pistol, and shot the man point-blank in the side of the head.

At the sound, the chaos enveloping the grounds of the mansion seemed to stall, as if the gunshot had stunned the crowd into sub-mission. As quick as a heartbeat, the fight resumed, and this time pistols appeared alongside knives and fists. Most of the masks were gone, revealing men and women of all races clashing with no appar-ent order. All around Ettore, blood smeared the freshly fallen snow, and he stumbled away, horrified by the violence.

A bullet whizzed right by Ettore's head, and Stefan grabbed him by the arm, his eyes gleaming brighter than Ettore had ever seen them. Where Ettore would have expected to see fear or even shock reflected on the German's face, he saw instead a feverish, wild, almost feral excitement.

"Come!" Stefan said, pulling Ettore along as he raced toward one of the domed stone huts, turning to shoot over his shoulder. Stefan ran behind the hut to pull open a door as two bullets thunked into the wood. Multiple voices called out Stefan's name as he ushered Ettore inside, closed the door, and threw an iron bar over the latch.

Inside the domed structure, a stairwell descended into dark-ness. Still holding the gun, Stefan pulled a flashlight out of his coat and bounded down the stairs. Ettore followed on his heels. Behind them, someone pounded against the door, and Ettore heard a rend-ing sound, as if someone was using an ax to get through.

"Where are we going?" Ettore managed to say. He felt as if he might be sick. "What happened?"

"We've been betrayed! I confess I didn't think they had it in them. Can you believe they attacked with knives before they drew their pistols? They still think we're playing by the same rules." Stefan threw back his head and laughed as they descended to a concrete underground tunnel.

Ettore could not imagine how anyone could laugh in such a situation. "What rules?"

"All bets are off, though I'll wager they'll honor sacred ground. In fact, I'm staking our lives on it."

A resounding thud came from above, as if the door had fallen. Voices poured into the stairwell behind them.

"They're coming!" Ettore said.

"Of course they are," Stefan said as they raced down the escape route. Though Ettore had no idea what the German was talking about, and could not see his face in the darkness, he had the strange feeling that Stefan was grinning.

The nightmare refused to end. Ettore lost track of time, but not long after they descended into the tunnel, some of the longest minutes of his life, their route dead-ended at a concrete wall. Thinking they were trapped, pure terror welled up inside him until Stefan reached up to pull on an iron ring embedded in the ceiling. As multiple boots pounded the floor behind them, Stefan lowered a trapdoor, jumped to grab the lip of the circular opening, and pulled himself through. He helped Ettore up before replacing the cover, which merged seamlessly with the rougher concrete floor of their new environs.

"Unfortunately," Stefan said, "there's no lock."

They had emerged into an underground chamber with no visible end. Wide concentric archways supported by brick pillars extended into the darkness, as if they had climbed into the middle of a vast underground cathedral.

Puddles of water slicked the floor. The air was cold and damp and fetid. Ettore saw a rat scuttle away from the light and said, "Where are we?"

"The cisterns. Hurry, now. Would you like my coat?"

"I'm fine," Ettore said, though he felt ridiculous racing around in a robe, and his blistered feet were aching. But those people were still behind them. He was too scared to take the time to change clothes.

Without pausing to get his bearings, Stefan raced through the archways to a set of steps that paralleled a sloping embankment. As they bounded up the stairs, a shout echoed through the cistern, and Ettore looked back to see two men and two women brandishing pistols near the trapdoor. They were waving flashlights in the gloom, searching for their prey. One of them noticed Ettore halfway up the steps.

"Stefan!" Ettore croaked. "Behind us."

Stefan turned to fire at their pursuers as he fumbled to extract a key from his coat. A blond woman in a green coat returned fire with a gun that shot bullets at a rapid-fire pace, terrifying Ettore.

"Automatic pistol," Stefan said grimly, pulling him up the steps.

They had ascended high enough that a wall now protected them from gunfire. They continued racing up the steps until they reached a door. Stefan rushed to fit the key into the lock, trying to escape before they were caught with no protection.

The footsteps behind them drew closer, echoing in the cistern.

"Hurry!" Ettore cried, backing into the wall.

At last the lock clicked open. Stefan threw the door open and burst outside, Ettore right behind him.

"Where to?" Ettore asked, gasping for air. "How far must we go?"

"Not far."

"Has someone called the police?"

"We never involve the authorities. Now save your breath."

Ettore knew he was slowing the German down. Ettore almost never exercised, and his legs felt as if they had weights attached. Fear coursed through him like an electric shock, and he wasn't sure how much longer he could last. *Oh God, how I wish for this night to end.*

They had surfaced in a courtyard with a view of spires and stately brick walls. When Ettore glanced over his shoulder, he saw that the door through which they had exited was one of many along the side of a hulking granite building. Perhaps they had surfaced inside the grounds of one of the palaces in the city center.

They cleared the courtyard and entered a wooded green space dusted in snow. Stefan shoved Ettore against a tree, put a finger to his lips, and took aim. As the first pursuer burst through the same door on the side of the building, Stefan fired and hit a woman in the chest.

Stefan tugged at Ettore's shirt. "That won't slow them for long."

After winding through a maze of buildings and cobblestone courtyards riddled with hedges and fountains, they exited on a street that ran alongside a canal. Above them, Ettore saw a spiral ivory tower supported by a pair of dragons, jutting above the city like a curling unicorn's horn. They fled across an icy footbridge, into a plaza surrounded by lanterns glowing atop stone pillars. A bullet thunked into a wall beside them, causing Stefan to hunch as he ran.

The German shoved Ettore down a colonnaded brick walkway. Ettore thought they might have ducked into the palace again. He had no idea. It was all he could do to stay on his feet. "Why don't they use the automatic gun?" he managed to gasp.

"They might," Stefan said, "if they have a clear shot. But the survival of us all depends on staying in the shadows. No one must know we exist."

"But the gunfire at the house—won't it attract attention?"

"Many rules were just broken. The safe house will be moved, our influence in high places strained to corral the damage. But make no mistake, Ettore—after tonight, everything has changed."

They followed the walkway through an arched opening in a wall and into another green space fronting a squat red-brick building with cathedral windows.

"We've arrived," Stefan said. "Hurry now."

"Is this a church?"

"It's a library."

They dashed toward the ivy-covered entrance of the building. Instead of using the main door, Stefan veered around the corner to an inconspicuous side door.

"I don't hear anyone," Ettore said, glancing back as Stefan extracted another key.

"By now, they know where we're headed," Stefan said. "The question is whether they'll break our oldest law and follow us inside. If they don't, we'll wait until morning to exit, or until reinforcements arrive."

"And if they do?"

Stefan opened the door, exposing a lightless interior that secreted the musty smell of old books. "Then we see who has the better aim."

Alexandria

— 19 —

Late that night, after the conversation with her father, Andie grabbed a lamb shawarma and a piece of pistachio baklava from a walk-up window, then holed up at a pension ten blocks behind the Eastern Harbour. She grimaced when she opened the door to her room and saw a giant orange cockroach scuttling beneath a floorboard. But the sheets were crisp and white, the bathroom spotless, and the ambient light from the harbor gave her a sense of connection to the world as she peered out of the sixth-floor window.

The flimsy lock on the door made her nervous, so she shoved an armchair in front of it. After a hot shower to wash away the grime, she flinched as she wrapped herself in a towel and stared into the bathroom mirror, dreading another vision. Even without her strange affliction, she always found looking at her own reflection a disorienting thing, almost an out-of-body experience. As if the doppelganger of her reflection was another creature entirely, an entangled soul summoned to the glass by her gaze.

Nothing happened, and she took a moment to examine her drawn features. There was no doubt she had her father's green eyes, strong chin, smattering of freckles, and unruly cowlicks. While she did not have her mother's ethereal beauty, it was impossible not to see the resemblance in the long face and aquiline nose. She was their child, all right.

So why did you leave us, Mom? Where did you go? What happened to you all those years ago? Why did Dr. Corwin have a photo of us in some strange city?

The divots beneath Andie's collarbone were even more hollow than usual. She did a half-turn and regarded the sixteen stars of the Andromeda constellation that hovered between her shoulder blades. At times she regretted tattooing a symbol of her own name on her back, but mostly it made her feel more connected to the universe. And, if she were honest with herself, it ensured she never forgot both the memory and betrayal of her mother, a legacy she wished were different but knew she could never change.

Andromeda. In Greek mythology, the name belonged to the daughter of Cassiopeia and Cepheus, king and queen of Aethiopia. Cassiopeia had drawn the wrath of Poseidon by boasting that her daughter's beauty surpassed even the Nereids', his beloved sea nymphs. In response, the angry god had unleashed a monster that threatened to destroy the kingdom. Andromeda's parents chained her to a rock by the sea in an attempt to appease Poseidon, offering her up as a sacrifice to the beast.

The Greeks used the name Aethiopia to refer to the known parts of Africa at the time, including the Upper Nile region. With a little shiver, Andie thought about how, right that very moment, in a run-down hotel in modern Alexandria, she was standing in the homeland of her mythological namesake.

A daughter served up as a sacrifice. Some legacy.

After considering the liter of bottled water she had picked up at a corner shop, Andie cracked a can of Sakara Gold lager she found in the minifridge. *God, I need a drink.*

She sat on the bed with her back against the headboard and debated going to Cairo. It was less than three hours by car. Yet what would she do once she got there? Walk into the desert and try to sneak inside the caverns beneath the Sphinx? She supposed she could do some research and come up with a better plan, but that could take days. Before she went that route, she wanted to try something else.

Andie did not think much of the Hall of Records theory. It bore little historical weight, and smacked of amateur science. Yet if it related to the Star Phone puzzle in some way, she had to play the game.

But she didn't have to play it by herself—and she knew someone who specialized in conspiracy theories. *That irrational guide I was looking for.*

She exhaled and set her burner phone in her lap. So far, Cal Miller had proven trustworthy and helped her stay alive. Trusting anyone was hard for Andie, especially on the run, and with someone she had never met in person.

What if someone online was impersonating Cal? What if it was a setup or an elaborate con?

Yet if that were the case, wouldn't someone have caught up with her by now?

Weighing all the angles, she decided it was better to make contact. She wished she knew how hard it was to track a burner. She imagined it was pretty damn difficult, especially if the trackers didn't know in which country she had bought it. Even if they did know, they would have to threaten someone inside the carrier.

Unfortunately, she had great faith in her enemy's ability to accomplish that task.

So be it. She decided to take the risk. After logging into Twitch, she sent Cal a message and received a response from Rhodies4ever351! within minutes.

Good morning, or afternoon, or evening. Did you get where you wanted to go?

I did. Thank you for your help. It was invaluable.

You're welcome, A.R.

Andie jumped off the bed, clutching the phone as she stared down at her own initials. *He knows who I am.* Chills flowed through her, and a million thoughts dashed through her mind. Before she could decide how to respond, another message appeared.

It wasn't very hard to figure out. Puck described you, and I made a few calls. Seems a certain Prof's mentee hasn't been seen since his murder. Your secret's safe with me, I promise. I assume they already know who you are too.

She supposed he had a point. It was more the shock of having her identity outed before she was ready, after days in hiding. She chewed on her thumbnail and decided to play it cool.

I could use your help with something.

Of course. Though I'm worried about continuing this line of communication.

Me too.

Where does that leave us?

I don't know.

You should know I've decided to leave LA.

To go where?

Dunno. But I've been thinking. The only real place I want to go is where I can further my investigation. And if my guess is correct, then that might be wherever it is you are.

Andie kept pacing, gnawing harder on her nail. It was not that she hadn't considered this option. It was just that, again, it hadn't been staring her in the face.

He typed some more.

Since these people are trying to silence us both, I thought it might behoove us to join forces.

She ran a hand though her hair, still wet from the shower, then clutched the back of her neck. Despite her guarded nature, and despite the grave price of guessing wrong, her instincts told her she could trust this guy.

They also told her that if she kept plowing ahead on her own, she might be dead before the end of the week.

Cal was a former investigative journalist. He could be a helpful ally, something she desperately needed. She began typing.

I've found another piece to the puzzle. But still missing some.

What puzzle? Can I help?

Have you ever heard of the H*ll of R*c*rds?

It took him a moment to respond. As in, lost knowledge of the ancients? Africa? Up denial?

That's the one.

Why Mercuri, I didn't realize you were a fan of my show.

So is it real?

You don't mince words, do you? The legend is real, that's for sure. Pliny mentioned a hidden cavity beneath the Sphinx over 2,000 years ago.

Andie frowned. I read about the excavations. Not that impressed.

Those tunnels and shafts are authentic, and the government has been weirdly cagey about it. Why close it off? Also, too many reputable experts have questioned the weathering and watermarks around the Sphinx to discount out of hand theories of a far older origin than is commonly believed. We're talking 10 to 15,000 years. I do believe there's more than meets the eye, but that Edgar Cayce nonsense is for amateurs.

Then what isn't?

Oh God, there are a zillion theories out there, from all the usual suspects. Prediluvian civs to the aliens. Some think the hall is one of dozens found in ancient sites around the world, from Tibet to Machu Picchu, a vast repository of lost knowledge. It sounds sexy but I have my doubts. Contrary to what you might think, I don't believe everything I put on my show. I just don't discount things out of hand. Anyway, right now I'm more concerned with conspiracies that affect my health.

If the hall *was* real, where would you look?

I honestly have no idea. I'll tell you where I wouldn't look: Giza. Far too obvious.

What if I told you I have reason to believe the hall is connected to the Sphinx?

Then I'd tell you that, contrary to popular belief, sphinxes were ubiquitous in ancient Egypt. Are you sure it's *the* Sphinx, and not *a* sphinx?

Andie paced the room. It was a good point, one which she knew from her research was correct.

True. I'll think about it.

Anything else I can help with? Running for my life means I'm kinda short on freelance gigs.

Andie continued to walk back and forth in the tiny space, now rubbing her temples as she thought. She trusted him more and more, and didn't have to feel guilty about endangering him, because he was already a target.

A security breach seemed inevitable if they kept communicating like this, and what did she have to lose?

With a deep breath, hoping she was doing the right thing, she wrote:

Were you serious about your offer?

Me? You? A gin joint in a town somewhere in the world?

Yeah.

Then you bet.

OK. Assumption of the risk, though.

Of course. Want to tell me where u r?

Andie's hands hovered over the keypad for a very long time. If she were wrong or if someone were listening, then she could doom herself by giving away her location. She took her bottom lip between her teeth and told herself she was doing the right thing.

You can already guess the country. HEAX. Let me know when you're here and I'll give you more.

Understood. Be there as soon as I can. If you don't hear from me in a few days . . . then you probably won't.

In the lobby of the pension the next morning, Andie hovered over an Egyptian coffee as thick and sweet as maple syrup, so strong it felt like mainlining a shot of adrenaline. The door to the outside was propped open, letting in a cool morning breeze before the sun blasted the city.

The lobby, which doubled as a café, had dingy red carpeting and smudged photos of Abu Simbel, Siwa Oasis, and the pyramids displayed on the walls. Halfway through her coffee, a young couple strolled arm in arm down the staircase and took one of the adjoining tables. They spoke French, and Andie eyed them as she asked for the check. Why had they sat so close to her?

The combination of paranoia and caffeine left her shaking with nerves as she grabbed her backpack, left the hotel, and walked hurriedly down the street, glancing over her shoulder every few steps. Though it was too hot for her jacket, she had her hijab in place, along with black jeans and a white T-shirt.

The clue to her location she had given Cal, HEAX, was the International Civil Aviation Organization symbol for El Nouzha, Alexandria's other principal airport. As opposed to the more familiar IATA codes—used for reservations and baggage tags—ICAO codes were simply a different standardized form of international airport recognition. Just another layer to throw her pursuers off, should anyone be scanning the internet.

Even if Cal had jumped on a flight last night, she figured she had at least a full day to figure out where to rendezvous before he arrived.

If he arrived.

Her next port of call was the Alexandria National Museum, which her research and the hotel receptionist informed her was the best source of information on the city's history.

The museum was a ten-block walk due east from her hotel, about a mile south of the library. Within minutes, the facade she recognized from a flyer in the lobby came into view: a three-story white Italianate mansion plopped like a lost pearl amid a sea of dilapidated apartment blocks. The gated compound included a garden with a handful of Egyptian sculptures scattered on the lawn, as if left outside after a frat party.

She climbed the curved staircase that led to the entrance,

bought a ticket, and found herself in a foyer with gray marble columns. According to her information booklet, the museum was a restored palace focusing on the history of Alexandria from antiquity to modern times.

Though Egypt's pharaonic era predated the city—Alexander the Great laid the groundwork around 330 BCE—Andie began her tour by heading downstairs, to the exhibits from the time of the god-kings. Dark-blue walls symbolized the journey to the afterlife, and the pursed lips and curved eyes of an eerie sandstone bust of Akhenaten, husband of Nefertiti and probable father of Tutankhamen, drew her eye as she wandered the floor. After finding nothing of interest among the wealth of artifacts, as well as no sign of life from the Star Phone, she headed down another staircase to a chilly subterranean chamber, where a statue of the jackal god, Anubis, lorded over two painted sarcophagi. On another day, she would have lingered over the exhibits, but she had come with a purpose, and the secluded basement made her nervous.

Back on the ground floor, working her way through the centuries, she turned a corner and came face-to-face with a diorite sphinx that stopped her in her tracks. Excited, she pointed the Star Phone at it, circling to hit it from every angle, but nothing affected the device. She also noticed an exhibit on the ruins of the Serapeum, which included a photo of two huge sphinxes right inside the city. Remembering that the Serapeum might have housed a portion of the library's collection, she decided that would be her next destination, if nothing else turned up.

She continued browsing the impressive collection of Greco-Roman relics, then continued upstairs to the Coptic, Islamic, and modern eras. Her frustration grew until, just past a series of black-and-white photos of nineteenth-century Alexandria, she found an exhibit highlighting the discovery of the Catacombs of Kom el-Shoqafa in 1900, a trilevel funerary site considered one of the wonders of the medieval world.

The builders of the catacombs had tunneled through a hundred feet of solid rock in the second century AD to construct the underground complex, and the placard's description caused a tingle of excitement to spread through her.

> The catacombs are riddled with loculi—cavities in the stone walls reserved for family burials—and include a chamber called a triclinium, where relatives could sit on stone couches and enjoy refreshments while paying respects to the dead. Some theorize the subterranean galleries might have given rise to the apocryphal legend of the Hall of Records, perhaps as a metaphorical veneration of ancestral knowledge that persists through the centuries and into the afterlife.

The Star Phone revealed no further secrets, but Andie studied the photos and the text of the exhibit for a long time, thinking about how much the phrasing of the placard imitated the themes of her search.

Knowledge of the ancients persisting through time.

The collective wisdom of planet Earth, lost and suppressed until only myth remains.

After finishing her tour, Andie left the museum deep in thought, intrigued by the Serapeum but debating whether to visit the catacombs first. So far, the Star Phone had illuminated two sphinxes, and the only connection to the Hall of Records was her own interpretation of the message. Yet something about it rang true. Dr. Corwin loved patterns and meanings hidden beneath the surface, and had always approached his work on the cosmos as if it were all one grand puzzle to be solved. He used to love telling Andie over coffee about the veiled themes and clues embedded in his lectures, and even his scientific papers.

She sat on a bench in the garden and pulled out her prepaid phone. According to Google Maps, the catacombs were nearly an hour's walk to the southwest, still in the thick of the city, not far from the ruins of the Serapeum. Instead of choosing between the two ancient sites, she decided to walk over to the library to see if its col-lection on either of the locations contained another clue.

The library was nearby. Though the day was growing late, the evening sun caused lines of sweat to trickle down her back. She loos-ened the hijab as she walked. The route took her past the El-Nabih cistern ruins, through a busy commercial section full of cafés and bookstores that ran alongside the university, and then straight onto the grounds of the library. Just as she was about to cross the court-yard leading to the entrance, she glanced up at the elevated walk-way and froze when she saw a very tall woman with ebony skin and chiseled features talking on her cell phone. The woman was staring down at the entrance as if keeping an eye out for someone.

It was the same woman from London. Zawadi. There was no doubt in Andie's mind.

Her heart hammering against her chest, Andie ducked behind a concrete pillar and debated what to do. How had they found her? Could it possibly be a coincidence?

Wishful thinking.

She risked another glance and saw Zawadi hurrying down the walkway with her long stride. After she disappeared inside the building, Andie took the opening. She darted back into the street and aimed for the largest crowd of people she could find. After slowing to a fast walk, she made two more turns and jumped into a cab parked outside a hotel. The driver was a middle-aged man with glasses perched on a thin nose, a bead of moisture on his top lip, and a red-and-white checkered keffiyeh draped loosely around his neck.

"Are you free?" she asked the driver.

"Yes, please. Your destination?"

Andie paused for a beat, then went with her gut. "The Catacombs of Kom el-Shoqafa."

"You are sure? We may not arrive before the close."

"It's okay. Do your best."

He darted into the traffic, then apologized over and over as they hit a series of roadblocks caused by congestion. The entire way,

Andie sat low in the seat and kept a constant eye out for signs of pursuit. She did not think Zawadi had noticed her, but her presence in the city caused Andie's pulse to quicken and a lump of dread to settle deep in her chest.

A sidewalk market that had spilled into the street cut off their route. Everything from hubcaps to used clothing to goat heads hung from wires stretched between stalls in the hot sun. The driver cursed and veered into a lane so narrow Andie thought the car would scrape the sides of the flimsy wooden shacks lining the road, built into the sides of concrete towers in various stages of ruin. The slum only worsened as they drove through. Andie swallowed at the families living in caves scooped out of sections of collapsed buildings, mothers drying clothes on piles of rubble as their children clambered atop mounds of garbage.

After they cleared the slums, the city opened up, and soon they were climbing a dusty hill ringed by midrise concrete apartments with men sitting at tables out front smoking shisha. At the apex of the hill was a courtyard with low Roman columns denoting the entrance to the catacombs.

Fifteen minutes until closing time. Andie asked the driver to wait, but he apologized yet again and said he had to rush to the airport. With a final nervous glance behind her, and no easy escape route in case someone had followed, she walked through the iron entrance gate. A bored guard waved her in. Half a dozen tourists were still milling about, and a feral cat slunk beside her as she made her way across the sunbaked courtyard to a flat-topped mausoleum.

Wondering where to find the ticket booth, she noticed a sign in front of the entrance to the catacombs. She drew closer and read the English translation.

CLOSED FOR REPAIR

Great. There was no telling how long that would take. A day, a week, a month? She asked the guard, but he claimed to have no idea. Whatever the duration, it was time that Andie didn't have.

After taking a few steps away from the mausoleum, she took out the Star Phone. As soon as she focused the lens on the pyramidal piece of stone adorning the top of the doorway, the device activated, conjuring a familiar three-dimensional image.

Another sphinx, looming at the entrance to the catacombs.

Guarding another secret.

20

In the wealthy suburb of Kafr Abdou, known for its shady palm-lined boulevards and quiet cafés, a world apart from the grime and chaos of the urban sprawl ringing Alexandria, Omer lowered his binoculars from his perch atop a rooftop patio.

A satisfied smile lifted the corners of his lips. Under a false alias—procured on the city's black market as soon as he arrived—Omer had rented a top-floor penthouse across the street from Allenby Garden. If Omer stood at the very corner of the glass-walled balcony, faced northeast, and trained the binoculars just right, he had a view overlooking the entrance to his former organization's safe house in Alexandria.

Are you listening, Ascendants? Soon you will hear me roar.

Omer entered the penthouse through a set of double French doors, heading straight for the private elevator. The fruits of his eighteen-hour vigil had just ripened. When he arrived in the city, he had found no trace of the target. This did not surprise him. Alexandria was a vast metropolis of five million people, most of it off the grid, a quagmire of derelict neighborhoods and sprawling bazaars. Entire districts lacked proper street signs, or had not yet been mapped. A nightmare scenario for locating someone who did not wish to be found.

Even if Omer still had access to all his resources, Alexandria existed in a different technological universe from western Europe.

After the Arab Spring, in an attempt to deter terrorism, the Egyptian government had issued edicts to bolster scrutiny of its citizens. Yet the edict was taking time to implement, and would still fall far short of the Big Brother surveillance used in London.

Still, if the target remained in Alexandria long enough, Omer felt confident he could locate her. She was an amateur, a Westerner, and would have limited options. On the other hand, if she came and moved on quickly, he might lose the trail.

Which was why he didn't plan on spinning his wheels to locate the target himself. He might not know Andie's current location, but he knew who wanted to find her, and where *they* were. He would let his former colleagues do his work for him.

As suspected, they were right behind him. He had just seen Kumal enter the safe house with a travel bag. Omer guessed he would link up with one or more of the agents local to the region, perhaps Ahmed or Mirette. Though not as physically impressive as some of the others, Kumal was intelligent and extremely resourceful, and should not be underestimated.

When he reached the ground floor, Omer nodded to the doorman and stepped into the brutal midday sun. He was already dressed for the mission: wrapped neck to toe in a white *bisht*, a flowing Arab cloak, worn over a *thawb*. A gray keffiyeh covered his head, kept in place by a black *igal* made of goat hair. A typical outfit for a devout local Muslim or a visiting Arab businessman. His attire left only the oval of his face exposed, and even that was recessed within the voluminous keffiyeh, and further concealed by a false beard and sunglasses.

A bisht was also an excellent choice of attire for concealing weapons. Omer took full advantage by bringing two boot knives and a Tariq semiautomatic pistol he had purchased from the same black-market source, a British veteran of the Iraq War, who ran a brothel near the Western Harbour.

Outside, a private driver awaited in a black Citroën that Omer had hired for the week. The Citroën was perfect—nothing too fancy in case they needed to follow someone on the sly inside the city.

After climbing into the back seat, he ordered the driver to circle the block and park down the street from the safe house. Once in position, Omer waited patiently behind the tinted windows of the Citroën, listening to an international news podcast as he kept a sharp eye on the door.

Less than an hour later, Kumal emerged wearing dark slacks, a linen shirt, and a russet Sikh turban wrapped around his head. He stepped into a waiting green sedan that wound its way through the neighborhood, then drove along the coast on El-Gaish Road into the heart of the city. Omer's driver did an excellent job of trailing him as they looped onto Suez Canal Road near the Bibliotheca Alexandrina—dangerous territory—and headed south before veering east on Abou Quer. Moments later, the sedan slowed to a stop at the entrance to the Alexandria National Museum, a handsome Italianate mansion that Omer had never visited.

This excited him. He guessed Kumal had tracked the target to this place and wanted to know what she had done, to whom she had spoken, and when she had left. Omer knew she wasn't still inside, because the target would recognize Kumal's face from the V&A Museum, and they would not take her against her will in broad daylight. Not here.

Omer released a small breath. If they had known her exact location, Kumal wouldn't have bothered to stop at the museum. The window of opportunity was still open. Omer had no idea why the target had come to Alexandria or where she had gone, but he felt confident that if she had not left the city, his former colleagues would hunt her down within days, if not hours.

And then Omer, like a vulture circling above a fight to the death on the savanna, would swoop in to collect his prize.

21

Two miles north of the Catacombs of Kom el-Shoqafa, just south of the bow curve of the Eastern Harbour, the battered remnants of El-Tahrir Square's grandiose architecture devolved into Alexandria's main souk district, a human beehive of buyers and sellers shouting, haggling, and cajoling over the price of every foodstuff and household good imaginable. Andie experienced sensory overload as she burrowed into the nest of backstreets and alleyways, inhaling the aromas of exotic spices and sizzling animal fat, incense and shisha. The more pleasant smells were undercut by cat urine and stinking offal and the unwelcome perfume of thousands of busy people rubbing shoulders in a confined space during the heat of the afternoon.

Feeling claustrophobic, longing for the warm sea breeze that beckoned a few blocks to the north, Andie pressed through the bazaar, aiming for the destination she had scouted that morning— right after she woke up and saw the message from Cal that he had arrived in the city.

The previous day, standing at the entrance to the catacombs, Andie had decided not to attempt to enter the ruins alone at night. Not until she read up on them and knew what she was getting into. Not with the sighting of Zawadi less than an hour prior.

Just before she had fallen asleep, lying in bed wondering if her fear of going in alone had affected her decision, she answered her own question.

Hell, yes, I'm scared. What kind of lunatic wouldn't be?

It was 5 p.m. She had asked Cal to meet her at six, when the crush of humanity in the souk would be at its peak. The souk was not a tourist bazaar, catering to cruise ships or wealthy Europeans. The streets and stalls were packed with local Egyptians going about their daily business. After Cal had described his clothing—jeans and a gray Clippers T-shirt with a blue logo—it had given her the idea to meet him in the souk. She could spot him from a block away, and if things went south, she thought her hijab would garner more sympathy from the crowd than Cal's Western attire. Even if not, she preferred the chaos of the bazaar to a more isolated location. If she didn't like the vibe, she could disappear before he saw her.

For the meeting spot, she had given him the name of a silversmith at the end of a covered lane in Zinqat As Sittat, "the Alley of the Women." Yet instead of waiting at the silversmith, she was standing outside the entrance to a tea shop halfway down the dead-end lane, waiting for Cal to show.

Throngs of women, some veiled and some not, flowed into and out of the stalls and shops lining the alley. There were dressmakers, bakeries, herbalists, spice vendors, florists. Right on cue, two minutes after six, Andie saw a man fitting Cal's description appear at the entrance to the alley, dressed as promised. He was taller than she had expected, standing half a foot above most of the crowd and drawing stares.

She stepped behind a pair of potted dwarf palms as he passed, disguising her presence as she watched for signs of anyone following him. It had not escaped her that Zawadi had appeared soon after Andie had revealed her presence to Cal.

Then again, they had found her in London even more quickly. And if Cal had wanted her harmed, she asked herself for the thousandth time, why help her escape? Why supply her with a passport?

You've been through this already, Andie. You've made your decision.

Own it. You have to trust someone, despite Dr. Corwin's warning.

After ten minutes passed with no sign of trouble, she walked down to the silversmith, found Cal examining an engraved plate, and tapped him on the shoulder.

"Hi, Doc."

Startled, he turned and took her in, seeking out her eyes inside the hijab. "Aloha, Mercuri. I thought you'd bailed."

She curled a finger. "Come on."

"Where to?" he asked, but she had already slipped back into the crowd.

Once they reached the alcove signaling the entrance to the tea shop, she turned and said, "Care for some refreshments?"

"I was going to insist on some caffeine. I tried to catch a catnap on my flight but couldn't fall asleep."

"Jet-lagged?"

"Confused, a little afraid, stiff from squeezing into a pillbox for eighteen hours. And, yeah, jet-lagged."

The tea shop was built into the vestibule of an old high-ceilinged arcade. If restored, the scuffed tile floor and ivory marble walls would have been stunning. Another two archways, each supported by cerulean pillars decorated with gold-leaf edging, connected to hallways leading to different parts of the souk. Escape routes that Andie had sourced ahead of time.

They both ordered coffee served in tiny glass cups, set on saucers with a sugar cookie on the side. Groups of people were crowded around small round tables spaced throughout the café. As they took a seat near the middle, Andie took a better look at her companion. She had seen photos of him online, but he was older and better-looking in person. Not her speed at all: she didn't go for the glib, life-is-basically-easy, former-jock type that his first impression exuded. Yet at least she could relate to the cynicism lurking behind his approachable blue eyes, and the way he canvassed the crowd with suspicion. Time would tell whether those traits belonged to him or to the situation.

"Well," he said, after a greedy sip of coffee, "this is a bit awkward. I've met sources under strange conditions before, but this is a first."

"I'd hope so."

"I don't know where to start. Maybe with 'Congratulations on staying alive'?"

Andie looked him in the eye. "You should know that yesterday, soon after we talked, I saw one of the people who's after me. A woman who . . . killed someone in London."

His eyebrows lifted. "Here in Alexandria?"

"That's right."

"Killed who?"

"Another professor. A friend of Dr. Corwin's. I wanted to see if he knew anything useful, and—" She expelled a long breath and looked down.

"You're afraid it got him murdered."

She nodded.

"You can't let yourself go there."

"Why not?" she said, eyes flashing. "I made the choice to put him in danger." And then, more quietly: "Though I think he might have already been involved in some way."

"What do you mean?"

Instead of answering, she pressed her lips together and gave him a long stare. "I think I'd like you to go first."

He cocked his head. "Still don't trust me?"

"I just met you."

"Hey, it's fine. I don't trust people either. Though I gotta tell you, if I had nefarious intentions, I would have taken a better flight."

"Maybe. Maybe not."

"Tough crowd," he said, and hovered over his coffee for a moment. When he looked up, he said, "You said this person arrived just after we talked. You're wondering if I had anything to do with that, aren't you?"

"Trust me when I say I'm not taking *anything* for granted."

"Hey, unbridled suspicion is a trait near and dear to my heart."

He tapped his fingers on the table. "Have you changed hotel rooms in the city?"

"No."

"Then they didn't trace our call or they'd have you already. What about your phone? Same one as in London?"

"I bought a new one at the airport when I landed."

"Good. So it's probably not a trace on your end . . . Have you made any other calls? Or contacted anyone besides me?"

She hesitated. "Just once."

"Who?"

"It doesn't matter."

"It might, if it's someone you know well."

After a moment, she said quietly, "It was."

"Were you in your hotel?"

"I was on the street."

"That's a relief." He leaned back. "I'm guessing they didn't track *you*, they tracked someone else. They've probably got ears or eyes on everyone you know. Family, close friends, boyfriend."

She swore softly and didn't bother correcting him, horrified and enraged at the thought they might be tapping her father's phone or even watching his house. Thank God she hadn't told him anything useful.

Or had she?

"No more calls to whoever it was, okay?" he said. "Not unless they're secure."

After a hard swallow, Andie looked down at her hands. "Is this really happening? God, I hate these bastards."

"Believe me, I know. Listen, Andie . . . if this is going to work, we're going to have to trust each other. Quickly. I appreciate this meeting spot you scouted, but I'm starving and could use something a little stronger to drink. Have you eaten?"

"Not since breakfast."

"What do you say to finding someplace a little more private and talking over dinner? I mean really talking. I'll start, and I promise I won't hold back. To be honest, I've got nothing left to lose."

"Except your life."

"I don't have much of one left. Oh, and you might have to pick up the tab, unless you want to wait for me to wash dishes. After the flight, I'm kinda flat broke."

She finished her coffee and set down the empty cup, then searched his eyes and realized that while they might be two very different people who under normal circumstances would never have entered each other's orbits, and who still might not turn out to be friends, there was an earnestness about him, as well as a quiet desperation beneath the self-assured surface, that made her want to trust him.

"Dinner sounds good," she said. "My treat."

They decided to walk over to the harbor and eat in one of the tourist restaurants so they would not stand out. Despite the kitschy sign and a lobby full of replica swordfish, the place they chose, a seafood joint on the ground floor of an art nouveau apartment building, had a classy vibe and a cozy interior invisible from the street. The waiter apologized as he led them to a booth wedged into the corner, half hidden by an aquarium, but they relished the privacy.

"Would you care for the beverage list? A carafe of wine?"

"Just a glass of house red," Andie said, with a glance at Cal. "Unless you want to share a carafe?"

"My heart's set on a cold beer."

The waiter returned with their drinks and an icebox on wheels displaying the fresh catch. After they ordered, lingering over the drinks, Cal took her all the way back to his investigation into PanSphere's black-site lab, the mysterious disappearance of his source, and his fall from grace. She listened in shock as he told her about finding the connection to the Leap Year Society and his own dossier on Elias Holt's computer, and the attempted abduction at the planetarium.

"I'd call you crazy," Andie said, "if my story wasn't just as disturbing."

Cal raised his glass. "Misery loves company."

The waiter returned with a bowl of olives and a grilled shrimp appetizer arranged on a wooden platter. Andie stabbed a piece of shrimp as she thought about his story. "I assume you've researched the Leap Year Society?"

"It's like trying to peer inside a black hole. The evidence tells me it's there . . . but I've got no idea what's inside. Who the hell are these people? How can anyone be so good at staying off the radar? Dane— my techie friend—thinks they have a team of people scouring the internet to remove any references that pop up. But there's got to be a record somewhere in the world, in some kind of medium. If it's old-school, hidden in some dusty crypt or an abandoned Soviet building, then even better. I'm an old-school kind of guy."

"The Leap Year Society was mentioned in Dr. Corwin's journal," Andie said. "I'm sure it was their symbol I saw in the V&A, and it matches what you saw on Elias's computer. What I can't figure out is if Dr. Corwin was part of the club, then why was he murdered? Did he have a change of heart? Did he want to keep the Enneagon for himself? Was he trying to protect someone?"

"Whoa, there, Tonto. V&A? And what the hell is an Enneagon? You're getting ahead of me."

"Yeah. I suppose I should catch you up."

"It'd be helpful."

Over the delicious main course, a whole fish battered lightly in bran, Andie told him the entire incredible narrative, all the way up to her visit to the closed catacombs. Getting it off her chest made her feel less like she was going insane. The only things she held back were her visions and the photo of her mother. She did show him the ink drawings, and told him about her visit to the bookshop, because she knew they related to the puzzle in some way.

Cal's eyes grew wider and wider. "And I thought I had a good story. If I hadn't seen what I've seen . . . I guess my instincts were spot-on."

"About what?"

"About using my last dollar to fly halfway across the world for someone I've never met."

"Just chasing a lead, huh?"

He sat back.

"Are you going to be on *my* side," she said, "or the story's? Since lives are at stake, I'd rather know at the beginning."

"Wow. I thought I wasn't a trusting person." After a long swallow of beer, he set his elbows on the table and leaned forward again. "Listen. I'll admit I came here, first and foremost, to save my own skin. Not that zI don't want to help you—but like you said, we just met. I get the sense you value someone who's a straight shooter, so I promise I will be. And if you're asking me whether I'm an ends-justifies-the-means type of guy . . . well, no, I'm not. But do you want to hear me say that, or would you rather see it for yourself?"

"Fair enough. Though it does help to hear it."

"Let me know, and I'll shout it whenever you want."

The waiter arrived to clear the plates. They passed on dessert but ordered coffee. Once they were alone again, Cal said, "So you think this Star Phone is some kind of puzzle that leads to the Enneagon? What kind of puzzle?"

"I don't know."

"Can I see it?"

With a glance around the restaurant, she took the device out of her pocket and handed it to him. He tapped and probed the hard shell, then turned it on and studied the image of the scroll and the alphanumeric code that had led Andie to Egypt.

"How very interesting," he said. "I'd love to see the guts of this thing."

"Me too."

He rubbed the stubble on his chin as he handed it back. "It's got that feel of importance to it. Who makes something like this? This thing and the Enneagon . . . what if it all connects back to my original story in some way?" He sat back, kneading his hands atop the table with a faraway, covetous look in his eyes. "What the hell have we stumbled into?"

"I don't know, but my first priority is finding out whether Dr. Corwin is alive. I wish your friend could look at the Star Phone and try to trace the message."

"He might be able to, but we'd have to go to him. And I don't want to put him in danger."

Andie had thought about it before, searching out a similar expert. Time and opportunity, as well as trust, were the problems. She also doubted whether someone unfamiliar with the device, maybe anyone besides Dr. Corwin or Lars Friedman, could hack it.

"I need to tell you something else," he said. "I looked into Quasar Labs."

She sat up. "And?"

"The buck doesn't stop there. After a hell of a lot of digging, I found a parent company. A holding shell. It started to remind me of the layers I waded through to find the black-site lab."

"Who owns Quasar?"

"I haven't gotten that far. But I found a sister company called Plasmek, located in Bangalore and connected to the same international tax haven."

"And? What'd you find?"

"Plasmek's focus is researching speculative phenomena in the electromagnetism realm, such as the Hutchison effect."

"I'm sorry—the what?"

"There's a Canadian inventor—this Hutchison guy—who claims to have discovered new properties of metals while trying to re-create Tesla's experiments. Objects that spontaneously fracture, jellify, defy gravity, and float to the ceiling. Weird stuff to say the least."

Andie frowned. "Is he still alive? Is there any truth to it?"

"Yes, and I don't know. As far as I can tell, they're not working with him, just co-opting his research. They've experimented with Tesla coils and a Van de Graaff generator—"

"Both real," she interrupted.

"—to create some kind of special electromagnetic current, possibly tapping an unknown energy source that's apparently causing these effects."

Andie frowned. "There are far more states of exotic matter in existence than people realize, but I'd have to know more. It sounds pretty out-there."

"I only mentioned that one because I didn't understand the others. But quantum physics sounds pretty far-out-there too. Or how babies are made, for that matter."

Andie waved a hand. "You're dissembling. I could toss around all kinds of unbelievable facts about science. But they'd be proven ones, from reputable sources."

"Reputable sources? Like, say, the *Journal of Applied Physics*?"

"Um, yeah, that would do."

He leaned over, dug into his backpack, and removed a stack of paper bound with a metal clip. Curious, she took the stack of paper, which was an article from a recent edition of the *Journal of Applied Physics*. The title of the article was "Electromagnetic Properties of the Great Pyramid: First Multipole Resonances and Energy Concentration."

"What's this?" she said.

"Read for yourself."

She took some time to browse the article, reading enough to glean that scientists had recently discovered that, for unknown reasons, the design of the Great Pyramid at Giza had the effect of scattering electromagnetic waves entering the structure and then collecting them inside the chambers hidden within, as well as in the region beneath the base.

"Okay," she said.

"Okay? An international team of physicists have discovered that a pyramid built five thousand years ago hoards pockets of electromagnetic energy, and all you have to say is 'okay'?"

"Nothing in here says or even suggests the collection of energy was intentional."

Cal stared at her. "As we speak, scientists are trying to re-create these effects on smaller objects, including nanotech devices. We're not talking about some extraordinary design in the natural world we're trying to replicate. This is manmade."

"You do understand that electromagnetic energy is everywhere, all around us, all the time? Sunlight is electromagnetic energy."

"So, what—they got lucky?"

"I'm just saying don't jump to conclusions. Strange things like that happen in science a lot more than you think. Sometimes it takes years or even centuries to understand it. But I grant you, it's odd, especially given everything else going on."

He said, "You've heard of the pyramid light theory?"

"I'm afraid not."

"It so happens that, among the building materials available to the ancient Egyptians—including copper—they chose limestone to cover their pyramids. Limestone is an incredibly good conductor of light at higher frequencies. The ancient Egyptians could have learned this by trial and error, sure. But it's highly curious that they built the Great Pyramids at the exact geographical center of the Earth, because—"

"Land mass increases the emission of electromagnetic radiation," she said. "A fact known to antenna designers worldwide, and which an ancient Egyptian would have no way of knowing."

"Exactly. So why build in that precise spot?"

"I can think of a number of symbolic reasons. Anyway, they would hardly need an entire planet to light up their pyramid."

"Unless they wanted someone to see it from outer space."

"You can't be serious."

"I don't understand all the science, but according to the theory, each of the chambers, shafts, and passages in the Great Pyramid plays an important role in conducting light. Something about emitting free electrons into the ionosphere. Look, I'm not saying aliens built the pyramids. I'm saying what if the designers knew far more about the properties of light and electromagnetism than we think?

What if they were trying to light up the night sky and send a signal to the stars, or gather electromagnetic energy into those chambers just because they could, even if they didn't understand it?"

Light up the night sky.

Cal's words bore an eerie similarity to the conversation Andie remembered with her mother from all those years ago, sitting in the desert as they gazed in wonder at those monolithic structures.

"Why are we talking about this?" she asked.

"When you told me you were in Egypt, my research on Quasar and Plasmek made me think of all those theories I've heard on the pyramids. Granted, most are nonsense. But I did a little research and saw that article in the *Journal of Applied Physics* . . . Didn't you say Professor Rickman speculated that Dr. Corwin might have been trying to connect his device to the body's energy field?"

"I did," she said slowly.

"What if he invented some kind of conductor of electromagnetic energy, just like the pyramids but more sophisticated and on a much smaller scale? And then found a way to connect it to the human body? Maybe he didn't even know what the effects would be for sure until he made it. I dunno, I admit I'm reaching."

"I'll keep an open mind," she said quietly, more disturbed by his speculation than she cared to admit. She had a knee-jerk aversion to pyramid theories, though she had to admit her research into the knowledge lost at Alexandria had made her rethink her opinion of science and progress in the ancient world. "But you have to remember I'm a scientist, Cal. I deal with facts and have very little patience for conspiracy theories or wishful thinking."

"Sometimes you've got to dream a little to reach the facts."

"Maybe you do. But you can also lose the thread and get lost in the labyrinth."

Cal blew out a breath. "All this talk about weird energy, this device everyone's chasing, and those ink drawings some crackpot in London thinks are connected to some *other* place . . . this is getting heavy."

Andie didn't respond, lost in her own uncomfortable thoughts about how her mother, Dr. Corwin, and her own visions might relate to all of this.

Cal fiddled with his empty coffee cup. "I'm sure we've both got a million more questions. But someone's trying to kill us and we need to keep moving. For now, I agree that following the Star Phone might be our best bet to finding the answers we both want. So you think the catacombs is the next step?"

"I do."

"When do you plan to explore them?"

A grim smile lifted the corners of her lips. "How about tonight?"

"Surely it's after hours. And didn't you say they were closed for repairs?"

"Didn't you say you wanted your life back?"

He settled back in the booth, lips compressed, eyeing her for a long moment. "Mercuri," he said finally, "I think I like your style."

Leipzig
——o 1933 o——

On the curb outside his apartment, Ettore stomped his feet to stay warm as he waited to meet Stefan for the first time since the horrific night in Copenhagen.

No one had pursued them into the library that night, and Stefan had walked right out the side door once the sun rose, pistol in hand and a grim, satisfied twist to his lips. A car with two armed guards had retrieved them, and Stefan had said very little on the drive to Ettore's hotel, deep in thought and writing furiously in a notepad. Ettore was set to depart Copenhagen the next day, and Stefan promised to contact him in Leipzig before the end of the week.

True to his word, the day after Ettore returned to Germany, Stefan had sent a man in a belted coat and top hat to hand-deliver a note to Ettore while he was on his way to work. The note informed him—did not request—that Stefan would meet him at 7 a.m. that Saturday outside Ettore's apartment.

Ettore tried to concentrate on polishing his particle theory as he chipped away at various projects with Werner Heisenberg. But thinking of the impending meeting with Stefan had caused Ettore to lose focus. His hope was that the chaos of that awful night would keep the German occupied until Ettore returned to Rome.

While fascinated by aspects of the Leap Year Society, Ettore was traumatized by the violence he had witnessed and the terror of running for his life. He wanted no part of such a dangerous lifestyle. In fact, he had come to the decision never to attend another meeting of the Leap Year Society. All morning, he had tried to work up the courage to tell Stefan.

On the other hand, that ancient glass ball he had seen in the mansion had sparked Ettore's imagination and given him an idea he was excited about. He had no doubt there was *something* hidden down there between the quarks and neutrinos, layers on layers on layers, a cosmic onion that Ettore suspected science had only begun to unpeel. Yet the thought that technology might not progress fast enough for Ettore to uncover better answers in his lifetime depressed him thoroughly. He *had* to know why the quantum world worked as it did, why the numbers aligned with such symmetry and perfection.

Recently, someone had invented a microscope capable of much greater magnification than previously available. Still, Ettore doubted an amplification device would be invented for many generations to come that could reach the world of atoms, not to mention the subatomic realms beneath them.

But what if there was another way to probe the nature of reality? After all, one did not necessarily have to *see* a thing to experience it.

What if, he thought, one could harness the quantum fluctuations that occurred on an ongoing basis within one's own mind?

Ettore revered the work of Nikola Tesla and had studied it closely. What if one could somehow connect the body's own mysterious energy field to those places in between, or even to another dimension?

Inspired by the strange gray world mirrored inside the bauble, an idea had started to form in Ettore's mind: a synthesis of his own particle theories, Tesla's research, and Ettore's belief that something mysterious and unseen lurked at the edges of human experience.

Expecting to take a long walk with Stefan, as was their custom in Leipzig, Ettore was surprised when a black Mercedes pulled to the curb. When Ettore opened the door and stepped into the back, he found Stefan awaiting him in an unusually somber state. The bottoms of the German's eyelids were dark and pendulous as if from lack of sleep, dirt crusted his nails, and his light-blond hair was not as neatly trimmed as usual.

"Good day, Ettore."

"Yes, good day. Is that . . . is that blood on your coat?"

Stefan absently flicked at a splotch of barely dried crimson on his right sleeve. With a shrug, he said, "And how is the institute upon your return?"

"The same as before. Good. And the Society . . . has it survived?"

"The blow they struck was a nasty one, but now that the cancer is uprooted, we will rebuild stronger than ever. Thank you for the concern, but do not worry. *That* war has only begun."

"And what of the other?" Ettore said, with a glance at the Waffen-SS emblem on his friend's shoulder.

"That, too, I'm afraid."

"Will they come after me?"

"They would never destroy a mind such as yours. And we have people in place to dissuade any . . . counter-recruitment . . . attempts."

"What does that mean? You're *watching* me?" When Ettore didn't receive an answer, he swallowed and said, "Where are we going?"

Stefan turned to look out the window as if the weight of the world were on his shoulders. "There is something I wish for you to see."

"Which is?"

"Things have progressed further and faster in my country than I believed possible. It is imperative that we act with clarity, and with great alacrity."

"Can you not speak plainly?"

After a moment, Stefan said, "Do you know what a concentration camp is, Ettore?"

"Is it not a place of detention during conflict?"

The German passed a hand through his hair and spoke very softly. "Whatever you think you know about the capacity of human beings to visit evil on one another, I assure you, you know nothing at all."

Whatever Stefan meant by that cryptic remark, Ettore had the feeling he had been speaking not just to him but to the world in general. When the German failed to elaborate, Ettore repeated his earlier question. "Can you please tell me where we're going?"

"We are driving," Stefan said, "to a town called Dachau."

The trip took much of the day. In the late afternoon they pulled into a pretty little Bavarian town with cobblestone streets winding up to a well-preserved castle atop a hill. Ettore quite enjoyed the scenery and interrupted Stefan's brooding to tell him as much.

"Yes, it's very beautiful," Stefan replied. "A picture-perfect *Heimat.*"

Ettore knew the German word meant "homeland," a term subverted by the Third Reich's nationalist propaganda. "There is a concentration camp here? In this picturesque place?"

"All too often, the deepest darkness is paired with great beauty, just as a thin line separates love from hate, chaos from order. It's as if human beings and nature, maybe the universe itself, cannot exist without polar extremes, and the closer we come to one, the stronger grows the potential for the other."

The driver skirted the town and took a smaller road to the east. After driving through the forest for several miles, the trees broke to reveal a piece of cleared land housing a cluster of low uniform buildings that resembled barracks. An electrified barbed-wire fence surrounded the complex. Watchtowers and guards ringed the perimeter. After a pair of unsmiling armed men in brown uniforms interrogated Stefan, they let him enter, and the Mercedes passed beneath a fanciful curved sign erected over the entrance.

ARBEIT MACHT FREI, the sign read.

Work will set you free.

Stefan gave directions to the driver, then lowered the windows as they drove slowly through the camp. A sharp chemical disinfectant undercut the fresh air. Guards observed every inch of the property, and all around them, prisoners performed a variety of menial tasks: digging a ditch just behind the fence line, cleaning latrines, carrying crates in and out of buildings. The bunkhouses had a flimsy appearance, out of character for the Germans, which made Ettore think they were built for animals, or for someone they did not expect to house for very long. As he stared at the forlorn faces of the prisoners, the gaunt cheeks and shaved heads and hollow eyes that would not lift to meet his own, a sense of foreboding overcame Ettore, and he had the strange feeling the souls of these men had already begun to depart from their bodies. He could almost see the sad pale halo of their essence dissipating into the wintry air.

"This is all I can show you," Stefan said, raising the windows as they completed the circuit. "It was risky for me to bring you at all. But I wanted you to see for yourself, no matter the lies that will be told in the newspaper. I'm afraid this is only the beginning."

"The beginning of what? Why would they lie? Is this not a prison like any other, if perhaps a bit grimmer?"

Stefan stared out the window for some time before speaking. "Just after our return from Copenhagen, I met with a man named Heinrich Himmler." At the mention of this name, Stefan gave a visible shudder, which surprised Ettore. He had seen nothing, not even an assassination attempt and a nighttime flight though Copenhagen while pursued by armed gunmen, that had rattled the daring German.

"There are factions within the Nazis even more extreme than the others," Stefan said. "Men who do not see other men as human beings. A great darkness is coming, Ettore. Worse than you or anyone can possibly imagine. If my superiors have their way—and I do not see who will stop them—men, women, and children will be slaughtered like sheep at these places, and worse."

"What is worse than death?" Ettore muttered, lowering his eyes at the thought of such barbarism.

"Death is a welcome relief to those undergoing great suffering. I am speaking of torture, mass starvation, sterilization, medical experiments on children—"

"*Children?*"

"A man is whispering in Himmler's ear, a devil who committed horrific atrocities during the war. Injecting prisoners with neurotoxins, slaughtering women and babies with bayonets, burning entire villages alive. I have met this man myself. He recounted a tale to Himmler, right in front of me, of a campaign on the Eastern Front, where he made the decision, in order to alleviate the filthy state of his troops and raise their morale, to carve up their female prisoners and boil their fat to make soap."

Ettore felt as if he might be sick. "Good God," he whispered.

"I myself . . . I myself saw a gypsy child gassed to death by these men in an underground facility. As an experiment for future 'exterminations,' as they called it. While I speak the truth, I admit I am telling you this to shock you. You need to be shocked. Unimaginable horrors are coming, and we damn ourselves if we do nothing and let them happen. I had a feeling, after the night of your initiation in Copenhagen, that your resolve to aid the Society might have wavered."

The abrupt change in topic caught Ettore off guard. Now he understood the true purpose of the visit to Dachau. It was as if Stefan had read Ettore's mind and taken steps to reclaim him.

"You're our great hope, Ettore. We must develop a weapon with sufficient power to combat the coming evil."

"I thought you wished for me to help you find the Fold?"

"We believe that, yes, once it is properly understood, the Fold could be the key to all things—including a superweapon. By all means, include it in your research if it helps. But the truth remains that we know almost nothing about it." His face twisted. "And our spineless former compatriots have hoarded what knowledge they have."

"A weapon . . . What would you do with it?"

"Let me worry about that."

"But I wouldn't even know where to begin!"

"Do you not? You're aware, I'm sure, of the concept of a nuclear chain reaction?"

"The concept, yes, of course—"

"And that the American president has publicly stated that it might be possible to create a bomb the size of an orange that can destroy an entire town with one stroke?"

"These are speculative ideas."

"Tell me, Ettore, of your own speculations. What do *you* think science can do with the energy contained in the atom?"

Ettore pressed his lips together and looked away. Already, labs had induced nuclear transformations by bombarding atoms with accelerated protons. He and Werner had discussed the world-changing possibilities of harnessing such awesome power.

But a weapon of mass destruction?

It was a vile thought, and Ettore wanted no part of that madness.

"I know you're set to return to Rome," Stefan said. "We have people there as well. I'll be in close communication and ensure you have the resources you need."

Somehow, though spoken without inflection, Stefan's words seemed to Ettore more like a threat than an offer of assistance. "But I don't understand how I can—"

"You'll find a way, I'm sure. We just need a blueprint. An idea we can use. You possess one of the most brilliant minds in the entire world, Ettore. Perhaps *the* most brilliant. On my end, I'll work to wrest what knowledge of the Fold we can from the others."

Ettore wanted to tell Stefan right then and there that he never wanted to hear the name of the Leap Year Society again. But he hadn't the nerve. He would wait until he was back in his own country, safe and secure, and then pass Stefan a letter.

Stefan squeezed a gloved fist at his side. "As it has always been, the race to acquire technology is the true war. Yet the stakes are far higher than in the past. Unimaginably so. This is a war, Ettore, that must be won at all costs."

The next day, when Ettore walked into work, still disturbed by the conversation with Stefan, he noticed a pall of gloom hanging over the hallowed halls of the physics institute. No one seemed to want to meet his gaze. Werner gave him an abrupt greeting and walked off in the other direction. Had Ettore done something wrong? He had a sudden, terrible thought—what if someone had discovered his personal relationship with a member of the Waffen-SS?

As soon as Ettore reached his cubicle and read the headline of the journal article that someone had placed on his desk, a message loud and clear, he understood at once the situation was far worse than someone learning of his meetings with Stefan.

It was worse than anything Ettore could have dreamed.

He took the journal article in both hands, read the entire thing without taking a seat or moving an inch, and then sank into his chair, his hands trembling so badly he dropped the article on the floor.

The discovery of Paul Dirac's positron, the name given to the negative-energy sea of antimatter predicted by the Brit's wild theories, had just been confirmed by independent sources. In contradiction to all conceivable logic, it appeared that every time a particle of matter was created in nature, its existence was accompanied by an equivalent particle with opposite quantum characteristics—an antiparticle. Bizarrely, in all but a rare few cases—less than one in a billion—the twin particles annihilated each other at the moment of their creation, transforming mass into pure energy.

The import of this discovery was as yet uncertain. Yet one thing was very clear indeed: Dirac's particle theory was in direct contradiction to Ettore's. The beautiful infinite tower that Ettore had trumpeted to the world—the most important achievement of his life—was as dead as the concept of a flat Earth.

Ettore had staked everything on his theory. He had publicly mocked Dirac, and his peers had jeered right along with him. Yet now it was Ettore who had become a laughingstock, a disgrace, a pariah in the scientific community.

His career, and maybe even his life, was finished.

—o **22** o—

Another taxi dropped Andie outside the entrance to the Catacombs of Kom el-Shoqafa, this time under the watchful eye of a yellow moon so vivid it bulged out of the darkness as if tearing through the fabric of space. Both she and Cal carried backpacks with their few possessions inside. Andie could not deny her relief at having Cal by her side as she took in the remnants of the old necropolis slumbering atop the hill, ancient and brooding, a far more permanent fixture than the flesh of the human beings interred beneath the stone courtyard.

Not knowing what to expect, she was unsurprised when a husky young man in a khaki uniform exited the guard shack as they approached, holding a rifle and standing just inside the iron fence. Earlier in the day, she had seen no sign of video surveillance. That boded well for the planned excursion—if they could manage to get inside.

As the taxi drove away, Andie and Cal stopped ten feet before the fence, holding up their palms in a sign of peace.

"Hi," Andie said to the guard. "Do you speak English?"

"Closed."

"We know. Listen, I don't mean to startle you, but we're video travel bloggers and are dying to get a few pictures of the catacombs at night. Our channel is focused on mysterious sites around the world, and authentic footage goes a really long way."

"Come tomorrow. During day."

"That's the thing . . . We really like night shoots. I know it's underground, but there's no one around after dark, and this courtyard is so atmospheric . . . We'd be in and out quickly. I promise."

Annoyed, the guard waved the rifle toward the road, then started walking back to the shack.

"We'll pay you," Cal said.

The guard paused with his hand on the doorframe.

"One hundred US dollars."

Though Andie had hatched the plan to bribe any security guards they encountered, Cal, who had experience paying off officials of all sorts, had suggested the amount. Not too high to raise suspicion, not too low to waste anyone's time. Just enough to pay for a week or two of groceries, a couple bottles of liquor, or a nice gift for a wife or girlfriend. To Andie's great annoyance, Cal had also said that an Egyptian guard would take a request from a man more seriously.

The guard remained still for a long moment, facing away from them so they couldn't read his expression. At last he turned and said, his eyes flicking nervously toward the road, "Two hundred."

"One fifty."

"No."

Cal released an exasperated sigh. "You're cleaning me out, man. Can't we talk—"

"Two hundred or leave now."

"Okay, okay. You missed a career as a Hollywood agent, my friend."

"Money now."

Cal reached into his pocket, took out his wallet, and counted out ten twenties. As he approached the gate, holding the bills in the air, the guard insisted they both hand over their backpacks. With little choice but to comply, they squeezed the packs through the gate and let the guard search them. Andie had the Star Phone safely in her pocket. During the search, the guard took out a six-pack of Heineken. "I take these too."

Earlier, not knowing what awaited, Andie had devised a plan consisting of three parts: bribe money, a pair of bolt cutters purchased at a hardware store near the harbor and which they had dropped in the bushes once they had seen the guard, and the beer to sweeten the deal if the bribe faltered.

"Sure thing," Cal said. "We were going to celebrate with that later, but they're all yours."

"Consider it a tip," Andie said.

The guard raised a bottle in salutation, grinned, and unlocked the gate to let them through. "One hour. No more."

"Fair enough," Cal said.

Andie felt relieved. She had been worried he might limit them to five or ten minutes. On the other hand, she knew the contents of the catacombs had been looted long ago, the place was deserted, and the guard probably didn't care if they stayed all night.

Andie and Cal retrieved their backpacks, and the guard relocked the gate and led the way across the courtyard toward the mausoleum. Though surrounded by a city of millions, the silent scattered ruins of the necropolis—isolated atop the hill and swathed in darkness—made her feel as if they were exploring an archaeological site in the middle of a wilderness dig.

After the guard had retreated to the guard shack, Cal said, "Do you take all your guys to the graveyard on the first date?"

"Let's get this over with," she muttered. She was thinking of the three levels of catacombs lurking beneath the surface, as if the mausoleum were the petrified hand of a corpse reaching out of the soil in a shallow grave, a portent of what lay unseen beneath.

The noise of a tram in the distance followed them inside, then faded into silence. The air felt heavy with dust and stone. Andie reached into her backpack and took out their final purchase of the night, also from the hardware store: a handheld flashlight with a beveled edge and one thousand lumens of illumination. She still had her pocketknife, and Cal had purchased a small wooden club he had stuck in his backpack. Neither of them knew much about guns, or where to get one in Egypt.

The flashlight revealed an interior with rough stone walls, dominated by a well of darkness looming in the center, a central shaft used to lower bodies into the tomb. Scaffolding covered the wall to their left.

Andie stood at the edge of the shaft and shone the light down. Thirty feet below, they could see the faint outline of a stone floor.

"I guess we're doing this," Cal muttered.

"Even if the catacombs were open, photography isn't allowed inside. This is the best option to see if the Star Phone has something to show us."

On one side of the cylindrical shaft, a set of stone steps spiraled down into the catacombs, separated from the main shaft by a wall. Darkness lived and breathed at the edges of the cone of amber light as they navigated the staircase. Windows cut into the stone wall provided glimpses of the central well as they descended, and the air grew more damp. At the bottom, all traces of moonlight disappeared, leaving them utterly dependent on the flashlight.

A short passage led to a rotunda supported by columns hewn out of the bedrock. Andie slowly turned about the room, illuminating two more corridors and another shaft that, she knew from her research, dropped to the flooded bottom level. Since entering the catacombs, she had peered through the lens of the Star Phone several times, but nothing had changed.

"If we weren't down here alone at night with assassins on our trail," Cal said as he took in the underground sepulcher, "I might appreciate the atmosphere more. How big is this place?"

"Not that large, though archaeologists think this could be one of hundreds or even thousands of catacombs hidden underground nearby. This whole section of the city might have been one giant necropolis."

"That's a lovely thought."

She stepped through the opening on their left, into a hall lined with stone benches and the broken remains of pottery still littering the floor. "I read this was a banquet hall where relatives came to toast the deceased."

"Down *here*?"

"I don't know. It seems more authentic than a funeral parlor with flowers and elevator music."

"Authentic. Yeah, I wouldn't argue with that."

They found nothing of interest in the triclinium. After returning to the rotunda, they tried the remaining corridor, which led down a set of stone steps to the main burial chamber. Floor-to-ceiling pillars marked the entrance, resembling the front of a Greek temple. Atop the open portal was a frieze depicting a winged sun flanked by a pair of falcons. Bearded serpents carved in bas-relief guarded the sides, and above each serpent was a shield in the likeness of Medusa, a mythological creature whose stare could turn human beings to stone. Wards designed to deter would-be tomb robbers.

Wooden planks, laid to preserve the floor, led through the portico into the burial chamber, as well as into two side passages exiting from the sides of the vestibule. Andie stepped into the passage on the left and shone the flashlight down a corridor honeycombed on both sides with empty square slots, each just large enough to fit a sarcophagus.

The claustrophobic passage lined with tombs gave her the shivers. Her imagination ran wild, envisioning all manner of things lurking in the darkness, ready to crawl out of those holes as soon as she turned her back.

Stop it, Andie.

"The maps show this passage wrapping around the burial chamber," she said.

"It doesn't look very inviting. Do we need to explore it?"

"Maybe. Let's try the main one first. There's more iconography inside."

The wooden plank beneath their feet creaked as they stepped warily between the pillars and into a chamber decorated with Greco-Roman statues and carvings hewn from the rock walls. The statues felt eerily alive in the gloom, and Andie felt as if their eyes were following her about the room.

They found three stone sarcophagi inset into the walls, each with heavy stone covers. Cal walked around the room with the flashlight, illuminating the ancient art as Andie followed behind with the Star Phone. Just as she was wondering whether they would have to pry open one of the coffins, Cal called out to her.

"Andie," he said. "Check out the tip of that spear."

"Where?"

"On that statue to your left."

At the edge of the cone of illumination cast by the flashlight, she saw the jackal-headed statue—Anubis—to which Cal was referring. The Egyptian god of the dead was depicted with the uniform of a Roman legionary, an ode to the syncretic beliefs of the time. The muscular statue was holding an upright spear and facing the doorway. Andie had to step closer to see the sphinx carved into the handle of the spear, just below the point.

"Hold the light steady," she said, holding her breath as she aimed the Star Phone at the sphinx and pressed it to her eye.

The room spun as if tilted on an axis. Andie's familiar dizziness was exacerbated by the lower level of illumination. Yet once she got her bearings, a thrill passed through her when she saw a new image replacing the statue of Anubis. The familiar scroll representing the library remained in place, yet instead of the alphanumeric string below it, two new symbols hovered: a sun in the form of an ouroboros rising over water, and a cross with a loop at the top.

"What is it?" Cal asked.

After sealing the image in her mind, she handed him the Star Phone and let him see for himself.

"Holy shit," he said, taking a few wobbly steps back and forth while he gained his equilibrium. "This thing is for real. What's that snake-eating-its-own-tail thing called?"

"An ouroboros."

"And the ankh—"

He was cut off by a loud thump from somewhere behind them, as if a heavy object had fallen down the central shaft.

Cal's face was rigid as he returned the Star Phone to Andie and waved the flashlight through the entrance to the chamber, illuminating the stairs beyond. "What was that?"

"I think we should go see," she whispered.

"I think we should get the hell out of here."

"What if someone's waiting for us to climb those stairs?"

"So what do you suggest—hiding out here until morning?"

"I don't know," she said. "I don't like the thought of doing anything without knowing what made that noise."

She gave brief consideration to hiding somewhere in the catacombs, but the only place she could think of, squeezing into one of those hollow cavities in the passages around the central burial chamber, seemed more dangerous than staying put. If anyone came looking for them, their hiding place would become their tomb. She supposed they could slip into the murky waters of the flooded lower level, but that was an absolute last resort that terrified her just thinking about it.

After a moment, Cal raised the miniature bat with his right hand and took a step toward the doorway. "Let's go take a look then."

Andie gripped her pocketknife and followed him out, pointing the flashlight at the floor. Side by side, they passed through the vestibule and crept back up the stairs to the rotunda. Everything was as quiet and undisturbed as before. Disturbingly so. *What had caused that thump?*

She aimed the light into the flooded shaft at their feet. Not the faintest of ripples disturbed the ominous dark surface.

"Maybe a piece of scaffolding fell," Cal suggested. "Or one of the stones broke away."

"Maybe."

Emboldened by the thought, Andie sucked in a breath and led the way down the final passage. Just before they reached the spiral staircase leading to the surface, the flashlight illuminated a motionless form crumpled on the floor at the bottom of the central shaft. It only took a moment for Andie to realize the figure was the guard who had let them in, his neck bent at an unnatural angle, blood spreading like a dark nimbus on the floor around his head.

23

As Andie stifled a scream, backing away from the body, Cal gripped her arm and said, "It's not the guard."

Swallowing, Andie watched as Cal pointed the flashlight directly on the dead man's features. He was right: though the clothes and general build were the same, she gasped as she recognized the darker skin tone and chapped lips of the Indian man who had followed her throughout London. "I know him."

"What? Who is it?"

"His name was Kumal," said a cultured voice with a slight Middle Eastern accent, from somewhere in the darkness behind them.

Andie spun, gripping her knife as fear and adrenaline spiked through her. Cal raised the bat and whipped the flashlight wildly about the chamber.

A dark-haired man in a green windbreaker emerged from the gloom of the corridor leading to the rotunda. He was composed and very handsome, and inspecting them with a raptor's gaze that Andie knew from past experience missed nothing.

Cal took a step toward him, brandishing the bat. In response, the man calmly raised the bottom of his jacket and removed a handgun tucked into a holster. Cal slowly lowered the bat. "Who are you?"

"The man who's been chasing me," Andie said. "What do you want?"

"To deliver you."

The statement, along with the casual certainty with which he had uttered it, sent a chill creeping down Andie's spine.

"*Deliver* me? To whom?"

The slow, thin-lipped smile that spread across his face unnerved Andie even more than the fresh corpse lying on the floor behind her.

"I thought he was your friend," she said, glancing back at the body.

The man took the gun out of his pocket and waved it toward the spiral staircase. "Up the stairs."

"Why?" she asked. "Where are we going?"

He pointed the weapon at Cal. "He lives to ensure your compliance. If you both come peacefully, I'll release him once we arrive."

"Sure you will," Cal said.

"Your voice was silenced long ago. What do we have to fear from a disgraced journalist?"

"Is that why you followed me around LA and tried to kidnap me? Because I'm silenced?"

"Cal," Andie warned. "I'll go. Don't tempt him."

"He's lying, Andie."

She turned to lock eyes with Cal, trying to convey that she already knew that, but with a gun pointed at them, what could they do except try to survive a bit longer?

The dark-haired man aimed the gun at Cal. "If you're seeking another reason, American deaths raise questions, even those of disgraced journalists. And I don't have time to dispose of the body. But I will kill you, right this very moment, if you both don't drop your weapons and start climbing."

With one hand raised, Cal set the bat on the ground, handed the flashlight to Andie, and reached to open his backpack.

"No," the man said.

"I've got another flashlight—"

"Move. Now."

With his other hand, the man flicked on a silver penlight with impressive illumination. Left with little choice, Andie dropped the knife and let Cal proceed first up the spiral staircase, hoping he might have a chance to run away. Their captor made her start climbing right behind Cal, and then stayed on her heels, limiting her options. She debated a swift kick to his face, but he was just out of range.

Though dazed by the turn the night had taken, fear and adrenaline sharpened Andie's focus, and she thought furiously through her options. If the man wanted them dead, the catacombs seemed a pretty good place to leave the bodies. He had already dumped one inside.

And why *had* he killed the other man? Did they have a falling-out? A different agenda?

A more important question loomed: Should she let their captor take her somewhere, or fight to the death right now? Neither option boded well for her future, but she agreed with Cal. In the end, the man wasn't going to let either of them live. Maybe it was true he didn't want to leave the body of an American in public, but he could just shoot Cal in the head when they reached his car and stuff them both in the trunk.

Either way, they probably had a better chance of escaping right now than wherever he planned on taking them. A shiver of dread coursed through her as she decided to fight as hard as she could before they reached his vehicle, and a desperate plan took shape.

After they had climbed in silence for some time, nearing the top, Andie asked, "Why me? Whatever it is you think I know, I don't."

No response.

"You're with them, aren't you? The Leap Year Society?" She took another stab, remembering the name in Dr. Corwin's journal. "Or is it the Ascendants?"

She glanced down to gauge his reaction, but his expression remained neutral. When she looked back up, Cal had reached the last step and was about to exit the shaft.

"What's the square root of one thousand and fifty-six?" Andie asked, right before she clicked off her flashlight and threw it straight down on their attacker's head, hoping to crack his skull with the beveled edge. There was a faint thud as the flashlight struck home.

"Run!" she screamed to Cal.

Though the man did not cry out, darkness consumed the space around them as the light from his pen spun downward into the shaft. She prayed he had fallen to his death. Above them, a sliver of moonlight illuminated Cal's hand reaching down to help her up the last few steps.

To her left came the sound of flesh slapping on stone. As she reached for Cal's hand, she looked over to see the man pulling himself through one of the windows cut into the wall that overlooked the shaft from the staircase. A liquid blackness—blood—gleamed on his forehead. The bastard must have vaulted across the inside of the shaft when he fell. As he bounded up the stairs, Andie and Cal fled the mausoleum, screaming for help as they ran through the courtyard, knowing the real guard was either dead or tied up.

Sensing they were about to get shot in the back and then dragged to a waiting vehicle, Andie felt as if she might vomit as she screamed again, "Help! Someone help us!"

A gunshot rang out, causing her to flinch. But she felt nothing, and Cal hadn't slowed. Their attacker didn't seem the type to miss at close range, even in the moonlight. Another gunshot caused her to glance over her shoulder, revealing a scene that both gave her hope and confused her.

Though he had never uttered a sound of discomfort, the dark-haired man was holding his bloodied right arm and diving behind a waist-high pillar. Two more gunshots caused chips of stone to fly off the ruined column. Andie whipped her head to the left. At the edge of the courtyard, she saw a tall woman, her complexion as inky as the night sky, taking aim with a compact handgun. When their attacker finally managed to return fire, the woman spun with the economy of a leopard stalking its prey, then melted into the darkness behind a concrete sarcophagus.

When Cal jerked her arm forward, Andie realized she was gawking at the scene.

Zawadi?

"Let's go!" Cal said in a rough whisper. "This is our chance."

She didn't need to hear it twice. After snapping out of her paralysis, she sprinted into the darkness, through the open iron gate at the entrance. The guard was nowhere in sight, and the door to the guard shack was closed. An ominous sign. She didn't want to know what was inside.

Andie and Cal looked side to side as they ran, searching for a place to hide in case whoever survived came after them, or more assailants were waiting on the street. Yet no one appeared when they reached the road at the top of the hill. More gunshots filled the courtyard, farther away than before. They fled down the cracked pavement, fearing a dead end if they tried to cut through the courtyards of the tall apartment buildings ringing the hill.

"Let's try for the main road," she said as she ran. "More choices."

"Okay," Cal said.

Andie let gravity do the work as she dashed down the hill, running so fast she feared falling face-first if she hit a loose stone or a patch of gravel. Cal was ten feet behind her, breathing heavily.

When they reached the road at the bottom, Andie looked back and saw no one following them. The gunshots had stopped too—which could just mean the survivor was chasing them. There was obviously dissension in the ranks, judging by the dead man at the bottom of the shaft, and Andie feared Zawadi no less than the dark-haired man.

Andie slowed enough for Cal to catch up. Soon they saw signs of life all around, pedestrians and an open coffee shop and even a gang of rough-looking youths, whose presence filled her with immeasurable relief. Still, she did not relish trying to escape the maze of streets and alleys in a dodgy neighborhood, at night and on foot, and she thanked the universe for small miracles when a black-and-white taxi pulled alongside them, the driver leaning his head out to ask if they needed a ride.

Andie gripped the cloth seat as the taxi wound away from the cat-acombs and through a maze of inner-city neighborhoods so bleak she wondered if they had not exchanged one crisis for another. They entered a particularly grim patch with neither street signs nor electricity, prowled by roving gangs of youths and stray dogs. The potholed alleys were barely wide enough for the sedan to squeeze through, strewn with trash and parked mopeds and laundry hanging overhead. She began to wonder if they were being kidnapped by someone else. When they questioned the driver, he assured them it was the fastest route, and she sat white-knuckled in the back seat until they exited the poverty-stricken neighborhood and emerged onto a busy multilane highway.

Soon they were speeding toward the harbor. Knowing she couldn't return to her pension, Andie asked the driver to take them to a major hotel chain, to buy some time to think. Both she and Cal had most of their belongings in their backpacks on the seat between them. The rest, some odd clothes and toiletries, could be left behind.

The radio was blaring an electronic mix of Egyptian folk music, which was grating on her nerves. Andie gripped the Star Phone. As with the sphinxes, the display of the two new symbols in the crypt had been temporary. Once she stopped pointing the device at the tip of the spear, the image had reverted back to the scroll and the alpha-numeric GPS code.

Another marker.

Yet as she stared down at the empty cursor spaces, willing the device to divulge its secrets, she had to believe they were close to the end of this particular journey. *How many steps would there be,* she wondered, *before the endgame?*

How many mysteries to uncover?

"That woman was the same one I saw in London," Andie said.

Cal started. "The one who killed the professor?"

"I'm sure of it, unless she has a twin. I think her name's Zawadi."

"She is rather unforgettable. Does this mean she's on our side?"

"I think they're fighting amongst themselves for some reason. I don't trust any of them."

"Probably a good policy. About London, though . . . you didn't actually see her kill him, right? What if she showed up later?"

"Walking out of his apartment just after the murder? I think Professor Rickman knew her and let her inside, and it got him killed."

"I suppose. But what if there's a power play going on inside the Leap Year Society? If we find someone who could help us, it might improve our chances of staying alive."

"And get you closer to your story?" she snapped.

"Is that such a bad thing?"

"If it puts our lives in danger more than they already are, then yeah. Anyway, why would anyone help us?"

"I don't know," he said, letting his head fall back against the headrest in exhaustion. "I'm just exploring ideas."

Andie did the same, pressing her hands to her temples and closing her eyes as she slumped in the seat. The stress of the night, compounded on top of everything else, washed over her like a tidal wave. "Sorry. I'm not thinking straight right now."

"Are you sure you don't want to take our chances with a fancy hotel? Bubble bath, clean sheets, stocked minibar?"

"I'll settle for a hot shower and a cup of coffee."

Andie soon got her wish. After spotting a budget hotel on the way to the harbor, about ten blocks off the water, they told the driver there was a change in plans and tipped him well for plucking them out of danger.

A pair of Siamese cats lounged on the rose-colored carpeting in the lobby of Cleopatra's Chalet. Yes, the obsequious man behind the counter told them, they had a business center with free internet. Yes, they had hot water and coffee and sugar for the gentleman. No, a credit card was not required, and they accepted cash deposits for incidentals.

Sold, Andie thought.

As much as they both wanted to crash, they knew they had no time to spare. Cal speculated their pursuers had traced Andie forward from the airport, or from the call with her father. Either way, they couldn't afford the luxury of a full night's rest.

After her shower, Andie changed T-shirts and slipped into the same jeans as before. At least she had washed away the grime of the city.

"How do you like your coffee?" Cal asked when she emerged. "A little milk? Sugar?"

"I prefer if gravity can't escape," she answered as she entered the bedroom.

"What?"

"Thick and black."

Andie sat on the bed, which reeked of cigarettes, as Cal brewed a pot. The hotel was not in the best area and was laughably cheap, less than thirty bucks a night. This would account for the smell and the small family of orange cockroaches she had spotted in the room. She had to chase two out of the shower before she entered, and one almost dropped on her from the ceiling.

"Ready to head to the war room?" he asked, handing her a paper cup of coffee.

She took a greedy sip. "I am now."

"It's pretty terrible."

"I don't even care."

Downstairs, the "twenty-four-hour business center" turned out to be a brown-walled cubicle with a concrete floor and a single desktop computer that looked as if it might predate Windows. Cal still had his laptop, but they didn't want to risk using it unless they had to, even with the protective software Dane had installed.

Cal brought another chair from the lobby. "At least we have the place to ourselves," he said, closing the door behind him.

The arthritic computer shuddered to life when she depressed the power button. Two minutes later, an interminable wait to Andie, the home screen popped up.

She set a piece of paper on the desk between them. It was a rough sketch she had made of the two new symbols above the scroll that the Star Phone had displayed in the catacombs.

An ouroboros sun rising over water.

The cross and loop of the ankh, the ancient Egyptian symbol of life.

"Here's my theory," she said. "Together with the scroll, I think the three symbols represent locations in the city. What if, in keeping with the GPS theme, we're supposed to trilaterate a location among them?"

Cal put his palms on the desk as he leaned over the drawing. "It's clever," he said slowly. "In fact, I'd say it's a pretty damn good guess."

"Besides the obvious one—the scroll representing the library—I have no idea where the ankh might be, or what the rising sun represents. Any ideas?"

"Not offhand," he said, "but hold on." He left the room and returned with a stack of guidebooks and pamphlets from the lobby. "I'll look through these while you search. Maybe something will jump out."

"Okay," she said, already typing in the search bar.

All through the night, taking turns on the computer when someone's eyes got too bleary, popping out every hour or so for more coffee, they researched the meaning of the symbols and tried to correlate their findings with specific locations in the city. Thankfully, no other guests appeared in the middle of the night to use the computer. Neither did Zawadi nor the dark-haired man burst into the room brandishing a firearm, the thought of which made Andie loath to leave the shabby little hotel. Cleopatra's Chalet felt as safe as a womb compared to stepping back into the exposed streets of the city.

Hours later, they felt good about what they had discovered.

The most prominent ankh in the city, as far as they could tell, belonged to a statue in a park in the Anfushi district. A squiggly piece of land straddling the Eastern and Western Harbours, known for its mosques and a necropolis, the neighborhood was only a short cab ride away. The statue itself, unearthed from the waters offshore, like so many other Alexandrian treasures, was a bronze cast of Cleopatra holding a large ankh upright in her right hand. In addition to being the most prominent ankh they could find, the involvement of the legendary queen seemed a fitting ode.

The third symbol, the ouroboros sun rising over water, proved more challenging. Tying it to Egyptian iconography was the easy part. The ouroboros had symbolized renewal and purification for millennia. A good choice, she thought, to form a sun, which itself represented both Ra—the classic sun god—as well as Aten, the original name for the incarnation of the sun itself, later deified in its own right. During the New Kingdom, pharaoh Akhenaten had taken the worship of Aten a step further, abandoning polytheism and instating Aten as the sole creator god.

Sometimes Ra and Aten were syncretized. Sometimes they weren't. Sometimes they were depicted together, and sometimes apart.

There were others too. While Ra objectified the daytime sun, Horus symbolized the sunrise, and Amun symbolized the sun in the underworld. And sometimes, in certain art and motifs, the sun was simply the sun.

The symbol might even refer to a site outside Alexandria, for instance the ancient city of Heliopolis. Obelisks, often built to catch the first rays of the sun in honor of its life-giving power, were another option. Yet one of Alexandria's most important obelisks now rested in London, another at the Vatican.

It was all very confusing, and they didn't have time to consult an Egyptologist. In the end, they decided to stay in the city, pick the most prominent edifice they could find, and run with it. They agreed the ruins of the Serapeum presented their best option for the ouroboros. Founded by Ptolemy I around 300 BCE, destroyed by a Christian mob seven centuries later, the temple was dedicated to the Greco-Egyptian sun god Serapis. Plus Andie had already discovered that the Serapeum was the reputed landing site for many of the works of the Library of Alexandria.

All the pieces seemed to fit.

"So we've got our three points," Cal said. "The library, the ankh in Anfushi, and the temple. Or at least we think we do. How do we triangulate them?"

"We don't. We tri*laterate*."

"What's the difference?"

"Triangulation uses angles. Trilateration is, well, more sophisticated. Give me a few minutes, and I'll handle it."

As she worked, he paced behind her and said, "So the Star Phone is some kind of map or puzzle that leads to the location of the Enneagon . . . and the Enneagon itself is a device or new technology Dr. Corwin developed? Something game-changing enough to drive these people into a frenzy."

She gave a grim nod.

"If the Enneagon is really what they're after . . . have you considered giving the Star Phone to them? In exchange for your life?"

"What do you think?"

"That you've made your bed, for better or worse. And that even if you gave it up, they probably think you know too much."

"Good answer."

He put his palms up. "Just checking."

"If we can find the Enneagon first, we'll use it as leverage to free Dr. Corwin or hold someone responsible for his death. And you'll have your story."

"And after that? You think they'll just let it go?"

She swallowed. "I haven't gotten that far."

"Me either," he muttered.

Though Andie knew what free websites and calculation tools to use, the sluggish computer was maddening. It took her far longer than she had intended—they had agreed staying off their phones and Cal's laptop was a good idea—but at last she was able to use the GPS coordinates of the three locations to derive a fourth one in the geometric center of the others. She pointed it out on the map to Cal.

"Smack in the middle of the city," he said. "El Attarin neighborhood. Do you know it?"

"No." She zoomed in as close as she could. As best she could tell, the location was a place of business called Misr Petroleum. She frowned. "A gas station?"

Cal raised his palms. "They can put a QR-type code on almost anything, right?"

"Sure, but it wouldn't *mean* something."

Just to be safe, Andie selected five more sites they thought best represented the sun rising over water, then performed similar calculations. With the new information in hand, they choked down cold cereal and stale pastries at the continental buffet in the lobby, downed another cup of coffee, grabbed their bags, and emerged from the hotel squinting like newborn babes in the morning sun.

They caught a taxi within minutes. Exhausted but hopeful, they sat quietly during the drive to the gas station, eyes latched on to the road for signs of anyone following them. Andie took the time to retie her hijab.

"Here?" the driver said as they approached a busy corner in a nondescript commercial sector of the city. Across the street was the gas station they had glimpsed on Google Maps. The grimy exterior and attendants in blue shirts with blue-and-yellow logos looked identical to dozens of others they had passed.

"Thanks," Andie said, paying before she stepped out.

The streets were packed with cars, trucks spewing noxious fumes, bicycles, scooters, motorcycles, and pedestrians risking their lives to dash across the street. She realized it was 8:30 a.m. The middle of rush hour.

After ten minutes of feeling foolish waving the Star Phone around, seeing nothing that felt remotely right, they gave up and tried the second place on the list.

And the third.

And the fourth and the fifth.

"Something's wrong," Andie muttered over a table in a shisha joint with hookahs embedded in the centers of the tables. The casual lounge shared space with an internet café in the back. They were ensconced in a quiet corner, hidden from street view by a faux alabaster pillar. Each time the front door opened, they craned their necks to get a nervous glimpse of the new customer.

"Every second we stay in this city feels like borrowed time," Cal said.

"What are we missing? The scroll has got to be the library. I feel reasonably good about the ankh, but the ouroboros sun . . . not so much."

Cal tapped his fingers against the side of his teacup. Both of them, feeling strung out by coffee, opted for an inexpensive koshary tea. Mostly they had come inside to get off the street, and in case they needed a computer for research. "Let's talk about the ankh. What exactly does it represent?"

"Life and immortality mostly, but it's all over the place. The enigmas of heaven and earth, male and female genitalia, the sun coming over the horizon. It was used to mark necropoli and provide divine protection for temple walls, believing the ankh was the key—one interpretation of the curious shape—to the afterlife."

Cal thought for a moment, and then his fingers stopped tapping against the teacup. "Did you say they once marked necropoli?"

"All the time, inside and out."

Cal sat back in his seat, his jaw slack with disbelief.

"What?" she said.

"I may not have your big brain, but I'm pretty good at seeing the obvious. We might be overthinking this. Let's say the first symbol is still the library, and the ankh represents a necropolis—we know one of those around here pretty intimately, wouldn't you say?"

"The catacombs," she murmured. "Okay, that's one interpretation . . . Oh my God, I see where you're going. What if the three symbols represent places the Star Phone *has already led me in the city?*" She thrust her palms on the table. "It makes perfect sense. A final trilateration of the stages of the journey. But how does the rising sun fit with the National Museum?"

He flicked his eyes toward the rear of the establishment. "Let's go find out."

Moving as one, they picked up their teas and hurried to the row of computers shielded from view by a beaded curtain. On their left, at the end of the row, a pair of teens huddled around a social media website.

Thankfully, the late-model Toshibas in the café were far faster than the dinosaur of a computer in the hotel. After a quick search, Andie found what she was looking for: a painting in the Alexandria National Museum depicting Ra holding a serpent by its throat. She had assumed the ouroboros was part and parcel of the sun imagery, a creative interpretation, but she had been wrong. In Egyptian mythology, the serpent symbolized Apophis: an ancient god of darkness, chaos, and destruction, and the mortal enemy of Ra.

The god of light holding the god of darkness by the throat. She had the feeling there was a message there.

More importantly, they had found their serpent.

The museum itself was the third symbol.

Cal let out a small whoop. "That's got to be it!"

Andie was already pulling up the trilateration website. "Let's see where it takes us."

After typing in the GPS locations for the library, the catacombs, and the museum, she was able to pinpoint another site in central Alexandria, not far from where they were. When no commercial establishment popped up on Google Maps, she switched to a street view, which allowed her to identify a structure near the middle of the road, a nondescript house or building.

"What the hell is it?" Cal asked.

After making a careful note of the location, Andie logged off and turned to face him. "I don't know. But let's go find out."

Twenty minutes later, another taxi dropped Andie and Cal in front of a residential villa surrounded by a high, crumbling stone wall covered in desiccated brown vines that snaked across the surface as if trying to squeeze the life out of it. Through the closed iron gate, Andie spotted a brick walkway overgrown with weeds. The walkway led to the stoop of a three-story mansion with arched Moorish windows, balconettes on the upper two stories, and stripped gray walls with hints of the original mauve plaster.

A similar state of entropy defined the neighboring properties. The entire street was a nursing home of forgotten glory, dying a slow death from neglect, eerily calm and deserted. It felt like a living time capsule cordoned off by decree from the rest of the city, awaiting discovery from some future civilization.

"Okay," Cal said. "What now?"

As Andie stepped up to the gate, aiming for a better look at the grounds, she felt the Star Phone vibrate in her pocket, followed by the buzz of an electronic lock. With a click, the tall iron doors slowly parted, offering them entry. Andie whipped the device out of her pocket and scanned the grounds, but the face was unchanged.

There was no one in sight. No cameras they could see. Heavy drapes on the windows protected the interior of the mansion from view.

"I liked the gas station better," Cal muttered. "This looks more like a field trip to a haunted house than a step toward uncovering the Leap Year Society."

"I don't like it either, but the gate opened for us."

"Maybe it has an automatic sensor. Anyone could set it off."

"The Star Phone buzzed in my pocket at the same time."

He gave her a sharp glance.

"We're supposed to be here," she said.

As the gates started to close, forcing their hand, Andie glanced nervously down the street before stepping inside. She could always climb back over, she reasoned. After mumbling something under his breath, Cal slipped through as well.

Crickets chirped from the high grass as she kept to the brick path. The grounds sprawling a hundred feet to either side must have once been magnificent, but now they were a mess of shaggy palms, overgrown foliage, and dry stone fountains.

"What do you want to do?" Cal asked in a low voice.

"Whatever this place is, it's connected to the Star Phone. If the people chasing us knew about it, they'd be here already."

"Maybe they are."

Andie had come too far to stop now. Shoulders straight, she waded through the weeds choking the walkway and climbed the marble steps to the front door. Cal stayed close at her heels, and she knocked on the door with no response. After a louder knock, she called out to anyone who might be home.

Nothing.

No one.

She bit her lip as she scanned the grounds again. Not knowing what else to do, she reached for the brass handle that had long since lost its gleam. The wooden door was outlined in weatherworn but beautifully carved trim, with metalwork inserts shielding stained-glass panels in the center.

After a groan of complaint, the door pushed right open.

24

The creak of the door as it opened caused little fingers of unease to creep down Andie's spine. A musty odor wafted out of the house, from decades of mildew and rotting floorboards. She took a step inside and found herself in an empty foyer with a patterned tile floor, thick gold carpeting, and a faded fresco on the ceiling of nubile Egyptian maidens lounging around an oasis, guarded by men with the heads of scarab beetles. A wire cord dangled a foot down from the center of the fresco, the remnant of a chandelier.

After making sure it did not lock from the outside, Cal closed the door behind them, cutting off the rays of sunlight that had penetrated the old home. As her eyes dilated in the gloomy interior, Andie felt as if they had sealed the door to a tomb. Two side corridors led deeper into the house, and she used the light on her phone to illuminate a wide staircase with an ornate iron railing on the far side of the foyer.

"What do you want to do?" Cal asked in a low voice.

"I suppose we explore."

"You sure about that?"

"Of course not," she said. "You have a better suggestion?"

"Why is no one here?"

"Maybe they are, and we're supposed to find them. Maybe Dr. Corwin is trapped inside, or set this place up and couldn't return."

He shook his head. "I think you're reaching. If the Star Phone hadn't opened the gate, I have a feeling you'd have climbed over anyway."

"If we don't do something to change the narrative, they'll hunt us down and kill us."

Cal ran a hand through his hair and turned in a slow circle, peering down the dark corridors. "I don't like it one damn bit, but I guess we should look around."

They decided to start with the upper floors and work their way down. On the third-story landing, they stepped through an arched opening at the top of the staircase and into a sitting chamber with dull wooden floors. Thick crimson drapes matched the wall paneling, and a mirror hung from the wall above a limestone fireplace. The floor-to-ceiling drapes reeked of cigar smoke.

Cal gripped Andie's arm. "The mirror."

Unsure what he meant, Andie aimed her light at the glass and then caught her breath. The reflection was inversed like a typical mirror, but instead of seeing herself and Cal surrounded by threadbare furniture, she saw the room as it must once have been: clean and bright, with gleaming mahogany floors, filled with people in Victorian dress holding cocktails. She lightly tapped the smudged surface. It felt like glass, and the three-dimensional image seemed real. "That's just . . . creepy."

"At least the people aren't moving. Then we might have issues."

There were no ashes in the fireplace or other signs of recent occupancy. As she had outside, Andie tried the Star Phone, pointing it at the mirror and then at the rest of the room, to no effect.

They returned to the hallway branching off from the landing. The first door on their right was open, and they walked into a bedroom with built-in bookshelves, a four-poster bed, and forest-green velvet furniture with gilded edges. As Cal moved to inspect the bookshelves, Andie stepped across the Oriental rug to a powder table in the corner, facing another mirror. Her reflection was normal.

Displayed on the powder table was a goblet made of a strange, milky emerald substance that resembled smoked glass, ornamented with gold leaf shaped into the figure of a bearded Greek god. When Andie flashed her light on the goblet, it turned bright crimson, illuminating the figure with a hellish glow. The light had also added a pair of ram's horns, cloven hooves, and a tail to the figure. She nervously replaced the cup on the powder table.

What is this place?

The rest of the house contained more of the same. Upstairs and down, they found textiles and period furniture in various stages of decay, and in each room, a single object was displayed that looked very old and exhibited some bizarre characteristic. In a bathroom on the second story, they found a rectangular crystal the size of a bar of soap, so heavy they could barely pick it up. A hall with pitted concrete floors and stained-glass windows on the ground level harbored a pair of ancient ceramic urns engraved with runes, lying on their sides on a wooden table. The bottoms of the urns were composed of copper plates that merged seamlessly with the clay. The plates each had a hole drilled through the middle, with a wire that connected the two and extended out through the tops, giving the impression of a primitive battery. Andie had never seen anything like it. The blending technique on the copper plating looked far too advanced for whatever time period had produced the urns.

When they finished browsing the aboveground stories, finding no sign that anyone had lived in the house for years, if not decades, Cal and Andie stood in a hallway behind the kitchen, poised atop a tight staircase leading to the basement. The light from their phones revealed a closed door—the only one inside the house—at the bottom of the steps.

"Don't they make horror movies about this sort of thing?" Cal muttered.

Andie didn't answer. She was listening to her instincts as much as for sounds of life from below. Along the way, she had come to suspect the Star Phone was not just a puzzle box of intellectual hoops and exotic destinations that led to the prize of the Enneagon. Dr.

Corwin never did anything without meaning. For reasons known only to him, she knew he was trying to tell her—or whoever possessed the Star Phone—something important along the way.

"Maybe this is the end of the line," Cal continued. "Just an old house with some weird artifacts."

She didn't admit it out loud, but this was her greatest fear. That the Star Phone did not lead to retribution, or to Dr. Corwin himself, if he was even alive.

Maybe the device was nothing but a sophisticated toy, the Enneagon a myth or a spark in her mentor's imagination. But she knew in her heart how absurd this line of reasoning was. People were dying, she and Cal were running for their lives.

Yet as she stood before that unopened door, Andie realized how much she had always sought to ascribe meaning to her past. Just as fear shadows love, she had a festering dread of losing what she most desired. More than anything, she wanted to know why Dr. Corwin had a photo of her mother in some strange city in his desk drawer, what the ink drawings meant, and, most of all, she yearned to understand why her mother had abandoned her.

Except *yearn* was too soft a word, she realized. Too pure and fluffy, like a child waiting by a white picket fence for a lost golden retriever to return. Sometime over the past week, now that the possibility of answers might be within her grasp, a dam had burst inside her, a high-walled bulwark she had carefully built over the course of her life, brick by stoic brick, to keep the emotions at bay.

No, she didn't long for those answers, or yearn for them, or really, really hope, pretty please Mommy and Daddy, that she wouldn't be disappointed one day.

She fucking *craved* them.

"Are you coming or not?" she asked Cal, her voice rougher than she intended.

"You're not worried it's a trap?"

"Of course I am. You're not worried we'll miss the whole point of finding this place?"

After a muttered curse, he followed her down the steps. Despite her bravado, she was very afraid and wished she had a weapon to defend herself, though she doubted anything would help against the likes of Zawadi or the dark-haired man.

The wooden door at the bottom was reinforced with iron studs and arched at the top, as if leading to a dungeon. Yet when she pulled on its iron ring, it creaked open as easily as the front door. Unlike the main entrance, another door lay behind this one, a chunk of solid steel that looked as thick and impenetrable as a bank vault.

Before they had time to ponder this new dilemma, the inner door clicked and swung silently inward to expose a tubular corridor with walls, floors, and ceiling made of steel. Andie felt as if she were staring into a giant pipeline, or the cold core of a nuclear reactor.

"What the hell?" Cal said.

A faint glow emanated from an opening on the right, thirty feet ahead. Cal called out for her to wait as Andie strode down the dark corridor, her footsteps echoing on the steel.

She could not see where the passage ended, but the light was coming from a room revealed by another open steel door. Andie blinked in surprise as she peered inside to find a cube-shaped room lined with onyx partitions embedded in the walls, divided at six-inch intervals by laser-like slivers of light.

The main source of illumination was a cylinder of violet light in the center of the room, stretching from floor to ceiling. Like the walls of the Bibliotheca Alexandrina, the cylinder was filled with words from many different writing systems, projected in a swarm of motionless white characters.

Andie moved closer and spotted a phrase in English.

The store of all knowledge is the memory of humankind.

"Welcome."

Andie jumped at the sound of the computerized voice. She looked up and noticed a tiny speaker embedded in the ceiling, at the top of the cylinder of light. "Hello?" she said. "Is someone there?"

"My name is Hypatia."

From her research at the library, Andie recalled that Hypatia was an ancient philosopher and astronomer, the first female mathematician of note recorded in the annals of history. She was also reputed to be the last keeper of the Library of Alexandria.

Cal whispered, "Is this some kind of AI?"

"I guess," Andie whispered back, then said in a louder voice, "Hi, Hypatia." The exchange of pleasantries with a voice assistant in an abandoned house felt bizarre in the extreme.

Not abandoned, she thought. *Staged, for some unknown purpose.*

Unsure what to do, she navigated the perimeter of the room, noting the symmetry of the onyx partitions and the cool sterile air. "This is a data storage room, isn't it?"

"Indeed," Hypatia replied.

"Is this the Hall of Records?

"It appears to be more of a square than a hall."

Andie felt as if someone unseen were laughing at them. "Then what is it?"

"All libraries, in all forms, are an attempt to mold chaos into order. A library is a physical symbol of the soul. A torch lit by the fire of Prometheus. The most powerful creation of humankind."

"Do you know anything about Dr. James Corwin?"

"I am a keeper of lost knowledge, and do not concern myself with modern affairs."

"Can you at least tell me if he's dead or alive?"

"I am a keeper of lost knowledge, and do not concern myself with modern affairs."

Andie raised her voice in frustration. "Hypatia—and whoever else might be listening—if you know anything about Dr. Corwin, whether or not he's still alive, or where the Enneagon is—if you know anything at all that might help, then please tell us."

"I am a keeper of lost knowledge," the voice repeated, "and do not concern myself with modern affairs."

Cal shook his head, and Andie sucked in a breath, working to corral her anger. "Fine," she said. "What kind of lost knowledge do you protect?"

"The library preserves the fruits of humanity's intellectual labor, as well as higher secrets."

"What secrets?" Cal said. "Who preserved them?"

"Over time, as methods of transcription increased in sophistication, an abundance of knowledge from many different cultures was preserved. Yet opposing forces were at work. War, migration, successions, natural disasters. The destruction of information became more and more commonplace, and fearing even more devastating losses, the decision was made to preserve the most significant works in a safe location, shielded from the capricious forces of nature, the ravages of time, and the whims of kings and tyrants. Even today, such destruction continues in many parts of the world."

"You're not telling us anything," Cal said in frustration.

Andie laid a hand on his arm. "Was the knowledge in the Library of Alexandria preserved somehow?"

"Over time, as methods of inscription increased in sophistication, an abundance of knowledge from many different cultures was preserved. Yet opposing forces were also at work. War, migration—"

"Yeah, yeah, we got that," Cal said. He took out his phone to take a video of the room. "That's weird. The camera isn't working."

"No recordings of the premises are allowed," Hypatia said. "Violators will not be allowed to leave."

"There's probably a security system," Andie said in a low voice. "Better not to risk it."

Startled, Cal looked over at her. "Can they do that? Jam my camera?"

"I don't think it's public yet, but, yeah, there's remote camera-blocking tech out there. Concert venues have lobbied for it for years."

"I'm sure the government would love it too. Scratch that: I'm sure they have it." He slowly lowered the phone, his eyes flicking about the room as if searching for a hidden camera. "I should know better. I'm never leaving the house without my SLR again."

"What happened to the library in modern day?" Andie asked Hypatia.

"With the methods of preservation unbound by traditional restraints, information can now be encoded in the grains of matter itself, the building blocks of the universe."

"Is she talking about the cloud?" Cal said.

"I think she's implying they're beyond that," Andie said. "Maybe she means storing information on atoms, but that's brand-new . . . Nothing approaching this sort of scale."

Andie had to admit the implication of Hypatia's words—centuries and even millennia of knowledge hidden away from the general populace—was an incredibly tantalizing proposition. A sudden thought hit her. What if Democritus's theories on the atom had not been abandoned after all, but kept alive by whoever had started this library?

And he was but a single philosopher among the legions of thinkers and inventors lost to the ravages of time. What if there was an entire parallel track of scientific knowledge and progress unknown to the vast majority of the world?

Andie walked to one of the walls and placed her hands on the smooth onyx surface. It was solid. She waved a hand in front of a violet beam. No heat, no variance in the light.

"Can we look at the records?" Cal asked Hypatia. "Take any of this out of here?"

"Do you possess archival access?"

"Yes."

"Then please step forward so I may scan your retina."

"Um, maybe I don't."

"I'm afraid the knowledge in this library is unavailable to those without archival access."

"What are the objects in the house?" Andie asked. "In the rooms upstairs?"

"Objects in the personal collection of the Keeper."

"But what *are* they?"

"Objects in the personal collection of the Keeper."

"Okay—who's the Keeper?"

"I am the avatar of the Keeper. But please, if you prefer, call me Hypatia."

As intriguing—and maddening—as the conversation was, Andie had the feeling she was supposed to do something here. Something to move things forward.

Maybe she was supposed to ask the right question. "How much information is in here?"

"We have carefully curated our collection, as a librarian is at risk of being swallowed by her own library. According to Jorge Luis Borges, an Argentinian literary figure who lived from 1899 to 1986, a library in which every book exists is simply called 'the universe,' a place of infinite possibility that is impossible to comprehend."

"That's pretty deep, Hypatia, but I have to disagree," Andie said. "We don't *know* yet what might matter."

"Are you arguing with a voice assistant?" Cal asked.

Andie paced back and forth, shredding a thumbnail. "I'm just trying to figure out what we're supposed to do."

"Try showing her the Star Phone."

Andie had been debating how much to reveal, but she reasoned anyone listening behind the scenes would at least know about the Star Phone, since it had granted them entry. After taking out the device, she slowly circled the room, aiming it first at the onyx partitions, the ceiling and the floor, and then finally at the violet cylinder. "Nothing's changed."

"Hypatia," Cal said, "have you ever heard of a Star Phone?"

"Indeed."

"What is it?"

"That which allowed you to enter."

"Yeah. We got that. Anything else?"

"A path of wisdom for those who seek."

Andie stepped right up to the cylinder with the Star Phone. "What else is it?"

"Over time, as methods of inscription increased in sophistication, an abundance of knowledge from many different cultures was preserved."

"Dammit!" she said.

"Please respect the sanctity of the Keeper's chamber."

"Wave it through," Cal suggested.

"Why?"

"I don't know. Just try it."

"Where does the Star Phone lead?" Andie asked.

"It is a path of wisdom for those who seek," Hypatia said.

"And where does this path end?"

"Only with great foresight and vision may the path of humanity be altered."

"What do you know about the Leap Year Society?"

"I am not authorized to discuss this."

Clenching her hands in frustration, Andie did as Cal had suggested, reaching out to wave the device through the stream of violet light. As soon as she did, she noticed movement on the face of the Star Phone. She edged closer, stepping inside the swarm of languages, watching in shock as a new code typed itself into the cursor spaces. As before, the nine-digit code locked into place, now revealing the image of a blue zero in the middle of a shape resembling a double helix. Inside the zero, in turn, was a curious symbol outlined in crimson: the number 3 with a looped tail, set beneath a curved horn or claw lying on its side and cradling a square or hollow box.

As before, the previous code disappeared, reverting to a blinking cursor.

"Good suggestion," Andie said to Cal, slowly stepping away.

"What did you see?"

After showing him the altered face of the Star Phone, which caused him to whistle, Andie peppered Hypatia with questions until she grew tired of hearing the same answers over and over, with little variance except for a historical factoid now and again.

"Hey," Cal said, touching her shoulder. "We're not getting anything new, and I'm worried we're overstaying our welcome." He gave the steel door a nervous glance. "I don't want to be stuck in here when this vault closes for the night."

She realized he was right, though she had to vent some frustration. "Who the hell are you?" she shouted. "Show yourselves, dammit! *Help* us!"

The silence of the underground vault was deafening.

"The real Hypatia would have come in person," Andie said in disgust, then turned on her heel and left.

They left the house without incident. Trying to decide what to do next, Andie and Cal ducked into an unassuming restaurant wedged between a shoe store and a corner market, a dozen blocks south of the not-so-abandoned villa.

Or maybe it was abandoned. Maybe the owners of the house and the keepers of the digital library controlled events from a remote location, watching over every visitor, playing God in their little universe. Andie was torn between falling to her knees with awe at the life-changing promise of secret knowledge the library offered, and a scoffing suspicion that it didn't actually harbor the information Hypatia suggested it did. Either way, someone had put the hologram in place, and Andie's blood boiled at the thought of someone watching from the shadows as she and Cal entered the house and choosing not to intervene.

Or maybe Dr. Corwin himself was the keeper of the library, and the house had been abandoned since he disappeared.

That didn't quite make sense to her, since Dr. Corwin lived halfway across the world. Surely someone else was involved.

She didn't know what the hell was going on.

After choosing a table in the basement of the restaurant, a white-walled room with a giant projector screen playing Egyptian music videos on one of the walls, Andie and Cal decided to split a greasy but delicious layered pastry called a *fateer*.

"We've got to find a way to go back," Cal said. He seemed dazed by what they had seen. "Imagine what they might have stored in that vault."

"*If* they have what Hypatia implied, and *if* they wanted to share, they would have released it a long time ago."

"They can't just keep it to themselves in that dungeon."

"Apparently, they can. And they have."

Cal took a long drink of *karkadeh*, a cold hibiscus tea that came with the meal, then stared down at his hands. "I only got a glimpse of what was going on in that black-site facility I investigated. How many governments and companies around the world are conducting experiments and harboring research we never hear about?"

"Your point is? I'm not here to save the world."

"Maybe you should be."

Andie pushed her plate away. While the fateer was satisfying at first, the grease was starting to get to her. As was the conversation.

"Look," Cal said after a moment. "I'm just trying to get a handle on all this. I know it's extremely personal to you—but it is to me too."

Andie steepled her fingers against her mouth, closed her eyes, and let out a deep breath. "I know."

After the waiter swung by to drop the check, Cal said, "I can let the library go, but we need to get out of this city. Has anything changed in your mind?"

Still corralling her anger, she opened her eyes and stared at the video screen behind Cal without really seeing it. "I'm confused as to how it all fits together. Was Dr. Corwin part of the Leap Year Society, or did they shoot him? Are there two different factions? More than two? Either way, they're not trying to kill us for no reason. Everyone seems to want the Star Phone and whatever it leads to, so I still think following it is our best bet."

"I have to agree. Do you have any idea what the next clue means? Where we might need to go?"

"The zero makes me think of Aryabhata. He was an Indian astronomer and mathematician—fifth or sixth century, I think—"

"Pre-JC, or post?"

"Post. He wrote an incredible work of genius called the *Aryabhatiya* when he was only twenty-three. Among other things, he's credited with advancing the conceptual framework of the absence of a measurable quantity. The zero. He didn't come up with it himself—it was a process, one which the Mayans, and the Babylonians before them, were also undertaking—but Aryabhata devised a number system around it. He was also one of Dr. Corwin's favorite historical figures. It's a good place to start."

"And the rest? The DNA thingy and those squiggly lines?"

"I don't know about the double helix. The other symbol looks Hindi or Sanskrit to me, which fits with Aryabhata. In fact, let me check on that right now."

When Andie pulled out the phone she had purchased in the Alexandrian airport, she decided to quickly check her email. There was still no reply from Dr. Corwin—she had almost given up hope on that front—but there was a new message from a sender called Cassi with a subject line that read Invitation to a Masked Ball.

The sender's return address was Cassi14159@gmail.com. Thinking it was spam, she started to delete it, but something about those numbers and the odd subject line made her pause.

As a frenetic EDM video played in the background, she stared at the address for a moment before it clicked.

"One four one five nine. Those are the first five numbers of pi after the decimal point."

"What are you looking at?" he asked.

"Hang on."

By the time Andie finished reading the short email and realized the import of the sender's name, her face had gone white, her hands trembling as they clutched the cell phone. Instead of responding to Cal's repeated inquiries, she handed him the phone and sat rigid in her chair, trying to process the storm of emotions whipping through her with the force of a hurricane.

> Dear Andromeda,
>   I just received word of the unfortunate situation in which you're involved. I have intervened on your behalf and arranged for you to attend a soiree in

Venice this weekend, where it is my greatest hope that all differences will be resolved. You'll find first-class tickets with EgyptAir for you and your friend waiting at Borg El Arab International Airport.

You have my word you will arrive in Venice unharmed and under my protection. Yet I must impress upon you that, if you do not accept my invitation, I will not be able to protect you. I wish it were not so, but there are powerful forces involved—extremely powerful—who are beyond my ability to influence.

I'm so terribly sorry the first communication you've received from me after all this time should arrive in such a manner, and I won't attempt to convey in an email the depth of emotion I feel about the prospect of seeing you again. I love you more than you could ever know, Little Mouse, and implore you to come to Venice so we can reconnect in person and work together to resolve this unfortunate situation.

To attend the ball, simply wait atop the Ponte dell'Accademia at midnight on Friday night, and someone will transport you. You may dress however you wish, though I suggest formal attire befitting your truly remarkable beauty. I'll never forget how lovely you looked carrying father's crystal angel. Finally, it's extremely important—imperative—that you bring the device called the Star Phone.

Love forever,
Your mother

 PART FOUR

25

As the Egyptian sun crested the horizon, bathing the hillside around the Catacombs of Kom el-Shoqafa in honey, Omer emerged, soaking wet, from the closed entrance to the mausoleum, startling an early-bird tourist so badly she tripped and fell as she fled across the courtyard.

There was no sign of anyone else. Even if Zawadi thought he had survived, she would never risk exposure by sticking around this long. After giving the shuttered guard shack a sidelong glance—the morning shift would arrive any minute and discover the body—Omer hurried through the gate and walked down the hill, reflecting on his escape as he searched for a taxi. The long submersion had destroyed his cell phone.

Under any circumstance, Zawadi was a feared opponent. If the odds were even, Omer did not know who would prevail between them. But Zawadi had shot him in the shoulder before he even knew she was there. Fearing others nearby and knowing she had the superior position, Omer had had no choice but to cower behind a ruined pillar in the courtyard. When Zawadi had flushed him out, instead of running across the open courtyard as she wanted, he had doubled back into the catacombs, hoping she would not give chase.

Yet she had bounded down the spiral staircase after him, forcing him to take the only option he saw left: a desperate dive into the murky waters of the flooded lower level.

Omer could hold his breath for an extraordinarily long time. Yet Zawadi would leave nothing to chance. She might divine where he had gone and wait around to ensure he never surfaced.

What she would not do, however, was follow him down. That would be suicidal—as he knew it might be for him. Not knowing if he would ever take another breath, Omer filled his lungs with air before he dove, lowered his respiratory rate, and swam through the submerged catacombs, using his waterproof penlight to guide the way as he searched for another exit. Beneath him, shards of broken pottery protruded from the sand-covered floor. He suspected the sand had flushed in with the groundwater, and that this level had never been excavated.

Long minutes later, on the verge of having to risk surfacing in front of Zawadi, he found a sagging portion of the ceiling down one of the ruined passages. He used his boot knife to pry loose one of the stones, and just before he blacked out, he got another stone loose, and then another, and managed to poke his head through the hole. Air, sweet air! He had no idea if he had broken through to the next level up or found another section entirely. It didn't matter. Instead of climbing out and risking exposure, he floated in the chilly water for hours, returning to the hole for air as needed.

To stop the blood loss from the gunshot wound, he took off his windbreaker and made a crude tourniquet. Used to submerging his body in extreme temperatures, he withstood the cold, imagining his flesh as a suit of armor encasing his body, keeping him warm and dry. His greatest fear was infection from the filthy water, but there was nothing he could do about that until he surfaced.

When he finally climbed out of the flooded level, half-alive and barely able to climb the stairs, Zawadi was nowhere to be seen. Just to be sure, he waited inside the mausoleum until sunrise and tried not to stumble when he emerged into daylight.

A modicum of strength returned as the sun warmed his skin,

and his relief at surviving the ordeal turned to anger and then satisfaction and, finally, to his first moment of true hope in days.

The enemy had sent their best to kill him and had failed.

Not only that: they, and any Ascendants who were watching, would *think* they had succeeded.

Twelve hours later, in the city of Amman in Jordan, Omer watched in the darkness as Juma Qureshi opened the door to her top-floor suite. By the stillness of her presence, he knew she had noticed the red pinprick of light on the left side of her chest, just atop her breast.

"Come in," he said softly, from an armchair in the living room

"Can I turn on the light?"

"Please do."

Juma closed the door behind her as she stepped inside the suite and flicked on the track lighting. On the other side of the living room, Omer was sitting in a chair, holding a black handgun with a laser sight under the barrel. Behind him, outside a plate-glass window, the glowing towers of the Al-Husseini Mosque sat like a golden crown atop the city.

"My God, Omer, you look like hell. Why is your shoulder bound? Did you get shot?"

He pointed at a low-slung chartreuse sofa to her right. "Sit."

They had been lovers and comrades in arms for almost three years, and he knew her stress reactions as well as she did. As she stepped hesitantly out of the entrance hall, entering the open-floor-plan living room, he nudged his head to the left, his eyes never leaving hers. "On the side by the table. Take off your coat and leave your gun on the floor."

"Is this really necessary?"

"I won't ask again."

Moving in slow motion, she removed her Glock G17 from its ankle holster and laid it on the floor. After shrugging out of her belted red coat and draping it over a chair, she took a seat on the couch. Beside her was a glass end table with a single cup of tea. Juma was quite fastidious and did not miss details. She would realize she had not left it out, and what it portended.

"Drink," Omer said.

"What is it?"

"A sedative. We're going to talk. What happens after you fall asleep depends on what you say."

"It doesn't have to be like this, my love. Why don't we step into the bedroom—"

"And give you an opportunity to catch me off guard? I think not."

She shook out her lustrous dark hair as she sank into the sofa, her lips puckering as she crossed her legs. "Tie me up first, if you like."

"As attractive as that sounds, I might as well give you my gun."

She took her bottom lip between her teeth and looked away. "I trusted you."

"And I, you. Circumstances change."

"I should have changed my code."

"You should have, but it wouldn't have mattered. Drink the tea, Juma."

After stroking the ceramic cup with a fingernail, she lifted the mug and took a sip of the tepid beverage. It would taste like peppermint, he knew.

She pursed her lips and drank the entire contents, then showed him the empty bottom of the cup.

"Good," he said. "Thank you."

"What do you want? You know I don't have access to anything more than you once did."

"I don't think that's true. In fact, I think you're slated for Ascension."

Juma laughed. "You think so much of me? I don't know where the target is, Omer. I swear it."

"Whether or not you're telling the truth, I have a different strategy. Where is the Archon?"

"What? The *Archon*? I've no idea."

"Do you not? I have a feeling something very important is underway, and security will be heightened. There's a packed suitcase in your bedroom. Where are you going?"

"New York. A mission."

"To do what?"

"You know I can't say."

"Where is your phone?"

After a brief hesitation, she started to reach into her yellow leather handbag.

"Give me the whole purse."

After she complied, Omer pulled out a silver cell phone identical to his own. He slid it across the tile floor. "Unlock it." When she didn't respond, Omer kept the gun trained on her and slid a serrated knife out of the side of his boot. He asked again.

"What are you hoping to accomplish, Omer? Are you on a suicide mission?"

"On the contrary. I aim to get my life back."

"My God, you're still trying to deliver the target. Do you actually think they'd take you back? That will make it worse!"

"They'll reconsider once I stage an attack on whoever is holding her, blame that bitch Zawadi, and emerge the hero."

"If the Archon even suspects you have done this and questions you—"

"That's a chance I'll have to take," he said evenly.

"You'll kill me either way, won't you? They know of our past, and if there's any doubt, I'll be interrogated as well."

"As I said, what happens next depends on you. Now, I'll ask again: Where is the Archon?"

Juma sat mute on the couch. With a sigh, Omer took the knife and stood. "You don't have to give me a location; I wouldn't have trusted you anyway. But you do have to unlock your phone."

After another long pause, Juma reached down to pick up her phone, then used the retina scanner to unlock it. She passed it across the floor. Omer searched through the phone with one eye trained on

Juma, then looked up in satisfaction.

"Venice," he murmured. "Yes, I've heard rumors."

She didn't respond.

"I can see it in your eyes, Juma. Maybe someone without our history could not, but I know you too well. You're getting sleepy, aren't you?"

"I don't want to die," she whispered.

"Nor do you have to."

"But I haven't given you anything."

"I never planned for you to. But the only way I can let you live is if you leave them. Tell the Ascendants you're disappearing, Juma. Forever."

"You—you can't ask that of me."

"Call them. Tell them right now." He tossed the phone on her lap as her eyelids grew heavy. "Do you want to live or not?"

"That is not a life, is it? It's why you're here in the first place. I'm so tired, Omer."

"Do this before you sleep."

"Look at me, my love. Both of us have yearned for the same thing for so long! When I lose consciousness, remember what we have and find another way. I beg you. We can do this together. I will help you. No one ever has to know. We'll be as we once were and join them together."

She refused to take the phone, pleading with her eyes until her body sagged and her breathing became full and steady. Once sure she was asleep, he laid her gently on her back, kissed her on each eyelid, and held a pillow over her face.

Venice, Italy

—○ **26** ○—

Mainland Italy receded from view as the vaporetto left Marco Polo Airport and chugged through the lagoon toward the famous floating city. The cramped interior of the water taxi, combined with the roll of the waves and the stifling humidity, was starting to nauseate Andie. She fought her way to the railing of the uncovered section near the front of the boat and took deep draughts of air, ignoring the flustered stares of two Versace-clad women she had displaced to get there.

Cal stayed put. They had spoken very little since Andie had declared she was going to Venice, brushing aside his heated objections.

Trust no one, Dr. Corwin had told her. *Not even your own family.*

Andie knew it was a trap and didn't care. It was her *mother.* She was going to the damn ball.

Cal's most stringent argument was that her mother may not have actually written the note. Despite the use of the nickname Little Mouse, Andie had harbored this exact concern when reading the email for the first time, thinking the language was stilted. Though what did one say under the circumstances? How did you explain a twenty-year absence? Yes, she'd had her doubts as she read it—right until she encountered that telltale line near the end.

I'll never forget how lovely you looked carrying father's crystal angel.

When Andie was very young, five or six at most, she had accidentally broken an angel figurine her father had inherited from his grandmother. It was very expensive, a prized possession he kept on a display shelf in the dining room. One weekend morning, when her father was on a long walk, Andie had gotten a little rambunctious and crashed into the bottom of the shelf. The crystal angel had toppled over and shattered. Andie was mortified and couldn't stop crying, knowing how upset he would be.

When her mother found out, she gathered Andie in her arms and said it was better if she took the blame instead. Andie cringed in her bedroom when her father returned and shouted at her mother. As far as Andie knew, he had never discovered the truth.

This one line, incongruent with the rest of the message, had erased all doubt in Andie's mind. Not just that, but she was sure the line harbored a hidden message. All those years ago, when her mother had diverted her father's wrath, she had been protecting Andie—and now she was trying to do so again.

Everything that had happened between those two points in time was a mystery Andie desperately wanted to solve. She could only assume her mother was a member of this shadowy organization. But at the moment, the mystery was secondary to the present reality: her mother knew she was in trouble and had reached out.

And nothing had ever felt quite so good.

"Fine," Cal had said, as they retrieved two tickets at the Alexandria airport, just as the email had promised. Somehow, Andie's mother knew about their false passports, because their tickets were issued under those names. "Maybe only your mother knows about the crystal angel, but someone could have tortured her for the information."

"In that case," Andie had replied, "I *really* have to go."

After throwing up his hands, Cal gave up trying to dissuade her. She knew he was just as terrified as she was, and almost as motivated.

Well, he didn't have to come to Venice.

None of this meant Andie didn't intend to take precautions. It was already four in the afternoon on Friday, eight hours before the appointed meeting time. Just enough time to recoup over dinner, establish what safeguards they could—and find a place to hide the Star Phone.

Andie's first impression of Venice, under a searing blue sky as the vaporetto approached the fabled city from a distance, was of a smear of pastel chalk. But as the buildings clarified and the water taxi pulled into Piazza San Marco, her breath caught in her throat and she stared slack-jawed at the sight. Despite heaving with tourists and vendors, the massive seaside plaza ringed by domes and spires and multitiered arcades, sprinkled with elegant green lampposts and soaring columns, was a fantasy made real. Backed by the turquoise expanse of the Grand Canal—much wider than she had imagined—the splendor of San Marco was overwhelming, the wealth of centuries compressed onto a dollop of land that had been the most powerful real estate in the world for over four hundred years.

Andie couldn't stop gawking at the view. Piazza San Marco was a snowflake cast in marble by Bernini, an outdoor chapel to art and beauty and the genius of humankind, and one which still, as far as she could tell, set the gold standard.

As the vaporetto pulled away and entered the Grand Canal, the Doge's Palace and Saint Mark's Basilica receding gracefully from view, she wrenched her mind to the task at hand. The message had said to wait atop the Ponte dell'Accademia at midnight. The Ponte dell'Accademia was a footbridge—one of four spanning the Grand Canal—that linked the tourist mecca of San Marco with the quieter neighborhood of Dorsoduro. Soon, after a glimpse of the sumptuous old mansions lining the Grand Canal like a succession of Renaissance paintings, the water taxi crossed to the Dorsoduro side and pulled right up to the Ponte dell'Accademia—also a vaporetto stop.

Andie and Cal shouldered their backpacks and exited the boat with a crush of other tourists as the canal water lapped against the barnacle-encrusted pilings supporting the city. Seagulls whirled in the sultry air, an accordion player dueled with a violinist by a public waterspout, and the heady smell of jasmine competed with the sweet stench of the canal.

While quieter than San Marco, the modest plaza fronting the bridge was still a beehive of activity. A signpost guided the way to the Gallerie dell'Accademia, the Peggy Guggenheim Museum, and other sights. There were no roads or new construction in Venice, not a hint of blacktop in sight. Change the clothing and take away the tourist trinkets, and it could have been the fifteenth century.

They were both starving. After taking some time to orient themselves, wandering the narrow lanes and tight *campi* between the Grand Canal and the Giudecca Canal, they found a quiet little pizzeria down an alley with white mortar showing through the bricks.

A waiter led them to a courtyard table beside a wall covered in blooming star jasmine. Andie ordered a glass of wine to calm her nerves, Cal ordered a beer, and they decided to split a gorgonzola-and-onion pizza and a caprese salad.

As Andie fiddled with a coaster, Cal leaned toward the table. "You ready for this?"

"Of course not."

"Yeah. Bad question. As ready as you're gonna be?"

"At this point, I don't see an advantage to overthinking it."

In truth, they had already installed what precautions they could. Cal's friend Dane had sent Cal a link to install remote tracking software on both their cell phones. Cal was not going to the ball, and they had developed special distress signals for each other in case they were forced to text or call under duress. While she was at the ball, Cal planned to roam the back streets of the city and find a place to stay out of sight. If things went south, he would alert the authorities and try to reach Andie.

When they parted ways after dinner, the soft dusk sky streaked with lavender, Andie disappeared into as many dark alleys and hidden courtyards as she could. She did this partly because such unexpected perambulations were inevitable in Venice, but mostly to throw off anyone watching her as she looked for a safe place to stash the Star Phone.

Dorsoduro was a maze of twisting cobblestone lanes, footbridges spanning tiny canals, hidden steps and archways, courtyards, secret gardens, saints peering down from alcoves, and masses of purple and crimson bougainvillea framing wooden shutters. She felt as if she were walking through an impressionist painting weeping tears of grime, a floating city of stone and flowers, a watery journey into the imagination. Yet as she delved into the quieter sections of the neighborhood, far from the madding crowd, she saw a different side to the city, one held together by spit and grit and history. Everything fading and peeling, shirtless men hanging out of windows to drape clothes on wires that stretched across the canals, children licking gelato and playing soccer in ruined plazas, balconies with striped canvas window sheets, the lilt of Italian and the clang of dishes, the smell of tobacco and shellfish.

Night descended on the city. As Andie walked the lamplit streets alone, the city dreamy and inchoate after dark, her long-repressed emotions bubbled over, filling her with so much nervous energy she felt electrified. She was about to see her mother for the first time in twenty years! It took an act of willpower to remind herself of the kind of people she was dealing with.

Half an hour before midnight, the claustrophobic streets hemmed in by canals and lagoons started to feel oppressive. There was no park or forest to run to, no easy way to stretch her long legs if she needed to escape. Andie was distressed she still had not found a good place to hide the Star Phone. If she took it with her, she would have no leverage.

After passing by the Ponte dell'Accademia for the umpteenth time, she stepped inside the public restroom near the bridge. There were plenty of people around. When she finished using the facilities, she paused before she opened the stall door, then turned to inspect the toilet. Moving as quietly as she could, she gently removed the lid of the tank and set it on the closed seat. It looked the same as any other on the inside: two valves and a rubber ball floating atop the water. Just to be sure, she flushed the toilet again and noticed the water level did not exceed the top of the cylindrical valve.

With a furtive glance behind her, she took out the Star Phone and wrapped it in a shirt from her backpack, then set it atop the flat surface of the valve. She carefully tapped the device on either side to ensure it would not slide off. It was a ridiculous place to hide something, but she hoped that would work in her favor. Who would suspect a public restroom? Plus, it closed at midnight. With any luck, Andie could retrieve it first thing in the morning, before anyone else went inside.

She exited the restroom and acted as normal as she could. If her pursuers wanted to trace her route in Venice and search every single place she might have hidden the Star Phone, they had a huge task in front of them.

Like a disappearing childhood, the appointed hour arrived before she knew it. At five minutes to midnight, panic surged through her. What if her mother hadn't sent the message after all? Or worse: What if she had sent it to lure Andie to Venice, but wouldn't be there to meet her?

What if she was abandoning her just like before?

That thought caused a sharp pang in her stomach. Andie shook it off with a snarl, striding up the steps to the long footbridge arching over the Grand Canal. To either side, a corridor of darkened buildings pressed against the glossy surface of the water. She was wearing her jeans, running sneakers, and the same military-green hoodie she had worn for most of the journey. She might be acceding to her mother's request, but Andie wasn't about to play little princess and dress up for the ball. She didn't care if she stood out, or embarrassed her mother's friends.

Andie was going as herself.

Despite the late hour, a steady flow of people passed across the Ponte dell'Accademia. Andie waited at the apex of the bridge with folded arms, trying not to look conspicuous as she eyed everyone who passed, feeling very awkward standing alone amid the throngs of young Venetians and nighttime tour groups and couples strolling arm in arm across the canal. Precisely at the stroke of midnight, she was startled when a mustachioed gondolier—dressed in the classic black pants and navy-blue-and-white striped shirt—touched her elbow as he passed her on the bridge. "Come with me," he murmured.

After pausing a beat, Andie followed him to the Dorsoduro side of the bridge, then down a short flight of concrete steps to where a few gondolas were moored along the canal. No one paid them any mind as the gondolier extended a hand to help Andie aboard his vessel, a black-lacquered gondola with silver trim and an iron feather at the head of the prow.

When she was young and searching for answers to her visions, Andie had studied a number of ancient symbols. To the Native Americans and other cultures, a feather represented freedom, inspiration, and travel, not just with the body but with the mind and spirit. A symbol of evolution to a higher plane.

An ascension.

She took a seat on a red-upholstered bench strewn with cushions. The gondolier untied the boat and poled away from the wooden pilings jutting out of the water.

"Where are we going?" she asked.

He did not answer or even glance her way. Instead he stood atop a platform at the rear of the boat and pushed the gondola through the Grand Canal with slow, even strokes. They were headed away from the lagoon, deeper into the city. A shadowy tunnel of palatial buildings hovered on either side. The silence was broken only by the water lapping against the sides of the boat, the creak of wooden vessels moored along the canal, and the whisper of the gondolier's oar as it dipped in and out of the water. Besides the moon, the only sources of illumination were the oily glow of the streetlamps reflecting on the edges of the water, and every now and then a wink of light from another gondola slithering past in the darkness.

As the Grand Canal inscribed the beginning of its S curve, Andie suspected the gondolier would take her down one of the labyrinthine side channels and disappear into the bowels of the city. After passing beneath the golden glow of the Rialto Bridge, her guide did veer left into a narrow waterway, but he surprised her by pulling alongside one of the lavish estates lining the Grand Canal, and mooring beside an arched loggia that stretched for half a block.

Andie looked up and caught her breath at the sight of the pale marble facade illuminated by the moon. Each of the four stories had different styles of balustrades and ornamental pillars, rising to a flat roof topped with a field of delicate sphere-tipped spires, which belonged more to a wedding cake than to a building.

The gondolier was a perfect gentleman as he extended his hand to help her onto the limestone walkway. A man in an ankle-length overcoat and a wide-brimmed hat stepped out from one of the darkened archways of the loggia, bearing a handheld copper lantern. His face was obscured by a creepy ivory mask that tapered down to his chest like the snout of an anteater. The mask had eyeholes but no openings for the nose or the mouth. He swept a gloved hand toward the interior, signaling for Andie to proceed.

The gondola had already slipped into the inky waters of the canal. Andie swallowed and turned to face the man in the mask. "Who are you?" she asked, realizing it could be a woman behind the disguise.

It could even be her mother.

In response, the figure beckoned again, then turned and disappeared into the loggia. Andie clenched her fists and followed, walking beneath one of the towering archways, footsteps swishing on stone as they approached an ornate wooden door with a brass handle.

A deep male voice behind the mask startled her. "Your phone, please."

"Why?"

"Protocol demands."

"Whose protocol?"

No answer.

"And if I refuse?"

"You won't be allowed to enter."

With a smirk meant to hide her growing unease, Andie dug in her pocket and handed him the prepaid phone she had purchased in Egypt. She thought he would refuse and ask for the Star Phone, but he accepted the burner phone with a nod, took a black scanner out of the inside of his coat, and ran it over her clothes. It beeped outside her other coat pocket. She removed her pocketknife and handed that over as well.

The scanner did not go off again, and he reached for the pull ring. Andie breathed a sigh of relief. She had lost the tracking software on her cell, and what little protection the pocketknife offered, but at least she was going inside.

One step closer.

The open door revealed a flight of marble steps. Light spilled down from above. In the background, she heard distant laughter and the faint sound of classical music.

On either side of the stairwell hung dozens and dozens of elaborate masks. Interspersed among the Venetian Carnival–style pieces were masks of a more macabre variety, some of them similar to her guide's, some depicting Death in its many incarnations, some depicting an eerie blank face with no markings at all.

"Choose any you like," the man said, as he led the way up the steps.

"I'm fine."

"As you wish."

"What are these . . . other masks . . . for?"

"The ball is a prelude to the Redentore Festival, which marks the end of the plague in Venice."

"Is anyone going to tell me whose party it is? The Ascendants? The Leap Year Society?"

Again, there was no response. Andie seethed in frustration, hating that she had to play their game, growing more and more doubtful she would ever see her mother. *Cal was right. I don't know how they did it, but they impersonated her somehow. I'm never going to see her, and they'll never let me leave.*

Yet the possibility that she was wrong kept her going, and she knew her internal debate was pointless. She had come this far. She was seeing it through. *Who the hell are you people? What have you done with my mother and my mentor?*

They emerged into a foyer with an enormous hanging lantern suspended from the ceiling, greeted by a stone knight with a coat of arms carved on a shield. French doors opened onto an interior courtyard. A hallway beckoned on either side, and a staircase wide enough for a team of horses led into the higher reaches of the mansion. The sounds of revelry steadily increased as they climbed to the second story, exited into another foyer, and passed into a grand ballroom the size of a gymnasium, filled with hundreds of people.

Andie tried not to gawk at the scene. Greek and Roman statues lined the perimeter, interspersed with busts, vases, and other decorative art set on pedestals. Stunning Renaissance frescoes with a pink-and-silver theme adorned the long side walls from top to bottom, mostly sensual nudes performing a variety of tasks in ancient centers of learning. The floor was white marble, and a domed ceiling soared far overhead, punctuated by a stunning blown-glass chandelier. On the higher levels, revelers gazed down on the festivities from interior balconies. Andie didn't know much about classical music, but she thought it was Vivaldi's *Four Seasons* playing through the hidden speakers.

The majority of partygoers wore masks and formal evening attire. Yet some of the guests—including all of those carting silver trays of drinks and hors d'oeuvres around the room—wore racy and outlandish carnival outfits, designed to showcase their incredible physiques. Not ten feet from her, a young woman wearing a feathered headdress and covered in gold body paint, which left nothing to the imagination, was offering champagne to a crowd. A bare-chested man wearing silk pantaloons and a jester's cap trailed behind her with a plate of langoustine tails.

Maybe only the gorgeous ones were allowed to forego masks. Or maybe they had hired a bunch of supermodels to cater, or they all had incredible genes. Andie didn't know and didn't care. Being perfect had never appealed to her.

It's a good thing, because I've got a long hill to climb.

Despite her general disdain for the scene, she felt more awkward than she ever had in her life—standing on the edge of the ball looking in, with tired bags under her eyes and in dire need of a wash, dressed in travel-worn jeans and a green hoodie as the cream of society swirled about her, pairing off to dance to the music or just wandering confidently about the room, sipping champagne and nibbling on caviar. No one was using the high-backed ebony chairs carved with red roses that lined the walls, and she debated disappearing into one. After several minutes, when no one had spoken to her or even glanced her way, she began to wonder if she was invisible. Maybe the entire ball was a grand illusion, or behind a pane of one-way glass that cordoned off the section in which she was standing.

But then someone stepped out of the crowd and began to walk Andie's way. Though wearing a creepy mask similar to the man who had brought her in—a number of people had them on—Andie could tell it was a woman by the sway to her walk, her shimmering silver dress, and the delicate turn to her wrists. As she passed one of the servers, she set her wineglass on his tray without missing a beat, started walking faster, and whipped off her mask as she approached Andie, revealing a smiling face with an undeniable similarity to her own.

"Mom?" Andie managed to croak, just before her mother dropped her mask on the floor and swept her up in her arms, pressing her tight to her breast and sobbing as she stroked her hair. "Little Mouse," she kept repeating. "I've missed you so much."

Despite the danger and Andie's resolve to stay calm and focused, despite the looming question of why this woman was standing there of her own free will but had waited twenty years to contact her, Andie couldn't stop the tears from flowing. She clutched her mother tight and gave in to the moment, shuddering as years and years of pain and self-doubt poured through her: the silent suffering as a child when she had watched her friends' parents drop them off at school, the struggle of being a teenager with only an alcoholic father to guide the way, the ever-present dagger in her heart from the belief that she was not even worthy of the unconditional love of her own mother.

"Andie, oh Andie."

Oddly, no one seemed to be paying attention to the scene they were making. Andie didn't care. She wasn't there for anyone else. "Mom, I've . . . I've got so many questions."

"I'm sure you do. You look like you could use a drink too."

"Yeah, I could." Andie hesitated. "You've barely aged."

"Thank you, dear. I'm afraid I can't say the same of you, since the last time we met! But you're as beautiful in person as I knew you were from all the photos I've seen."

"Photos? What photos?"

"Do you think I haven't followed your every move? Wished every second of every day that things were different? But all that can change now. Come. Let's see about that drink."

Reeling, confused and wary and dizzy with happiness all at the same time, Andie followed her mother across the room to a window overlooking the Grand Canal, showcasing the magical glow of Saint Mark's Basilica. When Andie broke off her gaze, her mother extended a glass of amber-colored wine. "This varietal is only produced on a single hectare in the entire world, on our private island nearby. This is the wine the doges used to drink, Andie. It was lost to time until our viticulturists revived it."

Andie started to take it, but at the last second, she grabbed a glass of red wine off the tray of a passing server.

With a sad smile, her mother slowly retracted her offer. "That's fair."

Though Andie's heart felt ready to burst, she had not forgiven a lifetime of abandonment in a moment, or forgotten why she had come.

"Why, Mom? Why did you leave?"

"We'll talk about that soon."

"No. I want to know *right now.*"

A look of infinite weariness and regret passed across her mother's visage, quickly consumed by a fire in her sapphire-blue eyes as she swept her gaze across the room. "This, Andie. I wanted to give you all of *this*. But I couldn't do it from home, in our situation. It isn't that kind of organization."

"But I don't want any of this. I never did. I just wanted you."

Her mother's mouth quivered with emotion, and she worked to regain control. "That's because you don't understand. Not yet. But I promise you will."

"What do you mean?"

"I asked you here to join us. Become one of us, stay with me forever, hold the world in your hands." The spark in her eyes returned to flare even brighter. "The world and even more."

Andie was stunned. "Join you? Why now? I have a career, a life…" She put a hand to her temple. "Mom, what happened to Dr. Corwin?"

"I've no idea," she said, "and I'm as devastated as you must be. I was very close to him once."

Andie looked her in the eye. "You don't know? You swear that?"

"I admit our organizations are rivals—that's a very long story—but all I know is that he disappeared. We're hardly murderers, Andie. Our goal is to *eradicate* such evils of society."

"Then why all these weird masks? Why was someone trying to kidnap me? 'Deliver' me, as he called it?"

"Omer was only trying to bring you in to talk. If he was armed, it's because a dangerous game is being played, Andie. One with the highest stakes imaginable. But as I said, all will be revealed in good time." She took a drink of wine, picked up her mask, and smiled. "I assume you must have felt a little disturbed, if you've never seen this style of mask before. The full costume represents the clothing worn by the plague doctors, intended to protect them from the horrible disease ravaging the city."

Andie was trying to process what her mother had told her about Omer, who she assumed was the dark-haired man. But why hadn't someone just approached her in a normal manner? Or were they so afraid of Zawadi—whoever she was—they had to take extreme measures?

"Plague is the ultimate expression of the cycle of nature we desire to escape," her mother continued. "Our masquerade ball is a paean to death and human frailty, meant to remind us that, despite all we've accomplished, we still have far to go to fulfill our aims."

"Which are?"

"To conquer death, for one. To transcend our humanity."

"Good luck with that one."

Her mother's gaze bored into her. "We are in the Anthropocene age, Andie. We humans have transformed our world, our environment, beyond all recognition. We are more in control of our destiny than has ever been dreamed. We've raised electric buildings to the sky, split the atom, created artificial intelligence to do our bidding, begun to explore the stars, unraveled the skein of life, gained the ability to *ignite* life. We've come far, but the ultimate journey has just begun."

"Not much for home and family in that philosophy, huh?"

"On the contrary," she said quietly. "We desire those things very much. Love and life itself are our most precious gifts. But why settle for scraps? What if we could enjoy our loved ones in full health until their deathbed, or for decades longer than is currently possible? Centuries even? What if there were higher dimensions to explore together, where time does not exist as we know it, where we could live in our minds forever once our bodies crumble into dust?"

"What are you talking about? This Fold place?"

Her mother blinked. "Where did you hear about that?"

"Drawings," Andie said after a moment. "Historical accounts of a shadowy realm like ours but different. I saw it in Dr. Corwin's journal after he died. I went through his things in his office. I know he's searching for it."

"And what has he found?" her mother said, with a catch in her voice.

"I have no idea. What do you know about it? What *is* it?"

"I've only heard rumors . . . There's someone among us called the Archon, Andie. Our leader. That's who encouraged me to reach out to you."

"The Archon? Does this person have a real name?"

A flicker of fear passed across her mother's visage. "It's kept secret for a reason."

"Don't you think that's a little odd?"

"There's a lot of symbolism involved—everything we do has meaning. But mostly, the hidden identity is meant to inspire loyalty and discourage backstabbing and political intrigue. The Archon is the most accomplished among us, and when he or she is ready for a successor, then a committee of high-ranking members—I don't really know who, I'm not that high in the organization—names a successor."

"Why does it seem like you're a little bit afraid of this person?"

Andie's mother took a long drink of amber wine. "The principal aim of our society is to acquire knowledge at all costs. To better humanity and ensure we do not destroy ourselves before we ascend to the beings we are destined to become. The higher one rises in the organization, the more of our knowledge, accumulated throughout history, one is given access to. The Archon knows things the rest of us . . . do not."

"What kind of knowledge?"

Andie's mother squeezed her arm. "Let's not talk about that. Not now. I'm curious: What else did you find in Dr. Corwin's office?"

"A photo of the two of you in a city I've never seen before."

Her mother opened and closed her mouth. "I suppose there's a lot for us to discuss," she said, her voice almost a whisper.

"Yeah. There is. How about we start right now? First question: If you wanted me to join you, why did you wait so long?"

Her mother stepped so close their faces were almost touching. Her smile dazzled more than ever, but behind the eyes Andie could see the fear had returned. "To make sure I could protect you," her mother whispered as she leaned in to kiss Andie on the forehead. To anyone watching, it would appear as if she had never spoken.

Her mother pulled away and said, "Why don't we go someplace a little more private to catch up? I'm afraid it may take all night!"

"Let's," Andie said, unnerved by her mother's behavior.

After slipping an arm around Andie's waist, her mother guided her back into the crowd, toward a hallway across the room. The scent of her mother's hair from when she had kissed Andie's forehead still lingered, and Andie felt as if she were a child once again, loved and protected, secure in her mother's embrace.

As they neared the center of the ballroom, her mother said, "There's only one thing we have to do before we leave."

"What's that?"

"You did bring the Star Phone, as I asked?"

Andie stopped walking and turned to face her. "I'm afraid not."

Her mother's arm fell away, her face slowly crumbling. "Please tell me you did."

"Nope."

"Why, Andie? Was I not clear how important it was?"

"You were clear. I chose not to bring it." All of a sudden, Andie noticed that a circle of masked revelers had surrounded her and her mother. Andie looked side to side as she backed away. "What's going on?"

Her mother shook her head, eyes pleading. "I can't protect you without it. Why didn't you listen?"

Someone grabbed Andie from behind. She gasped and tried to jerk away. When she couldn't free herself, she twisted and saw two people in cow's-head masks holding her by the arm. Andie felt a prick in the back of her neck, as if someone had jabbed her with a needle. "What was that? Let me go! *Mom!*"

"Andie, I'm so sorry. I never wanted this to happen."

"Sorry? You're *sorry*? Get these people the hell off me!"

"Give them what they want, and you won't be harmed. I promise, Little Mouse."

"Don't call me that."

"Stay strong, Andie," her mother said in a soft voice. "It's out of my hands now. Remember what I said, give them what they want, and we can be together. I swear it."

Her captors dragged her through the crowd as the music and the party continued unabated around them. Andie continued to struggle but felt the enervating effect of the drug start to overwhelm her as the other guests sidestepped the two people in cow's-head masks and their prisoner without a word, reaching for more drinks and pretending not to notice. Only her mother was watching, standing in the center of the room with a forlorn expression, and as Andie screamed for her to intervene with a failing voice, twisting in her captor's grip, a single tear fell from her mother's eye and slid unhindered down her cheek.

Rome
──○ 1934-1938 ○──

"Everyone makes mistakes."

Enrico Fermi, director of the Physics Institute on Via Panisperna, had said this to Ettore after his return to Italy. "Even you, Ettore. The problem with you—with almost always being right—is that you never see the big one coming."

While Ettore would be the first to admit he was hopelessly incompetent in many areas of life, his chosen field was a different story. Once he had truly committed himself to an idea in physics and worked out the numbers, Ettore in fact did *not* make mistakes.

He simply didn't.

Yes, it was true his career was ruined, at least for the moment. But the truth was he had never cared much about that anyway. What bothered him was his pride—wounded beyond repair—and the glaring error in his calculations that gnawed at him like an ever-present rat scurrying through his mind, taking little nibbles of his self-worth, scratching at his confidence, twitching its nose in doubt every time Ettore dwelled on his theory.

How had he been so wrong?

What had he missed?

Or had he been wrong at all? This was the idea that he couldn't let go. It was undeniable that Dirac had been proven correct about the positron and the existence of antimatter. Yet what if Ettore was right too? What if the two theorems were not incompatible, as the world believed, but somehow worked in harmony, at a deeper level than anyone presently understood?

Over the previous year—a time span in which Schrödinger, Dirac, and Heisenberg had all received the Nobel Prize—Ettore had sunk into a great depression, ostracized in the scientific community and barely speaking to his friends or family. The only escape he saw was to prove everyone wrong by building this insane bauble he had conceived of in Leipzig, a device which unlocked his infinite tower of particles and connected to the body's energy field. If his theorems were correct, then . . . well, he didn't know exactly *what* would happen.

Ettore became more and more obsessed with the idea of the Fold, and its analog in science. He knew, deep down, that such a place existed. The place where the building blocks of matter lived, a world of dreams and eternal time and the interconnected fabric of the multiverse.

There was a popular philosopher who had famously pondered whether anything we can imagine is real. Ettore, unlike the vast majority of his peers, gave the idea credence.

And why not? How else to account for the infinite bazaar of the human mind? What was imagination but a piece of reality birthed by neural synapses, as extant as any other thing, whether or not it lived in the physical world as we know it? Perhaps it was *more* real, an embryo of possibility untethered to corporeality, allowed to gestate and thrive and branch a quadrillion times again in the quantum soup of the subconscious.

He was getting ahead of himself. He didn't need to uncover the ultimate answers all at once. He just needed to make a simple connection.

And he thought he knew how to do it.

There were just two problems. The first was the Leap Year Society.

Over the course of the next few years, while Ettore toiled in isolation, the Society sent a number of people to remind him of his duty and coax him into making their weapon. Always he put them off, by promising development and showing them theorems they didn't understand.

It seemed to satisfy them, until he left his house one night for a walk, on a mild December evening, and found Stefan waiting for him on the street outside.

"Stefan! What are you doing in Rome?"

Dressed in his typical double-breasted wool coat, though without his Nazi insignia, the German officer's arms were folded, and he leveled his hawkish stare at Ettore. "It's been a while, my friend."

All of a sudden, Ettore felt much colder than the weather warranted. Though Ettore hadn't thought it possible, Stefan looked even more intense than ever, and there was a darkness shadowing his eyes that made Ettore want to turn and run in the opposite direction, as fast and as far as he could. These were eyes that had seen too much violence and depravity, too much human evil on display. They were eyes that, even if well-intentioned, had stared into the abyss for too long.

He's become a fiend. A mad, demonic fiend.

"I hear you've been unwell," Stefan said.

"I'm fine," Ettore mumbled.

"It's unhealthy to remove oneself from society, Ettore. No man is an island."

"Every man is an island."

"Tsk, tsk. You must take better care of yourself. Walk with me."

Ettore shuffled along behind Stefan as he stepped into the festive streets of Rome, surrounded by families out for an evening stroll, the shop windows and streetlamps festooned with Christmas decorations.

"I'm sure you've heard the Joliot-Curies have discovered artificial radioactivity," Stefan said. "It's nothing less than transmutation! Modern-day alchemy!"

"I've heard."

"And this doesn't excite you?"

Ettore's lips twisted into a sneer. "Do you have any idea what might happen if other elements are manipulated in such a manner? What sort of power might be unleashed?"

"Which is why *we* must be the first to unlock the doorway. To ensure the world does not burn."

"And who's to say you won't be the one to burn it?"

Stefan whirled around and grabbed Ettore by the collar, lifting him on his toes. He jerked him closer, face-to-face. "I've seen your designs. They're nowhere close to finished. Don't toy with me, Ettore. I'm warning you."

"I would never do that."

"Do you know who betrayed us in Copenhagen? The night we announced our split?"

Ettore swallowed. "No."

"*I* did. I leaked the information and knew our spineless compatriots would stab us in the back. It was the only way to convince some of my associates to take such a drastic step. So you see, my friend, if I could make a decision that led to the deaths of my closest allies for a cause in which I believe . . . then you should have no doubt I won't hesitate to kill you."

"I don't," Ettore whispered.

With visible effort, Stefan composed himself and released Ettore's collar. "Our time is short. German scientists are working around the clock. I wish you no harm, but . . . you must come through for us."

"I'm getting closer. I've been exploring antimatter collision as well. I think it shows great potential."

"Ah, yes. An intriguing avenue. When can I expect a blueprint? One with actual merit?"

"Soon, I promise. Within a year."

"A *year*?" Stefan looked as if he might fly into a rage again, but instead he turned his head upward, toward the yellow sickle of the moon. "One year. No more." He stopped to let his stare bore into Ettore a final time. "I'll be watching."

After that ominous proclamation, Stefan walked swiftly away and disappeared into the night. Disturbed, Ettore spent the rest of the evening wandering the streets of Rome in a half-aware state, oblivious to the Christmas cheer, the laughter of friends and families.

Yes, Stefan and the Society were a problem, but they were also a solution. Ettore didn't have all the materials to make the device he wanted to build. So the Society, he decided, would do it for him. They owned a private lab in Rome dedicated to their own projects and scientists, ready for Ettore's ideas. Making the device right under their noses would be walking a dangerous tightrope, but no one else would fund his idea. The work was too speculative. Convincing the Society to build his device was his only chance at redemption.

Unfortunately, his second problem was even more serious than trying to fool Stefan.

Ettore couldn't get the math to work.

He was so close to having a finished theorem, a conceptual idea of how to unlock his tower of infinite particles. Artificial radiation was indeed the key. And the proper application of electricity, channeled through the right medium, should—in theory—allow the mind's eye to experience the effect. It was all theoretical, of course, and that was okay. Ettore just wanted to give his theorem a chance to succeed.

But that last little tweak in the numbers that would tie it all together . . . the final key . . . maybe Dirac had it right after all, and Ettore was just plain mistaken.

They were calling him mad, he knew. His family, Fermi and the other scientists, everyone. This caused Ettore to cackle. Mad? Was anyone paying attention to theoretical physics? Because if anyone really thought about what scientists had discovered in the last few decades about the inner workings of nature and voiced their opinion on the street, then they would appear as unbalanced as that megalomaniacal buffoon Mussolini.

Particles in two places at once, their futures uncertain until observed? Communicating somehow across space and time?

Madness. Sheer madness.

And it got worse. According to Ettore's calculations, if a particle and an antiparticle were indeed two sides of the same coin, it was probable that a quantum superposition like Schrödinger's famous cat would result, except one moving in *all* directions of time, all at once. Ettore angrily shook his head. Those putrid scientific materialists. How vulgar to think the gears of the universe were set into motion by mindless chance. It was so . . . *impossible.* The further he dove into the rabbit hole of his ideas, the more convinced he became he was drawing closer to a deeper reality.

How much easier, he thought, *to give in to the world.*

How much easier to believe in the illusion.

Over the next year, as fascism gripped the country like a bad fever, Ettore barely left his room. Unable to focus on anything besides his work, he let his hair and beard grow to absurd lengths, shocking those who saw him. Fractals and whispers of inchoate formulas filled his head, the numbers still not aligning. Chaos, madness, perfection, annihilation . . . circling the drain of his skull . . . He couldn't stop the flow, he couldn't shut it off, he couldn't get it right.

And then one night, the stranger appeared in his dream. Freud would have said that Ettore's own subconscious provided the solution; Jung, the collective wisdom of the universe manifesting in response to his yearning for truth. The mystics of the world would have their own opinions, each as varied as the patchwork cloak of a gypsy.

What Ettore knew was that late one night, gripped by the psychosis of his failure, drunk on wine and despair and contemplating suicide for the first time in his life, his incomplete theorem stomping about in his head like a perverse general who refuses to recognize defeat, Ettore fell asleep without knowing it, his head slumped on his desk as a full moon hovered outside the window. Later, he couldn't say how the dream started or ended, but he remembered a figure appearing in his bedroom dressed in a gray traveling cloak, a young dark-haired woman, her eyes burning in the depths of the cowl like pinpricks of starlight in a night sky. He had never seen her before, and for some reason in the dream he couldn't explain, she terrified him. Ettore tried to stand, but she strode to his desk before he could react, placed a gloved hand on the back of his neck, and held him in place. When she put her other hand atop Ettore's own, he remembered thinking he was going to die. That perhaps she was an incarnation of his own darkness, come to consume his mind and leave his body a withered husk for the world to mock. Yet instead of harming him, she guided Ettore's hand toward his pen. He picked it up, and together they filled the page with a calculation that Ettore somehow, in the impossible way of dreams, recalled the next morning. He did not remember the stranger leaving or ever speaking to him. He only knew that once he started writing, the numbers aligned at last.

He had discovered the missing piece to the puzzle.

In disbelief, Ettore jumped to his feet and whooped as if he were a small boy. *This was it!* By some miracle of the subconscious, his mind had taken all of his frenzied work over the last few years and assembled the pieces while he slept. It was not that unusual, he knew. There was evidence for this sort of phenomenon.

What mattered was that he had it. This was the core of his device, whether the theory itself was valid.

Yet he dared not go public with the knowledge. Not until he tried it himself.

This placed Ettore in a perilous situation. After some thought, he conceived of a desperate plan to give the Society's engineers the blueprint for his silver sphere, tell them it was an essential component to a new weapon, and promise delivery of the final plans once he was sure the core was viable. The engineers wouldn't understand what it was. No one would. And before they discovered his treachery, Ettore would be gone.

If his hypothesis was correct and his device unlocked a hidden pathway, then he had no idea what would happen.

If it was wrong, or if his betrayal was discovered too soon and his contingency plan failed, he had no doubt Stefan would kill him.

As 1937 drew to a close, Ettore took steps to implement his plan. Out of the blue, he applied for a professorship in Naples, dusting off a paper he had kept in a drawer for years. The paper laid the hypothetical groundwork for the neutrino and shocked the scientific community with its brilliance. He won the professorship with ease.

Ettore thought moving to Naples would relieve some of the pressure from the Society. And he was right. He no longer felt watched at every turn. Yet on the first day of the New Year, a visitor to his home reminded him they were still watching, and that Stefan had not forgotten Ettore's promise. More than a year had passed since Stefan's visit, but Ettore had submitted a blueprint for the device and the Society's engineers were working on it. Stefan was appeased for the moment, but the reprieve would not last.

And then, in March of 1938, he received the news for which he was waiting. The prototype of his device was finished and needed only his approval. Claiming his professorial duties did not allow him to travel, he asked them to deliver it to him in Naples.

Giddy with anticipation, he withdrew a large sum of money from the bank and worked hard to appear busy at his job. Just before the prototype arrived, he bought a ticket to Palermo on a mail boat, and left a note for his superior.

> Dear Carrelli,
> I made a decision that has become unavoidable. There isn't a bit of selfishness in it, but I realize what trouble my sudden disappearance will cause you and the students. For this, I beg your forgiveness, but especially for betraying the trust, the sincere friendship, and

the sympathy you gave me over the past months. I
also ask you to give my regards to all those I learned to
know and appreciate in your Institute, especially Sciuti:
I will keep a fond memory of them all at least until 11:00
tonight. Possibly later, too.

E. Majorana

According to Ettore's wishes, someone from the Society
hand-delivered the prototype of the device to his house. His request
to keep it overnight was granted. The Society was not worried—they
had the blueprints.

Ettore's heart fluttered when he saw his silver bauble for the first
time. That very afternoon, as soon as the emissary left, Ettore inserted
an initiator he had managed to build himself, which was far ahead
of its time and contained the key to his core theorems, into a slender
opening atop the device. Next he attached a dozen filament wires with
electrodes at the ends. The blueprints he had handed over were a red
herring. The technology inside the sphere was already in circulation,
albeit more streamlined and using cutting edge materials. Without the
wires and the initiator to unlock his infinite tower of particles, the true
purpose of the device would be impossible to discern.

With an effort of will, he resisted the urge to try it out right then
and there. He reminded himself of the plans he had in place, an atmosphere befitting the gravity of the moment. Yes, he would ignite the
device far from prying eyes, alone on the sea, beneath a starry sky.

Shaking with anticipation, he boarded the ship for Palermo that
very evening, to cement the final details. On the return journey,
when at last he was alone on deck, with only the trillion twinkling
eyes of the universe to bear witness, he closed his eyes and pressed
his fingers into the trigger points of the device, overcome by the
beauty and emotion of the moment, unsure if his eyes would open
onto this world or another.

27

Cal thought he was dreaming. Yet when he blinked his eyes to clear his mind, catching a strong whiff of rosemary, the robed figure standing in front of him with the golden face was still there, regarding Cal in impassive silence.

"Greetings."

The voice came from behind the face, which Cal realized was a close-fitting mask or helmet that covered the person's entire head. The contours of the mask approximated an androgynous human face. The only openings were two eyeholes, behind which Cal saw nothing but darkness.

As with the golden mask, the voice left the gender unclear. It did not sound digitized, though it possessed an oddly neutral inflection.

Cal realized he was sitting in a high-backed wooden chair with no restraints. The floor, walls, and ceiling within his line of vision were all painted a warm shade of blue. No doors or windows he could see. As he started to rise in anger, the eyeholes of the mask shifted to lock on to his gaze. "Remain seated."

Though he didn't really want to, Cal followed the suggestion, sinking back into his chair.

Where am I? The last thing he remembered was walking at night along a tiny canal in Dorsoduro, staying out of sight, waiting for Andie to contact him. Right before he crossed a bridge, he heard footsteps approaching from behind. He was sure he had turned and seen someone's face, but he couldn't seem to hold on to the details. He frowned and tried to concentrate, but the memory was an eel slithering through his subconscious, slipping away from his grasp.

"Who are you?" Cal said, trying to quell the panic. "How the hell did I get here?"

The masked figure was standing five feet away with hands clasped behind its back. Heavy white robes extended from the bottom of the mask all the way to the floor, leaving no skin exposed. The person behind the disguise was even taller than Cal.

"I am the Archon," the voice said. "My associates have delivered you to me."

Cal didn't like the sound of the word *delivered*, as if he were a piece of chattel brought here by this person's servants. "Do you have a real name?"

"Do you mean an arbitrary appellation given to a child at birth, or a grouping of letters that better reflects the true nature of an individual?"

"Where am I? How long have I been here? Where's Andie?"

"All unimportant concerns. What matters is where you will next awaken."

"I gotta say I don't much like the sound of that. Is there a choice involved?"

"Our lives are full of choices. Even in cases where our physical actions are restrained, the mind remains uninhibited. That is, except for those rare instances in which you encounter someone with the ability to overpower your freedom of will and deny the conscious mind its due."

"Okay, I'll bite . . . I suppose you're one of those people?"

"I am indeed."

There was no boast to the voice, no change in modulation.

It scared the hell out of him.

"Well, this is creepy and all, but I think I'll walk on out of here and see about some of my other choices."

As Cal started to rise again, the Archon held out a palm, then slowly inverted it. As the palm turned downward, Cal found himself returning to his seat again. For some reason, the only physical action he wanted to take was to stare at that golden mask. Before he could ponder the absurdity of the situation, the voice spoke again.

"I believe you know who we are, Calvin Miller, just as we know about you."

"I know that you ruined my life."

"Have you ever thought that perhaps this life you hold so dear, your old life, was worthy of ruination?"

"I was kind of partial to it."

"You're a resourceful man, and one who shares many of our principles: a thirst for knowledge, dissatisfaction with the status quo, reticence about the course of humankind."

"Now you're putting words in my mouth. I'm only opposed to people like *you*, who think they're better than everyone else."

"Someone who believes the ends justify the means?"

"Exactly."

"In the right circumstance, everyone does. Parent fighting for their children. Leaders waging war for their nations."

"Those are hardly analogous."

"Aren't they? Tell me, please, beyond a difference in scale, how they differ. How about a journalist who breaks laws to repair his reputation?"

Cal waved a hand in annoyance. "I wouldn't have had to do that if you hadn't destroyed it."

"A rationalization that suits your own selfish purpose. We wouldn't have noticed you in the first place if you had not involved yourself in the concerns of others, and which are far above your head. You have *no idea* what is at stake. You judge so easily, yet we, too, believe our means are justified. That our goal is for the greater good. And I daresay our interests are far less egotistical than your own."

Cal snorted. "I have my doubts."

"Our ultimate aim is to preserve the future of humanity, of all our lives on this precious planet."

"With yourselves at the top of the food chain, of course."

"That is a necessity of present circumstance. We wish deeply it were not so."

"Listen, Archon person. If you give a damn about me, or want me to give any credence to anything you're saying, then let me out of here and give me my life back."

"This is not about you—though what I have to offer may serve both our goals."

Cal spread his hands. "I'm listening."

"Join our organization. I cannot install you as a full member, not yet, but I will set you on the path we have all walked."

"Join you. Uh-huh." He started to tick off his fingers. "One—you haven't told me where Andie is. Or where I am, for that matter. Two—I'm trying to expose you, not join you. Three—I think you're full of shit."

"I assure you the offer is genuine. The path to Ascension is a long and arduous task, one with a small likelihood of success. But you will be forever changed by the journey, of that I assure you. And why not learn the answers to those secrets you so desperately seek, help impose order on the chaos that surrounds us, escape the prison of your own unseeing mind?"

"Sure. Just let me discuss it with Andie first."

"She has her own choice to make."

"Then let me talk to her about it."

"My time and patience grow short, Calvin. What is your decision?"

Even if Cal thought the offer was genuine, it held little appeal. The purpose of his career in journalism, and even the conspiracy show, had never been uncovering secrets. That was the short-term aim of both endeavors, sure. But Cal was a simple man. He didn't need to understand the inner workings of the universe. He just needed a cold beer, a freezer full of bone-in rib eyes, his dog at his side, mild winters, and lower level tickets to the Clips.

Yet there was something which did motivate him in life. Most people would call it a noble trait, but Cal didn't think of it that way. He thought of it as a mark of basic humanity that everyone should have, a calling magnified by certain events in his own past.

To him, the goal of his professional undertakings had always been clear.

What Cal cared about was justice.

"Say I decide to join you," he said. "What do you want in return?"

"Leaving this room is dependent on providing us the location of the Star Phone. To leave this *place*, you must renounce your past life and embark upon the path I set. If that is your choice, further instructions will be given."

"Is that all? Renounce my past life and do whatever you tell me? Why don't I just make this easy for all of us: Go to hell. And I have no idea where the Star Phone is."

The Archon stood in front of him, unmoving, for a long moment. Cal thought about trying to stand again, but to his great annoyance, he couldn't bring himself to do it. In fact, he couldn't even seem to turn around to see if there was a door behind him, or stop looking at the vacant eyeholes of that damned golden mask. It was almost as if those two bottomless orbs were an extension of himself, and he could no more look away than he could separate himself from his own optic nerves.

The Archon's hands swung to the front, revealing a pair of black gloves, then clasped at the waist. "You choose not to join us?"

Cal laughed.

"I'll ask a final time: Where is the Star Phone?"

"Go. To. Hell."

"Then I'm afraid I'll have to ask another way."

"Whatever suits you."

"Stand, Calvin Miller."

He opened his mouth to retort, but instead of speaking, he found himself sliding out of his chair and standing motionless in front of the robed figure.

The Archon raised a gloved hand in front of Cal's face. The hand unfurled to reveal a swarm of multicolored lights dancing in the open palm, flickering in and out, a swarm of disembodied fireflies flashing in Cal's vision. The effect lasted only an instant, but it dazed him, and as the hand disappeared from his line of sight, the eyes of the mask seemed closer than ever, as if Cal were being drawn into a vortex.

"Sleep," the Archon commanded.

All of a sudden, Cal was wobbly on his feet, his eyelids too heavy to keep open. He let them close and felt his consciousness slipping away, as if a powerful sedative had overcome his mind.

"Open your eyes. Be with me."

Cal's lethargy disappeared and he stood rigid, his gaze blank and unseeing, in front of the masked leader of the Ascendants.

"What is your name?"

"Calvin Miller."

"With whom did you come to Venice?"

"Andie Robertson."

"Did anyone else come with you?"

"No."

"Good. Now that we are one, I want you to think very carefully and tell me exactly what I wish to know. We will start with your visit to the house of Elias Holt and work our way to the present. You may begin."

Without hesitation, Cal started to speak, and over the course of the two hours, pausing only to wet his lips from a bottle of water that somehow appeared in his hands, he found himself doing exactly as the Archon had asked.

When Andie regained consciousness, she found herself in a small room with every available surface painted rich walnut brown. She was sitting in a straight-backed chair and wearing the same clothes as before. The last thing she remembered was someone poking a needle in her neck and dragging her out of the ballroom.

The warmth of the room and the faint scent of an exotic spice, maybe cardamom, invoked a snowy night at a cabin curled up by the fire. In sharp contrast to the cozy vibe of the room was the person dressed neck to toe in long white robes befitting a Greek philosopher, standing five feet from Andie, on the other side of a wooden table.

An eerie, snug golden mask with open eye sockets shielded the figure's face and head from view. Andie couldn't even make out the gender. A glass of red wine was on the table between them, and she wondered if she would be made to drink it.

"Hello, Andromeda."

"My name is Andie. Where the hell am I? Where's my mother?"

"Samantha won't be joining you again tonight. Not unless an agreement is reached."

"An agreement about what?"

"I think you know."

"Why don't you enlighten me? You're this Archon person, I assume."

"Where did you hide the Star Phone?"

Andie smirked. "Now that's a good idea. Hold on one second, and think about how stupid it would be for me to give you my only bargaining chip." She jumped to her feet and pointed a finger at the Archon's face. "I want to talk to my mother. Now."

"I'm surprised she inspires such loyalty after giving you up so easily."

"I don't know what you have on her, but you people are holding her against her will."

"I assure you that is not the case."

"You can assure me of whatever the hell you want."

"Sit, Andromeda."

"I think I'll stand." Andie turned to find an exit, but saw no doors or windows in the room. She walked to the nearest wall and started probing for a seam. "How do I get out of here? Where's the secret door?"

After watching her in silence, the Archon said, "Your companion does not know where you hid it. I suspect only you know the location."

"He wouldn't tell you if he did."

"Oh, I believe he would."

Andie did not like the matter-of-fact tone of the Archon's answer. Everything about this person creeped her out, from the golden mask to the rigid stance to the oddly neutral voice, as if the entire persona was constructed to embody something less than—or more than—a human being.

"I know what an archon is," Andie said, continuing to examine the room as the figure circled in place to watch her. "I came across it when I was researching Democritus. It had a couple of meanings in antiquity. One was 'a lord or ruler in ancient Greece, often the magistrate of a city-state.' Another—the definition used by the Gnostics—referred to someone who acted as a proxy between humanity and whatever transcendent force created the universe. So which is it? You seem like an ambitious type—maybe it's both."

"It's rude to speak of matters in which you are unversed."

"So enlighten me. I'm a good student."

"We wish you no harm, Andromeda."

"I told you not to call me that."

"As your mother said, we wish for you to join us. The offer is genuine. I believe once you understand the larger picture, you will come to embrace our cause."

Andie returned to stand in front of her chair and crossed her arms. "I'm not much of a joiner."

"Only someone who has never worn the mantle of responsibility prefers to stand apart."

"And only narcissistic pricks want to control other people."

The Archon lifted a gloved hand. "You're a scientist. An astrophysicist."

"I'm a PhD student."

"You understand far better than most what a miracle it is that we exist at all. How fragile our position in the cosmos. A single wayward asteroid could plunge us into another ice age, and eventually our sun will fail. Yet we both know that long before a celestial disaster occurs, the human race will destroy the planet through negligence, or with technology it misuses or does not understand. This fate is imminent unless steps are taken—bold steps—to avoid it."

"I'm going with the Gnostic definition."

"We're devotees of knowledge. Enlightenment. Progress. Imagine a shift in perspective from belief in the individual to belief in the potential of humankind. When the best of us band together to propel the human race forward, stripped of loyalty to country and ethnicity, miracles can be accomplished. In the last century, human achievement has increased at an exponential rate. Yet we are at a crossroads in our evolution. If changes are not implemented, and a shortsighted government or a rogue organization or perhaps even a well-meaning scientist unleashes technology on the world that it is not prepared to handle, then our precarious balance will be destroyed."

"And you think what? The Enneagon has the potential to unlock forces beyond our control?"

"We do not think it. We know it."

"How?"

"Join us, and we will share the knowledge."

"Or you could just tell me."

"Knowledge without perspective is worse than meaningless: it's dangerous."

"So the Star Phone leads to the Enneagon?"

"It does."

"Where's Dr. Corwin?"

"We wish we knew. We would talk to him directly."

"So you didn't murder him?"

"Of course not."

"Then who did?"

"We've no idea."

"What *is* the Enneagon?"

"The distillation of the next frontier in science. A key to the unlocking of human potential. And, above all, a portal."

"A portal to where?"

"Imagine, child, the millions of lives lost through the wars, disease, poverty, inequality, and greed that has plagued our species. The exploitation of human capital and planetary resources that still occurs on a daily basis, around the world. We are so remarkable and yet so flawed. Is there not a better way?"

"Who gave you the right to make the rules?"

"If you better understood our position, I'm confident your viewpoint would change."

"I'm standing right here."

"As soon as we acquire the Star Phone, you'll be released and an offer will be extended to join us formally. Of this I swear."

"I want to see my mother. Right goddamn now."

The Archon's gloved hands reclasped in front of the white robes. "We know of your visions of the Fold, and how they trouble you."

Andie stilled. "What are you talking about?"

"Come forward. Peer into the wineglass."

"Why?"

"To prove that we possess answers to your questions."

Wary of a trick and keeping an eye on the Archon, who remained motionless, Andie stepped to the edge of the table, leaned over, and glanced into the long-stemmed wineglass.

She looked up. "It's a glass of red wine."

"Look again."

With a frown, Andie lowered her eyes a second time—and gasped. Somehow, impossibly, the ruby-red wine had morphed into a semi-transparent, variegated gray surface that mirrored the room in which they stood. Andie and the Archon were represented as tiny figures standing on either side of a three-dimensional cube-shaped lattice the same height as the table. Chalky ripples in the gloom indicated the floor, walls, and ceiling. Beyond the borders of the room loomed a mass of deepening shadow, which seemed to expand the farther she stared into its depths. There was movement in those nether regions, the same haunting, inchoate forms she had glimpsed at the edges of her visions.

Andie's head jerked up. "What— How did—"

The Archon passed a hand above the glass. When Andie looked down once again, the image was gone, the surface of the wine returned to normal.

"You feel as if you're being watched when it happens," the Archon said, "and the universe seems infinitely larger than you could imagine. We can help you understand."

Andie sucked in a breath. "Don't forget feeling lost, terrified, and horribly alone. Why would I ever want to learn more about such a place?"

"Have you ever considered that you've only seen a small portion of the whole? That your vision is flawed? Incomplete? A condition of your unique mind that can be explored and reconstituted?"

"I don't know how you did that . . . but it's all in my mind. It always has been."

"No. The Fold exists."

Andie started to say something, then grimaced and shook her head.

"It's a place that appears as beautiful and wondrous to others as it does mysterious and frightening to you," the Archon said. "A place, perhaps, that encompasses all things. A place glimpsed by seers, mystics, and gifted anomalies like yourself since the beginning of time. I am one like you, Andie. I can manipulate the minds of others and see into places they cannot."

"You're lying."

"Ask your friend. When the time is right, I will teach you these things. Join us. Unravel the secrets of the universe with us by your side. With your *mother*."

Andie swallowed, barely able to believe that someone else had seen this place she thought lived only in her mind. Seeing the ink drawings and accounts in old books was one thing, but to see it right in front of her, somehow brought to life in a wineglass, even if it was just a trick of the mind . . .

"All I have to do is tell you where the Star Phone is?"

"We will begin there."

"And if I don't?"

"I hope we don't have to discuss such matters."

"That's what I thought. You know, it sounds like such an easy choice. These are things I've wanted all my life."

"I'm pleased to hear this."

"There're just a couple of problems."

"Perhaps we can work through them and come to an understanding."

Andie raised her hands. "Maybe. One issue is that my mom left me high and dry when I was a little kid, while Dr. Corwin has been there for me my entire life. I love my mom, but giving up the Star Phone means I'll never see Dr. Corwin again. Or if he's dead, then the people responsible will never be held accountable. An even bigger problem is that despite all this great stuff you're telling me, I have no reason to trust you."

"It is the truth, Andromeda. Whether you to choose to believe it or not."

"I told you," she said with a snarl, "*that's not my fucking name.*"

Andie lashed out with her foot, overturning the table and shattering the glass. As wine spattered the bottom of the white robes, the Archon opened a palm to reveal a spray of dancing colored lights. The polychromatic display had a mesmeric effect, sucking in Andie's gaze like a vacuum, but she blinked to clear her head and stalked forward, keeping the Archon's robes at the edge of her vision. Andie's hands were up and ready, knees bent, adopting a kickboxer's stance.

"Intriguing," the Archon said.

Andie stepped beside the fallen table to attack from a side angle. Uncoiling her body like a spring, she unleashed a powerful side kick, hoping to drive the Archon back, end the fight quickly, and find the exit.

Right before Andie's kick connected, the robed figure swiveled faster than any opponent Andie had ever faced, sidestepping the kick and letting Andie's momentum carry her forward. As Andie tried to regain her balance, the Archon slid behind her, and Andie felt a blow just to the right of her neck, above the shoulder blade.

A painful tingling shot through her body, and then she felt nothing at all.

28

"Morning, sunshine."

Still groggy, Andie groaned as she opened her eyes. Her neck ached as if hit by a sledgehammer. The light was very dim, but once her eyes adjusted to the gloom, she wished she had kept them shut.

She was lying on the damp floor of a room whose pockmarked stone walls, spotted with grime and mildew, looked as if they had stood since the Dark Ages. Across from her, through the grid pattern of an iron portcullis set into the foot-thick wall, she glimpsed a hallway just as grim. Water plopped in the distance, and the dungeon smelled as rank as a sewer.

Steel manacles, bolted to the floor via two-foot lengths of heavy chain, secured her ankles. She managed to stand but barely had room to step away from the wall at her back.

"Over here," Cal said. "In the guest suite."

She looked to her left and saw him chained to the back wall of a tiny alcove connected to her cell. A pile of oversize bricks was stacked neatly beside the alcove. She took a step forward, testing her manacles. They felt as solid as they looked. "How'd you get here?"

"Someone ambushed me in Dorsoduro. They got my laptop."

"I'm really sorry. Are you injured?"

"Just a bump on my head and my pride. What about you? Did you meet your mother?"

It was Andie's turn for silence. "Yeah," she said finally as the events of the night flooded back. "I met her."

"Not a Hallmark moment."

Andie pressed her lips together. "There was a party, a grand ball. Almost everyone was wearing masks . . . and then she walked over to me, just like I remembered her. We talked. She tried to get me to join them." She swallowed. "She said I had to give them the Star Phone if I wanted to leave."

"Judging by your present location, I can guess your answer. That must have been hard."

After releasing a long breath, Andie forced away her emotions and tried to think things through. What if she had intuited the wrong rationale in the email from her mother?

What if the reference to the crystal angel was not an offer to protect Andie but a cry for help herself, from a powerful father figure who was displeased with her?

"Something's wrong, Cal. She didn't seem like a prisoner, but I think she's gotten herself into something she can't get out of. I think she needs my help."

"Maybe she's afraid of that creep in the golden mask."

"You met the Archon?" When he didn't respond, she said, "Cal?"

"Yeah. Right before I ended up here. Don't ask me what happened, because I'm not sure. My memory is foggy for some reason. I think I answered a bunch of questions . . . though I'm not really sure why." He sounded embarrassed. "I must have been hypnotized. I think I told them everything, then woke up chained to this wall."

The memory of the encounter with the robed figure caused Andie to shudder. "I think the Archon tried to hypnotize me or something too, then hit me in the brachial plexus when it didn't work."

"The brachial plexus?"

"It's a nerve center that if struck really hard can knock you the hell out."

"Why do you think—"

Cal cut off at the sound of footsteps splashing through water in the hallway. Both of them fell silent as a man in a white tuxedo and a green plague-doctor mask appeared outside their cell with a tray of food. He was too short to be the Archon. It took him a moment to unlock the padlock securing the iron portcullis, which creaked as it swung open.

The masked figure stepped inside and set the tray by the door. Andie noticed a glass of water, plastic utensils, and a pile of pasta in a white sauce, which smelled delicious.

"Hungry?" the man asked her.

She glared at him.

"I'll bring this over as soon as I'm finished." He strode to the pile of oversize bricks next to the alcove, picked two of the bricks up, and set them down at the base of the alcove.

"What the hell are you doing?" Cal said, with a catch in his voice.

"Research has proven time and again," the man said as he started building a wall to seal off the alcove, "that torture is not the most effective method of eliciting information. The problem is one of veracity. Most people will say or do anything to stop the pain. It's not very helpful to have prisoners lie or embellish the truth to save their own lives. On the other hand, those rare individuals who can withstand prolonged torture also tend to lie. Invariably, they're protecting someone or something, a loved one or a cause or a country, that compels them to remain silent or provide false information."

The entrance to the alcove was quite narrow. The bricks were already stacked a foot high. Cal jerked on his restraints, his eyes roving side to side. "Let me out of here!"

"What *has* proven effective," the man continued, "is the torture of someone who the possessor of information cares about."

"I barely know this guy," Andie said. "We met all of five days ago."

The man shrugged. "Even so, we believe you're the sort of person who will not allow his distress to continue." She seethed in silence as he stacked brick after brick, slowly hiding Cal from view. "I'll leave a tiny opening for air to enter, and so you can hear his pleas for help.

He'll dehydrate long before he starves to death. In this damp and humid environment, I estimate four days at most." When Andie snarled and jerked on her chains, he turned to face her gaze. "As soon as you reveal the location of the Star Phone and we recover the device, you'll both be released."

"He's lying, Andie," Cal said.

"Let him go," she said. "Put me in there. He doesn't know anything."

"Yes. We know." He finished walling up the opening, leaving a sliver of space between the bricks and the apex of the alcove. "Let's hope it doesn't rain, or the dungeon will become most unpleasant."

He picked up the tray and set it in front of Andie. She tried to kick it away, but he jerked it back at the last moment. "I wouldn't do that, unless you want the rats to come. I advise eating everything on the plate, as quickly as possible."

When he set the tray down again, Andie quivered in rage but didn't lash out.

"I'll return in the morning," he said.

By the end of the second day in captivity, Andie couldn't take it any longer. She wasn't sure if two full days had passed; she was going on what their captor had told them, the regularity of the meals, and the toll the imprisonment had taken on Cal.

For the first few hours, she had talked to him, to keep his spirits up and to brainstorm an avenue of escape. As the hopelessness of the situation set in, they had stopped planning for the future, and then gradually, after the first day, stopped talking at all. The last time she had called out to him, his voice had grown so weak and hoarse he sounded like an elderly smoker whispering on his deathbed to a priest.

Twice a day, the man in the plague-doctor mask brought in food and water. Andie continued eating and drinking, to keep her strength up and because she believed his claim about the rats. She could hear their scrabbling in the hallway outside the cell, and at times she saw the shadows of their plump gray bodies scuttling across the stone floor. So far, it had rained twice, causing water to rise to her ankles in the cell before it settled into rank puddles. She was cramped and exhausted, and overcome with despair.

Yet she was far better off than Cal.

"He'll be here soon," Cal croaked in the near darkness, startling her. It was the first time he had spoken since the last visit.

"I know."

"Don't tell him anything. They're going to kill us anyway. Or at least me."

She didn't respond.

"Andie," he said, trying to make his whisper sound forceful. Instead it cracked at the end, causing him to choke and fall silent. It made her want to cry and scream, and tear her captor's face off.

"Listen to me," Cal said, when he regained his voice. "*They will not let us go.*"

"I'm not going to listen to you die. We're not getting out of here on our own. I'm telling them where it is."

"That's selfish."

"It's better than *this*."

"What if the Enneagon is as important as they think it is? What if they find it and use it for God knows what?"

"That's not my problem right now. You are."

She heard the faint rattle of chains. "Don't, Andie. Please. They know I'll never stay quiet, and I don't want to die for nothing."

Andie stared in silence across the cell.

Despite the damp conditions and her soaked feet, the cell was hot and humid. Andie had long ago removed her jacket. Each time her captor entered, he wore the same green plague-doctor mask, though he usually changed suits. This time he walked inside wearing a black tuxedo with a peak lapel.

"Are you ready to talk?" he asked her.

She glared at him.

"He won't last much longer." He walked over and slapped the bricks of Cal's prison. "Still with us?"

There was no response, and Andie eyed the set of skeleton keys in her captor's hand as she prepared for her last desperate attempt at freedom.

"You're killing him," the man said.

Andie was lying on her side, her field jacket bunched in her left hand and supporting her head. Though the position of the jacket looked random, it was carefully arranged, and her hand was twisted tightly around one of the cuffs. As their captor bent to set the tray down, Andie raised her head, flicked her left wrist, and snapped the jacket behind his legs, catching the thick cotton of one of the sleeves in her other hand. She almost missed, but she had practiced the movement over and over in the long dull hours of her captivity, and she managed to grasp the cuff between her thumb and index fingers. Before the man could react, she pulled the jacket taut and jerked hard, catching the bottoms of his ankles. He dropped the tray and fell, stumbling within her reach.

Andie released the jacket, grabbed his pant legs, and yanked him toward her. As he twisted to get up, she gripped a handful of hair behind the mask. He shrieked in pain as she pulled him even closer, wrapping her knees around his waist to secure the grip and feeling the hair strain at the roots as she came face-to-face with the snout of the awful mask. She didn't have a plan except to punch and bite and do whatever else it took to get those keys. As the man bucked to free himself, she threw a straight right that caught him on the jaw, dazing him. She swung again, going for the knockout, but this time he ducked his head, causing her to connect with the top of his skull. Pain flared in her hand. She tried to headbutt him, but he had found his footing, and he pushed hard on her chest as he pried her legs apart and scooted backward, out of reach.

"You shouldn't have done that," he said, breathing heavily as he adjusted the mask.

"Go to hell."

He took off his soaked tuxedo jacket and laid it across his arm. "And you enjoy the rats. I'll be back tomorrow. Or maybe not."

As he turned to leave, she swallowed and said, "Wait."

He took a moment to straighten his cuffs, and she glanced at the brick wall shielding the interior of the alcove from view. The silence on the other side was ominous. "I hid the Star Phone in a restroom," she said quietly. "On the Dorsoduro side of the Ponte dell'Accademia."

"Where?"

"Inside a toilet. Third stall from the left. Lift the lid to the tank and you'll see it."

She could feel the satisfaction oozing out of him.

"Let him go now," she said.

"If you're telling the truth, I'll return."

"I said, *let him go*! He may die before you get back!"

"Then you should have told me sooner."

Andie cursed and jerked at her manacles as the man spun on his heel to leave. Ever since her capture, she had harbored a foolish hope that they were bluffing, or that her mother would return for her. Andie would never forgive herself if Cal died because she had waited too late to talk.

As their captor walked out of the cell and bent over the padlock to secure it, there was a flash of movement in the hallway. Andie thought she was hallucinating when a tall, sleek form in a wetsuit emerged from the darkness and shoved something into the man's back. Andie heard an electric crackle as he stiffened and then convulsed, his face pressed against the bars. Still applying the stun gun, Zawadi opened the latch on the iron grate and shoved him inside the cell. She pulled him to the ground, put a knee on his back, and finally clicked off the weapon. He stopped twitching and laid still, his head lolling to the side.

Zawadi ripped the keys off his belt, walked over to Andie, and bent to unlock the manacles securing her ankles.

Once Andie realized Zawadi wasn't going to kill her, she jerked her head toward the brick wall. "My friend is dying in there! Get him out first! Please!"

"Are four hands not better than two?" Zawadi asked in a rich accent that sounded African. She found a key that fit, the manacles dropped away, and she bent toward the other ankle.

"I suppose you're right," Andie said, not caring how or why Zawadi had freed them. She just wanted Cal out of that death box. "Is the guard dead?"

"No. But he won't stay unconscious for long, and I'd prefer not to kill him."

As soon as Andie was free, they worked together to rip the bricks down and found Cal slumped against the back wall, breathing shallowly with his chin on his chest. When Andie ran to him, his eyes slowly lifted. She took his hand as Zawadi approached, reaching into a waterproof pouch at her side and handing a bottle of water to Andie. She held the bottle to Cal's lips and helped him drink as Zawadi worked to free his bonds.

"That's enough," Zawadi said. "He won't be able to handle too much. Stop and give him two white pills from the green bottle."

"What is it?"

"Adrenaline."

"How about a Twinkie?" Cal said, with a weak grin.

After Zawadi eased him out of his chains, she rubbed his arms and legs to invigorate them as Andie gave him two of the adrenaline pills and more water.

"The pills take a minute," Zawadi said. "Can you walk?"

Cal took a shuddering step forward, stumbled, and fell into Zawadi's arms.

Zawadi put an arm around his shoulder. Andie hurried to support the other side. "Can't you just make sure the guard sleeps a little longer?"

"It's not just that. They have strict protocols, and his failure to return will raise an alarm."

"Where are we going?"

"Away from here. Is the Star Phone really where you said?"

Andie gave her a sharp glance, wondering if Zawadi had freed them only to retrieve the device and kill them herself. Yet if that were the case, and she had overheard the location, why free them at all? Maybe she wanted Andie as insurance, in case she had been lying, and had only freed them to gain their trust.

"It's okay," Zawadi said quietly, as if reading her thoughts. "You can hold on to it. But we need it to help Dr. Corwin, if he's still alive."

Andie caught her breath. "You think he might be?"

"I haven't seen him since the day he arrived in Bologna. But I haven't seen his body either."

"What about the morgue?"

"The Italian police are still conducting an inquest, and the Ascendants have contacts in high places. No one seems able—or is willing— to tell me exactly where the body is."

"Are the Ascendants the same as the Leap Year Society?"

"They're a rival faction. A story for another time."

"And Professor Rickman? Why did you kill him?"

Andie was hoping Zawadi would deny the charge, but instead she said, "I killed him, yes. But not for the reason you think. He was the one who betrayed James."

"What? Why? Who *are* you?"

"Come," Zawadi said. "We must leave."

Frustrated, Andie resisted the urge to kick the prone form of their captor on the way out, and they half dragged Cal down the dank, fetid hallway. Zawadi refused to answer more questions and kept glancing at her wristwatch. More cells appeared on either side, and rats chittered in the background. When they approached a sewer grate set into the floor at the end of the corridor, Zawadi eased away from Cal, and Andie supported him as he gripped her shoulder. She thought his eyes looked a little brighter.

Water lapped at the edges of the sewer grate and spilled onto the stone floor. Andie noticed the bolts holding the grate had already been cut. "How'd you know we were down here?"

Zawadi knelt to remove the rusty bars. "Quickly now."

"Can he swim in this shape?"

"I'll help him. We're not going far. Please, just follow me to the surface."

"I can swim *and* talk," Cal said, his voice stronger than Andie had heard in some time. "The adrenaline is kicking in."

"Go ahead," Zawadi said to Andie. "I'll replace the grate."

Wary of the murky water, but far more worried about getting caught, Andie forced herself to stick her legs into the dark abyss lurking below the dungeon. The water was colder than she expected. After a deep breath, she lowered herself through the grate, submerging fully. Once she got over the shock, she opened her eyes and spied a giant wooden piling five feet from her face, its bottom unseen in the lightless depths.

Cal followed her down. Andie held on to him as Zawadi dropped through the hole and held a penlight in one hand while she replaced the grate. After that, she linked an arm through Cal's, and Andie helped on the other side.

The waterproof penlight cast a faint halo in the cloudy water. Following Zawadi's lead, Andie and Cal kicked a dozen or so feet to the side, until they reached the submerged corner of the building. Zawadi pointed straight up, and long seconds later they broke the surface beneath a crescent moon, emerging in a narrow canal walled in by decrepit buildings with laundry hanging from rickety stone balconies. Andie took deep but quiet breaths to recover her oxygen. Clumps of debris floated on the filmy surface of the water, and the stench of the sewer filled her nose. When Zawadi flicked off her penlight, the moon was the sole spark of life in the decaying corpse of Venice.

"Where are we?" Andie asked. It felt bizarre to find the city so quiet. She was confused by the late hour and realized the guard must have tried to disorient her by feeding her at odd times. Had three days really passed?

"The Venetian Ghetto," Zawadi said. "Hurry now."

Canoes with motors, fishing dinghies, and other dilapidated watercraft were moored along the canal. Zawadi swam across the water to a walkway of wooden planks. As Andie climbed out, a flash of movement startled her, but it was only a crab scuttling through a pile of fish guts.

Zawadi hurried down the splintered planks, stopping when she reached two of the larger fishing boats shielding a pair of objects that resembled large foot scooters. The odd contraptions were standing upright and floating atop the water, attached to the sides of the boats with metal clamps.

"What are those?" Cal asked.

Zawadi pressed a button on one of the clamps, causing it to release in her hand. "Modified hydroboards." She stuck the clamp onto the long steering stem of the strange vessel, where it attached like a magnet. Another button between the handlebars caused a quiet motor to erupt underwater, beneath the foot platform.

She passed the hydroboard to Andie. "We can't all fit on mine."

Andie's eyes widened. "I . . . I'll do my best."

"It requires some balance, but you'll get the hang of it. Faster now. We have to escape the city."

As Zawadi held the stems of both hydroboards upright, Andie grimaced and stepped onto the one Zawadi had given her, grasping the handlebars with both hands. When Zawadi let go, Andie wobbled and fell over. The engine kicked off and the hydroboard bobbed in the water.

"Hold it upright," Zawadi said quickly, "start the motor, and climb on with a knee to start. It brakes and throttles like a motorcycle. Have you ridden before?"

"Plenty."

"Good. The engine's electric and decelerates as soon as you ease off the throttle."

Andie fell again, and she wanted to scream in frustration. Zawadi cast an anxious glance down the canal.

C'mon, girl. You can do this. You have to do this.

At last Andie found her balance and moved precariously into the main canal, wobbling but not toppling over. As Zawadi had said, the throttle worked by torquing the handlebars, and Andie felt comfortable with that.

Zawadi swooped in beside her, Cal hanging on to her waist. "Follow me."

"Where to?" Andie said.

"To the Ponte dell'Accademia, and then to the mainland."

"This thing will go all the way across the lagoon?"

"Oh, yes. And if you fall off, don't panic. Just find the board and climb back on."

"I'll do my best."

Zawadi flashed a tight smile.

They followed the canal for some way, ducking beneath three arched stone bridges and a tangle of low-hanging laundry lines before reaching a plaza surrounded by canals and anchored by a hulking marble church. The side canals were empty, and only a few stragglers roamed the city streets. Before long, the expanse of the Grand Canal loomed ahead. Andie glanced over to find Cal leaning on Zawadi's back for support. As they entered the huge channel dissecting the city, Andie felt as if she were starting to get the hang of the hydroboard—right until she almost ran into a gondola slinking through the water. To avoid it, she veered sharply to her right, and the sudden change in direction caused her to fall off.

Salty water filled her mouth and clogged her nose. Choking, she spit it out and desperately tried to find her hydroboard as salt stung her eyes. The board was bobbing a dozen feet away, and Zawadi zoomed over to hold it in place. Cal urged Andie to hurry as the gondolier gawked.

Shaken from the fall, Andie managed to reclaim her balance and speed back into the canal. A couple of small boats plied the water, but there was no sign of pursuit. They reached the base of the Ponte dell'Accademia without further incident, but Andie had never felt so exposed.

"Get the device," Zawadi said. "We'll wait here."

"Won't the door be locked?"

Zawadi hesitated, then killed the motor and had Cal wait with both boards on the stone steps leading out of the water beside the bridge. Andie followed her across the piazza to the public restroom, where Zawadi used a set of tools in her pack to pick the lock on the door. She accomplished the task much faster than Andie could have.

As Zawadi returned to the bridge, Andie entered the restroom, her stomach bottoming when she entered the third stall. What if the toilet had clogged and someone had found the Star Phone? What if it had slipped off and was ruined?

She held her breath as she eased the lid off, sagging with relief when she saw the device sitting right where she had left it. She grabbed it, she replaced the toilet lid, and hurried back to the others.

Zawadi was waiting by the steps down to the water. Andie cringed as the other woman moved toward her, wondering if she would take the phone and turn the stun gun on Andie and Cal. Instead Zawadi tossed her a canvas pouch with a strong seal. "Waterproof," Zawadi said.

"Thanks," Andie said, sealing the phone inside.

Zawadi waded into the water and climbed onto her board. Andie followed suit, and they returned to the Grand Canal, racing back the way they had come. She had thought they would continue past Piazza San Marco, but as she recalled the maps of the city, she realized the fastest way to reach the mainland was to follow the Grand Canal back into the heart of Venice and cut north on one of the smaller canals, which the vaporetti and other large boats couldn't navigate.

It was smooth riding until a pair of sleek powerboats with searchlights swung into the canal behind them. A powerful white beam hovered right on them, causing Zawadi to utter a rash of harsh syllables in a foreign language.

Andie was right beside her, squinting in the bright illumination. "You're sure it's them, and not the police?"

"The police would have sirens and strobe lights, and they've likely been paid to stay away. Follow me."

Zawadi cut sharply to the right, on a direct path to the shore. Andie executed the same maneuver and felt the board give way beneath her. In a panic, she fought to keep the hydroboard upright. It wobbled, but she clenched her thighs against the stem and barely hung on. The searchlights cut off, but the sound of the engines behind them increased. A shiver of fear whisked through Andie when she looked back and saw the powerboats closing in. Multiple figures stood along the sides of the boats.

Right before they reached the edge of the canal, Zawadi shouted, "Get ready. We're porting the boards."

"What do you mean?"

Zawadi killed the engine at the last moment, pitching Cal into the water as she almost slammed into the stone wall at the base of another bridge. She helped him ashore, then lifted the hydroboard. Andie landed with far less grace, and Zawadi helped her out of the water while Cal picked up her hydroboard.

Soaking and exhausted, their shoes slapping on the worn paving stones of Venice, they followed Zawadi down a succession of silent streets, running across footbridges spanning fingerlike canals and through empty moonlit piazzas.

"Are we hiding somewhere?" Andie asked.

"I told you, we must leave the city. It's too dangerous."

"Where are we going?"

"The same place as before. I've already arranged transport."

When they reached a canal lined with shuttered trattorias, Zawadi set her hydroboard in the water and jumped on. Cal put Andie's board down and climbed on behind Zawadi, with a backward glance as they sped off to make sure Andie was keeping up.

Clutching the handlebars, Andie worked hard to follow as she darted through a mazelike series of canals, deeper and deeper into the city, before emerging on a larger channel with lights hovering in the distance. Zawadi whipped to the right and accelerated. Soon the shadow of a body of water appeared at the end of the waterway.

The wind whipped into Andie's wet clothes and hair as she

urged the hydroboard onward, tracking Zawadi as she zoomed past a marina and into the choppier waters of the Venetian lagoon. Andie almost lost her balance again, but this time she clamped her thighs against the stem as soon as she started to tilt.

Soon after they entered the lagoon, the whine of a powerboat sounded in the distance, followed by another. She knew the mainland was a few miles away. As speedy as the little hydroboards were, Andie knew the powerboats would quickly overtake them in open water.

They would never make it in time.

Yet Zawadi kept going, heading straight into the lagoon. Bobbing searchlights appeared on their left, still some distance away, as the first powerboat rounded the head of the island. *They're going to catch us,* Andie wanted to scream.

A huge shadow materialized in the darkness ahead of them, growing larger and larger. It couldn't possibly be the mainland yet. Nor did Andie think they were close enough to Murano, a small island renowned for artisanal glassmaking, just north of Venice.

The landmass started to take shape beneath the amber light of the moon. Andie spied the corner of a massive stone wall stretching into the darkness, and the vague, bushy outline of treetops clumped beyond the wall, as if it were enclosed parkland.

It was clear Zawadi was aiming for the gated entrance to the walled compound, a bulwark of stone topped by a statue of an angel and bookended by squat towers. It could have been the entrance to a medieval cathedral.

Zawadi sped onto the boat ramp fronting the entrance, killed the engine, and leaped off the board in one smooth motion. Andie missed the ramp and fell on her side at the edge of the limestone staircase half submerged in the lagoon. She pulled herself onto the steps, slipping on the algae at the bottom, as Cal grabbed her hydroboard. Across the water, the roar of the powerboats drew closer, the searchlight probing the lagoon.

"Where are we?" Andie said, as they hurried toward a tripartite arched entryway cut into the face of the wall. "What's going on?"

Zawadi put her fingers to her mouth and whistled like a song-bird, then handed her stun gun to Andie. "Take this. Just press and hold the button if you need it. It's water-resistant, but try not to swim with it."

"Why?" Andie said, reluctantly accepting the device. It was so small it fit in the palm of her hand.

"Because this is where I leave you."

"*Leave* us?" Both Andie and Cal stared at her in shock.

"I can't evade them with the two of you in tow, but you can escape, and I might have a chance on my own. Whatever you do, keep the Star Phone safe."

"I don't understand. What are we supposed to do?"

In the darkness on the other side of the arched entrance, through a tunnel of stone, a gate swung open. "A boat is waiting to ferry you to the mainland," Zawadi said. "I let them know we're in danger and can't risk going directly to the launch site. They've sent a friend to take you to the boat—a monk who lives on the island. A car will carry you to Bologna. If I can, I'll meet you there."

The powerboats drew ever closer, three of them now, all with searchlights sweeping the lagoon.

"*Bologna?*" Andie said. "Who are these people?"

"You can trust them! Go now! Inside the gates before you're seen!"

Zawadi set her board in the water and raced back into the lagoon. She angled north, away from the stone walls and toward the main-land. The woman was extremely resourceful, but what chance did she have on a floating skateboard against three powerboats loaded with weapons? Andie sucked in a breath, confused and sick with worry.

Cal spoke in a harsh whisper. "We have to go!"

He was halfway to the iron gate. Andie ran to catch up. Once she got close to the archway, she was finally able to make out what lay on the other side of the wall. Clumps of cypress dotted the islet, but instead of encountering a city park with graceful paths and hedges, Andie found herself staring at a sea of white tombs, an island cemetery stretching as far into the moonlight as she could see.

29

On the other side of the archway, a man dressed in a monk's brown cassock was waiting for them, holding the iron gate open. A voluminous hood shielded his face from view.

Cal hurried through with the hydroboard. Despite the danger driving them onward, Andie hesitated as the waters of the lagoon lapped against the steps behind her. What if nothing but a fresh grave awaited them inside the cemetery? What if Zawadi had switched the Star Phone with a fake, led them into a trap, and was speeding away to safety?

What if? What if? What if?

At some point in her life, Andie knew she had to learn how to trust. It didn't help that her own mother had just betrayed her. Or had she? On some level, yes, she had lured Andie to Venice and handed her over to the Archon. But Andie did not believe, *could* not believe that her mother was acting under her own free will.

What strange hold did the Archon have on her? Or perhaps her mother truly thought the only way to save her daughter was to bring the Star Phone to the Ascendants.

More than ever, Andie was determined to see this through. *If* Zawadi was truly on their side, and *if* they made it to Bologna, then somehow, some way, Andie was going to continue searching for the Enneagon. She knew she could use it to bargain for Dr. Corwin and her mother. She might not find it, she might die along the way, but either option was preferable to living her life without trying to help the ones she loved.

Cal's rough whisper cut through her thoughts. "Andie! Come on!"

A final glance at the lagoon revealed the lights of the powerboats swinging north, veering away from the cemetery. Clenching her fists, she turned to follow Cal through the gate. The man in the cassock secured the lock behind them, then headed down a wide path leading through an orderly section of tombstones covered in flowers. A copse of trees obscured the area to their left from view. The silence of the darkened grove made Andie nervous.

The monk waved them forward, pressing ahead at a fast clip.

"Have any of these people heard of a meet-and-greet?" Cal muttered as they hurried after him.

"How are you feeling?" she asked.

"Starving, exhausted, and made of rubber."

"The adrenaline's wearing off?"

"Yeah."

"Hang in there."

"Not much of a choice."

"Want me to carry the board?"

"I'm good for now."

She walked beside him as they cut straight through the heart of the cemetery. The air smelled of sea and stone and fresh flowers. The man in the cassock was not using a light, and the gloom deepened as they entered a more wooded section. Tombs of all shapes and sizes filled the gaps between the foliage, accented by crosses, memorials, and statues of angels and weeping saints. When they angled toward the wall on their right, the fresh flowers on the graves had disappeared, the undergrowth was unkempt, and headstones leaned to the side in the tall grass.

The buzz of a cell phone broke the silence, coming from within their guide's cassock. He was a few feet ahead of them, and without stopping, he reached into the cassock to quiet the phone. As he did,

Andie noticed something in the moonlight that made her blood run cold and her knees feel watery.

When the monk had reached for his cell phone, she had caught a glimpse of his right hand, and it sparked a memory that stretched all the way back to the night in Durham when a man with a gun had appeared at her house.

The man in the brown cassock, the man supposedly leading them to safety, was missing a pinky.

She studied his form in the darkness. He had the right build and the same predatory walk as the intruder she had seen in Durham and then the catacombs. If she got this wrong, it could be disastrous. But what were the odds that someone else had the same disfigurement? Her mother had called him Omer. It had to be him.

And Andie had to act on the knowledge.

She dared not whisper or even gesture to Cal. Every now and then, their guide turned to make sure they were with him. If he suspected an attack, then they were doomed. Maybe they were already. But she had to try something before they reached their destination, and she had to do it fast.

Why had he not just shot them? She guessed he was tasked with bringing them back and had somehow learned of Zawadi's plan. Maybe he had arrived on a hydroboard himself or hidden in the cemetery before it closed. Maybe a boat still awaited Andie and Cal, and a monk had indeed been supposed to meet them, and Omer had ambushed him to get close enough to the boat with Andie and Cal in order to fool whoever was waiting to take them to safety.

Up ahead, the trees thinned as the cemetery opened up. Andie decided to make her stand as soon as she had room to maneuver. The next hundred feet seemed to pass in a heartbeat, and then they were crunching on pea gravel with low gravestones all around, clear of the dense foliage. After a silent deep breath to work up her nerve, Andie rushed forward, gripping the stun gun Zawadi had given her.

The man whirled and raised his hands, causing the hood of the cassock to fall back and expose his face. It was Omer. He saw what was happening, but not in time to stop it. Andie lunged forward like a fencer, pressing the button to ignite the device and catching him right in the middle of the chest.

When the stun gun connected, Omer seized up and stumbled backward. Yet instead of falling over, incapacitated, he twitched for a moment and then brought his muscles under control. Andie tried to follow up, but it was too late. Before she could shock him again, he reached into the cassock and withdrew a black handgun.

She was sure the end had arrived. Omer leveled the firearm at her chest, causing her to shrink back. At the same moment, Cal leaped out of the darkness, swinging the hydroboard by the handlebars with all his might. He caught Omer in the shoulder with the heavy engine beneath the board. The blow caused the handgun to go flying and dropped their assailant to the ground.

Andie ran up and stunned him in the back again. As Omer rolled to get away, shuddering through the current, Cal pulled her by the arm. "Run!"

She knew he was right. Omer either had protective gear under his clothing or superhuman powers of resistance, and neither of them had a chance against a trained assassin. Gripping her weapon, Andie took off down the path, Cal right beside her.

Behind them, Omer cursed and gave chase. She glanced over her shoulder and saw a long, serrated knife in his hand. He was twenty yards back and gaining ground, gritting through the pain.

Andie's heart thumped against her chest, fear propelling her forward. When the path turned sharply, she plowed ahead through a quadrant of low graves, leaping over tombstones as branches whipped into her face. Cal was right with her, face pale with exhaustion, arms pumping, sprinting for his life.

In the distance, she noticed a break in the wall surrounding the cemetery, revealing an expanse of dark water. If an escape boat was moored offshore, then surely it was there. She looked back. Omer had closed half the gap. He was surging ahead with an unhinged but confident expression, sure they wouldn't make it to the water.

As Andie drew closer to the breach in the wall, she spied a basin of water indented into the island where it spilled into the lagoon—a tiny marina for a boat to pull inside and dock. Yet there was no sign of a watercraft.

Omer's footsteps pounded the gravel path. She could hear him breathing behind her and knew the chase was over.

"Help!" she cried, in case anyone was listening. "Help us!"

As the lagoon materialized, Andie despaired when no one was waiting to save them. She felt Omer's hand on her shoulder, pulling her toward him, and she whipped around to jab the stun gun at his face.

He anticipated the maneuver, batting Andie's arm away. The blow felt as if it had shattered her elbow. She dropped the stun gun, and he kneed her in the solar plexus, sending her crashing to the ground and paralyzed from the sudden loss of breath.

Cal roared and rushed Omer with his bare hands. Andie pushed to her knees and tried to scream at him to stop, but only a croak escaped her lips. It was a brave but foolish last charge. A small smile parted Omer's lips as he pointed the knife at Cal and prepared to lunge.

A gunshot echoing through the night caused Andie to cringe. The sound of the blast was reduced by a silencer but still loud and shocking. Instead of seeing Cal gutted on Omer's knife, Andie saw their pursuer slump to the ground like a puppet who had just lost its strings. It took her a moment to notice the hole in the center of his forehead, blood pouring from the wound, and she looked up in shock to see a blond man standing at the edge of the wall where it opened onto the lagoon. He was holding a gun and urgently waving them over.

Omer was staring straight ahead, eyes glossy and unblinking, and his body had sunk into the gravel as if deflated. Cal backed away from him. Andie's eyes lingered on the body for a moment, revolted by the violence but feeling no remorse. Her breath returned in ragged gasps as she ran beside Cal, toward the man waiting by the wall.

Whoever he was, he had just saved their lives, and they had little choice but to accept his help.

Their rescuer was standing on a stone walkway that extended along the base of the wall, wrapping around the edge of the lagoon. "Zawadi sent me," he called out, further easing Andie's fears. "Quickly, please."

The man was tall and lean, maybe forty, with quick brown eyes and a strong Scandinavian jaw that matched his accent.

"Did she escape?" Andie asked.

"I don't know. But if they catch her and don't find you with her, the Ascendants will send more boats into the lagoon. We should be safe if we hurry."

Once they had cleared the wall, they saw a cigarette boat moored just out of view. The man hopped onto the sleek prow of the boat, ran down it, and untied a rope slung around an iron post jutting out of the wall. Andie and Cal followed him on board and into the cushioned seat in the center of the boat.

The man fiddled with his cell phone as he took the helm. "I don't know if he tapped our phones or discovered the poor groundskeeper's true identity, but I'm shutting down communications. Do you have phones?"

"We were prisoners in a medieval dungeon," Andie said. "So no."

"If you hadn't resisted, he would have taken me by surprise. We would all be dead."

"How'd you know?" Cal said to Andie. He was slumped in the seat beside her, his eyes hollow with hunger and exhaustion.

"Just math," she said with an ironic, melancholy twist of her lips. She was thinking of her mentor, the five-digit passcode to the folder housing his MUT research, and the contents of the wall safe behind the Ishango bone that had launched her on this insane journey.

"What?"

"Omer was missing a digit. A finger. I remembered it from before."

His eyes widened in surprise and admiration. "I didn't even notice."

As the speedy vessel darted into the lagoon without its navigation lights, the engine purring at a low hum, Andie twisted her body to stare at the receding walls of the cemetery, grateful to be alive but overwhelmed with emotion.

Soon the lights of Venice were a speck in the distance, and as her mother grew farther and farther away, Andie turned toward the mainland, facing a future as terrifying and uncertain as the mounting mysteries of her past.

Naples, Italy
March 1938

As the mail boat drifted in at first light, its crew working hard to secure the vessel, Stefan took up a position at the front of the wooden dock. He shoved his hands into the pockets of his coat to warm them. Behind him, the blasted dome of Mount Vesuvius loomed high above the Gulf of Naples, a constant reminder of the fragility of civilization.

According to his sources, shortly after Ettore received the core of the device from the Society's engineers, Ettore had taken an unauthorized trip to Sicily. Before he left, he had emptied his bank account and penned a strange goodbye letter to one of his associates.

Stefan had contacted the port authority in Palermo and confirmed that Ettore had reboarded the ship for the return journey. Still, sensing something amiss, Stefan had arrived at the dock well before dawn. As soon as the vessel anchored, before anyone had disembarked, Stefan rushed aboard and, in his most commanding voice, told the captain he was searching the ship. The captain took one glance at his Nazi credentials and stood down. Mussolini fawned over Hitler, and no one dared question a high-ranking member of the Third Reich. Everyone stood meekly about while Stefan interviewed the crew and passengers and, quivering with rage, inspected every single inch of the boat.

Ettore was nowhere to be seen.

In fact, except for the crew member who had shown Ettore to his cabin, no one even remembered the quiet professor of theoretical physics. That was Ettore's tragic flaw, Stefan knew. His inability to communicate with others throughout his life, despite his obvious yearning to do so. *There is no need to reach for the stars if we are content with that which is right beside us.*

Had Ettore fooled them all and absconded with his invention? Had someone from the crew of the mail boat, perhaps a plant from the Society, helped him escape? Or had Ettore simply jumped overboard and put an end to his sad life?

What exactly had happened in the middle of the open sea?

The only thing of interest to the German soldier was a piece of silver filament wire he found pinched between a pair of wooden crates stacked along the sidewall of the pilothouse. At first glance, the wire was so thin he mistook it for a piece of string. He again questioned the crew and passengers, but no one claimed to know who or what the wire belonged to.

It could be nothing, Stefan thought. A random piece of flotsam washed onto the deck in rough seas, blown in by the wind, or a meaningless item left by a passenger on a previous journey.

Or it could be everything.

What game was Ettore playing?

Furious, Stefan pounded a gloved fist against the railing. How many years had he wasted on this man? How much had he damaged the cause? If Ettore was still alive, Stefan vowed to find him and flay him alive for his betrayal, then toss his bones to the dogs. Yet despite his rage, Stefan had to admire the scientist's ingenuity and courage, and for acting so out of character. *I didn't think you had it in you, Ettore.*

As Stefan stepped onto the creaking wooden dock, clutching the strange piece of filament wire, bewildered by the find and sensing it held the key to a greater truth, he wondered just exactly what it was that Ettore Majorana had convinced them to build.

EPILOGUE

Dr. James Corwin's world was black and silent.

Odorless, unending.

After his capture, the Ascendants had kept him sedated until he woke in a white padded cell. They interrogated him every day until he managed to lift a cell phone off a guard and send a desperate plea for help to the Star Phone. As punishment for his actions, his captors had placed him inside a sensory deprivation chamber.

Dr. Corwin had no idea how long he had been inside. Time had ceased to have weight, and he was losing his will to resist.

He knew that a typical isolation tank involved floating in water that contained enough dissolved salt to obtain a gravitational field of approximately 1.275, rendering the body weightless. But he wasn't in water. He was being held in a chamber as dark as a cave, suspended a few feet off the floor, naked, upright, his arms outstretched. A metal helmet was affixed to his head; metal bracelets were on his wrists and ankles.

None of his bonds were attached to the walls.

At rare intervals, the force keeping him suspended in midair would shut off and he would crumple to the padded floor. By groping around with atrophied limbs on these occasions, he had discovered the contours of his cell, and that a tray of bland food and water awaited him. He would eat and drink and massage his muscles in silence as a computer-generated voice interrogated him from unseen speakers, seeking the hidden location of the Enneagon, claiming his suffering would never end unless he told them.

And he believed them.

Oh, how he believed them.

The source of his imprisonment was not magic. Nor was it science fiction. He surmised that powerful magnets, which attracted his metal bonds, were embedded in the soundproof walls. Pushing and pulling in equal measure, the force adjusted to his body weight to keep him suspended. Every time he finished eating, he had tried to resist the electromagnetic levitation, but the current would turn back on and he would slowly, inexorably rise into the air and return to his suspended position.

He knew that prisoners kept in prolonged isolation in normal jails—in full command of their external senses—suffer mental and physical health problems, often severe. Some commit suicide to escape the ordeal.

Dr. Corwin was trapped in a waking coma in absolute stasis, with no release or stimulation. A never-ending plunge into the ceaseless dark of the void.

So when a fluorescent light appeared for the first time in what felt like a lifetime, it flared like a sunspot, blinding him. When he regained his vision, he saw someone standing in the middle of the room, wearing a close-fitting golden mask and a white robe that brushed the floor.

A modulated voice spoke from behind the mask. "Do you know who I am?"

Dr. Corwin's mouth felt stuffed with cotton. After a time, he managed to croak out a reply. "I know they call you the Archon."

"Then you know why I am here."

"Are you? I'm not really sure of anything right now."

During his imprisonment, weird patterns of light from his own retinas had flooded his mind, phantasms that caused him to question his present reality.

"I understand your confusion. But I assure you I am not a hallucination."

"That's unfortunate."

"We've never held anyone in this state for so long," the Archon continued. "Even I do not know how long your sanity will persist. No matter: I can bring you back if I choose—as long as you answer my questions."

Dr. Corwin had heard enough about the Archon to know the identity of the person behind the disguise was a closely held secret. He had long suspected the leader of the Ascendants was someone he had once known, an adversary from his own past. "Hans? Is it you?"

"Perhaps this will help," the Archon said, and raised a hand.

The light in the room was extinguished except for a golden glow emitting from the mask, which now seemed to hover in the darkness below Dr. Corwin. A strange liminality between worlds that restored some of his equilibrium, anchoring him better than the artificial lighting.

"An improvement?" the Archon said.

"I suppose, all things considered."

"Excellent. As you have probably surmised, I have come to speak with you myself, since our interrogation has thus far proven ineffective."

"I'm honored. Where are we exactly?"

"Where is the Enneagon?"

The Enneagon. The Enneagon. It took Dr. Corwin a moment to recall what it was and how he had hidden it—even from himself. *Ah, yes. The Archon isn't going to like that very much.*

"The thing is," Dr. Corwin said, "I can't for the life of me seem to remember."

The Archon took a step forward. The pupils behind the vacant eyeholes should have been visible in the darkness, but instead the circular openings in the mask seemed to stretch to infinity. "You found the Fold, didn't you?"

"We found it long ago."

"You know what I mean," the Archon said. "You *found* it."

"You have no idea what you're talking about."

"I know far more than you think. I know about stepping, and the ones who roam. The walls of knowledge are crumbling. The old guard is dying, burdened by their failure to bridge the gap and reach the infinite. But I will find what you have made. Catalogue and absorb it. Improve upon it. I will save the world from itself and fulfill the destiny of our species."

"You're mad."

"Mad? I am supremely rational. I'll ask you again: Where is the Enneagon?"

"Who are you? Remove the mask."

"Your fortitude is impressive. But I will strip the knowledge from your mouth and mind, or I will bring Andromeda here and break you in another way. As you know firsthand, the brain withers and dies without light. The same result occurs when observing the suffering of a loved one."

"Don't you dare touch her—do you hear me? She's innocent! She has nothing to do with this!"

"None of us is innocent. Did you not involve her yourself? I'm afraid your plea to moral authority falls flat."

"Damn you!" Dr. Corwin struggled to free himself, though he knew it was useless.

"It will be curious to see which route is more effective. I ask a third and final time: Where is it?"

Dr. Corwin's laugh escaped his dry throat as a rasp. "You don't understand—if I still knew, I would tell you to save her. I can't give you what you want."

Suddenly a mass of snakes the color of dry grass appeared and writhed around the golden mask. The snakes hissed, a susurration that echoed around the room and drove needles of pain into Dr. Corwin's head. Unable to move, he could only shut his eyes until the terrible sound dissipated.

When he dared to open them again, the snakes were gone and

there was no more light in the room. He was unsure if the hallucination had originated from the Archon or his own mind.

"What did you do?" he whispered, now barely able to speak from the effects of isolation and the residual pain in his skull. "Who are you?"

"You're an old man who no longer fears for his life," the disembodied voice of the Archon said. "This I understand. But there are fates worse than death—for you and for her. It is life itself you should fear. Given time, you will tell me what I wish to know. Of that I assure you."

"Only the unwise are very sure of anything," Dr. Corwin rasped.

In response, the flare of light returned, and then the snakes and the pain.

To Be Continued Fall 2020 in
Volume II of the Genesis Trilogy!

Be sure to visit unknown9.com to stay up to date
on both the Genesis Trilogy and all of the other
stories set within the Unknown 9 universe.

ACKNOWLEDGMENTS

I have a lot of people to thank. To Alex Amancio: I have nothing but mad respect for the creative genius, business acumen, and sheer determination it took to bring your vision for Reflector Entertainment to life. Thank you for giving us a world to create in. Simon: it's been a wild ride, and I appreciate your ten hands and twenty fingers that do a little bit of everything yet never seem to sweat. Anwdrea: thank you for picking up that Dominic Grey novel! Noémie, Andre, Ben, Marc-Olivier, Iléana, Matthieu, John, Jesse, Julie, Oliver, Pascale, Georgia, Ari, and the rest of the Reflector team: I appreciate each and every one of you, and I feel incredibly lucky and grateful to be working alongside so many smart and talented people. I also want to give a shout of thanks to the other artists from a wide range of media who provided excellent companionship and incredible creative energy to the U9. I can't wait to see the final products.

On the novel side, I had lots of expert help: David Downing, Elizabeth Johnson, and Varsana Tikovsky provided A+ editing support; the Book Designers, Justin Branch, and Kristine Peyre-Ferry were invaluable resources throughout the project; Emi Bataglia and Rosanne Romanello are the sort of publicists authors dream of working with; Ayesha Pande Literary is, as always, a guiding light of encouragement and sage advice; and I hope I haven't left anyone out.

As always, beta readers John Strout, DJ, and Rusty Dalferes were beacons of support who I simply could not do without. Bill Burdick and Dan Ozdowski provided priceless insight into the tech world. A special thanks to the über-talented Kim Belair for her guiding hand in the early stages of the novel. And finally, to my wife, who provided amazing comments to the manuscript, was the finest of companions as we tripped around the globe for research, and deserves a medal of honor for putting up with my coffee-and-wine-fueled rants on quantum physics, radical theories of consciousness, the nature of the universe, what Andie should be wearing at any given moment, and how it's so unfair that Italians get mortadella and we get stuck with bologna.

AZMXGTKFDZS
QKGRSVTOCDC
EWDQABJMEKB
LGKWISKXUPV
JBMRHJHBKGG

—THE BEGINNING

ABOUT THE AUTHOR

LAYTON GREEN is a bestselling author whose work spans various genres, including thriller, mystery, suspense, and fantasy. His novels have been nominated for numerous awards (including a two-time finalist for an International Thriller Writers award), optioned for film, translated into multiple languages, and have reached #1 on genre lists in the United States, the United Kingdom, and Germany.

In addition to writing, Layton attended law school in New Orleans and was a practicing attorney for the better part of a decade. He has also been an intern for the United Nations, an ESL teacher in Central America, a bartender in London, a seller of cheap knives on the streets of Brixton, a door-to-door phone book deliverer in Florida, and the list goes downhill from there.

Layton lives with his family in North Carolina. You can also visit him on Facebook, Goodreads, or on his website:

www.laytongreen.com

ALSO BY LAYTON GREEN

THE DOMINIC GREY SERIES

The Summoner
The Egyptian
The Diabolist
The Shadow Cartel
The Resurrector
The Reaper's Game (Novella)

THE BLACKWOOD SAGA

Book I: The Brothers Three
Book II: The Spirit Mage
Book III: The Last Cleric
Book IV: Return of the Paladin

OTHER WORKS

Written in Blood
A Shattered Lens
The Letterbox
The Metaxy Project